THE MANDELA PLOT

BOOKS BY KENNETH BONERT

The Lion Seeker

The Mandela Plot

THE MANDELA PLOT

KENNETH BONERT

Houghton Mifflin Harcourt

Boston   New York

2018

For information about permission to reproduce selections from this book,
write to trade.permissions@hmhco.com or to Permissions,
Houghton Mifflin Harcourt Publishing Company,
3 Park Avenue, 19th Floor, New York, New York 10016.

hmhco.com

Library of Congress Cataloging-in-Publication Data
Names: Bonert, Kenneth, author.
Title: The Mandela plot / Kenneth Bonert.
Description: Boston : Houghton Mifflin Harcourt, [2018]
Identifiers: LCCN 2017060208 (print) | LCCN 2017050070 (ebook) |
ISBN 9781328886156 (ebook) | ISBN 9781328886187 (hardcover)
Subjects: LCSH: Mandela, Nelson, 1918–2013 — Fiction. | Politics and
government — Fiction. | Political violence — Fiction. | Jewish
families — Johannesburg (South Africa) — Fiction. | Johannesburg (South
Africa) — Fiction. | Political fiction. | BISAC: FICTION / Literary. |
FICTION / Coming of Age. | FICTION / Jewish. | FICTION / Political.
Classification: LCC PR9199.4.B6743 (print) |
LCC PR9199.4.B6743 M26 2018 (ebook) |
DDC 813/.6 — dc23
LC record available at https://lccn.loc.gov/2017060208

Book design by Greta D. Sibley

Printed in the United States of America
DOC 10 9 8 7 6 5 4 3 2 1

FOR NICOLE

It is a haunting truth, not to say a tragedy, that the story of a family or a nation is nothing but a succession of echoes. All human patterns repeat, all return to overlay and re-present what has already been — only the *style* of each repetition may vary. Different actors may interpret an ancient text yet the essential drama remains beneath, as unmoving as the rock of the place in which it must play itself out, again and again. All that stands against this is the flimsy weapon of memory, as fragile as a web of dreams.

— H. R. Koppel, *A Light for the Abyss*

La haine est le vice des âmes étroites, elles l'alimentent de toutes leurs petitesses, elles en font le prétexte de leur basses tyrannies.

Hatred is the vice of narrow souls. They feed it with all their smallness. They use it as an excuse for their vile tyrannies.

— Honoré de Balzac, *La Muse du Département*

NOTE TO THE READER

A glossary appears on page 456 for the benefit of those unfamiliar with South African terminology.

Neither the township of Julius Caesar nor the suburb of Regent Heights can be found on any map of Johannesburg. They are fictional locations that are wholly the product of the author's imagination. Both places contain schools — the Leiterhoff School and Wisdom of Solomon High School for Jewish Boys, respectively — that are just as fictional and imaginary as their locations. Needless to say, the characters populating these nonexistent places are also entirely fictional creations of the author, as indeed are all the characters in this novel.

THE NAME

Here they come in the night with their long boots and heavy machine guns, their steel helmets and wolf dogs on chains. The megaphone booming raus-Juden-raus and I'm sprinting down the passage and they keep dropping over the garden walls like giant snakes. Bambam they're at the front door, bursting it, splinters flying, a sledgehammer smashing the mezuzah. My brother has made it outside but a spotlight freezes him and he's kneeling on the lawn in his underpants, hands laced behind his neck, rain dripping from his bowed face. Now explosions of smashing glass from the big bedroom where Ma is screaming and I turn and run through the kitchen to the back door. Backyard's empty. Just reach the fence. Climb it and escape. But when my fingers touch the door handle I am stone.

Zaydi.

They haven't got to Zaydi yet, in his room at the far end. The megaphone voice won't stop saying all Jews out now move it Jews out get out.

They're inside. But Zaydi. I have to go back.

1

I'm playing slinkers like always and then this weird thing happens—
I start winning. I'm stocking points left and right and they can't stop
me. My heart pops like fireworks and whenever the toe of my polished
Jarman touches the slink it shoots exactly where I want it to. I start
giggling like a spaz. Meantime Pats and Ari have gone all quiet and serious. They won't look at me.

Slinkers is this game we invented, it's a combo of soccer with
snooker with golf plus chess. But it's like a million times more lekker
than any of them, I swear. I mean it's just the best, hey. I can't even explain how good. One day we are ganna organise selling it and it'll be
bigger than rugby even, once the people try it out, no jokes. Me and
Ari Blumenthal and Patrick Cohen—to be honest we started it cos shul
is so bladdy boring. You sit and sing in Hebrew or you stand quiet
till your feet hurt. Fat Rabbi Tershenburg gives his blahblah. It takes
hours and when it's finished everyone goes into the foyer and the hat-
ted ladies come down the stairs from the women's gallery. They kiss
their husbands good Shabbos and they get hold of their kids. Then the
whole lot herds off up the path to the kiddish hall where they fress off
paper plates piled with kichel and herring and gargle down little bottles
of Coke and Fanta. Not us. Our folks don't come to shul on Shabbos.
Instead we've saved up the bottlecaps from those little bottles. We've

rubbed the tops of the caps like mad on the rough steps outside, like we're trying to set them on fire, which gets them all silver and smooth. A ready one is called a slink.

All the time the people are in the foyer the three of us are waiting all ants-in-pants but pretending not to show it, pockets full of slinks. When they're gone, old Wellness, the Zulu caretaker, he comes limping in and switches off the big bronze chandeliers one by one. When the last one is out and it's darkened and Wellness has hopped off, we three jump in like a shot and start our match. It's like this every week. We use the patterns on the foyer's marble floor for lines and goals. Slinkers is complicated, hey. Got like a million special rules. Pats always says it's not just scoring a goal that's the hard part, it's getting *to* the goal. Well not for me! Not today! I score another one off a free kick and I'm giggling so hard I have to lie down. When we start the next round it hits me like an uppercut to the body (a *liver smasher*, Marcus calls it) that I am about to win the whole bladdy match. I look at my friends. They're still not looking at me. Not a good feeling. Basically I only have these two friends, ukay, my shul friends. I mean that's it. I don't really like to think about why that's so, but it's the truth.

I miss blocking Pats's slink and so I lose the next point and then the next. Now my friends start smiling and talking again. Soon we start arguing. We always argue. This one is about our air force and how we have Mirage fighter jets and whether they are better planes than the Cuban Migs we are fighting on the Border. The Mirages were used by Israel in the Six-Day War but the Migs were invented by a Jew. Ari says Mirage. Pats says what bulldust. I say what my brother Marcus would tell me, that it depends which model the Cubans are sending to fight us cos our Mirages are quite old and no one will sell us new ones cos of sanctions. In a little bit we are shouting like usual. It echoes in the roof which is round up there, like the inside of one of those helmet hair dryers old ladies sit under, but super dark without the lights. In the end I lose the argument, like usual. And then I carry on losing slinkers points and the more I lose the more the okes start laughing and patting me on the back and that. And then I lose the match, like usual. And then I lose the argument about which way to walk to Pats's house. Basically, I always come off third out of three with my two friends. That's my place. But today is the first time I'm seriously wondering why.

2

We are walking to Pats's house, taking Route Alpha Kilo Leopard. We have these code words for all our routes. Sometimes we argue about how long we would last if we got tortured for our codes. It's a vote of two to one that I'd be first to talk, but it's three out of three that the worst torture is the one where they stick pins in your balls. We walk cos you have to walk to shul on a Shabbos, you're not allowed to drive on Shabbos anywhere, obviously — it's against the Torah — so it would be chutzpah deluxe to rock up at the shul in a car. Old man Meyerson did it one time, got a lift with his son Neil who dropped him off outside, and no one talks to him anymore.

We reach the Emmarentia Dam by one o'clock or so and I feel the wind fresh in my face with the hot sun. The water is sparkly and full of little waves. The fishermen put nobs of mooshed bread on their lines so they can see them stretching from the rods. Kayakers are going hell for leather and windsurfers are falling and getting up and bending over to pull up their heavy sails. Ice cream man has those fat round granadilla lollies like cricket balls on sticks and he's also shouting to sell "cendy floss, cendy floss, anybody loves cendy floss?" and we're walking on the roadside next to the parked cars. All along on the grassy bank people are lying on towels with oil on their skin. White people trying to get brown. The African sun is happy to cook the hell out of them and I smell coconut sun cream and baby oil and sausage smoke. The air gets all bendy over the hot road. A radio from one of the parked cars is play-

ing "Do You Really Want to Hurt Me?" and I think of Boy George singing, with his hat and his girl's make-up, on *Pop Shop* which we always
tape at home — Fridays at five. I remember old whatsisname saying on
Pop Shop that 1986 belongs to New Wave, which sounded lank cool, but
I don't know how our year can belong to anything or what New Wave
actually means, really.

A yellow Volkswagen Golf, not the GTi fast one but the one that
Da says only ladies buy, is slowing down behind us. It makes me super
tense, I swear. It's happened lots of times before that someone shouts
antisemitism from the back of a car at us. Ari is wearing his yarmie, he
keeps it clipped in his hair and never takes it off because he's more religious than us two. Pats sometimes wears his outside of shul as well, he
wants to test himself to be proud to be a Jew. Pats is full of weirdo ideas
like that, he gets it from Laurel, his sister who's a drama student at Wits
and lights black candles in her room and that. But even me, obviously
I'm wearing my shul clothes which look completely funny here at the
Dam on a nice Saturday — my smartest shirt with long sleeves and collars and a pair of smart brown long pants and a pair of leather Jarmans
that are like the most expensive things Ma ever bought me which she
is always telling me — so they know what we are even without yarmies
on our heads. The last one shouted *Yo! Bladdy fucken Jewsss!* I remember the face sticking out the window, some blond oke with an earring.
He didn't look cross, he looked sort of happy when he saw me looking
back at him. Like he'd just swallowed down some lekker strawberry ice
cream with chocolate sauce. Sometimes I think about what he must
have seen, I mean what *my* face would have looked like to *him*. And
why would it make blondie so happy to shout that antisemitism at us?
But we just ignore them when it happens. What could we do? Anyway
this yellow Volksie passes us with no hassles and I feel better.

Then when we reach the far side where the road starts going up
away from the Dam, I see something hectic down in the willows and I
have to stop. Aloud I ask, "You check them down there?"

Pats shades his eyes, wrinkling his pointy nose while he looks. "Who're they?"

"That's a Solomon rugby jersey he's wearing," I say.

"No," says Pats.

"Ja, those are the colours," I say. "That's what he's got on, I swear. Solomon."

"So what?" says Ari.

I take a breath. "Let's go say howzit to them."

"You know them, hey." It's not a question, Pats is being majorly sarcastic.

"Ja, I do," I say. Sometimes lies just fly out of my mouth by themselves. Pats laughs and the two of them carry on walking but I don't move. I'm back to thinking about slinkers and how I've never won a single match since we started playing when we were little all the way till now when we've already had our barmies and become proper men of thirteen and high school is coming round the corner. It's specially nuts cos I'm the oldest of us — man, I'm ganna be turning fourteen years old this year, *soon*. So why couldn't I win the match today when I was so unstoppable? Why must I *always* come last? Something inside of me like a car alarm light on a dash keeps blinking an answer that I don't like. *It's because it keeps them happy.*

Meantime the okes have stopped on the road and are looking back and calling to me as if I've lost the plot. But I don't move. My heart's boombooming. "Come on, okes," I say. "Follow me." I start walking down to the place where the grass hits the willow trees. There's this huge kukload of trees here, so thick it's like a mini jungle, I swear.

When I look back, they're actually following. It's a hell of a surprise, on a level, but then all-a-sudden I start feeling lank chuffed cos I *want* them to see this, I really do. Want to mash their bladdy faces right in it.

3

I reach the willows first. The trees hang their whippy branches down into the water and there are more trees behind so they block you off like a wall. I catch a whiff of cigarettes but I can't see into the shadows cos you know how it is when you look from the bright sun into shade — it makes you into an instant Stevie Wonder. So I'm still blinking and trying to see when these three okes step out. Straightaway I've got a tingly feeling I should leave but Ari and Pats are coming up behind me and then I see the colours again — they belong to only one high school in Johannesburg. A skinny oke who's older, like fifteen or sixteen, steps up to me pulling a cigarette from his mouth. He's got one of those floppy mouths where the lips are about two sizes too big for his face and the bone part of his forehead by the eyebrows sticks out, making me think of a picture of a skull I saw this one time except that skulls look like they smiling with all their teeth and this oke has no smile for me. Instead he *pokes his hot cigarette straight at my eye,* I swear. It only just misses cos I use my reflexes to bend back. When I get my balance I see the other two have gone around and they've got Pats and Ari inside a circle.

"What you lighties doing down here?" says the skull face.

I say, "I was — I just saw him wearing that Solomon rugby jersey." And I look around to point to that one with my chin. "Do you okes all go to Solomon? What Standard are you?" I'm trying hard, grinning away, but this is all wrong, it's not how it should be.

"Oh, sweetie," says skull face. As he says this his other arm is busy coming up and around and something explodes bang clap almighty *hard* over the whole of the side of my face. I go away for a second and when I come back all three of us are being pushed into the willows by the three older ones. Duck poo is everywhere here. There're suckholes in the dark muck round the bottoms of the long weeds by the water and millions of dragonflies zipping and hovering like tiny helicopters. No one else is here, everyone's back there in the sun on the grass. I'm cold and start to shake but it's not from the shade. My face on the side feels as thick as the blue rubber they make slipslops out of, throb-throbbing like mad. The tall one's hand is scratching down the back of my neck, grabbing my collar. I look around and he's reading the label on my shirt. One of the other ones says to him, "What is it, Crackcrack?"

Crackcrack says, "This is OK Bazaars he's wearing. True's God. It's bargain-bin, polyester special. His mommy goes to jumble sales. She shops with the shochs, I bet you anything."

I hear Pats arguing with them, I cannot believe how calm he sounds. He is saying something about all of us being Jewish, that they must be also if they are Solomon boys, so let's just mellow out. The one with the rugby jersey grabs Pats's head and bangs his own forehead into it, chopping like he's an axe and Pats is wood. Pats goes white and stops talking. Without looking at me, Crackcrack pinches my chest so sore that I want to shout but I don't do anything. "My shoes are handmade calf leather," Crackcrack says. "Bet your daddy drives Toyota. I got my own Maserati. My driver Edson is parked up there for us, I got him till I get my licence. We go cruising and chicks stare. You goody-goody rabbi boys come from shul and scheme you can cause shit with us."

He pulls me round by my chest skin and lets go and I nearly fall into the rugby jersey one. "Present for you, Polovitz," Crackcrack says.

"I don't want him," Polovitz says.

I see the other one of them has got hold of Ari's red yarmie. I know it was a special present from his old man. Ari covers the top of his head with his hand and looks ready to bawl big time but he's holding it in and he says, "Ja, but you okes are breaking the Shabbos. That's all HaShem cares about. I feel sorry for what He will do to you." Everyone sort of freezes for a second. *HaShem* is a strong word, a shul word. It's Hebrew for The Name and we say it aloud instead of God's *real* name, which only ever gets written down in the proper places, like the Torah.

Then Crackcrack grabs Ari's ear. "Sweetie," he says. Twisting, he makes Ari go down to the ground. He takes black mud and slaps it on Ari's cheek, smears it all over his face. "Now you look like the shoch that you are," he says. "Be quiet, shoch." Ari can't hold it in anymore and starts to bawl, the tears running down the mud as he sobs like he's having an asthma attack. He doesn't even notice that the other two are using his special yarmie for a Frisbee. Meantime Pats is just parking there with his face still white as Tipp-Ex except where his forehead is growing huge red bumps out of it like giant chorbs on their way to being the worst case of blackheads in history.

Crackcrack looks at the water and says, "What you reckon, Russ?"

This Russ gives a big happy smile, looking down on poor Ari with his face all muddy and snotty. Russ says, "Bath time for the babies."

Crackcrack flicks his cigarette and slowly lights up another one from a gold lighter. The way he keeps his shoulders up and his eyes nearly shut as he does it, trying to look cool, I reckon he's practiced it from movies. Then I see the pack is American Camels. I don't think you can get Camels in the shops anymore cos of the sanctions. But he's showing off *he* can, it's more than just money. And like the other two he's got on Puma and Lacoste and Fila — a kind of uniform. All-a-sudden it whacks me like a good one from a cricket bat how much *less* I am than them because I don't have those logos on me. That they come from another world I don't know anything about. And straightaway that makes me think of Marcus.

"Oright," Crackcrack is saying. "Time to boogie. All a you little rabbi boys get your arses into that water."

Nobody moves.

"Shift it, you pusses. I won't tune you again. You got till three or we will fuck you all up solid."

I look behind and see the mucky water in the weeds is full of floaters, slimy moss and strings of duck shit and cans of Lion Lager and other pieces of nodding rubbish. I look at the three of them in front of us. I think of hitting them — like seriously hitting. And in my head I see my brother pounding his heavy bag in our backyard, whacking it *buff! buff!* with the sweat flying off. Me, by myself, I've tried to do it a few times, but my shots are just these tiny little pokes with my bony knuckles into the hard canvas that I can hardly dent. I look at their faces and try to imagine doing it to a real nose, a chin, and the idea makes me feel weak and nearly sick, as if I am melting down and down, into my socks.

"One," says Crackcrack.

There's a little gap between two of them, on the left. I start going for it slowly, turning sideways, and Pats says, "Don't try, Helger. You'll just get us more hurt, hey."

It's that word, that third word. *Helger.* It goes off like a bomb. I mean I see it in their faces — *kaboom.*

All-a-sudden I'm thinking faster than Jody Scheckter doing three hundred kays an hour at the Kyalami racetrack. I walk to the gap and I know they won't try to stop me now. I pass between them and they do exactly zilch, they just stand there like a couple of frozen blobs of shit, with their mouths open. I look back at Ari and Pats. "Come on, okes," I tell them. "They won't touch you. Let's duck."

Polovitz says to Russ, "Bladdy hell. It *is*, hey."

"Can't be," says Russ. But he doesn't sound like he did a few seconds ago, his voice is all high like a girl's.

Crackcrack steps up to me like he's ganna sort this nonsense proper right this second. "What's your name?"

"I'm Martin Helger," I tell him.

"What crap."

"Oh hell, Jesus," says Russ. "It's the brother. Little brother."

"He doesn't have one," says Crackcrack.

I feel everyone looking at me while I stare back at Crackcrack. "My brother goes to Solomon," I say. "Maybe you know him. His name is Marcus. Marcus Helger. I was going to ask you all if you knew him. Before." There's dead quiet. I tell them my brother Marcus is in matric—that's Standard Ten, last year of high school, and so he's older than them, eighteen now. I ask them again do they know him, but I already know the answer. Something huge has swelled up under my throat. I feel like I'm standing on a tower above them, looking down.

There's a noise from someone. It's like a yawn but different. It reminds me of a noise Ma once made that time in Rosebank when we saw this young black guy running down the street and a cop shooting at him from behind, the running man sprinting so full-on like I'd never seen before, with his head down and his arms going like mad and his jacket flying out straight behind him and the cop holding his big gun with two hands in front of him going poppoppop and we couldn't believe it and Ma made that sound I can't forget. Russ makes *that* kind of sound again, staring at me with his eyes all big like Meccano wheels. "I didn't touch you, hey," he tells me. "Not me." He turns around and takes like two or three big steps and then he just sprints away and he's gone and Crackcrack says to me, "You bluffing." Polovitz starts to say something but then he stops and turns around and also runs. Just like that.

Crackcrack is sloping off, chewing on his thumbnail. Ari grabs his arm. "Leeme go," says Crackcrack, but he keeps looking at me and he doesn't try to pull his arm away. What he does try is a smile, but it looks (Ma would say) just ghastly. He tells us he was only charfing when he said he was ganna put us in. They would never have actually done it. "Was a joke, hey okes, just a joke."

Ari says, *"You called me a shoch."* The way he says it makes it sound worse than bad, like the worst thing you can do is call someone that. And it *is* pretty bad but I think he added much worse with the mud didn't he. The tip of Crackcrack's tongue pops out to take a quick spin round his sausage lips and then he swallows hard and sticks out his hand. I can see it trembling. "Here, man," he says to Ari. "I am sorry. Put it there." He looks at the rest of us. "Sorry, okes. I'm lank sorry."

Ari ignores the hand. Crackcrack offers it to me. Ari says, "Don't be crazy, Helger. Don't let him off."

I stand there for quite a while staring at the hand. Then Pats surprises me by saying in my ear, "Just let him go, hey. Let him go and overs."

Ari hears him. "It's not overs," he says. "No way!" There're bits of drying mud still stuck all over his face and the rest of it looks red and swollen.

All the time Crackcrack's hand is still out for me. "Come on, china," he says—calling me his mate now, making like we are best buddies. "China, you don't need to say anything to your boet, don't tell Marcus. We all men, hey. We keep it here. I said sorry. I am."

I stare at him. "Don't," says Pats. But I already hear my voice speaking, sounding deep and rough, like someone else's in my pounding ears. "But you're not," I say. "You bladdy liar."

4

Afterwards we're walking single file on the path through the bulrushes taller than us, our feet squishing on the mud. It's hot like being in a greenhouse and I'm sweating big time and when we come out it's like someone peels plastic off my skin as I feel cool air on me and it opens up so we can see out all across the fields behind the squash courts to Letaba Road. I am still shaking. Pats turns and says to me, "How could you do that?"

"I don't know," I say. "I just did."

"It was wrong, hey," says Ari. "Lank wrong."

I feel my face twisting. "Ja, *now* you say that. That's not what you said at the time. You were all like go for it."

"I wasn't!"

"Ja, you were."

"How could you do it, Mart?" Pats says. "It was sick."

I look away. There's a buzzing in my head. "I don't know," I say. "It was like someone else was."

"You did it," says Ari.

Then Pats starts telling me how terrible I am again and I feel some of the other feeling coming back into me and I say, "Fuck him. He deserved. *He deserved what he got.*" There's this sad little bush to my right, minding its own business. I go over and grab it and start yanking, but it's tougher than it looks. I grunt and jerk, losing skin on my hands, until the roots rip completely out of the dirt. Then I turn and chuck the whole thing away into the bulrushes. I spit and wipe my mouth, breathing like I just ran a cross-country.

They're staring at me. "There's summin wrong with you," Pats says softly.

I point. "You were both in it also. Fully."

Ari rubs his nose, says, "They were all shitting themselves like I have never seen. Your brother must be some main man at Solomon, or what."

I say, "I don't know. If I did I would have said who I was straightaway." Which is true cos Marcus never talks to me like when we were little, not for years, not since starting at that high school.

"How can your brother be going to Solomon?"

There it is, hey. After all this time. I kept it from them as a secret and I could because they're shul friends who never come to my house to play and Marcus never goes to shul and they never ask me too many questions about my family anyway cos they're always talking about themselves. But I always knew they'd find out eventually — maybe that's why I did it today, why I went down there. I put my hands on my hips and look away. Just waiting now for what must come next.

"What high school are *you* going to next year?"

It feels good in a way, to spit the secret out like a rotten tooth. "I'm ganna be going to Solomon also."

They kind of smirk at me for a while until they see that I am dead serious, then they look at each other like oh-my-God. Ari says, "How can you go to *Solomon*?" Pats says, "Why you been lying?"

"I was never lying," I say. But I know that's not exactly true. For years I've been letting them think I'm going to government high school just like they will. I mean I go to a government primary school like them so why wouldn't I go on to a government high? Plus they know I live in an old bungalow in Greenside *with no swimming pool* and Greenside boys don't go to Solomon. They'd maybe believe me if I'd said that other Jewish private school, middle-class — but not Wisdom of Solomon High School for Jewish Boys up in Regent Heights. Never ever. *I haven't been lying!* I almost say or shout again to my only two friends, but I bite my lips instead, my face hot. Not lying. I just wasn't saying. There's a difference, right? I was just keeping shtum about it until today when I saw the rugby jersey down in the willows. I wanted to stick it in their bladdy faces for once, show them they not better than me cos they're not.

I thought it would be like, *Allow me to introduce you to some fellow Solomon chaps.* And the Solomon chaps would say, *Oh how delighted to meet you. So frightfully delighted.* Cos Solomon is full of gentlemen scholars and I am going to be one too because that's what I want to be and have friends like and will have. I still can't believe those okes were really Solomon okes, except they were. Okay so they were some bad apples. But also, on a level, I'm not *that* surprised by them, I mean when I think of Marcus and how he changed so majorly when he went to Solomon, there's a part of me that sort of nods and goes uh-huh, exactly, that makes complete sense, but I don't want to listen to that part. I push it away. That part gives me a sick feeling all the way down into my balls.

Meantime Pats is saying, "Your da, he works in a scrapyard. He drives around in that old bashed-up bakkie." Straightaway I see him, my da Isaac Helger with one knobbly elbow sticking out of that rusted Datsun, driving rattly down Clovelly Road on his way home, whistling in his teeth, his thick forearm covered in ginger curlies like the ginger hair over his sunburnt face full of wrinkles and a blob nose and stick-out ears. I hate it that I feel embarrassed but I do.

"How can he afford?" says Ari, puffing up and pointing a finger at me like a lawyer in court on TV who is getting the bad guy in the end. "I mean financially afford. You have to be able to financially afford!"

"You are so right, hey," says Pats to him. "The Sheinbaums go to Solomon. The bladdy Sefferts go. *The Ostenbergs* send their kids there." He's talking famous names from the *Sunday Times* and that — like the owners of the diamonds and the goldmines, the ones who build the big casinos and own the larney shopping malls and the big companies on the stock exchange. There are only three hundred boys at Solomon, and they all come from families like that. Never Greenside scrapmen.

"Something," says Ari, "does not add up."

It's like I am not there, the way they're discussing me like I'm a medical case. In my head I can see them running home to spill the news about me, little Marty from Shaka Road, and finding out what I already know. That just cos old man Helger might look rough when you see him in shul on Yom Kippur with that old suit that doesn't fit and no tie and wrinkled neck and boiled-looking hands and face all sunburnt and drives around in a rusted truck doesn't mean he hasn't *got* — doesn't mean he is like them. Cos they're the idiots. They don't know that Isaac Helger *owns* our scrapyard. They don't know yet how a place can look dirty and ugly but that doesn't mean it's a poor place. Me, I know cos Da has said it so many times, *It's dirty fingernails that digs up real money.*

Ari turns to me. "They are ganna eat you alive in there, my bru."

Pats says, "And what year is your boet, again?"

"You know Marcus is in matric," I say. "Stop acting."

"I'm just saying he'll be gone next year, bru, when you get to Solomon. Those okes are ganna moer you for what you did."

For what *I* did. Like they weren't involved.

"Let's be honest," Ari is saying. "You don't have any friends. You can't do sports cos you're a full-on minco. Your marks are so bad you already been held back a year. You don't have really much personality, hey, I mean admit. And I mean look what you did today. Something is wrong with you, hey."

"No," I say, dry-mouthed. "It's what *we* did." I notice that I've started walking up and down, I can't keep still. It's bladdy amazing how much they know about me. And it's sick how right they are. It hits me that *everyone* who knows you probably always knows a lot more than they say to your face. Only when the kuk hits the fan do you find out, most probably.

"You the one who schlepped us down in the first place," says Pats all calm, touching the bumps on his forehead that are starting to turn blue. I see it then. What they want me to do. All I have to do is say sorry, like always. I have to say it was a hundred per cent my fault. I must do that little laugh I do through my nose and put my head down like I do whenever I lose, acting all *Oh well what can I do?* It makes me think of our dog, old Sandy, and how she rolls onto her back and shows her soft tummy to be scratched. I have to be that. I'm always that. If I do that now everything will be back to normal and we can all walk to Pats's house like usual, and play Risk after lunch and I'd lose and we'd play throwing stones in the pool to fetch and I'd lose that game too. All-a-sudden I get it — they're *jealous*. I feel my fingernails digging into my collarbone but I don't remember putting my hand there. "Oright," I say. "I'm going, hey."

"Going?" says Pats.

"Home," I say.

"Oright, go," says Ari, his face all squinchy like he bit an onion. "You go."

"I am," I say.

"Fine. Big wank."

"It's not your fault," says Pats.

"Is that right," I say. As I walk off I hear Ari asking what my problem is. My hands are fists in my pockets. No sports, no marks, no friends.

This one time in the Yard my da caught me out telling a lie. He'd asked me to watch an exhaust for blue smoke. I told Da there was nothing, but I wasn't even looking, I'd been reading this paperback book called *Tales of Mystery and Imagination* by Edgar Allan Poe. My da Isaac has these thick fingers and his hands are like sandpaper from all the calluses. He's old but those hands are so bladdy strong, man. They are like pliers, I swear. He squeezed my arm so I could feel the fingers digging in down to the bone, giving me five bruises that I remember lasted for like two weeks after. I remember every word he said too. *Your name is all you have in this world, boy. Once you lose your name, you can never get it back. People have to believe in that name. Helger. If you tell stories, that's what your name will turn into — bullshit. Don't ever forget that.*

Da is so right. Nothing more important. Look at how those two ran away from the name Marcus Helger, just the name. A name can be a real thing, like a gun or a knife. I will make one for myself at Solomon — for something. Whatever I have to do. I don't need Ari. I don't need Pats. I don't need anyone. My face is wet.

HaShem means The Name. The real name is too holy to ever say aloud.

The next week when I don't go to shul, Ma asks me why, and I tell her it's because I don't believe in The Name anymore.

THE NIGHTMARE

5

I'm doing my *Playing*—my most secret thing—in the garden when I hear the big gate being opened and the car pulling in. We have two gates, both made of steel with spikes, both always locked, obviously. It gives me plenty of time to stop and go inside, but I stay cos I'm so curious. I hear the main gate crashing closed, then a car door slamming, voices and footsteps. Now the inner gate is being unlocked and they walk in—for these few seconds as she comes around on the garden path I have the new girl all to myself. I'm ready to look bored, standing there. I knew it was ganna be a girl, but when I see *her* it's like all my blood turns into one solid thing and then someone invisible starts banging a hammer against it. Coming toward me is a full-grown woman, a serious beauty. She has that Middle Eastern look of black curly hair and olive skin with plump red lips. She's got big round ones under her tight T-shirt and her hips are wide in those green knicker-bockers and I see an ankle chain above open shoes with glittery straps and giant cork soles. She's got a rucksack on her back and a suitcase in each hand.

It's December 1988 and, God almighty, I cannot believe my luck.

After she's unpacked in the Olden Room she joins us at the supper table, sitting in Marcus's old chair, and tells us her name is Annabelle

Justine Goldberg, but call me Annie, uh? Please. And let's see, I'm an anthropology major at Columbia, which is in New York City, USA. And she's real excited about the teaching position she has arranged here in Johannesburg, South Africa. Her accent is TV and movies. It's Demi Moore, Michael Jackson, Sly Stallone, *Dallas-Dynasty*. America! It's juicy coolness exploding in her mouth compared to how we swallow all our words like we're ashamed of them.

"Teaching where, at Wits?" asks Arlene.

"University? No-oh," Annie says. "Elementary school."

"What's that, elementary?" Isaac asks. "Izit nursery school?"

"I think she means primary school," I say.

"Oh yeah," Annie says. "I mean primary, like early grades?"

"And whereabout's this school?" Arlene says as she double-stabs the potato salad with wooden spoons.

"Julius Caesar," says Annie. "It's a township?"

Arlene freezes in her murdering of the potatoes and just stares at Annie for like ten full seconds, I swear. It's Arlene who brought this Annie here. Arlene's been a member of the Johannesburg League of Lady Zionists for donkey's years and when they asked around for a host family to take a Jewish foreign exchange scholar for a few weeks, she went ahead and volunteered us. She said with Marcus away and Gloria passed on and still unreplaced because of Isaac's insane stubborn refusing to let us get another maid, the house was empty enough for a guest. The shock to me was how Isaac didn't start up another round of the shouty screamings over it. He just sort of shrugged. Maybe he's sick and tired of arguing—there was just so much of it after Marcus did his disappearing act, it took such a long time to reach this Quiet Age as I call it. During the Age of Arguing I started calling them Isaac and Arlene instead of Da and Ma. It was my way to try and remind them to act like grown-ups. As far as I'm concerned, now that I am nearly seventeen years old, we should all be adults in this household, and behave like ones. Arlene and Isaac and Martin. Obviously I don't call Zaydi by his first name, Abel. Zaydi is, we think, at least like ninety-two. He mostly sits in the garden clicking his false teeth and praying and talking to himself. It wouldn't feel right to call him anything but Zaydi, which is Jewish for Granpa. Anyway it bugged my folks for a while to be called by their names like adults but they got over it. And now it isn't just three adults and one senior anymore. Now it's four of us. It's plus Annie Goldberg. Annie the not-girl, Annie the full-grown woman *heading to a township*. Arlene is in shock, Isaac is boiling full of I-knew-I-should-have-stopped-this-bladdy-stuffing-nonsense. And myself? Man, I am still busy thanking my lucky stars. I mean *look* at her. And my school year is over, it's summer holidays for me now. We are talking *weeks*. And I am a virgin.

6

I jerk awake. Another bout of the Nightmare. I lie there groaning, feeling afraid. The clock says two oh five in red numbers. After a while I see some flickering in the gap in the curtains. I get up on my knees to take a looksee. My room is the crappest bedroom, not only cos it's the size of a closet but cos all the others face the garden while mine faces the backyard which is a concrete square, basically, with Gloria's old room in one corner, empty now obviously, and a steel windmill thingie for hanging the wash in the middle. Marcus used to train there. I used to watch him wrapping his hands in bandages, used to look up from my books of poetry and spy at him. Watch him skipping with the leather rope going so fast it was like a force field around him. See him smashing at that heavy bag, huffing like a steam locomotive. And then looking down again, reading, say,

26 KENNETH BONERT

In Xanadu did Kubla Khan
A stately pleasure-dome decree:

I've always liked the words of poems and how they look on the
clean white of the page. If you read them over and over you get this
airy, lifty feeling right under your heart, no jokes. So lekker. But I remember it was almost three years ago now, when I was thirteen — right
after that bad thing happened at the Emmarentia Dam with Ari and
Pats — that I put my book down and went outside and stood waiting
there for the round to end. I asked him, "You want me to time you?"
And my brother just shook his dripping head and stuck his gum guard
out. I said, "I wanted to ask you. About school. High school. What it's
like . . ." And Marcus just sniffed and wiped his nostrils with that huge
forearm, his biceps with the veins swelling up like a party balloon in
his cut T-shirt. Then he turned his back on me. So I never did tell him
about the Dam. I went inside to a mirror and lifted my sleeve, my face
disgusted.

Now I'm kneeling on my bed looking out and seeing the opposite
of my brother. I mean it's body movement but it's not violent — Annie
Goldberg is dancing on the concrete under the bright moon. She is
barefoot and has on jeans cut off into shorts and a blue shirt from some
sport which I have no idea of that says *Seahawks* and it's so bladdy clear
that she doesn't have a bra on underneath. She has headphones on and
a Sony Walkman clipped to her waist. The smooth way she dances, it's
like watching oil being poured, I swear. Her arms are going like snakes
around her hips, her hips doing that up-and-down fluttery thing that
only women seem to be able to. A feeling of pure, absolute *wanting*
rushes through me like a bush fire through dry grass. So strong like I've
never had before and all-a-sudden *she spins around and sees me.*

I make like Donald and duck back down so fast it feels like I've left
my hair behind. I lie there panting like our dog Sandy used to do on
a hot day, holding a pillow squashed to my face. Morning comes and

I stay in my room till I hear her getting ready and then I sneak out to the fig tree by the garden wall on the Clovelly Road side. Isaac and Arlene have gone to work as usual, and Zaydi has already made his slow way with his canes to the chairs under the plum trees. When Annie steps out, I'm up in the branches and nicely hidden. I watch over the wall as an old snot-green Chev 4100 picks her up. This is a car full of black people and the way, all casual, she jumps in with them — I won't say shocks me, cos I'm like all liberal and that, but let's just say it would shock anyone in the neighbourhood. Where we live in Greenside it's just full-on northern suburbs, just bungalows with high walls and gardens and pools, every family is white obviously cos this is a white area according to the law. There's hardly anyone ever in the streets, just sometimes maids standing on corners waiting for the chinaman to drive up in his old Opel with the fah-fee results or the wide ladies selling fresh mielies from big burlap sacks balanced on their heads, shouting, "Green mielies! Green mielies!" Anyway I bet old Mrs. Geshofsky across the road would just about have an absolute cadenza if she saw Annie hopping into this carful of blacks. And crazy Mr. Stein, who lives right next door, I don't know *what* he'd do, maybe come charging out with a homemade flamethrower or something since he seriously is meshugenah in kop as Isaac says when he says Mr. Stein belongs locked up in Tara, the insane asylum. Before Annie can pull the Chev's door shut, I catch a few plinky notes of the black music they're playing, and I notice dried shriveled things hanging from the rearview mirror. It's all smiles and laughing in the crowded back seat as they pull off.

I climb down. There's nothing but time in this long summer holiday, school being out for six weeks, a luxury of open hours and days stretching off till the new year. At the Olden Room, which is hers now, I reach for the door handle. *Don't do this,* I keep saying. But I turn the handle anyway. It's locked, thank God. But I know where the spares hang. *Do not do this, Martin.* It's like a magnet is dragging me to them. I'm shaking and need the toilet. When I find that the spare key is not there I'm majorly thankful. Cannot believe what I almost did. I rush back to the garden to spend the rest of the day *Playing*.

Playing is something I shouldn't do anymore. Goes back to when I was a little kid, in love with the garden, the hosepipe my favourite toy, watering Ma's flower beds, the strelitzias and the proteas, the prickly succulents. I was still in nappies when Gloria used to put me on Sandy's back to play horsey, the fur all silky under my fat little legs and Gloria's warm dark hands curved around my ribs, holding me steady and the nice smell of her and her Sotho accent in my ear. Later on I started walking around the garden daydreaming—more than daydreaming, more like *living inside stories I make up*, I swear. I didn't even know I was talking to myself and making funny faces and noises while I was doing it until I got told. That's about when I realised not everyone does this, and I started calling it *Playing*. It's hero play, basically. Finding secret tunnels under the apricot trees and jumping onto underground bullet trains, taking out the baddies like Bruce Lee in *Enter the Dragon*, and rescuing the women prisoners, carrying them off like Conan the Barbarian. Getting older I've kept trying to grow myself out of this addiction of *Playing* but all I do is hide it away so no one knows I do it (except for one). It got so bad at one time I couldn't do any homework and ended up plugging—failing that whole school year. After that I controlled it more but I still can't stop. It calms me down, hey, seriously. Takes away my jitters and makes everything feel happy-safe again.

Tonight Annie Goldberg starts speaking to me alone for the first time. It's happening in the corridor by the kitchen door, she just steps out and bang she's right on top of me, her voice soft like she doesn't want anyone else to hear. It's almost painful to look in her eyes. Annie has these lovely eyes, very big and the colour of caramel with bits of mint green in them. When she touches my shoulder, I feel like my blood is being set alight. "I'm still on New York time," is what she is saying to me. "What's your excuse, insomniac?"

Because I was up at two in the morning, watching her dance in the backyard. I think of how I must have looked to her in the window, all peeping tom, and I feel my face blushing like hot peppers. "Um. I get this nightmare that wakes me up."

"Is it always the same?"

The question is like a quick push that makes me lose balance cos I so totally don't expect it. She has to say it again before I nod. She smells of lemons. Looking down, my eyes run into the dark circles of her nipples underneath the blouse she has on and I have to look up again pronto. "Then you need to pay attention." She's stating this like it's a fact, an order. "Recurring dreams, they're the ones tryna tell us something big. Especially what we don't wanna hear. What's yours about?" I shake my head. "What happens in this nightmare?" But I won't answer.

I sleep badly all night and next morning when she goes to take her bubble bath I head straight to the Olden Room door again and this time find it's been left a little bit open. My heart goes muchu in me, banging around like the drummer from Iron Maiden, and I stand there for a minute, I even almost pull the door closed but then I think of her naked in the bath, her soft, perfect olive skin, and I can't stop my legs from moving me forward. It's cool and dark inside. The Olden Room is where we store all of Zaydi's old clocks. When Zaydi came to South Africa in nineteen hundred and voetsak from his village called Dusat, back in Lithuania where most all of us South African Jews come from, he only had holes in his pockets and he didn't speak any English and he still doesn't, only mameloshen, and he opened up a little clock and watch repair shop there in Doornfontein and that's where Isaac grew up, behind the shop, so super poor. Then when Isaac bought our house after he was in business with Hugo in the scrapyard, he built Zaydi a room on the side of the house with its own bathroom and Zaydi moved in there after Bohbi — my grandma that I never knew — had died. Zaydi brought with him all his clocks left over from Doornfontein. They put them all nicely in the big room at the back of the house, with fancy curtains and a huge Turkish carpet. We call it the Olden Room because the clocks are old, I spose. I've always liked it in here, it smells of wood and varnish and brass.

And it's quieter than ever now, cos all the ticking clocks have been stopped for Annie. Arlene put a mattress in the middle for her, and a wardrobe and a desk against one wall. My bare feet sink into the cool softness of the carpet. The sheets and blankets are all messy on the bed and clothes are lying all over the show. The desk is piled up with books and magazines and mugs and combs and stuff. As my eyes adjust I spot a pair of her panties lying under some jeans. It's surprising how lacy they are, all femmy, this side of her gets hidden under the tough jeans and the boy T-shirts. I kneel down and pick them up, my heart knocking, one eye on the door. Again I can't stop myself and I squash the panties against my face, covering over my mouth and nose as I suck in air that tastes of her crotch and her private sweat, God, what am I doing? I'm dizzy and moaning aloud. It's too much, the excitement, the wrongness, and I drop the panties and run out to do something else. When I come back a minute later, I am much calmer and she's still in the bathroom. I page through some of her books on the desk. Sociology, anthropology, boring-ology. I finger the chunky jewellery in the little box. My eyes start roaming back to the panties but a hair dryer switches on down in the bathroom and it's time to get the hell out. Still, I have this bold feeling all day, and in the night when she comes back home I look her straight in her caramel eyes and say, "Do you like your room?"

"I'm surprised I didn't get your brother's."

"He left it locked," I say.

"Yeah, I noticed. You think that's normal? Put a padlock on your bedroom door?"

"Not really."

"The army's done that to him. Screwed with his mind. You're going to have to face that fucking draft too, soon. Have you thought about it?"

The f-word shocks me, the way she just uses it like it's nothing. It's never been said in our house before — the folks would kill me, no jokes. "Marcus didn't have to go," I explain to her. "He'd already got deferment after high school, he was in varsity, did his first year engineering, but then he dropped out. He didn't tell anyone. He just went."

"I don't get it."

"He volunteered," I say. "Basically."

She opens her mouth wide, then closes it and walks away. I stand there thinking, *Well that didn't go too well.*

7

But Annie Goldberg *never* locks her door when it's her bathtime in the mornings, so I start going in there without fail. The hair dryer is my warning alarm. I know I'm doing wrong but can't help myself, it's like an addiction, like *Playing.* I shake just thinking about it, going into her things. Can't wait for the next morning to come fast enough — and then the next . . .

This time I'm leaving the room when I notice the wall clock by the door is hanging cockeyed. Maybe I bumped it. Straightening it, something heavy moves inside, falls over with a clonk. Behind the clock's little door in front are only the usual cogs. But when I pry the whole thing gently away from the wall something big drops out the back. A *shoe.* One of those disco kinds, with a huge fat sole made of cork, and glittery straps. I turn it around for quite a while, till I hear the whoosh of the dryer, and then I carefully put it back.

Can't stop thinking about that shoe and when morning comes again and she takes her bath I'm back in, searching carefully and —

bladdy hell—I turn up the second shoe of the pair. Hidden at the top of the curtains, stuck there with stickytape behind the wooden thingie in front of the rod. Who would hide a pair of shoes on top of curtains and behind clocks? What for? Then I remember she was wearing them the first time I saw her.

Thing is, I'm a hider myself. Means I now feel closer to Annie than ever. I want to show her loyalty, her secret is mine too now. *We're the same kind.* Every time I go in, I feel so tender toward her I can't even explain, as I search under the mattress and go through all her bags, fingering the linings, and digging in her cases and feeling the pillows and duvet covers and blankets and probing with toothpicks inside her tubes and jars. But there's nothing else to find except those obese cork shoes which I keep going back to, examining them carefully before replacing them exactly as found.

I start to really think, to work it out. If she was wearing them that first day it means she wore them at the airport. If she wore them at the airport, she must have put them on overseas. It's two plus two and it's obvious but it hasn't clicked in me before cos I must be a dummy: *she came through customs on these.* They don't feel heavy, don't rattle when shaken. But they're big enough—you could fit things inside. One sole peels away a bit from the instep, old glue stretching like pizza cheese. My curiosity grows, I seriously need to understand—so I get some carpenter's glue and a Stanley knife from the shed. As soon as it's Annie's bath time I'm in like Flynn. The blade splits the gap like butter, but I only peel it enough so I can angle it to the light. There's a hole dug out of the cork. Something in there is wrapped in bubble wrap. Looks black through the bubbles, white at the middle. I realise I've been staring for minutes, I've lost track. I have to either squeeze out some glue and stick the instep back or is there time to cut some more? The Stanley knife is shivering in my hand. I start cutting and peeling, exposing about half the bubble-wrapped thing. It's round, looks like a disc, like a little record? No, or maybe a roll of insulation tape. My fingertips can't

THE MANDELA PLOT 33

get under it. For some reason I look to my right and *Annie Goldberg is standing there in the doorway.*

She has her robe on and a towel around her wet hair and she's like a statue, her eyes huge and mouth open. Something hits my foot. I look down, I've dropped everything. Sweat pops out hot all over my body. Annie makes a sound in her throat and something snaps in me and I rush at her and slide past and run into the garden, into the bushes where I squat down and hug myself, shivering, my heart kicking like an ostrich. Zaydi is under the plum trees, as usual. I stare at the front door for so long my knees go numb. Still hugging myself I straighten up and sit down next to him.

Zaydi has his Russian tea, his canes, his holy book of tehilim. He is ancient and pale, the father of my father. He starts to speak in his thin voice. His lips tremble around the Yiddish words like he's taking hot soup. "In haym mir flekt nemen a brayt, a grosser brayt, azaviy . . . azo, un mit a bissel pooter . . ." It's the beginning of the story about the singing baker, Friedelman, back in Dusat. Zaydi has a million of these Dusat stories and I know them all cos he's been telling them since I was little. Zaydi—he's the only one I ever let watch me *Playing.* It's because I feel like he's not really there, he's living in his own fantasy world of that village on the lake. All his stories of white forests and frozen lakes with horses riding on them, they're just fairy tales to me. I mean they've never seemed *real,* not here—how could they?—under the hot African sun. But right now I want to interrupt him, make him look at me, and tell him I've done something so wrong, can he help me? Except he can't, no one can.

Across the lawn Annie is stepping out of the house fully dressed. She stands there on the patio staring at me and I get up like I weigh as much as an elephant and lumber slowly across the lawn. I speak to her shadow. "Listen. I'm so so sorry hey. It's disgusting. I should never have. I'm so sorry, Annie."

I look up and she's chewing on her lip, pale in the face with a blue vein twitching by her eye. She swallows and her voice is shaky and hoarse. "How long've you been snooping in my stuff?"

"I just. I'm sorry, Annie. I don't know what happened to me. I —"

"I asked you a question."

"I don't know, like a week."

"Aw Jesus, Jesus, Christ!" She isn't cross, she's *frightened*. And that scares me majorly — an electric shot in the chest. She's asking, "Have you told anyone else? About the — what you've seen."

"No."

"Did you tell anyone, Martin?"

"No, I didn't."

"Hey. Look at me. *Did you fucking tell anyone?*"

"No no no."

"How do I know I can believe you? You're a snoop, Martin. Did someone tell you to search my things? How did you know to look there? Jesus Christ, did somebody —"

"I swear to God, Annie, it's not like that!" My mouth's stretching itself down and wetness is burning in my eyes. "I would never tell anyone. I also. I mean I also have a hiding place and I hide things away — my secret things — and I can even show you it, in the garden, I've never shown anyone, or even told — I would *never* tell anyone, Annie, I swear."

She stares at me. "Why'd you do it, dude? How'd you like it if you found *me* in *your* hiding place?" When she says it like that I see how serious this is. It didn't feel that way when I was doing it — but now I see myself from the outside, a picture of me scratching in there like a bladdy monkey and I feel sick from it. Coughing into my hand even though I don't need to, wiping at my eyes that are starting to drip, I tell her, "Honestly, it's because. I think you're. Like I really like. *I like you,* Annie." But she's not listening. She has her hands to her head and she's walking away. "Holy mother *fucker*," she says. "What in hell am I supposed to do now? This is bad, *bad*."

"Annie, please don't tell anyone. My folks."

She looks at me sort of squinty, like she's not understanding. "*That's* what you're worried about?"

I rub my neck. "Well, ja."

"Lookit, Martin," she says. "You have to *get* this. It's not about your mom and dad being mad at you, okay. This is about you swearing to me right here, on your *life,* that you will never, *never* tell a single goddamn soul, alive or dead, about what you've seen in there."

"Absolutely. I swear I won't ever." I think about it a second and then say, "Why would I want to tell anyone? I'm the one who was snooping, Annie."

Annie is shaking her head, walking away. She stops and turns back. "Okay, I'm gonna need you to go over exactly what you've done. Everything, from step one."

"Okay," I say.

"Okay. Inside." I follow after her through the front door, into the cool dark of the house I grew up in.

§

In the Olden Room Annie swipes the desk clean and I watch her put the shoes down on it, the one with its instep flappy, next to the Stanley knife and the glue. She asks me how many times I've been into the shoes and I tell her today was the first. She doesn't believe me, prodding the glue and saying I've been putting them back together every time, devious me. I tell her the truth again, how I found them and then couldn't stop trying to work out why she would do it. That makes her face get clumpy and she sort of moans and walks up and down again, bending her fingers. "Exactly," she says. "If I'd left them out in the open this would never have happened. But it's an amateur mistake. Stupid rookie. *Idiot.*" She's not talking to me, it's for herself, tapping her head with her hand like she needs punishment. "An amateur," she says. "A *kid* finds it." She turns on me. "Have you done anything to them? When you take em out, do you, have you . . ." I tell her again I've only peeked in one single time, today, and I still have no idea what it is I saw, or why she'd put the thing there in the shoe and hide it. "Don't play dumb," she says. "You are not dumb."

Feels good to hear that, makes me want to show her she's right. "Well I did remember you came from the airport with them on. So I reckoned maybe it's something that you didn't want customs to bust you with?"

"Give the kid a gold star," she says. "So you took em out and —"

"No, Annie, I didn't! All I've seen, it looks like a little black disc thing in there."

"Bullshit."

"Annie, I swear."

"It doesn't matter," she says. "I goddamn *have* to trust you now. I have to assume you've seen it. And what do I do about that, Martin? About you." She's walking up and down again, shaking her head. She asks me why, why, did I have to go and do this? And I say sorry like another million times. She stops and looks at me. "Okay, Gold Star. Let's say you're telling the truth. So if it's customs I'm hiding it from, what do you think it is?"

"I don't know," I say.

"Don't give me that."

"Like drugs?"

"They have dogs that sniff that shit. No, not drugs. What else?"

"Diamonds?"

"Ha! Funny. If diamonds are getting smuggled they're going the other way, believe me."

"I don't know — like a bomb?"

"Dangerous, yeah," she says, "but these aren't literal weapons. But you know this already."

"No, Annie, I really don't. But if it's not drugs and it's not a bomb —"

She lifts her eyebrows. "What?"

"Has to be political."

"Bingo for the bright boy," she says. Then she looks around. "God. Hold up. You know what? I need a drink." I follow her into the kitchen where she takes out a cold Lion Lager then puts it back. She goes to Isaac's liquor cabinet in the lounge, but it's locked. I'm about to tell her where the key is hidden when she gives the cabinet a few thumps on top until the latch drops inside and the varnished doors pop open. I'm impressed. "How'd you know how to do that?" She doesn't answer. It's mostly Scotch in there but she finds a bottle of tequila at the back that was someone's gift long ago. In the kitchen she pours out two glasses of guava juice from the bottle delivered fresh by Nels Dairy that morning and then she mixes tequila into both, passes me one. "Let's go sit." So back to her room where we sit down by the desk and she's thinking hard because her forehead keeps wrinkling as she looks down. "Listen up, Martin. I may need your help for something."

"Ukay."

"But I want to ask you a question first off. I need you to get your mind right."

"Oright."

"Martin, you know the name of Nelson Mandela, am I correct?"

I pause. "Obviously. Ja. Of course."

"Tell me what you know."

"What d'you mean?"

"Just tell me what you think of him, Nelson Mandela."

Time for a long drink. The juice is sweet, the alcohol makes my belly warm. "Go ahead," she says. Then she says, "Mandela, Mandela. Man-deh-lah," like it's a magic spell, a whatchamacallit, an incantation. It scares me. The shoes are something political. Mandela. She keeps on chanting the word, asking me the same question. What does it mean to me? It makes me look down, at the cutting knife on the desk, and

I almost point to it and say Mandela is *that* thing, that comes in the night and slits your throat. Thinking of Julius Caesar township where Annie goes to teach and how on the six o'clock news just the month before she arrived we all sat in the lounge and watched a woman being burned to death there, the reporter saying she was trying to get to work when she was attacked by African National Congress thugs who wanted everyone to be on strike. They necklaced her — put a tire full of petrol around her neck and set it on fire. They danced around whistling as she fell over. She got halfway up again and a young guy kicked her in the head and her smoking jaw fell off. The reporter saying that was why our army was in the townships, to protect law-abiding residents like her from the ANC. All that is Mandela. And there was this white family of six that got found hanging from the rafters in their house only a few blocks away from us, nothing stolen, only slogans on the wall. Kill the whites. That's Mandela. When there're like ten thousand angry black people in the street pumping their knees up and down, going, "Hai! Hai! Hai!" that's Mandela. When I think Mandela, I think AK-47 assault rifle and RPG rocket launcher. I think of the Bomb Board at school saying REMAIN CALM. I think what happened to Solomon school bus number five on 29 September 1982. I think terrorist. But Mandela has some kind of power that protects him even in prison. Because President Botha has tanks and jet squadrons and nuclear bombs and secret police so why couldn't Botha just kill him? What's he afraid of? But he can't. The name Mandela is too powerful. Even his ferocious wife on the outside, Winnie, with followers who necklace people alive, she is protected from the police somehow by that magic name Mandela. It's a serious word, an illegal word, a word you whisper. Maybe Annie doesn't know this, that Mandela is banned. That nobody has ever seen a photo of him. Mandela is invisible but it feels like he's everywhere. Mandela's a hundred myths, a thousand rumours: they said already dead, not really in prison, replaced by an

agent, never really existed at all. Mandela is this joke Mervin Slapo-
letsky told at school one time which ended *when President Mandela
comes,* to mean the same as *when pigs can fly.* And Mandela was what
was coming to get me when I was little, if I didn't behave, according
to Gloria, making Mandela seem like the Tokoloshe, the monster that
used to live under Gloria's bed and was the reason she put the bed up
on bricks to keep it high off the ground.

My glass is almost empty. I've been mumbling. I look across at Annie
and I'm not sure how much I said aloud to her or what she understood
of it. She puts her glass down and moves in her chair and flicks her hair
and tells me, "It's what I thought. That's why I wanted to get to basics
first. Before we —" She looks at the shoes and back to me. She holds up
her palms. "Just listen to what I have to say, okay? Open mind."

"Okay."

"First off, it's Nelson Rolihlahla Mandela," she says. "The name Rolihlahla means the One Who Shakes Branches, the troublemaker. He's
a real person, Martin. Flesh-and-blood human being. Not a myth and
not a legend. Certainly not any kind of a monster. A person, a man, a
male African who is seventy years old and has been imprisoned con-
tinuously for the past twenty-six years of his life. Born in Thembu-
land in the Eastern Cape, with royal blood in his veins. In 1940 he gets
kicked out of Fort Hare, the only black university, tiny, with like a hundred and fifty students, started by white missionaries. He was kicked
out for being part of a protest, and he ran off to Johannesburg. A Jewish lawyer here, Sidelsky, gave him work and got him into legal training. He became a lawyer, one of the only black ones in this country,
and joined the African National Congress, which wasn't banned back
then yet, right, bet you didn't know that — ANC was a moderate organisation asking for the gradual increase of black rights going back to
the start of the century. Because as everyone knows, black people have
never been able to vote in South Africa, even though they are the huge

majority. Only whites like you can vote. Only whites can be the government. And blacks in South Africa have never been able to live where they want, they gotta stay in shitty reservations you call homelands or in the townships, the ghettoes outside the white cities. They have to carry passes to be in white areas. They're not allowed to have a decent education or get a good job. But in the fifties the ANC still had the idea of peaceful change. They burn their passbooks, they try passive resistance, strikes and stay-aways. They demonstrate peacefully but the government shoots them down like dogs in the street and brings in tougher laws, bans them. The government wasn't interested in talking reason, only domination, white supremacy, apartheid. That blacks should be serfs *in their own land.* So the ANC switched to a policy of armed resistance, and Nelson Mandela, he was the first leader of their fighting wing, called uMkhonto we Sizwe — Spear of the Nation. He never targeted civilians, get that straight. Military and infrastructure only. He is arrested in 'sixty-two due to a CIA tip-off to South African authorities — shout-out to the good old USA, thanks, guys — and then there was a trial with nine others for planning to overthrow the system. By the way, all the white conspirators charged in that case along with Mandela were Jews. And so was the weasel prosecutor working for the government, a certain Mr. Yutar, trying to get the death penalty for him. Man, South African Jews — you guys are only like a hundred thousand and change out of thirty million population but I tell ya, anything big that happens in this place and there you guys are. You pop right up. Gold, diamonds, apartheid, whatever. There's that inevitable Chosen One right in the middle of the action. They used to call Johannesburg *Jewburg,* you know it? Ha. But at that trial, called the Rivonia Trial, Mandela was expected to get death for sure. He shows up to court dressed in his traditional Xhosa robes, what a magnificent statement, and he gives a speech that you've never even heard of, which is a crime. It's theft of your own history as a South African. That speech. I mean dignity. Gravity. Speaking as a Xhosa king in his native land to that white judge, colonised to coloniser but eye to eye, right? What a moment. Telling it exactly as it is, for the record. Turning the trial around to be a trial of the *system* instead of *them*. He speaks for like three hours. People were cryin' in the bleachers. He ends by saying he is prepared to die for his ideal of a nonracial democracy. You can hear the people gasping. Putting it to the judge, almost daring him. Talk about true courage. Now, Martin, people have heard this speech all over the world, been inspired by it. But they haven't taught you any of this in that so-called school, this is the underground history of your country, Martin, the truth. Because, listen, Martin, Nelson Mandela is no monster, he is a moderate. He's not a myth, he's not some crazed killer, he is a cultured democrat. He is like Martin Luther King mixed with George Washington. They have to paint him as a bogeyman to keep you-all scared so you'll vote for em. But that power Mandela has, right, it is real simple, Martin, it's not a mystery, it's something called *legitimacy*. It's the reason there was a seventieth birthday party held for the man in Wembley Stadium, London, England, where seventy-five thousand people showed up and nine hundred million more watched it live on TV. It's the reason every college kid back home knows the name Mandela, the reason the single 'Free Nelson Mandela' has sold gazillion copies worldwide. This is what you don't see on your news. Everything's banned. You're in a vacuum down here. You don't realise what he *is* on the outside of this country. See, this whole nation of yours, Martin? *It* is behind walls. *You all* are the ones who are in a prison and *he's* the one who is part of the outside. D'ya follow me? Mandela is not only *not* a monster, he is *the only true leader of your country.* And everyone in the world knows it, man. Everyone knows it in their bones for a fact!"

She nods at me for a while. I'm not sure what I'm supposed to do so I put my empty glass down. I feel a bit light in the head but what she's saying is making my heart push blood through me in heavy pulses. I'd like to leave this room and go into the garden. "Go ahead," Annie says.

"Beg a pardon?"

"Go ahead. Finish what you started." She waves at the shoes. I stand. She's at my side. I pick up the shoe I've already cut a little and slip the blade in under the instep and start to cut around. Mandela. I really do not want to be involved in this. This American is some huge liberal who goes to the township in a Chev full of blacks. She doesn't know anything about what it *is* here in this country. I feel guilty, full of badness, even for just sitting here and listening to her go on about Mandela. Like terrorism is not a thing you should talk about like that. *Just avoid, avoid!* keeps flashing in me like an alarm. Meantime I put down the knife and peel the instep right off. There are *two* big holes, front and back. Both plugged by the same black things in bubble wrapping. The other shoe's the same. Four black things total. I wiggle one out of its little socket in the cork. Unwrap the bubble plastic.

"You know what it is now?"

I nod.

9

At the dining room table, the Stanley knife slits the label along the spine of a videotape — one from Marcus's old boxing library (*Mitchell v Morake 4*) — as I run the blade around the cassette seam. I check it's rewound all the way before stickytaping the flap down and using the screwdriver to take out the five screws in the back and lift off the face. It's a TDK E180, meaning 180 minutes of VHS tape. When I lift the reels out, I'm careful not to bring any of the little roller thingies with them. Annie hands me one of the four reels from inside the disco shoes. They're oddly narrow compared to normal reels cos they had to fit in her shoes, but still each one has forty-five minutes of tape on it. I unpeel some of the tape and lay it on the leader and cut through both with the razor to get the same angle so when I put them together they fit perfectly. All that's left is to put a little bit of stickytape to keep them spliced, and then both reels go back into the cassette. I look up and say, "I think I know what's on here."

"You think wrong," she says.

"Is it Mandela?"

She smiles.

"Interviews, speeches, biography, all that."

"There'd be no point to that. We're long past *that*."

"What's it, then?"

She says, "Now can we make the copy?"

"Let me do them all first."

She passes me the next tape, watches me fit it with another one of her shoe reels. It's not hard for me. As I told her before, our ancient Telefunken video machine eats tapes for breakfast, but Isaac still says it's "a hunned per cent fine"—that's why I've been fixing tapes and cleaning heads and that for years. I think of asking Annie why she couldn't just deliver the reels to whoever they're supposed to go to, why put them in cassettes at all? But then I already know the answer—she's going to hang on to these originals.

"Thanks for doing this," she says. "I mean for real. I've been going crazy trying to figure out how I'm gonna get this part done. You can't be too careful. The ANC's rotten with snitches."

I flinch. In my head the words *communist* and *terrorist* have both popped up in bright letters the colour of blood. But Annie hasn't seemed to notice my reaction, telling me the ANC's behind this tape mission, like it's no big deal. "It's going from comrade to comrade," she says. "I'm just the gal in the middle, passing it along. I'm also a techie moron. Told em that when they came to my hotel in London to give it to me."

"London?"

"Yeah, that's where it happened. That's pretty much the hub for the Movement."

"Movement," I say.

"Yeah, the Movement. As in anti-apartheid movement. I had a flight in the morning and I had to figure out a way to squirrel these videos away somewhere invisible real quick. What do you think of my shoes idea?"

"Good," I say. "Customs is looking at you and meanwhile you're walking right on it." I'm trying to keep my voice all casual, remembering the arrivals hall at Jan Smuts Airport when we came back from holiday to Israel that time, the customs men with their caps and moustaches and hard looks. "How come you even know ANC people?"

"Cuz I do. Told the ones who gave it to me, look, all I know is how to push play, that's it. They said improvise on the ground when I get there, find someone. But that's not as easy as it sounds."

"What would have happened if you'd been caught with this?"

"Still could happen, honey. I keep telling you but you're not listening. Why do you think I was so freaked out when I found you in my stuff? I thought you might report me. Or tell your folks and they'd do it."

"No ways," I say. "Never." But I'm not as sure as I sound.

She picks up the nearest tape. "This stuff is red-hot, Martin. Treat with extreme caution. Don't forget that. Do not think I'm kidding. If you get nailed with this, it'll be arrest, interrogation, prison time. The whole nine yards. I am not kidding you."

Well, she's an American and they exaggerate. I just nod like, ja, I get it, no problem, and use the video camera to make a copy for her, all four onto one 180-minute tape. Annie won't let me watch the TV during the process, so I can't see what's on the tape. Afterwards she asks me about my hiding place and I tell her she's the first other human being to ever know I have it. I call it the Sandy Hole because when Sandy was old and ready to die, she crawled into the papyrus reeds in the far corner. I followed her later, crawling inside. In the middle it was open, hollow, and Sandy was lying on her side with ants swarming on her black lips. I took a twig and touched her on her open brown eye and when she didn't blink I knew what dead meant. I dragged her out and went back to dig my secret hole in the mud. I put in a bin liner and put a big empty tin of Quality Street sweets down in there and covered it with a board with mud on top.

"And what's in the tin?" Annie asks.

"Secret things," I say.

She rubs her chin. "Nobody knows about it, uh? Nobody could find it?"

"Not in a million years," I say.

"These tapes — would you keep em in there for me for now? You proved to me my room is a joke. If the SB were to show up here and toss the place, I'd be screwed." She means the Special Branch, the security police. I try not to smile. It seems a bit much, hey, as if they'd ever bother with our little bungalow in Greenside. But I tell her sure, I'll stick the four original tapes in the Sandy Hole for her. "Swear on your life, Martin," she says, "that you won't watch em."

"Okay, I swear on my life."

She looks at me. "Good."

I say, "You're going to take the one tape with you, aren't you? Into the township today." She nods. I say, "That's where your contact is, to give it to." She doesn't say anything but her silence tells me I must be right. "What's it like in there?"

"It's tough but it's amazing. The girls are amazing. The people."

"Do you have to go through like roadblocks?"

"Oh yeah, there's police and army on the road into Jules. Any white person needs a permit, and I used to have to show them mine. But they're used to seeing us now, they wave us through. Course today could be the one they decide to search."

I think about this, looking at the video machine. "You should make it so if you do get stopped you can press a button and erase the tape."

She perks up. "Could that be done?"

"Why not? I'd just have to think about how."

"If you do," Annie says, "you should come with."

I fake a laugh to cover my shock. "Should I?"

"Yeah, you really should. Get off this movie set you live in here in the suburbs, Martin, this fake California. Quit pretending you're not in Africa. You're living inside a movie, my man."

"Oh ja? What's it called, the movie?"

"Whiteland," she says, not grinning with me. "You should, though —come with. I'll show you some things and change that screwed-up programming you have in there." She pokes at my temple.

"Screwed up, hey?" I say.

She says, "You think it's normal to get the same nightmare over and over?"

I wish I'd never told her about that. Ever since, she's been wanting to know what it's about. "That's just me," I say. "It's got nothing to do with where we live."

"No? Why don't you tell me about it and I'll see if that's true or not."

"Why don't you tell me what's on the video?"

She looks at me for a while, without blinking. "I'd have to show you some things first."

"In the township."

"That's right. You need to understand, gain the right mind frame."

I shake my head slowly. "Annie, you've been here like two and a half weeks, hey."

"That's right. And you've never been in a township in your life, true?"

"It's illegal," I say, feeling small.

"Exactly," she says.

There's something pushy about the way she's talking to me, I'm getting a teacher vibe off her that I don't like. It makes me want to push back but I don't have words to match hers, don't have the grown-up *knowing* that she's so chock-full of. So I say what I've heard so many others say. "It's not so bad when you compare them to the rest of Africa."

"Oh boy," she says, her eyes making circles. "You *really* need to come with."

I get hot in the face, but I go on quoting, all stubborn. "There're millions of em trying to cross the border and get in. If it's so bad why would they?"

She smiles very slightly. "Maybe you can ask them yourself, Martin. If you have the balls."

10

In the blackness I'm being slammed around and I'm suffocating but I tell myself it's just in my head, there's plenty of air, but I don't really believe myself cos everything tastes of hot dust and I feel dizzy. The Chev's suspension is utterly stuffed, the struts need replacing, it was bouncing hard before but then we must have hit a dirt road because ever since it's been insane. I hear stones ticking on metal and I cough on the dust and try not to hit my head on the lid by pressing hard with my legs. I feel the Chev climbing and then we are level and we stop and wheel around and reverse, the engine whining. The engine dies and there's silence. Doors slam and steps crunch close by. I can hear voices, but too muffled to understand. The trunk is what Americans like Annie call this. I am locked in the trunk of a car full of strangers, black people. We say boot. A boot or a trunk—it's just as locked and just as dumb to be in one either way.

But it's funny, what I regret most is telling her the Nightmare. I've never told anyone before. I feel like she owns it now, almost like she owns some part of me. It's not true, but I feel it. Like I'm in her clutches.

I hear the key scratching around the lock before it slides in. Then three loud bangs.

11

Always the whine of the brakes on the trucks and their heavy diesel panting. Always the soft rain. Always waking up in my own bed and believing it to be real, every single time. Then out of the dark the big megaphones boom German and the spotlights stab like lances through the rain. The noise of jackboots hitting the wet streets as the steel-headed soldiers in their dark greatcoats come off the back of the truck and rush to our walls.

"Achtung! Achtung! Aller Juden raus! Schnell! Juden rrrrraus!"

I'm up and in the passage and running. Jews out. Move it. Out. Wolf dogs are roaring. I see steel heads and greatcoats swarming over the walls and jackboots crossing the garden, trampling our flowers, Ma's prized proteas and strelitzias and geraniums. They've got Marcus in a spotlight on his knees already, hands behind his head. Arlene shrieks from the main bedroom but it's too late to help them. I can escape through the backyard and over the fence into crazy Mr. Stein's property.

I spring across the kitchen to the back door but I freeze there. Don't forget Zaydi! Glass is smashing everywhere. I swear and turn around and start running down towards his side of the house. All along the wet wind is blowing in the flapping curtains from shattered windows and the Germans with their blood-red armbands are at the burglar bars, slamming them with sledgehammers.

"Aller Juden raus! Schnell!"

I reach Zaydi's room, he is pawing at the glass containing his floating teeth, his wrinkled empty mouth chewing. I grab him and pick him up, he is so light his bones feel as hollow as the aluminium tubes of our folding garden chairs. I swing him onto my back. Just then his big windows explode. The Germans are hammering the burglar bars. I can see their big faces in the spotlights under their square helmets, screaming at me, spitting and roaring, and then an enormous black wolf dog of the northern forests launches itself, foam streaming from its fangs, and smashes so hard into the steel that the concrete gives way and the whole frame of bars rips loose and collapses into the room.

I turn with Zaydi on my back and I'm running as fast as I can, that wolf dog and the blood armbands close behind, and I know they don't want to shoot because they want me alive, us alive, they want to do medical experiments on all of us, to keep us in pain for as long as they possibly can.

Meanwhile Zaydi is getting heavier and heavier. As if his years are turning into kilos. It becomes so hard to carry him, he weighs almost as much as a whole century, I can barely hold on. But if I drop him they will have him. I kick open the door and start across the backyard to the fence. I can scramble over it by myself, easily. All I have to do is drop Zaydi. And if I drop him it will distract them. Drop Zaydi and get away — fly up over the wall and keep going and be free. That's all I have to do. Drop him, drop Zaydi . . .

"And then?" Annie Goldberg asked me.

"Then I wake up," I said.

"Do you drop him or not?"

"I don't know, I never reach a decision. But it's the worst part."

"Being forced to make that choice?"

"No," I said. "Being forced to hate my own grandfather."

EXIT GARDEN

12

The acid that Isaac keeps in the shed at home is for topping up car batteries and it's such staunch stuff it has to be kept in this special bladder. I have it with me, the tube running into Annie's bag with the videotape. If I didn't get the three knocks my job was to pump acid and burn the tape, wipe out whatever's on it. I don't know if that would actually work, but Annie believed me and that's all that mattered at the time. After I hear the knocks the boot lid creaks up and there's Annie. I pull out the tube and hand her the bag and then climb out of the Chev and I'm standing in a township for the first time in my life.

I see bare earth and a small yellow-brick schoolhouse. We are on a hilltop and I walk to the edge. There's hazy blue coal smoke and burning rubbish below, all these little houses hemmed in by koppies covered in yellow grass and stones. I see some bright yellow police Casspirs, long armoured trucks parked on the central dirt road, and then a brown army tank on a dirt soccer field. There are a bunch of combis, minibus taxis parked around a swarming marketplace. On the far side it's a solid field of corrugated iron and cardboard, the roofs of home-made huts with stones on top to keep them down — as if the land there has some bad skin disease.

Annie takes me into the little schoolhouse. It's bare concrete and brick walls, but new and clean. The principal is a short woman with big hair and veins in her neck, a wide smile and a painful handshake. Lindiwe Mokefi is her name. They run classes through the summer here, following their own curriculum. Annie already explained that this school is the first private English school built in a township, paid for by a Swiss charity, taught mostly by foreign volunteers, and free to the students. The only reason the government has allowed this place is cos it's so desperate to make our country look good to foreigners these days. This Leiterhoff School gives a decent education—unlike the other black schools ("slave trainers," Annie calls those)—but only to a small group of lucky girls.

She takes me to her classroom. The girls stand up together and sing *Good morning, Guest, good morning, Teacher.* They giggle when Annie sits me down at one of the long desks, the chair too low for my long legs. She gives me a textbook to read aloud from, a story of Heidi and Kurt, who live in a village on a mountain full of snow. When I try some yodeling I become a true hero. There's one girl, Ilona, who won't let go of my arm. At break time they all go out back and each gets a peanut butter sandwich and a tin mug of milk from powder. I stand there watching them swarm over a sandpit like ants, other girls are skipping rope like they are trying to stamp the earth to death, kicking up red dust clouds and singing *Umzi watsha, umzi watsha.* I ask Annie why they don't wear school uniforms and she says it's because it might make them targets when they go home, either to the Comrades, the radical youth who want all schools boycotted till education improves, or to cops who seem to think that all students are terrorists and arrest them off the street into trucks they call kwela-kwelas—climb up, climb ups —cos that's what they have to do.

Annie goes inside. I close my eyes in the sunshine and after a minute I feel a little hand gripping my fingers. Ilona. She has a flattened cardboard box with lines drawn on it, and some bottlecaps. We play Ludo, the bottlecaps reminding me of slinkers. Annie comes back out.

"You made yourself a real good buddy there I see." I notice she has her bag on her back. An older girl walks up. Annie says, "This is Nosipho, her sister."

"How do you do?" says Nosipho.

"I'm well, thanks, and how are you?"

"I am doing excellent," she says.

Annie takes me aside and says it'll be okay for us to leave the school for a while, she's arranged it with Mrs. Mokefi. It might be fine with the principal but straightaway my stomach starts zinging with steel butterflies. I ask where we're going.

"Show you where these girls live."

I'm eyeing the bag again and whisper with stiff lips, "Do you have *it* with you?"

She shrugs and I know that she does.

"What do you need it for?" I ask.

"C'mon," she says. I follow her, feeling numb. We head downhill on the dirt road. At the bottom there's this lonesome shop that looks like a knock-kneed old man with walls caving in and a roof like a squashed hat, spotted brown bananas hanging off like skin tags. One good cough and the thing will collapse. Old posters are curling. BUY STREPSILS. USE OMO DETERGENT. Get whiter than white. Then comes the first row of houses — grey concrete boxes the same and the same and the same like they were stamped by a factory machine. People are sitting on plastic chairs and watching us pass. There's music, shouting. A ditch piled high full of rubbish gives off a fruity stink — municipal rubbish trucks are targets in the war and don't come around. We wade through boys kicking a pup soccer ball, another boy too big for his bicycle rides up and circles, his thin knees pumping to his chin. He seems to know Annie, they exchange some words in African before he drifts off.

We reach this bend where on one side there's a field and on the other a crowd, women behind steam-billowing cast-iron pots of mielie pap and wire grills of pink meat and yellow chicken feet, charcoal whiff of burning fat. A barbershop flashes cracked mirrors, a shebeen blasts music with red-eyed drunks lolling in the dust outside. Some goats are grazing on garbage. Annie turns onto the field. Across is the shanty-town — that skin disease on the land, the slum of the slum, where people have built their huts out of trash. Annie's heading straight for it. *You go if you want but I'm effing not.* But when I turn away there's a group of young guys standing there, guys with those flat golf caps and those pants with pleats or else tracksuits. Looking right at me. A hurricane of fear starts up in my guts and I walk out onto the field without looking back. When I catch up to Annie I say, "Where in bladdy hell are you going? Annie Annie Annie. Wait. Annie."

"The school is needs-based."

"What? Stop. We can't go in *there*."

"It's where our girls live," she says.

Behind us the young guys are on the field also, following, spreading out. A headline flashes in my head, tomorrow's *Star*: TWO WHITE IDIOTS NECKLACED IN JULES. But her confidence sucks me along with her into the shantytown, taking a rough alleyway between the dinky huts. A naked little girl is standing in a ditch with fingers in her mouth and staring at me as she piddles down her chubby leg while a ribby, mangy dog laps the wet from her thigh. Looking away, I only just miss stepping on a mooshed rat with the worms of its guts all spread out. I try to keep my eyes on Annie's back. There's a flap of plastic hanging over a cutout in a hut and it flies up and a woman with wild hair sticks her head out. I say hello and she starts talking fast in what I think is Xhosa, her words all snapping and poppy in her mouth and she's not sounding happy to see me. I try to smile as I squeeze past. All the time I can hear Annie's bright American voice up ahead going hi, how are ya, how ya doing, hello, and mispronouncing *dumela, sawubona, how-zit, sharp-sharp*. It's kind of annoying to be led by an American cos this is my country, except it's not really, I don't know this part at all. And on another level I'm super glad she's American — they'll think I am too.

Annie makes a right, steps over a smashed-up old tin bath, some chicken wire, and then ducks through hanging sheets. We come into this small courtyard, with the hanging sheets on the laundry lines all around us. I can hear a humming. "I want to show you this," Annie says. "Before we go on. I need you to see it." She points to a kind of marsh to one side behind this droopy little fence. "Go on up," she says. I take a step and get clobbered in my nose by the motherlode of all bad smells. Annie's saying, "You understand?" And I just shrug and say it's gross. "No," she says. "That's not what I mean." Her voice has changed so much I give her a worried look. She puts her hand on my neck and steers me forward and we reach the sagging fence and on the other side is a pit and it's covered in about a billion shimmering flies. I have to put my hand over my mouth and nose. Some of the flies lift in a humming silver cloud but then drop right back down to their feast. The pit is piled full of mostly human shit but other things are rotting away. There's rice except it's not rice cos it's moving and I think so this is what maggots are. Annie's still got her hand on the back of my neck and it's nice to be touched but she's pushing a bit too hard. She points with her other hand. "You see the cans?" I just nod cos my mouth and nose are still covered. "Pick up that one," she tells me. She means that rusted lid sticking up, covered in fat blue flies and slimy ropes. This is where it all ends up. We're talking maximal shit. The smell is so thick it's like wet paint. I shake my head and Annie is saying, "Go ahead, what are you, scaredy? Pick it up." She pushes harder on my neck so I lean over the fence and like I'm dreaming I watch my hand go gliding down like it's not part of me and get hold of the tin lid between thumb and fingertip. When I pull, it makes a sucking noise before it pops loose. I turn my face to one side. "I'm ganna coch," I say. But Annie probably doesn't understand our word for vomit. "Just read it," she says. I don't have to.

I already know it's Pamper cat food, the blue tin, hearty beef and gravy flavour. I recognise it from the Spar, in the end aisle where Arlene and I used to buy Sandy's meals. I'm telling Annie this as I drop the can, automatically wiping my hand on my jeans before I can stop myself.

Annie says, "You think these people have cats? You think these kids here keep cats as pets?" She's right in my face, her eyes huge and shiny. "It's for *them*," she says. "It's all they can afford. I mean families here live on it. They have to *eat cat food*. You understand now?" I still have my other hand over my mouth and nose and maybe this bugs her cos she yanks my wrist. "Cats here live on the rats. With all the garbage and sewage they get giant rats breeding everywhere. These things eat the feet off children who have to sleep on the floor. I've *seen* it. And meanwhile you guys are piling up mountains of bloody steaks and sausages on the barbecue every Sunday." Annie is a vegetarian and she's making a horrible face which I think is because meat's disgusting to her but it's not that, the face, cos now she starts mimicking. It's *me* she's mimicking with a whiny voice, some of the things I've said to her. "Awww it's so hard at my fancy *private* school — nobody wants to be *friends* with me — ooh — I have to wear a stupid *uniform* — and the tests are so *hard* — and my principal is such a *dick* and wa wa *waaa* . . ." Almost as if she has one of those olden-day air raid sirens inside of her where you turn a handle and it goes faster and faster, like there is nothing I can do to stop it, and even worse I reckon there is nothing *she* can do to stop it either. "Oooh, we don't keep a maid," she's saying, all nasty. "Oh wow you deserve a medal!" I try to move around her but she stays in my face, so I put my hands on her shoulders but she goes all stiff and I can't move her. "All you care about is *this*," she says all hot in my ear and she takes my left hand and pulls it onto her tit, I swear. Just squashes it in. Her big soft tit. It's like an electric shock, I can't believe it, the feeling in my hand, the feeling of her, it goes all through me. It's not something I can hide from her cos she can feel it too, down there, what it does to me.

Next thing she's pushing me with her hips and I'm falling backward. The wires are behind my knees. I grab the fencepost but it's doesn't hold, it starts sagging. I twist half around and have to put out my hand and it goes straight onto the pit, nothing I can do. There's a horrible feeling of popping through and then it's warm slime and squelching and my hand going down, down, and all the ricey maggots swirl in around my arm. Getting gobbled alive. But when the slime touches my biceps my hand hits something a little bit solid underneath, I don't want to think what it can be, something soggy, but it pauses my sinking. Maybe Annie is trying to help me up then, I don't know, but I feel her weight coming down and I sort of panic, I'm thinking *This woman's gone nuts* and at the same time I'm like whatchacallit — flaying around — with my other arm and my bony elbow goes wham into her tummy. She makes a heavy *oof!* sound and backs off me and I can haul myself up, pulling my sucking arm out of the filth. I hold the stinking arm away from me and run to the nearest sheet hanging up. When I rip the sheet off and wind it round and round my arm it makes the laundry lines bounce and I see someone standing behind, close, and others behind him. He has a flat cap, black leather, and thin eyes watching me while he's chewing on a match. He's one of those who followed across the field. Annie's turtled up on the ground with her head down like a praying Muslim. I'm saying sorry but I don't think she hears me, I go to help her up, pulling on the bag which opens. The videotape's inside. Without really thinking about it, I take it out and stuff it quickly down the top of my pants under my shirt. Then I zip the bag and move off and start scrubbing like crazymad with the sheet around my arm. More young guys come out from behind the laundry and just stand there, staring at me, at us both. "Comrade," says the first one. "Are you all right, Comrade?"

"I'm fine," I tell him.

But he's not talking to me.

13

The shantytown runs along the bank of a muddy little stream and the people use that stream for everything. Annie and the guys wait for me while I find a spot that's not too bad—there's even a slither of laundry soap that I manage to pick out of the rubbish and clean my arm with till it hurts. On the other side of the stream there's more shantytown but not as much and past that it's just open veld, where the guys lead us.

It's hilly and hot in the open, all rocks and yellow grass and red ant-hills. I'm not looking at Annie as we walk, I keep playing over in my mind how bladdy nasty she got by that shit pit. Especially the mim-icking. When someone mimics you like that it's like a burn inside, it doesn't just stop hurting the second it's over. All-a-sudden I hear a big engine revving and look up and the guys tell us to run and we all run hard up the closest koppie and drop down in the high grass on top. Looking down, I see a yellow Casspir come around. Bladdy spaz-look-ing things they are, on their giant moonwalker tires. One of the guys says Mello Yello and I get that's what they call them, after the cold'rink which is also that bright yellow colour. Behind the Casspir comes a police truck. They both park and policemen get out of both and they open the back of the truck and bang on the sides. People climb down and stand there with their hands up, mostly school-age kids, some lit-tle ones, and older men and women too. The cops have shotguns or as-sault rifles out and are wearing khaki leopard patterns or blue peaked caps, some carry sjamboks. What surprises me is how most of these cops are black men. But the white ones look in charge, shouting or-ders. One of the whites has a German shepherd on a leash. A butter-fly hovers in front of me and I watch it for a while. The guy next to me slowly breaks a twig into twenty pieces. No one speaks. Annie is chewing on her lip. Down there, the cops are playing a game. Laugh-ing. They pick someone and that person has to run and get back in the truck. But there's a catch, the dog cop lets the big German shepherd go and I can hear him giving the order in Afrikaans every time to *vat hom nou* — take him now — so the chosen one has to try and make it while the unleashed dog hits them from behind and tries to drag them back, shaking and growling like mad. The males are mostly quiet but the screams of the females float all the way up to us so clearly. Then this one girl breaks from the group and starts running hard, all long legs, her skirt flying. A policeman moves fast across and hits her with his shotgun held sideways and she goes over and he gets her by the collar and drags her back to the truck. She's kicking and flopping. He pulls her up and swings her hard into the truck and when she bounces off he lets her fall on her back and the dog is on her. Her skirt goes over her head and a whip comes down on her dark thighs.

I look away and when I look back they're throwing her in the truck and looking for someone new when all-a-sudden one of the cops goes down on one knee, lifting the shotgun. I notice smoke on the Casspir. Then things bouncing in the air around it, dancing bits of bricks and rocks. The shotgun goes *crack!* Other cops are down low too, firing. Now there are flames also on the Casspir, licking there under the smoke, and its engine roars. As it moves I see men and boys popping up in the tall grass on the far side, up and chucking stuff, their arms bowling super fast, and I can hear the noise of things hitting the Casspir *bonk bonk* against the steel and also the *crish!* of breaking glass. There're more flames. I see a burning bottle spinning in the air. Now the men and boys are running hard the other way, back toward the shanties, whistling and spreading out, and the burning Casspir goes after them but all cautious on the slope, like it's an elephant walking on thorns.

Meantime the people by the truck are running in our direction. A cop spins round and shoots at their backs — towards us! One guy goes all stiff and then falls. A woman hugs a little kid to her chest. Annie dragged me into all this — she did it. *I could die.* All my fear gets turned into this big rush of pure rage against her, as the guys with us start moving and we all run downhill full stick. I have to press the video against my stomach to keep it from falling. There's a dirt road at the bottom and a BMW comes fast around on it, boiling dust and spraying stones as it sweeps to a stop. Annie's running to the window on the passenger side. She's talking there, touching her bag. I run around to the driver's side. Up close, the BMW's side window is missing, broken pieces of glass on the dash and wires dangling under the steering wheel. The driver is this kid, a boy. Two others in the back. But the man in the passenger seat is no kid and by the way Annie is talking to him, the way she's showing the bag, I just know this is him, this is the man, the connection for the tape. I stick my head in and speak to him across the kid driver. He turns away from Annie. Good. I'm so acid against her it's unbelievable. I mean who the hell does she think she is to schlep me into all *this*? Literally shoving me into the shit. And then mimicking me, which I truly hate the most. This American. I'm so cross I want to hurt her. Just having the tape with me is not enough. So I shout to this main man in the passenger seat, "Hey. *Hey.* She doesn't have it! I do!" He is probably thirty or so, wearing a black turtleneck, his face cannonball round and shiny-dark with a shaved head. "Who is this?" He's asking Annie but looking at me. I say, "I have it, hey." Annie's mouth is open but she can't speak, it's like she's been slapped. "She doesn't have it," I say. "I do." And I tap the tape under my shirt so he can hear. There's a hell of a bang from over the hill, then two more on top of each other. The passenger puts out his hand to me. "Okay, pass it, let's go."

Annie says, "Martin. Give it back and move away from the car. You don't know what you're doing. *Martin.*" But I'm not interested in listening to Annie Goldberg. I want to do whatever will rock her the most, make her feel bad for what she did to me and I'm opening the back door of the BMW and getting in before I even realise what I'm doing. Annie runs around the car to get to me. "Bye American!" I shout and the bald man in front laughs and points and the BMW shoots away, shaking its arse on the dust road, giving Annie a blast of red dirt.

14

The road climbs up and we pass groups of mature men walking down. They're all carrying sticks and spears with them, and some have animal skins on their shoulders or tied around their heads and I notice pieces of red cloth tied on everywhere and they're singing in their deep voices that way that makes your skin goosepimply. The driver kid gives them the old eff-you sign with the thumb sticking out of the fist. They shake their sticks, whistle and shout back. He swerves the car at them. Some have to jump to get out the way. As we drive away I look back and see a stick turning over in the air then it whacks the back window and bounces off leaving cracks in the glass. "Those dogs," says the bald man. "The time is coming. Chuh! Chuh! Chuh! Is coming." Every *chuh* sound he karate chops his other hand. "You know Buthelezi?" he says. "That dog. These men are his. They licking in the usshole of Botha. They lick Botha uss! The time is coming!" Buthelezi, Gatsha Buthelezi—he's the Zulus' man, I know that, with a beard and glasses. But I have a hard time picturing him kissing the arse of our white President Botha. Those older guys on the road must have been Zulus and when we drive up higher I see they've come down from this big red-brick building with a razor fence around and I click that this must be what a migrant hostel is, that I've heard of in the news. The Zulus with the red and the spears are from the hostel and they are older men and these in the car are township youth who live below and there's hectic aggro between the two, obviously, but I don't know why. The boy on the far side pulls out a handgun and points it out the window—the one in the middle sticks his fingers in his ears, I'm too shocked to do the same—and fires three times, all casual, pointing at the hostel as we zoom along its razor fence. The bangs hurt my eardrums and I smell something burnt that must be gunpowder. This kid did it so relaxed he might have been having a sip of col'drink instead. Nobody else in the car seems to even have noticed apart from fingers-in-ears. ". . . your name? Heh?" I realise the bald one up front is talking to me, his eyes in the rearview. Like a total dunce I give him my full, correct name. And he says, "Me, I am Comrade Shaolin. This one is Comrade Electrocute. Comrade Jaws. Comrade Guillotine."

"Pleased to meet you," is what I hear myself say.

The road goes around the back of the hill. It gets all overgrown and we stop and everyone piles out and walks. It's hot and the grass goes *bizzzzz* so loud from those insects with a name I can't think of since my brain has stopped working. Nobody says anything and I start to shit myself to the max. Telling myself do not panic but I cannot believe what I've gone and done. Marcus used to say there's no point in panicking, it just makes things worse. But it'd be pretty damn hard to get worse than this. Up here there's nobody else, nothing but sky and grass and in front an old rusted water tank lying on its side next to a concrete slab all cracked and black-and-white splotchy from bird crap. This's where we stop. There's a view down onto the concrete wall around the township, far underneath, and looking out I can see the long shimmery strip of the highway and then after that are the ivory-white roofs of the mansions in Sandton which is a suburb that makes *me* feel poor every day at school cos of how many Solomon students come from there — land of private tennis courts and perfect rose gardens and butlers serving sundowners. It's funny that they would build Sandton right next to Jules township. Funny, ja — like that Depeche Mode song goes, someone must have had a very sick sense of humour.

Shaolin walks out onto the concrete and waves me to follow. There's a spread tarpaulin on the other side, some folded chairs lying next to it. One of the kids picks up two chairs and sets them up on the concrete.

"It's nice here at night," Shaolin is saying. "We can look at the lights there where they have electricity. But they don't give us electricity. In here it's a dark city. Invisible city—what they want." He smiles at me. "We come up here and have nice braais some of the times." He points to the tarp and everyone laughs except for me. I don't get what's funny about a braai, we have one every Sunday. Kosher steaks and chops over charcoal. "Sit down," he says and I take a seat on one chair while he settles on the other, crossing his legs. He opens a striped pack of Stimorol chewing gum and tips three of the blue tablets onto his tongue. He chews for a while, then offers me the pack. "No, thank you," I say.

"I like fresh breath," says Shaolin. He scratches behind one ear then rests his cheek on his fist. "You are with Annie—you wants to be in the Struggle, the Movement . . . yuh?" I don't say a word. "Where are you from?" Shaolin asks.

"Greenside."

"Greenside. I know Greenside. Trees. So much green trees. We don't have any trees here like that, nothing was planted for us in Jules." He folds his arms, puts his chin onto his chest so his chewing makes him look like he's nodding, agreeing with himself. "No, they don't give to us any trees. Me, I used to think that is our . . . deprivement. But now when I look and I see these no-trees, I am thinking *good*. Because —know why?—I was in the Germany, Eastern Germany. Yes—you surprise?—yes, for trainings. I was in Berlin, in Dresden, in Potsdam. I was in Ukraine also, Odessa and Sevastopol. Receiving my military trainings and qualifications. Now, the fust time when I saw the forests over there, and the snows, and all the green-green trees, so many, I said I can't believe. They have the *same trees as Joburg*. Before, I didn't understand. Then I saw those trees and I grasped it, how when they came here, the whites, the Europeans, they put thousands and even millions of their own kinds of trees into our soil in order to make it like where they are coming from. To take this place and convert it to something else that is like their homes. Because our people, we never had trees before like these kinds of big, thirsty trees, so many, and they are none of them African. Not one. But here, here around Julius — look around, look, it is perfect the same how it was originally. The same hills, the same vegetations. It is not been changed. You see, they try to punish us with no trees but in fact they have done to us the favour. Here it is my home one hundred per cent, and me I am from here one hundred per cent, and here is still the real Africa, one hundred per cent, and me I am the real African. So we are proud to be in Julius. You understand?"

"Yes," I say.

"Hear my words," he says. "The one who gives the orders is not that police captain they say who is in charge. This Oberholzer. Oh no, no. But you see, me" — he thumbs his chest — "I am the real comman-dante of Julius Caesar township. The only one. And I am say for you, *this place is our place.* We are Young Lions of the Amagabane, the Com-rades. This is *our* zone. We are the ones who have make the Mzabalazo, the liberation war, and we are victorious. Now these other regime mili-tary can come in and drive around and do some raids but they go out the same way every night. We spit on their curfew. *We* are the law here, the justice who is ruling the people. It is our street committees, our people's courts. Not them. We had police living here before 'eighty-five, what we say in Xhosa was the Isiqalo — the Beginning. Since then we the people judged them and executed them by means of firebombings. We brought down their homes on their heads. We finished the police station. No, we do not tolerate traitor police families here in Jules, my area of control. The collaborators and the impimpis, informers, must all die. They can bring the army all day, put emergency state all day, but we the people are the only rulers of Julius township. It is *our* control. You see?"

"Yes," I say, and something Annie told me in the Olden Room about Mandela floats through my mind then, that word *legitimacy.*

"They are the thesis," Shaolin is saying. "We are the anti-thesis. After the victory of the liberation struggle it will be the *synthesis.* You

understand?" He stares at me. I shake my head. "It's Marx," says Shaolin. "The movement of history. The developments of freedom." He
leans forward, shutting one eye. "But are you a Majuta, like your friend
from U.S.?"

"Am I Jewish? Um, ja. Ja, I am."

"Then you should know Marx. Marx, he was a rabbi's son. Synthesis is the justice of history. We are the antithesis, they are the thesis."

"Okay," I say.

"You don't know," says Shaolin, leaning back and waving his arm.
"You have to read." I try to smile like I'll get right on that. Shaolin spits
out the gum and snaps his fingers. "Let me see the weapon," he says. I
say, "Weapon?" He creaks around in his seat, sideways, putting his leg
over the plastic armrest, and shakes his finger at me. "Ai, wena," he says
— hey, you — "do not play the games with me. If I'm giving the order to
show the weapon, you pull out that goddem weapon and you show the
weapon for us now."

I want to say I don't know anything about a weapon but what's the
point? I know what he means. I was all big-stuff about having it before,
but now I wish I'd never seen it in all my life. Wish I'd never met Annie
Goldberg. I say the word *okay* and I reach up under my shirt. Comrade
Guillotine is there straightaway with that handgun in his hand all casual, tapping on his brown leg under the shorts. I put my hands up so
fast it's like I'm a jerked string puppet. The others chuckle.

"Show the weapon," Shaolin tells me, "but be very careful."

"No problem," I say. "No problem no problem no problem."

15

The thing is trembling in my hands, held out like a beggar's hat.

"What is that?" he says.

"A video," I say.

"A vidyo."

"Ja, a videotape. It's what she brought."

"What is in it?"

"In it? It's a tape, that's all."

Shaolin's palm is still up, his lips get thin and then pop forward like he's going to kiss something and then get thin again. "No," he says. "It is explosive inside, she brings for us. Clever. Some new kind of Semtex?" I shake my head and I almost smile at how silly that is but then I get serious again really fast when I see Shaolin's face. "You play games with me you can get hurt. I have trainings in intelligence, boy. Look at me. If you want, we can interrogate you also, understand?" When he says that word *interrogate* the others sort of groan and move in closer.

I talk fast. "No, I just meant it won't blow up. I know it's video cos I—"

"Shut," says Shaolin. He speaks words I can't understand and Electrocute steps in and takes the cassette from me and gives it to him. He turns it around, flips up the plastic strip, and stares at the magnetic tape under it. Holds it to his ear and gives a shake. "This one," he says, "can be a transmitter. It can give the enemy a location, it can record what we are say."

"No," I say. "It's just—"

"Yes it can," he says. "Shut."

I shut.

"CIA," says Shaolin. "Americans," he says. "They think we are the stupid who can take this tape and then they can track us. Or else. Maybe it is a new kind of explosive. Very small. And when we put it in the machine and push play—boom! Like what the police did to Anton Nemanashi, our ANC lawyer, they send him a tape in a Walkman and he plays it and the earphones blows off his own head. So this can be . . ." He holds the tape and shakes it towards the others. "Can be veruh-veruh dangerous. You understand, gents? You must always suspect."

"Honestly," I say. "It's not ganna blow up. I helped put it together. It's just tape inside."

Shaolin stands up quick and lifts the tape like a hammer and I flinch back so hard I lose my balance. That cracks them up. Shaolin says, "Then why are you so frighten, if it's not a bomb? I am trained in the interrogation. If we have a problem with a comrade, a problem of internal security, we can bring him here for a nice braaivleis." He's using the full Afrikaans word for barbecue this time, stretching it out — not just braai but braaivleis, not just fire-cooking but fire-cook-ing-*meat*. Vleis being meat, like our English word *flesh*. The way they are laughing and staring at me, it makes my skin itch. "You like braai-vleis?" Shaolin is saying. I nod like crazy. "Gents," Shaolin says, "he likes braaivleis." They laugh even more. This is a joke I'm definitely not getting. I'm sweating like a sumo in a sauna. Shaolin asks me, "You have the braaivleis in Greenside?"

"Yes," I say. "Every Sunday."

They're killing themselves laughing now. Then Shaolin says two words and it stops and Guillotine goes to the tarp. Shaolin holds on to my arm friendly-like, his hand cool and rough. The tarp goes back, it's all charred black underneath like after a bush fire and then I make out these twisted-up wires on top. I keep looking and see a skull and some other bones, a jaw with teeth, ribs. It's not wire, it's people. When I see the melted rubber I'm sure. Necklacing. People burnt up alive here. "You don't want to tell lies to us, Mah-ten," says Shaolin.

My voice says, "Absolutely not."

"This vidyo, it's a trap, a trick. It is CIA. Not so?"

I have never thought so fast in all my life. "All I know," I say, "is that Annie the American? She brought it all the way here to Jules. It's some-thing special. And I took it from her bag. That is all I know, Comrade Shaolin. I swear to God that is all."

"Is that so?"

"Yes, ja, yes, absolutely," I say, nodding as fast as I've ever. "Because do you remember? Do you remember, hey, how she didn't want me, at the car, didn't want me to give it to you? Remember that, hey? She was tryna stop me, but I got in the car cos, you know, I thought, you, *you* should have it and not her, the American! To *help* you. I took it from her bag to help you guys out. Not *her*. Remember? Cos I'm *for* you guys aren't I? I mean I rather bring it to you myself. Hey? Izzen it?"

Shaolin steps back, cocking his head and wagging the tape in the air between us. Then he grins like a floodlight. "That is good one," he says. "Good one!"

16

Shaolin gives Jaws the tape and Jaws drives the BMW away and the rest of us go on foot along a different path, taking a "double up" — their slang for shortcut — across the veld where some fires are still making smoke from the violence before. But we don't see anyone, we move along carefully until we reach the mud stream and the shantytown again. Comrade Shaolin walks in front through the alleys between the huts and people pop out everywhere to shake his hand, touch his shoulder. We walk deep into the shanties and enter a hut. A pair of boys in shorts, one armed with an AK-47 almost as tall as he is, stand up and salute, lifting their fists. Shaolin does the same and they slide a corrugated iron wall to the side and behind is a big open hall full of people. Inside it smells of bodies and earth and paraffin, some light comes from lanterns but daylight's also poking through holes in the roof of corrugated iron held up by beams of stacked construction blocks. Up front there's a stage made of old milk crates covered by flattened cardboard boxes. People turn to look at Shaolin and they lift their fists and he salutes back. He talks to some of them, murmuring in ears, and they nod and run off. At the side there's a big easy chair with a rip showing stuffing. Shaolin sits and points and I take a plastic chair opposite.

There are even more people in here than I first thought and more keep arriving, a young crowd of mostly teenagers, standing room only.

I see red UDF and tons of yellow ANC T-shirts that are supposed to be banned. *Your bullets cannot stop us,* one shirt says. *Liberation before education,* says another. "You impress, this place?" Shaolin says to me.

"Yes," I say. "I am."

He nods. "We built this here in Klipkamp because is our fortress. They can't even watch from helicopter." Klipkamp is Afrikaans for Stone Camp and I reckon they call it that cos of all the stones on the tin roofs, here in the shantytown. "They cannot drive their armour vehicles in," Shaolin is saying, "so they will not enter." A woman wearing a black beret brings Shaolin a plate of fried something, oozing fatty smells. I feel my stomach moving and realise how hungry I am. Shaolin says, "You like some? Is good."

"What is it?"

"Is meat."

"What kind?"

"Pork meat."

"No thank you."

"Yes, Majuta never eats pig. Is the stomach part, this. Is good." He chews, licks his fingers. The grease shines in a thin line of sun across his lips. "Do you know," he says, "what my name is?"

"Shaolin? Sounds like kung fu."

He nods. "I will tell you. But the story is very long. You have to listen to all of it to understand. See, to start, my father, his job was a rubbish *boy,* and my mother she was a cleaning *girl.* We lived just here, I can show you, is still there. On Nineteenth Street, in yard fourteen. We don't have names for streets in Jules, they don't give us names, we are not worth names. My mother worked for a golf club in Edenvale. My father worked for municipality. They give to him a long piece of steel, like this, sharp one side, with a wood on the other to hold, and he would take a sack, and all day walk and stick the rubbish on the spike and put in the sack. Keeping the white parks clean for the white childrens. Salary, seven rands a week. There were nine of us with two rooms, like you can see, all sleep on the floor. My one brother died of TB. You know, coughing, tuber-closis? Yuh. My father got one extra job for a company which is stripping offices. He must pull out the edge carpets, you know what is underneath? Nails like little teeth. You are supposed to have things on your knees for this work, protections, but *they* gave nothing. One day my father put his knee on the nails. They are full of glue, poison. His knee went this big. He could not walk. He lost his job with the municipality. I was the clever one of all us, I learnt fastest, I remembered everything without trying. My mother was religious and even before school she taught me literacy because she wanted me to read the Bible, wanted me to be a pastor, a bishop one day. But my father said I should learn to read only so that I can understand the whites, the enemy. My mother wanted me to love my enemy like Jesus but my father didn't believe in Jesus. He said Jesus was another white man. He used to lie there with his bad leg up and he would drink. We didn't have money for pain medicines but there was the cheap skoki-aan, you know, the homemade stuff what you get, and he would mix that in with our kind of beer and he would drink all day. He was in a vast lots of pain. I think that the poison for those nails went into his bones. We only have that shit clinic and can do nothing, the drug is too expensive. He was a very quiet man but when he was drunk in that time he used to take that rubbish spike and pick up and say for me, 'You see, my son? My grandfather, your great-grandfather, he was a free man who had a *real spear* in his hand and he used that *real spear* to fight the white man with all his strength. But the white man, he has won and took away our spears and gives to us this *toy* instead. So now instead of stabbing the enemy we go around stabbing his rubbish with a little toy, like children. That is what we are in our own country, my boy. We fight rubbish for the whites. We are rubbish boys, not warriors. We are rubbish ourselves, to them.'

"With my father not working, I had to leave school very early. And I loved school. The books, the learning. I went into town and looked for work. There was a bioscope for our people, in Commissioner Street by the taxi stop to Soweto. The manager gave me a job to do the cleaning up between the films. Four double features every day, six hundred seats. In the white bioscopes, the Ster-Kinekor bioscopes, they show the good films from America, but for us it was the cheap films that come from China with the dubbing. Koong foo films. What you said before, kung fu fighting is Shaolin, from Shaolin temple, yuh. All this films, you see, the story is the same. There is a poor boy with nothing to start, who knows nothing. Then bad people with all the power, they kill his family or beats him up, or steal from him and he can do nothing. He is weak at the beginning, he is repressed under. But then he runs away and he finds a teacher of kung fu, you see, that power of Shaolin. And after he has it, he goes back and he uses it to smash up those bad ones. He breaks their bloody bones. Then he can get married and have a happy ending. I never was tired of watching those movies. You see, Martin, in those times I have had nothing in my head. No political matters, no understanding of anything. But when I started going into town then, that was how I started to see it for myself. How the whites live. How clean his big double-decker bus is, no crowds. The women with their make-up and perfumes and nice dresses. The shops full of all the goods and plenty of rands to buy what they want. The fat man in the restaurant drinking the wine from the crystals with soft, clean tableclothes. I am living here, down, down in the rubbish pit, why, because I am black, only because I am black. But I didn't choose my skin. Why must I be punish for my skin which is not anything I did to anyone? Black on my skin, black I can never wash off or get rid of. Yes, I tell you, those days I wanted to scrub it off and get on one of those nice buses, empty, and find a nice seat alone instead of squashed in and ride with it to the suburb with the big house with the swimming pool also. I also wanted to go to a good school with the best teachers. I thought to take sandpapers and rub my skin and make it bleed and will grow back white skin. The black skin the colour to me was the colour of dirt. My father was a rubbish boy. Like I belong to dirt and I can never get rid. I wanted to be white and clean and rich and everything easy and nice. I am telling you honest, you see? I was mentally sick. I used to have dreams — I never forget them — of taking off my skin like a shirt and burning it. Because that is what I am told I am every single day in town. When I was little all I knew was this place and I never felt it, but when I started in town and must take that goddem bus where you must fight for space, packed in, where there are tsotsis at the stop that can kill you for twenty cents like nothing, every day, *then* I know. Then I see myself. I am clever and I understand. I see where I am caught, where I can never come out. Like a trap. I am cleaning up the rubbish in the bioscope and I *am* my father again. They take away the real spear and they give to you a toy instead. And why must it be, heh? What have I done? Is it my fault? Why is it that I was born here in Julius Caesar township and you have been born white in Greenside in the same city, twenty minutes that way on the M1. Uh? What did I do? How am I wrong in myself? Can you *answer* me . . ."

Shaolin is leaning forward and I'm starting to worry because he's talking louder too, and others are listening. I look down, away from his eyes, and he reaches across and pokes my knee. "See me, look here, *look at me*, I give you the truth. My father fell drunk in the street and a lorry killed him. Or maybe he didn't fall. He was buried here, I can show to you — afterwards I looked through his things. There was the rubbish spike, lying there. The sack. I remembered everything what he said. Man, I wanted to take that spike straightaway to town and stab the first white man through the heart with it and go on stabbing all of them. I wanted to jump on that double-decker bus and go down the aisle and stab those eyes, who looked down at me. No, but I know what will happen. I can stab one, two. But I'm just a boy. Police will come, they will shoot me dead, or take me to John Vorster Square and throw me out of the tenth floor . . . So I went back to my work in the bioscope. I was down, in depression. Then, suddenly, I see it. No, it is *me* up there on that screen. They have stolen my land and killed my father. What I must do I must find a kung fu teacher for me, to give me the power. I was so young. I was looking for one actual chinaman. I know there was Chinese, some building for Chinese, some restaurant on Commissioner Street. I went looking in the windows, one day I see there some blue-and-white plates, fans, black furniture. I go inside the shop. I had it in my mouth to say hello in Chinese, which I learned some by watching when the dubbing was not good. So I said in Chinese *hello* but he was Indian, Mr. Prashad. He asked me what language and how did I learn. He called his wife. Prashad didn't know any kung fu, he was small and thin like a bird.

"But what is the power? One wise chinaman told us, said, *Power it is the barrel of the gun.* Yuh. But is it true? The gun is a metal tool which is made by what? The mind, the brain. Ahhh, the mind is the power behind everything, even every army, every police. Prashad, he taught me this. He had the Shaolin of the mind to teach to me. I was very lucky to find him. My life was coming true just like the film. I start to work for him. He would go in auctions and buy estates and put in his shop there on Market Street. And always he had books. Mr. Prashad and his wife, they lived upstairs. *Now,* these days, Group Areas, that law is not so strict in town, so it's many black and Indian also living there, and in Hillbrow. But *then* in that time it was only whites and Prashad he was fighting in the courts. And the other ones around, they used to throw his shop with stones, put dirt in his letterbox. But, see, Prashad wasn't like me, with rage, with hate. He was political. I didn't even know what politics *was.* He tutored me first there is no help to get angry, you must be in the politics, to organise resistance up from the gruss roots. He explained me the philosophy of what is resistance. To have the patience and the politics, to organise the people. One drop of water is nothing but if millions of drops are moving together you have a sea, waves, that even can wash a mountain down. Prashad explained he was a member of the ANC. I never even knew what ANC stood for, I mean literally, or the PAC, the SACP, I wasn't sure of it, the letters . . . For my work I was doing movings for the shop, there was a little place for me at the back. I didn't have any papers, any pass. When it wasn't busy, Prashad told me — those books, you go in and you read. I love to read before, younger, but he reminded me again of it, and gave to me the right books. He had banned books, he hid them in with the estate, in the boxes. If the police would raid and try to charge him, he can say, *Your Worship it is not my fault, I bought it from that estate.* Put the blame on some white man who died. Clever, see? Thinking, cautious. He taught me. And me, I was like someone thirsty finding water in the desert, you know. I started to understand my situation inside politics, what the political system is. The system of capitalist domination of the planet. Everything in the hands of a few rich and all the rest are just slevs to labour for them and steal for them the minerals of the lands. So I understand I am born in that class, also, it is my bad luck, it is not my fault. We are the majority, yuh, we exist for our blood to be used like petrol for those mines to get the gold out. The banks and the mines have everything and the people are dumb labour in their country. Yes we have a fence around us in Jules, why? Yes, because we are like the farm animals, the oxes and the cows. We must work the mines and be put back in the fence. No, they don't want us to learn this, of course. They don't want real education for us, only Bantu Education that is shit. To teach obedience and menial skills, to divide us the people by our vernacular languages. Because what will the farm animal do if they know they are going to be eaten? If they know they must only work to death. This is political awareness, step one. I would read and discuss with Mr. Prashad and Mrs. Prashad also. Prashad didn't teach to me how to kick someone but he was still my Shaolin master. He gave to me questions to make me think. Colonialism. If a thief come with a gun and takes your clothings he must go to jail. But if the thief is the Queen of Engerland, then nothing must happen? Violence and colonialism. And then with the Prashads we talked about history. I learned all about synthesis and anti-thesis. The freedom struggle that took place in India, also. But always I wanted to read best about China. Chairman Mao. The Little Red Book. The anti-imperial struggle for the people. This was the *real* kung fu movie.

"We would sit on the floor under the table after supper and listen quietly on that shortwave radio. Seven o'clock. This is Radio Freedom, from the ANC fighters over the border. You can get eight years in prison for listening to this. But yirrra! Starting with the sound of the machine gun *tuh-tuh-tuh,* and the warriors shouting amandla! ngawethu! *The power. Is ours.* I can never forget that, how it felt. I saw that everything I was learning is the truth. I was growing also, turning into a man. But not like my father. I said I must be disciplined to be strong. I started running. I must never drink or smoke. One day Prashad said, no, there is no future for you inside the regime. The state is too powerful, you can do nothing here, you need the trainings. He would help me to get out and find it, the ANC will provide. There is a way, if I can get to Swaziland, where my father's people came from, from there is a way to go more north. We have bases. In Mozambique, in Zambia. But Angola specially — many bases. Yes, and I went. I have been. What you will never hear on your televisions or your radios here, they tell you we are nothing, but it's not so. We have the bases. We have the fighters, the cadres, the infrastructures. We are engaging in border combat with the regime. I grew up in them, you see? That is why I am Comrade Shaolin and not the name I was born with. This is what the name Shaolin *means.* Do you understand, Martin?"

I nod. I feel hot in here. His voice in the dim light is pulling me down, down, making me sleepy. I want it to stop.

"Yes, what I always wanted was to go to China, of course, but I got my advance trainings in Germany and Ukraine instead. Is okay. Is good trainings. When I left it was Vorster was prime minister here, when I come back it is State President Botha. One Afrikaner regime and another one. One white man and another one. Nothing changed.

This Botha is trying to throw down some crumbs for the farm animals to feed on. Some little bit parliament for Indians he gives, and now you won't be put in jail for sex with another colour. Crumbs. Oh thank you, my baas, but, you understand Martin, he is only doing these because we are winning now. We have the youth uprising, the Comrades. We have the sanctions, the community actions, the armed resistance of the people's war. The liberated zones in our townships. We are winning this war. Our strategies are succeeding. The movement of history is with us. They can send the army here, but this — this is not theirs, this is ours, here. Like I have say for you, Martin. I am the commander here. The good revolutionary must swim like a fish in the sea of the people. Mao taught it. Wise man Mao. We are the antithesis to the white imperial presence. Synthesis is coming—" He turns his head, someone is at his shoulder, leaning down and murmuring. Shaolin looks at me. "We can start."

17

On the homemade stage, Shaolin lifts his fist and shouts amandla! and everyone else shouts back ngawethu! and he does that a few times while I think about the story he told wondering how much is really true. After the amandla shouts get really loud, he switches to mayibuye! and everyone shouts back iAfrika! — bring back Africa! Then he goes through a whole lot of vivas in English. Like he says, "Viva freedom viva!" And everyone in the room shouts viva! He vivas Comrade this and Comrade that, vivas the revolution and the people and the Struggle and the African National Congress and uMkhonto we Sizwe, the Spear of the Nation. He vivas so many things I lose track of the number. Then they sing African songs with most everyone dancing on the spot, doing the toi-toi which is this knee-lifting hop that I've seen on the news like a million times, only this isn't like TV. All those voices in that hot, dim place singing like mad and whistling and going *hai-hai!* together — man, I feel it deep in my guts and my skin gets goose prickles all over. Shaolin starts talking about missions that they have accomplished, he's speaking mostly Zulu, it sounds like, but he switches to little bits of English, it's a mishmash, even some Afrikaans. He asks different Comrades to step up and make reports. Everyone that gets up has to start with the same salute and amandla! and then a bunch of vivas and then maybe a song or two. I'm learning that these revolution types are into their speeches big time. If they have to do this like every week it must get lank boring. Like Assembly at school.

Then Shaolin starts talking about "the American" and my ears prick up. Now I see someone coming across from the side, up onto that low stage made of crates and moving into the lantern light — it's Annie. Next thing she is lifting her fist and shouting amandla! and they give the shout right back and she gives off a whole bunch of vivas and a whole lot of African words that I don't know. No ways is she just some courier. She starts talking, thanking the people for having her here in Julius Caesar, which she calls "a stronghold of resistance, a legendary place," and then she waits while Shaolin does some translating I spose for people whose English isn't that good, and then people start whistling and cheering. She tells them they are an inspiration to everyone in the world who is fighting oppression. Even in America, she says, we know the name of Julius Caesar township and the heroic resistance that is taking place here and she wants them to know that Americans are also in solidarity with their struggle. She starts talking about the "directive from Comrade Tambo in exile" and I know she's talking about Oliver Tambo who is the leader of the ANC, a terrorist that the government's been after since forever, I think. Apparently the ANC has been ordered to "make the country ungovernable" as their top mission, which is news to me. Annie says the ANC leaders in exile in Lusaka, Zambia, and London, England, have been "making great efforts to support you, the people, to fulfill the mandate of the directive and to expand the people's war. We need to work together to bring our struggle to the white areas also and ensure that South Africa *as a whole* is shut down! Shut down!" This leads to a minute or two of chanting and singing. Shut down, shut down. When the audience settles, Annie says, "Comrades, our leaders in exile have thought hard about how to bring the tools to your hands to win our *people's war.*" She says there's a new generation in the leadership, a young faction using technology — and they're behind a mission code-named Operation Fireseed.

Annie waits for Shaolin to translate, then she touches her chest and says, "Comrades, I come to you from overseas with the mission of educating you about Operation Fireseed. How we can all play our parts to carry it out here in Julius Caesar and throughout our entire sector." Her arms sweep out while Shaolin translates. Then she tells the people that there are a dozen couriers like her that have been sent into the country from overseas, each one carrying this — she holds up the tape, *my* tape — and each one responsible for its dissemination. "The leadership," she says, "they know they can't give the people enough weapons or trained soldiers to defend themselves from the regime. But they *can* provide these instead." She licks her lips, tosses her thick hair. "When Comrade Winnie Mandela says we have no guns, we only have matches and stones, she is not exactly right. This video will show you that we have more than we think." She says the tapes were made with the help of our friends in other liberation movements as well as former members of the regime, ex–South African military and police who have come over from the dark side.

She repeats that our first objective in Operation Fireseed is the wide distribution of these tapes — "these *seeds of fire*" — to every corner of this country. Meantime some others have carried a desk with a TV onto the stage, plus a video machine wired to car batteries. Annie taps the machine and says, "These are everywhere now. Even though more than twenty million people have no electricity in this country, there are millions of televisions everywhere, even in villages, even in places like this one." She flicks her fingers at the car batteries and the audience whistles and stomps. "It is estimated there are at least one quarter of a million VCRs, video machines you call em, that are in African hands, and that number is mushrooming fast." She puts her hands on her hips while Shaolin translates, and then she goes on. "Technology changes things, I mean totally. At one time there was no such thing as books, right? In those days the church controlled everything. Then the printing press came and people started to read for themselves and what happened? *There was a revolution.* This thing here — this is the real amandla ngawethu, the real power to the people." She's lifting up the tape, shaking it overhead as Shaolin speaks, his voice getting fast and excited. Annie shouts, "Viva victory viva!"

"Vee-va!"

"Viva revolution viva!"

"Vee-va!"

"Viva uprising viva!"

"Viva!"

"Viva Nelson Mandela viva!"

"Viva!"

"Victory or death!"

"We shall win!"

"Victory or death!"

"Matla ke a rona!"

Annie switches on the TV, showing a snow pattern as the car batteries hum. She sticks the tape in and the screen goes blue. Shaolin's right there and I'll bet he always knew it was no bomb — he was just being cruel to me up on that hill. Those burnt bodies don't have tongues but they can speak without making a sound and they say a truth in me that's louder than any of these fancy speeches. There are white lines on the screen now and then a picture, bulging and shrinking before it becomes a room with dirty wallpaper. A table in front has nothing on it.

From the left, a guy walks in, wearing dark glasses plus an Arab kefiya but wound round his face to make himself an invisible man. He holds up a box and pulls out a pair of rubber gloves like doctors use, snaps them on. Then he takes the gloves off and shakes his head and makes a sign like no no no. Then he puts the gloves back on and gives a thumbs up. The sign language makes me understand this is not meant to have a soundtrack. This other guy comes in. This one's got on a black ski mask and he also puts on rubber gloves and shows it's wrong not to. He starts laying out stuff on the table, one thing at a time. It's like ingredients, like a cooking show — cooking for deaf people. There's this bag of Wonderwerk fertiliser and a pack of Blitz fire starters. There's a yellow ten-pack of Lion matches, a sixty-watt light bulb, a bottle of paraffin. Things from ordinary shops that you can get anywhere. Kefiya takes out a razor blade and a pin, plus a strip of sandpaper and some wires and pliers and a frying pan. They start cooking, they go slowly, repeating their steps. They use big, obvious hand signals to show us when to give extra-special attention to something — the little details that must be important. I watch them treating the fertiliser with paraffin, watch them grating the Blitz as they include it in the process. At times Ski Mask holds up his wrist with the watch and points to it and then shows with fingers how long to wait for that part of the recipe. Kefiya fetches a little blackboard and draws a mushroom cloud and puts it on the untreated fertiliser, then he takes another board and draws a mushroom cloud that's much bigger and puts it by the cooked stuff and writes down 3X next to the cloud. He points from the one to the other —

Annie moves across and hits pause. "You-all get that?" she asks us. "Get what he's showing? The application of the flammable agents, it increases explosive power by a factor of three." People shout back yes, they understand, they want more. Annie says that the Fireseed idea is to make it simple to understand so that anyone can put it into practice, a kid or an adult, no language required. All they have to do is watch and copy. Comrades, you will study the tape lessons and then take copies to the people all across the sector. Then they can set up workshops and start to produce "effective arms" that can be stockpiled or "put into immediate action." She says, "Your uprising here, your Mzabalazo, has made a zone of freedom in Jules and there are many others like it across the country. But in the next stage of the people's war we must take our fight from the free zones into white South Africa. We must break down its power structures just as you have done here." There's a translation and huge cheers and some more singing and dancing. Then she says that you the Comrades can use your "people's courts" and your "street committees" to require that every citizen of Julius Caesar township *must* study the tapes and must *use* what they learn to produce their quota of weaponry. "We must mobilise the people to this task," she says, "and in this way the free zones will become the people's arms factories!"

They all cheer and she presses play again, stepping aside. The video men show how to scrape the heads off the Lion matches with razor blades, how to make a small hole in the light bulb and then to funnel the match stuff into the bulb until it's filled. They bring out Casio watches, FW87s in close-up, then circuit boards and batteries. They show how to solder a watch to the board, how to set the timer, how to wire it to the stuffed bulb. They show how to solder in series and in parallel. I rub my eyes, my face, it's like I'm dreaming. It's starting to land on me why Annie didn't want me to see this. I'm the one that copied this thing for her, this is my work up there too. Operation Fireseed.

I look to the screen again, it's showing a field that is too green and wet to be South Africa, the sky too white and low and the trees all wrong. It looks soupy and miserable — it must be Europe or someplace northern. What's strange is how all the goods they showed were South African. So it was shot overseas but meant for here especially, just like she said. Now we see this old barn close-up with cracked plaster walls. It looks Russiany or Polish, someplace like Lithuania where people like me come from. Kefiya puts a package down next to the barn wall.

Annie moves across and hits pause again. This time there's a groan from the watchers. I look around at their faces in the semidark. They're staring and eager. They burn down schools but they're like the best students in the world right now. "You have in this tape here," Annie says, "how to workshop firearms, mortars, flamethrowers, landmines, poisons. How to target these to destroy industry, to disrupt transportation and comms. To hit the enemy *where it hurts most.*" Fresh cheers are hurting my ears even before the translation gets finished. When Annie goes on she says more videos will come from the leadership in exile, with direct messages to the people. We have no TV station of our own but with distributing video we can establish "the people's broadcaster." I can see the sweat flicking off her nose as she swipes her hair back and the wet patches show in her armpits. She says, "Comrades, the regime controls us by controlling our information. Operation Fireseed will smash that control! Keep watching, Comrades. Keep watching!" She moves aside and onscreen the camera zooms in on the package. The audience waits like statues.

18

There she goes down a gap between two houses across the road. The American. Bouncing with every step. I don't even know why I'm still following her. She spins on me, her face still shining like she's onstage. "Evil little bastard," she says.

"I'm fine thanks for asking," I say.

"Dumbass. What got in your brain? You panic. Jump in a strange car, you don't even know what you're doing. With *my* property."

"Don't talk to me," I say, heading past her. Uphill will take us back to the school.

"From now on you stay near me and you do what I fucking tell you," she says.

"Aw, stuff you," I say, the brakes coming off my feelings as I whip around to face her again. "You're a bladdy maniac. You tried to shove me in a shithole for no reason. You're a brain case." I take a breath to go on but all-a-sudden my legs turn to pudding under me and my knees hit the ground. I'm full of buzzing, overloaded.

"Martin, get up," Annie says. "Don't be a drama queen."

"But I helped. And they could blow people up. I mean anywhere. I mean it could be me, Da, Ma, anyone. *Zaydi.*"

"Yeah, well, and your brother in the army is up there putting bullets in black babies, I never saw you crying about that. Get up now. People are watching us."

"You should've warned me."

"Martin, you're so brainwashed you wouldn't have understood until I took you through the looking glass first, okay? To see how the majority lives. To see that you live *off* that."

"*Bombs,*" I say, my voice climbing.

"Not only," she says. "Video will connect the street to the leadership in exile, to bring some discipline to the Comrades."

I look up. "You should have told me what you *are.*"

"Just a helper," she says. "A nobody."

"That's bull," I say. "Cos of you there'll be more bombs all over the show."

"Martin, look around, bud. These folks need a full-scale army to protect themselves. A couple of videos, we're only pitching pebbles at the machine." She watches me, hands on hips. "Dude, you should thank me for putting you on the right side of history. You will when you look back one day. Now get up, uh? You're making a soap opera of yourself. How old are you?"

I rise slowly and go on behind her, dragging myself. When we get to the top of the hill and come around the side of the Leiter-hoff School I catch a fresh shock. Parked in front is a Casspir, huge and bright yellow, with men of the South African Police sitting on it, some smoking cigarettes, their boots dangling. Annie waves, turning to me. "Just be cool," she whispers. "Wave at the fuckers, keep smiling." Then she hisses, "Don't *stare* at em like that, Chrissake."

Inside, we find there's a white police officer sipping coffee in Lindiwe's tiny office. He's a youngish fellow, early thirties—but what shocks me about him is that tin mug in his hand, one of the same mugs the girls get. I've never in my life seen a white man drinking or eating from a black person's utensil before, let alone a cop. This one's just parking there sipping his Frisco instant coffee like it's the most normal thing in the world. He smiles as Lindiwe introduces him. Captain Wilhelm Francois Oberholzer. "No, call me Bokkie," he says. It's a nickname meaning little antelope in English, but it also means a hotshot, a keener, someone full of enthusiasm. This Oberholzer is alien-tall when he stands up, heading towards seven feet, I swear, with long and gangly limbs like the poles they use for cleaning swimming pools. But his blue eyes are kind looking over his square glasses, and his smile is all loose and sloppy, making me think of a happy golden retriever. "How do you do, Mizz . . . is it Goldstone?"

"Goldberg."

"I stand corrected." His Afrikaans accent is thick but you can tell right away his English is good, this is an educated man. He could have been an accountant if not for the blue uniform. He's looking at me now. Annie says, "I'm staying with a family here, and he's kind of my, uh, little brother. Ha!"

Oberholzer says, "And whereabouts is your home, little brother?"

"Greenside," I tell him.

"You're a long way from Greenside! Hey? Hey?" He reaches out like he's going to touch my shoulder but then he leaves his hand hovering there. When he swallows his pointy Adam's apple gives a funny wobble in his long neck. I glance down—the cuffs of his blue combat pants are tucked into the tops of his boots and I bet it's because they're miles too short for him. Oberholzer's staring over Annie's head, as if he can't look in her face, her eyes. I know the feeling. "Principal Mokefi speaks so very highly of you," he says to Annie. "As a representative of South African Police, I want to let you know we are all very much pleased to have an American coming in here to help to do such important and valuable work as educating our young people. There is nothing more vital for the future of our country than education. This school is going to be a real boost here for the girls of Julius Caesar location."

Annie takes a second to answer. "I'm glad you, uh, feel that way, Captain."

There's this weird silence. Annie starts to talk and so does Oberholzer. "Oh sorry!" he says.

"No, you go on, please," says Annie.

"I'm saying I know you will be surprised by a lot of things you find here on the ground. I am fully up to date on the negative propaganda which I know a lot of Americans is unfortunately subjected to on the media over there. But the reality on the ground here is that my job and the job of my men is to make sure that the ordinary man and woman in the street is able to live their life peaceful, with law an' order, and free of intimidations. We will not tolerate any common thugs or gangs going round and trying to intimidate the populace."

A policeman calls from the corridor, in Afrikaans. Oberholzer says, "Wag net 'n bietjie daar, ek praat nou" — Wait a minute there, I'm talking now. "Our most important priority is that people can get to work, and also education and making sure that the schools are safe and running. That includes full protection for teachers, which I want you to know we are here for you."

"Well, thank you," says Annie.

"My pleasure. And here now is my card."

We all wait as he searches his long self. Eventually he finds it and gives it to Annie and he sort of bows and his glasses slide so his hands jerk up to catch them. "Any time," he says, "night or day. You remember. I am here to help."

"I'm sure I'll be right on that," says Annie.

Oberholzer goes stiff, slowly puts the glasses away in his pocket. "Lots of good policemen and their entire families have given their lives in this place. Since we've come in here in force, life's been much better for the general populace. Ask Principal Mokefi here. She knows."

Lindiwe smiles slightly with no teeth.

"Now let's talk about the video," Oberholzer says to Annie.

"Video?" Annie says, her voice tight as my heart decides to hold off on the next couple of beats while my armpits spritz, but then Lindiwe is saying that the captain is here to "make some video of our new school" and Annie smiles again and my heart can carry on. "Ja, therezit," says Oberholzer. "I am in charge of law and order here in Julius Caesar, and our good community relations is the key. We doing documentaries now, to let the world know the good things of what is happening, the positive side of life. How we are improving it every day. To balance all the other media lies about us, hey, isn't it so, Principal?"

"Yes," Lindiwe says, her face closed.

"Here we have a nice new school just finished being built, but is that on the television in America?" says Oberholzer. "I do not think so." There's a knock-knock from the door. A cop is holding a big video camera by his knee, like a suitcase. "I hope you'll say a few words," Oberholzer says to Annie. "Is jy gereet, Kaptein?" says the camera cop. Are you ready, sir?

19

Everyone is still laughing. The filming is over and the lighting guy made a good joke and Oberholzer is putting his cap back on, turning to go, when he turns back and plops his long veiny hand on my shoulder to say, "Hey, by the way, Principal, do you have a document of permission for this fine young lad to be here?" The laughing dies off like it's been strangled.

"He just came with Annie," Lindiwe says.

"Well we mustn't be naughty," says Oberholzer. "He cannot be in Julius Caesar and if he has no job at the school . . ."

"Please, Captain. We didn't know."

Oberholzer holds up his palm. "It's ukay, it's ukay. Dun worry. He is not being *arrested*. I will just give the lad a lift home, that is all." He winks down at me now. "That'll be nice hey, I'll take you back to nice Greenside and drop you off. Just like a taxi service, hey? You lucky fish."

"Thank you, Captain," I say.

There's a plain blue Ford Cortina parked behind the Casspir out front, and walking out with him into the sun with his hand on my shoulder like an uncle's, I feel relieved to be going home safe, getting away unharmed from this madhouse of a place. From Annie. She will stay and finish out the school day like always, pretending she's just a teacher and has nothing to do with any bombs or Comrades. The passenger door is locked, Oberholzer opens the back for me. Inside there's steel mesh between the back and the front and not much room for my knees. It pongs lank bad of old sweat and piddle. We drive in silence down the dirt road, only the radio crackles. I clear my throat. "Captain, may I ask something?" His answer is to bang the accelerator flat so the engine revs high and I go splam back into my seat. Next second he stomps the brake and I shoot like a rocket into the mesh, so hard that my teeth click and my head buzzes. "Jou kan jou bek hou, jou fokken stuk stront," is what Oberholzer says to me, now that we're alone. You can keep your trap shut, you fucking piece of shit. He drives on at normal speed. I guess that's all settled then and the answer is no. Any case, I can't remember what I would have asked him now. I rub my elbow and the side of my head, both stinging from the mesh. I don't say a word and neither does he until we get stalled on the highway in thick traffic. Then he says, "That American cow. Comes here and sticks her long nose in none of her business, blerry unbelievable. And those bunch a pusses upstairs, man if I was proper in charge she'd be where you are right now. I'd shove her on the first flight back to Jew York with my boot up her puss, the shit-stirrer. It is cunts like her that make all the crap for all the rest of us to clean up. It is them that puts all the ideas in those empty kaffir heads. Ja, burn down your schools and kill your elders and don't go to work, ja, great idea!" He thrusts his chin at the mirror. "Hey, you think you conning me, hey? Is that it, you think you got us conned so clever. I know what you doing there!"

"I'm not, Captain. I'm not doing anything!"

"You not, you not, hey? Ja ja ja. You know full well she's in there to stir up those munts. It's all my okes in the riot squad that are ganna get burned or shot cos of her! And you her little helper aren't you? What else you doing there? And lemme tell you something, I don't care who it is, if you go for my men, if you danger the lives of my okes, we are ganna come down on you hard. We gonna break you, man! We'll bust you every which way! You hear me?" I remember how Oberholzer's eyes had looked kind and blue back in the school, but now in the mirror they look dark, almost black, I swear. And he's knocking around up there. I think of an ostrich going mad in a cage, smashing. It's his long arms and legs and his cap that looks like a beak. All-a-sudden I'm not feeling jailed in by that mesh, I feel protected.

"You get yourself involved with American idyuts in a Swiss school of girls in the middle of Jules and what? What you think's ganna happen? You think they grateful? Boy, you will be the first one begging for help when they come to necklace your stupud arse. I am telling you, you are playing with fire, boy! And it pisses me off so much that me and my men we spend our lives on the streets to keep little brats like you safe in your nice clean beds! And this the thanks we get!"

"No, Captain," I say. "It's a mistake."

"I don't care how old you are, I can sling your arse inside on emergency detention for thirty days to start with! How'd you like that?" I bite into my wrist. He goes on, "I should take you and show you the things we have to deal with! Every day! It's us who stop the bombs from blowing the legs off your granny at the supermarket. It's us who is there to stop the Russian and Cuban brigades from parachuting into this country and putting you up against a wall! You know how many of us have died already to save your white arse? Do you know the pressure of this job? How many suiciders we get? How many of us end up blowing their whole family away and then save that last bullet for their selves? And they suffering for you! For you! This is Africa, boy! This is survival! If you weak, if you limp, those hyena come out and take you. There's no *democracy* in Africa, Jezus Chrise. That is for up there in bladdy frozen Swisserland or wherever, where it's easy cos everyone is nice and polite and white as yogurt anyway. Here we have got the real tribes of Africa, with the spears and the witch doctors and the *real* spells — man, Africa is war and survival and that is all!"

The back of his neck has turned watermelon red. His spittle on the windshield is like the soap spray from those guys at the petrol station. I try to keep very still and I'm praying that traffic will get moving pronto. The whole car is rocking. "You think I am a racialist," Oberholzer says. "That is such kuk. Firstly, I am an African also. We Afrikaners are the white tribe of Africa that have been here as long as any of them that came down from the north and we have had to fight for every inch of what we have. And we have built this country, piece by piece, nobody else did. It's ours, our sweat and blood and history. And nobody — *nobody* — else deserves to run it. Second, I don't mind a black, I work with them like family, I speak Zulu as well as most a them and that is a fact. They respect me and I respect them. Lemme tell you about these white liberals, these Jews in the northern suburbs who write in the papers and the books how wunnerful it will all be for this country if we just turn it all over to the kaffirs, just give em the keys to all what we built and say go have fun, you buggers. Lemme tell you, at one time — I am technical, me, right, that's what got me to where I am, improving myself, technology, like making the videos, ja, I mean I developed those skills — and one time a while ago, they asked me up to the ninth floor to edit tape. That's the Special Branch up there hey, security police. Those are the real main manne — wearing their cool suits, man, doing all the most hectic stuff. I used to go up there and help sort tapes they recorded from the phone and from the house of this woman who is a famous book writer and lives there nearby Greenside actually. She is also another Jew, big surprise. And, man, they *love* her in the overseas. Her and her husband both are big Jew liberals, ja. She thinks we don't know that she hides ANC rats in her backyard. We know, we know it all. It's she who duzzen know that the Branch has got at least a dozen transmitters stuck up her old puss and everywhere else round that property. But those people she hides are just too minor to arrest, it's better to listen in and see what's what, and besides half of them work for us anyway! Kaffir has no loyalty, remember that. Anyways, I'm sitting working, listening in on her, and I started realising why it is she is such a half-brained communist. Is because all of the blacks she knows are not ordinary ones. They the clever ones who know to act all nice to her to get her on their side and she can't even see through it. All these white libs in the north suburbs like her with their little knitted UDF scarves and freedom T-shirts, you notice they don't speak Zulu. Not one word! They write books like they big experts on this country but they can't even speak one single African language! What a joke! Don't speak Sotho, don't speak Xhosa or Venda or Tswana or Shangaan, nothing. Can hardly praat Afrikaans. They never been in the platteland, the real country. They don't understand Africa at all! They don't understand the real African, the common African. But I do. I grew up with them. And they wanna call *me* the racialist! Listen. More than half the men under my command are black Africans, ukay. We talking riot squad, active duty. These are men who would die for me. But that duzzen mean you mustn't watch them like a hawk and keep them in line. S'long's you do that, you okay, but if not—it's jiz like old Dingane who invited Piet Retief to supper in 1838 and when they left their guns outside and sat down, Dingane's warriors jumped them and gutted the lot. So you never turn your back. But they respect a man who is strong. Who fights like a man. Side by side. I am telling you as I sit with you here today, boy, on the blood of Jezus Chrise, I swear to you if people like me and my men were to stop fighting hard every day, you'd be finished! That is a fact! Where the *hell* is your gratitude?"

20

Captain Oberholzer gets off the multilevel motorway of the M1 and drives down Goch Road, underneath the stacked highways with the big concrete pylons on both sides. I realise, God, we are heading for John Vorster Square. It bakes a brick of fear in my bowels, I swear. John Vorster Square is at Number One Commissioner Street and it's an L-shaped set of buildings, and it's got these blue panels all over. People make sad jokes about this place, the Blue Hotel they call it, and all the prisoners that just happen to fall out of windows from the top floors or slip in the showers and "accidentally" snap their necks or manage to hang themselves. When we get there, Oberholzer drives through security at the back and down into underground parking. "See those spots," he says. "That's for SB personnel only." He shakes his head and whistles. "These security okes. They just like James Bonds hey, real-life James flippen Bonds. Unbelievable. You should check some of the motors these okes get to pinch from the stolen car pool. Like Porsches, man. Audis. Make the Flying Squad okes look like a bunch a wankers, even. Man, when I was up there on the ninth floor that time, I was like, the suits, the gold chains, the way they rock and roll — man, this is *it*, hey. *This is what I want.*"

He lets me out and we walk across to an elevator underneath cameras. When the doors open, I see two black men with bags over their heads and their hands raised, their wrists cuffed to a rail on the ceiling. Two large white men in suits who smell of Brut and cigarettes nod at the captain and ignore me. We all ride up, dead silent. Except I can hear wet snuffling noises from under the hoods. When I look down I see red droplets hitting the tops of their shoes, *pat pat pat.* The carpet has lots of old stains already. On the third floor Oberholzer and I step out. Oberholzer's all excited, whispering fast. "They going up to ninth, you see it? That's Branch only. Normally they take their own special lift that doesn't stop on any other floor. You check the lekker jackets? Style, man, *style.* Bladdy *nice.* Those prisoners are politicals. Those Branch okes, man, they get to hook the big fish. And you know the tenth floor is so top-secret there's no lift that goes there, only stairs from ninth . . ." He keeps whispering as we walk. "Tell you summin. Some okes round here, they don't like the security police, but me, I'm not negative, hey, I'm a positive person, you have to set goals in life. You ever read Napoleon Hill's book on success? You should, hey. Keep a positive mind. If you jealous and you look down on someone else's success yourself, then how you ever ganna be successful?" The corridor is wide, with a beige concrete floor, and the walls have two colours, the bottom dark blue and the top more greenish. I see a stairway curving up and the whole side of it is behind thick bars of another shade of blue. All the blues and the curving and the echoing noises of shouts and steel, plus the arches over some doorways plus a certain bad smell like must or dank — it makes me think of an aquarium. I imagine prisoners floating like bottled fish in their cells of blue. And I feel like I'm drifting underwater myself. Drowning.

I hear a typewriter clicking behind a door. "My office," Oberholzer is saying. "I got it the hard way, promotion from up the ranks. Developing my skills. My technical. My ideas. Good things happen if you work persistently, and Julius Caesar is the zone my unit is in charge of. I basically built this all from scratch, hey, a whole new concept in community relations and communications. You have to set positive goals in life, and you have to believe in yourself." A secretary greets us, we go to the right, and Oberholzer opens another door for me. It's bright through frosted glass. Parquet floor. Filing cabinets, a desk, a fan running. Oberholzer tells me to sit and goes to the files. "Ja," he says, "this community unit, we are still riot squad, still Internal Stability Unit, but the idea is *burger sake*—hearts and minds—but not just inside the community, but also the hearts and minds of the rest of the world, hey? Propaganda is what wins wars also. Photography, public relations. Especially video. And we may have been winning on the ground but in propaganda we are behind. The other side is devil good at it. That is how I put it to the general when I proposed my concept, setting this up, using my technical skills. I just went for it, hey. Others might have had the idea, but I took action, I spoke up, I had the guts—and here I am now, look at me, a full captain in corner office with the whole township under my command and control. See, you have to spring when you see opportunity . . . Ah-huh, here we are." He brings a file and gives me a blank card, tells me to write all my details in block letters. Name, addresses, birth date, and the same for all my family members. I want to say am I being arrested? I should get a lawyer, or talk to my parents, I should ask for that, at least. But I say nothing and start to write. Oberholzer calls the secretary for coffee, black. I write, MARTIN HELGER. 6 MARCH 1972. NUMBER 2 SHAKA ROAD GREENSIDE, 2193, JOHANNESBURG, SOUTH AFRICA . . . Oberholzer puts on his square reading glasses and writes in the file. The coffee comes. Not a tin mug this time. When I'm finished the card, I hand it across and he gives me a legal pad, telling me, "Now write down everything that happened that led up to you being inside Jules today. Everything. The story of how you came to be there at that school. Write nice and clearly, no cursive,

take your time." He goes out with the card. I stare at the pad. The secretary comes and asks if I want some Romany Creams. I really smaak
those crunchy chocolate biscuits and I'm hungry as hell but I shake my
head. She goes and after a while I start writing. *It all started when Annie
Goldberg came to live with us in Greenside, just two or three weeks ago.
I will have to check the exact date with my mother. My mother, Arlene
Helger, was the one who organised Annie to stay with us as an exchange
scholar from USA. She*

I look up, hearing these fast heavy steps outside, thump thump
thump, and then the door bangs open and Oberholzer rushes in. His
face pale.

21

We are back on the highway, zipping along above the city. I'm confused
but not stupid enough to ask any questions — it might make him change
his mind again. In the office he told me suddenly I could forget about
having to write anything down and instead he'd give me a lift back,
straightaway. We went down to the garage and when I stood at the back
of the Cortina, Oberholzer said don't be silly and opened the passenger
door for me. Like he's my chauffeur now. I look out the window. A bill-
board is selling cigarettes — THE NEXT BEST THING TO A LEXINGTON
IS ANOTHER LEXINGTON. Another one is for Iwisa mielie meal, proud
sponsor of the Kaiser Chiefs, kings of the soccer field. And there are
rooftops and tall glass buildings and then the yellow hills of the mine
dumps half covered in grass, hills made of all the sand they've pulled
up through donkey's years of digging gold up from under our feet cos
Joburg is one huge goldmine, more of it found here than anywhere.

We start changing lanes for the exit already, the sign says SMIT
STREET so I look at Oberholzer and tell him as politely as I can that

this isn't the best way to get to Greenside. He says, "Who said anything about Greenside?"

"I thought you taking me home."

"I'll drop you at your father."

I go blank and he says, "Your father is Isaac Helger."

"Yes, Captain."

"Lion Metals, according to what I looked up."

"Yes, Captain."

"Of course he is," says Oberholzer. "Of course it had to be." It's not just these odd words but the way he says them that makes my heart start to vibrate like banjo strings and I'm trying to think what to say but I have zilch. Meantime we drive into Braamfontein, passing the big train depot, and reach the bottom of De La Rey and make a right and head all the way up to the end. This is Vrededorp. The brick building at number 50A De La Rey is a full block wide and three stories high. The steel doors are peeling green paint with wire in the window glass on the ground floor, the burglar bars are shaped like diamonds. A sign says TOTAL ARMED RESPONSE. I can just see the side of the wall at the back as we come up, with the vicious hedge of broken glass along the top. This place is my childhood, hey, in the Yard with my da. I know the smells, the workers, the feel of it, everything. My da Isaac, he never went to school, he built this place from nothing with his two tough hands, basically. Him and his partner Hugo.

Oberholzer parks by the Salvation Army which is next to a tavern which is next to Mevrou van der Westhuizen's fish and chips shop, with its oily smells and potato peels on the sticky floor. Farther down are rowhouses with red metal roofs and white men with smudgy tattoos on their arms are sitting on the front steps and passing bottles. In the 5th Street park, skinny white kids who look as wild and tough as seagulls are swooping around and shouting, crashing shopping trolleys and throwing bricks around. Vrededorp is mostly Afrikaans. The ones who have jobs usually work for the railways or the cops or the post office. They call the Yard "die Jood se motor plek" — the Jew's car place.

I unlock the door. Oberholzer says, "Hold your horses." He touches something and all the locks suck down. "Your father, Isaac Helger, he must be getting on then. How old is Isaac Helger now?" I say seventy. He says, "Past the time for retirement, hey."

I shake my head. "No, not him."

"Everyone retires," Oberholzer says. "Then you'll be the one to take over, hey?"

"My brother, probably," I say. "When he gets out the army."

Oberholzer sniffs and lifts his eyebrows. "The army, hey. Ja. What's his name again, your brother?"

"Marcus."

"Marcus Helger," says Oberholzer, like he's tasting something. "Marcus. Helger. What's he doing there in the army, you know?"

"He's on the Border," I tell him. The Border — even just saying it I see the pictures in my head from TV and magazines. The bush war up north there where we are beating the hell out of the Cubans and the Angolan communists who want to take our territory of South West Africa away from us, for starters.

"Really now. And what unit is he with?"

"Not sure. I know he was in the parabats."

Oberholzer whistles. "Oh, a real grensvegter, hey?" Takes me a second to remember that *grensvegter* means a Rambo in Afrikaans, a super-soldier.

"Ja, I spose," I say. The parabats are the paratroopers, maroon berets and victory from the skies.

Oberholzer is staring off, at the front of the shop. Trucks being loaded for wholesale. One is an old dusty pantechnicon picking up parts to take out to Windhoek in South West, all the way across the Kalahari Desert, to judge by its plates. I recognise Winston and Oscar and Radibe — three of Isaac's senior guys — using straps to carry car doors and engine blocks up the ramp. Suddenly the door locks pop up. A hell of a relief, but I try not to show it, saying, "Well. Thank you very much for the lift, Captain."

"Tell me. Is your father, Isaac Helger, is he in there right now?"

"Ja."

"You sure?"

"He's always here at this time."

"Where, in his office?"

"No," I say. "He'll be in the back, in the proper Yard."

"And how comes you say that?"

I give a little shrug. "That's my da."

"Huh. That's your da. Isn't that nice."

There's a silence. "Well," I say. "Thank you again for the lift."

"Don't thank me yet," he says.

It's the way he says it, more than the words, that makes my mouth dry out. Softly I say, "Can't I go now?"

"Ja," he says. "Let *us* go."

"Captain?"

"I said let's go."

I clear my throat very carefully. "Please can you not? Can't you just drop me off, Captain? If I'm like not being arrested? I mean my father — like, please, he doesn't have to know, hey?"

Oberholzer smiles. "But I wouldn't wanna be rude," he says. "I come all this way."

22

I take us to the side, away from the high counters where the front staff like Mrs. Naidoo have their inky carbon-paper order books and their chittering adding machines and their cigarettes leaking smoke from dirty plastic ashtrays to the squeaky old ceiling fans while the lines of customers wait patiently — the thick-legged Afrikaans men in green or blue safari suits with short pants and socks pulled up to the knees (always a comb tucked into the top of the sock), the wiry black motorbike couriers with their arms threaded through their helmets, the mechanics in greasy overalls sipping col'drinks through their moustaches.

We go up on the old steel stairs and into the warehouse with racks full of exhausts and doors and radiators, gearboxes — every car part you can think of all filed like some kind of a library, with coloured paint written on the parts with the model and the year and the make, a big L or R for left and right. The wide freight lift at the back takes us down. Outside the sun rakes the open Yard. The earth is red and rock hard and the wrecks are piled on it in their long rows, smashed glass glittering and wrinkled steel bleeding oil and brake fluid. I used to play hide-and-go-seek with Marcus in here. There's a crusher and a crane in the back corner by the far gate, near the parked tow trucks. I'm leading Oberholzer off to the right and we run into three of the younger guys on staff, Dube and Zimbu and Orbert. The old guys still treat me like I'm a little mascot, the boss's boyki. But these younger guys are different, they usually just ignore me. Now they look at the captain in his uniform and their eyes get big. They tell us Isaac is down at the Old Cars. I'm not surprised. I go on with the captain. The Old Cars is by the Pyramid, the big stack of used tires. Lined up are the vintage cars that Da likes to work on when he gets a chance, restoring them and selling them off, usually working with Silas Mabuza. Silas has been with Da since forever. We get to the Old Cars and my father's short legs are sticking out from under a '31 Dodge. Other cars are under covers. There's one in the corner on stands that is Isaac's special prize, a 1936 Cadillac limousine. Funny, he always insists every old car has to be finished and done inside eighteen months max, but not that Cadillac, that thing's been there like a million years, almost as if he doesn't want to finish it. I look around and see Silas's tools are there, which doesn't surprise me. Him and Isaac are always together, the pair of them, he must have just stepped away. I call out and Isaac rolls out from under the Dodge and stands up, wiping grease with a cloth from his thick hands. The sun falls on his grey-salted ginger hair, flakes of rusty paint in the curls. The skin of his wrinkled face has that puffed, rubbery look from all the years of labour in the Yard, his eyes are slits that look like they've been cut into the rubber by a blunt knife, his nose is a blob that seems half melted. "What you doing here, Martin?" he says. He's not looking at me.

"I drove him here," Oberholzer says.

"And who you, then?"

"I detained your son today. He was inside Julius Caesar township."

"What the hell?" Isaac says.

I say, "Da, I went with Ann —"

"He was there illegally," says Oberholzer. "Your little angel."

"Now wait one second," Isaac says. "What you talking here? Coming here in my Yard with my boy. Martin, what is going on?"

Oberholzer smiles. "He is a very lucky little chap, you know. I could have —"

"I'm asking my boy!" His temper cracks like lightning. One thing, you don't mess with my old man, I don't care who you are. "Martin," he says, "you come stand here by me." I hesitate. "Martin — *get over here.*" I walk across and turn and face Oberholzer. Oberholzer is still smiling but it doesn't look like a real smile. His lips are moving like nailed worms on his pale face. He takes off his cap and wipes his hair back and puts the cap back on. "Listen," he says. "I don't know if you realise you talking to a captain in the South African Police —"

"Listen to *me*," Isaac says. "*I* dunno who the hell you are, but you wanna go for me, go for *me*, don't you go for my boy! He is a boy. He is a bladdy minor! Now what is your story? What do you want from me? Speak up, man!" Isaac takes steps forward and Oberholzer sways back. Caught by surprise. When he started with his talk of *chap* and *little angel*, it was like he was going to play with Isaac, poke at him. That's a mistake, hey. Big time. I could have told him that before. Isaac is all red now, his head down like a ram getting ready to charge. He's half the height but he looks twice as strong. "Ja, you a policeman," he says, "I see that, so what? Lots of policemen come here to buy. I sold Johann Malan some brake pads last week. You know who *he* is don't you? *Brigadier* Malan. Ja. Been coming here for years. And I reckon he outranks a captain by a little bit. He is a good friend of mine, matter of fact. So, I wanna tell you something, you come into a man's shop you should talk nicely or expect to get your arse chucked out on the street. I don't care what uniform you have on." He jabs with his finger. "Or what gun you come in here strapped on." Then he turns to me. "What happened, Martin?"

"I went with Annie," I say, "to see the school where she's working. In Jules. She invited me. Then the police came there and . . . he, like, arrested me."

Isaac shows his teeth to the sun, takes a breath. "You did *what?*"

"He was not arrested," says Oberholzer. "He was detained."

Isaac puts his hands on his hips and drops his head and looks at Oberholzer from the tops of his eyes, speaking more quietly. "What does that suppose to mean?"

"If he was arrested, he'd be in jail. Then we brings a charge in forty-eight hours. But we don't need charges to *detain.* Maybe you should ask your friend the brigadier to explain the Security Act for you. Section twenty-nine. Security police can detain a suspect for as long as they want. Which includes minors."

"Are *you* security police?"

The question comes fast and makes Oberholzer blink. He sniffs and says no. "I'm uniform, you can see that. Security police is Special Branch — the SB. The SB don't wear uniform. But —"

"So what the hell we even talking about then? I mean he went in to visit a school. He's just a kid!"

"Listen, Mr. Helger, don't play stupid also. You know it is illegal even just for a white to be in there in ordinary times, and Jules is a active unrest zone right now. Anyway, the new state of emergency this time applies *everywhere* in the country, ukay, I actually don't need to be SB to hold your boy right now, if I want. Suspicious activity under the emergency regulations is good enough, section three, if you really wanna know. And I can hold him for a whole month to start, just on that."

"Ach you talking such crap now," Isaac says. "How many harmless white schoolboys are you holding for emergency? Come on. I'll stick a complaint on you, man."

"I can hold him, Mr. Helger," Oberholzer says. "You better believe that."

Isaac rubs his neck. "It's that American girl anyway, who took him there, he said. So it's her fault. Go talk to her then. My kid just went along."

"That's *his* story," Oberholzer said. "That's why I'll detain him for questioning on the matter, hey. If I want."

That gets Isaac shouting again. He tells Oberholzer he's talking shit and to get the hell off his property.

"Know something, Mr. Helger," says Oberholzer, "I dunno what it is with you people."

Isaac stiffens. "What's that suppose to mean?"

"I come here to do you a favour, and drop your boy off with a warning. A normal father, he would be concerned what his boy is getting involved in. You should tell me thank you for what I have done. Believe me, I could have had Martin sent up to SB. Where they don't play games. Nothing you could do."

Neither one moves or talks and all I can hear is the sound of both of them breathing hard, skeefing at each other. Isaac says, "What is this *really* about?"

Oberholzer starts rubbing his right palm up and down against his belly. "Tell you what, Isaac Helger," he says. "You shake my hand. And you tell me thank you, Captain — for looking out so nicely for my son. And then I'll leave him here. If not, no, I will not detain you. No, I'm not ganna do anything to *you*. No. It is exactly your boy who will be detained. Exactly *him* and no one else."

"Who the hell are you?" Isaac says.

Oberholzer holds out his hand. "Shake my hand and tell me thank you." Isaac looks down at the hand. Oberholzer says, "I am Captain Wilhelm Francois Oberholzer. Ja, *Oberholzer* is my name, Isaac Helger. Now shake my hand and thank me proper."

"Oberholzer," says Isaac and his voice is so small. It gives me a scare and I almost run to him. His shoulders curl down and he sways like he's about to faint. "Oberholzer," he says. I've never seen my father this way, I swear. The captain's hand is pointing at him like a spear. Very slowly my father reaches up to it.

"That's right," says Oberholzer. "There's it. Now shake." My mouth is open as I watch the hands connect, my father's all limp. "And tell me thank you for what I done for you. Say thank you, Captain Oberholzer."

My father's voice is not his voice.

23

Isaac drives me home, saying nothing, but I can tell how upset he is by how his lumpy knuckles keep flashing white around the steering wheel. At home he does his usual scrub-up at the sink in the backyard, sluicing the grease off while I fetch him a Scotch and soda and clean clothes. Like usual we're all in front of the TV by six o' clock for the SABC news. It's Isaac in the big soft chair with his slipper feet up on the leather ottoman, it's Arlene in the chair next to him, her long ballerina's neck sticking up straight, it's Zaydi in the corner, and it's me with pole position as it's been ever since Marcus left, lying on the couch. We watch old grey-hair, square-glasses Michael de Morgan for about ten seconds — "the government today announced special measures" — before Isaac shouts his first "Bladdy schmocks!" of the evening. His legs kick and thrash on the ottoman and the old leather creaks like it's in deep pain. All these years of six o'clock abuse and you'd reckon the thing would have exploded into splinters by now. "Stupid bladdy idyats!" says Isaac to the TV. "Useless bunch of arseholes!" De Morgan reports another raid into Mozambique. Time on target eight minutes, twenty seconds, no casualties and eight terrorists eliminated. He moves on to another bomb blast, this one in Benoni, destroying an electric substation and killing two elderly women out for a walk. The women — Mrs. Eunice de Kok, seventy-eight, and Mrs. Marie Coetzee, eighty-one — were both white. Security police are investigating. Isaac yells and Arlene touches his arm and Zaydi says in Yiddish he must calm himself for the sake of his health but everyone knows that won't happen. Isaac's never exactly been a fan of the Nats, but the National Party have always been our government which is why he's never stopped his shouting. "Stuffing morons!" he yells now, and he's off again, his stubby legs chopping away like propellers.

After the news we wait for Annie for a while but it's clear she's not coming. Arlene says she could have phoned at least. Isaac has gone all quiet and won't look at me. He doesn't say anything about Oberholzer to Arlene. I wait till after supper, to get him alone when he's doing the dishes (which he always does right away as if to prove the point against Arlene that she was wrong when she used to say he'd be too tired to do maid's work). When I ask him if we should tell Arlene what happened, he shakes his head. "Don't talk about it to anyone. Especially your ma. The only person needs talking to is this American. I don't know who the hell she thinks she is."

"It's not her fault, Da. I went with her on my own cos I wanted to. She didn't want to take me. I asked her to."

"Why'd you do that?"

I shrug. "I dunno. I — I dunno."

"You're a sixteen-year-old kid," he says. "She could have said no. *She* knew what she was doing. It's a hell of a bladdy chutzpah to involve my boy."

I watch his thick hand scrubbing a pan with steel wool for a while, and then I say, "Did you know him, hey? That policeman. It seemed like maybe you did?"

He mutters something, shaking his head. But then he says, "Some things never go away. They get passed down, from father to son. It's in their blood and their mother's milk."

"What do you mean, Da?"

"What do you think I mean? I mean hating the Jews. I mean how it is a thing you cannot change no matter what."

"Who are you talking about? Oberholzer?"

His hands jerk so I get splashed with soapy water and he looks hard at me. "Don't you ever say that name in this house again."

"Sorry," I say.

"Forget it and don't think on it again," he says. "I'll talk to Hugo and we'll sort it out."

I don't sleep well. My dreams keep waking me. I see Kefiya and Ski Mask. I see the legs of old ladies in the street. I am forced to eat cat food and I am lost inside a shantytown where cops are setting dogs on screaming little girls. Oberholzer and Annie lock me up in a blue cell that fills up with water. The only bad dream I *don't* have is the Nightmare.

When Annie doesn't come home I start to worry about her, but Arlene says it's just rudeness, not letting us know if she'll be home for supper or not. Then Isaac says she is probably just too embarrassed to show her face around here after what she's done and Arlene says why, what has she done? So Isaac has to tell her I went to the township with Annie. Then Arlene asks me a million questions. I tell her it was nothing, just a visit to the school, that I asked to be taken. Isaac still doesn't say anything about Oberholzer at the Yard. At the end of it all, Arlene tells Isaac she doesn't want him to make a scene when Annie comes back. She knows his temper. Let's just leave it and move on.

But Annie doesn't come back the next day or the next and we reach the end of the week, Friday, and Arlene lights the candles and Zaydi says the kiddish for Shabbos supper and we sit down and start eating. But all-a-sudden the gates open and crash shut outside. It can only be her, she's the only one with keys. We all wait, not looking at each other. Annie Goldberg strolls in like a day at the beach. Hi, how are ya, guys. She takes her seat and starts piling salads on her plate. I get so tense my stomach doesn't want any food and I have to force the mouthfuls down. I keep checking Isaac and I don't like the way he keeps his head down, plus that vein in his neck is starting to twitch like mad. But the silence goes on to the point that I almost relax, like that's how it's going to be for the rest of supper. Then Isaac speaks up with his rough voice. "You know, uh, Annie. It's a funny thing, hey. I do the clean-up. I dunno if you noticed, we do not have a girl here."

"Sure," says Annie. "Arlene told me you guys prefer not to have a *maid* anymore."

"Gloria," says Da, "was with us since I bought this house in 'forty-eight. Now I decided a while ago, because I don't agree with the government we have, I don't agree with this full-on apartheid, that we will not participate and keep a girl in the back like every other white family. We will do our own cleaning at home. But we kept Gloria on here still, and the last I dunno how many years — hey, Arlene? — she couldn't even do much work, too old. So I was already doing a lot of the cleaning on my Sunday mornings even then. Izzen that so, Arlene?"

"It's true," Arlene says.

"But, see, I told Gloria, always, if you want to retire and go back to Lesotho, well and good — I'll settle you up with a nice lump sum for that. But if you want to stay here, also, if you happy in your room as things are, I said you're welcome to that. Her choice. Because I said one thing — ask Arlene — I said I will never kick her out of here, Gloria, never. I keep a loyalty to good people. And you don't know the times when the cops came here to look for her husband and I told them to get stuffed, they can't come in my house. I even hid the black gentleman *inside my own home.* And it's same thing as the Yard. Ask any a them. In Vrededorp there, you don't know this, but in Vrededorp when other businesses give the boys their pay packets, there's some of em will make em do a little dance before they get it, ja, just to rub it in. And I say that's disgusting. Other ones, you'll see some fat manager come out and shout at em, 'Load faster, load faster.' I say, 'You try it, fattie. You go ahead try.' Cos *I* do. Always have. By us, I bladdy work *in* there with my boys. They respect me. And I pay em a very good wage they would never smell anywhere else. That is why in forty years they never stole one cent from me, my boys."

Annie smiles into her plate. "Aren't they men? Wasn't the *girl* a woman?"

"Ukay, men. My *men.* You don't like my terminology, that's fine. It's just a way of talking. Maybe I'm ole fashion in my talking, but what do you know about real work, getting down in the hard dirt there and grafting hard with the men? There is respect you have to earn. You can never buy it. Ask *them.*"

Arlene says, "Ize, maybe not, hey? This discussion for another time?"

"Do you mind?" says Isaac. "I'm explaining something to her here." To Annie he goes on, "Like I'm saying, I do the washing up after supper here cos we don't have a girl. Sorry, a *maid,* is that better? And also I put away the leftovers you know. I put it all in whatchacallits, and I cover with tinfoil. I put the meat, the cold chicken. And it's a funny thing you know. When I get up in the morning, I don't eat any breakfast, I just take some tea. But when I open the fridge for milk what I see nowadays is the tinfoil is open and the meat is usually gone. It's bladdy licked clean in there. And I think that is a very odd happening. Cos I know what was there when I went to bed and when my wife was in bed and when Martin has gone to bed and my father also, I *know* what was there — so izzen it funny how the next morning the meat would be eaten up, and I wonder by who, if everyone else went to bed and you were the only one not home? Who came home at God knows what time and decided on a midnight snack. But then you're supposedly a vegitenarian, am I right?"

"What are you trying to say, Mr. Helger?"

"Call me Isaac."

"I don't think I see your point."

"I'm just looking at things," says Isaac. "I mean maybe, you know, maybe the Tokoloshe is the one that's chewing up all that meat, hey. You know about the Tokoloshe, hey? The African ghost that lives under beds and comes out creepy every night. Ja, maybe it was Toko-loshe ate the meat."

Annie says, "Or maybe it's someone from a starving family in Jules, who broke in to get a little something so their children could eat."

"Very funny," Isaac says.

"No," says Annie, "it is absolutely not."

Isaac sits up, his chair creaking. "You know the police brought my boy home from Jules on Tuesday, you know that, hey? The cops. My son."

"Izey," Arlene says. "Let's leave it. Friday night Shabbos."

"No, we are not ganna *leave it*. Because, Miss America, this happens to be my family here. My flesh and my blood. And if you ganna be schlepping my own son into your political gemors there, lemme tell you, you got another bladdy thing coming!"

Annie frowns. "And what exactly," she says, "is my political . . . chuh-what-is-it?"

"Gemors," says Arlene helpfully. "It means a mess."

"My mess, huh?"

"He's a kid," says Isaac, pointing at me with his fork. "And whatever it is you involved him with in that location on Tuesday—"

"Have you ever been there, to Julius Caesar township, Mr. Helger?" asks Annie.

"My name is Isaac, and missy, I been into the locations before you were wearing nappies. As a matter a fact I grew up playing with coloured boys, so don't try open a big bladdy jaw on me at the table in my own house."

"Ize, please," Arlene says. But I think we all know he isn't going to stop, not now. The fuse has already burned down.

"You think I don't hate the apartheid?" Isaac says. "Is that what it is? You think *I'm for the Nats*. Jezus Chrise! I was fighting and having the shit knocked out of me by Greyshirt Nazi bastards before you were born! Those are the ones who became the Nats, who were for Hitler back then! And I remember when they came in power in 'forty-eight, how we were crapping ourselves, the Jews—"

"Yeah," says Annie, "but it didn't work out too badly for you-all now did it? I mean admit it. Jews pretty much have it made here. Just like all the whites. Even better, mostly. Under the Natis, it has been a great life at the top of the heap for ya. Now you say you hate em, the Natis—"

"It's *Nats!* Not Nat*is!* That how much you know!"

"Nats, okay. Well if you are against em, and apparently you are, then logically you should be for the African National Congress—"

"Oh, God," says Arlene softly.

"You are bladdy well kidding me!" Isaac shouts. "You think I want those communist animals taking over? They would stuff this country out of sight in two days! They'll shut the whole economy down and send us all one-way into a ditch that we will never climb out of, black and white and yellow and blue, everyone!"

Annie is taking the shouting well, I think, her voice still calm. "Have you read the ANC's Freedom Charter, Mr. Helger?"

"You mean the same ANC that sets bombs to blow up little kids on their way to school? Ask my son sometime about what happened to school bus number five. You mean *that* ANC?"

"I just asked if you read the charter, Mr. Helger."

"Don't lecture me, lady. I've seen all that commie stuff from before the war even. Nationalise the mines. Take away everyone's property and give it to the state, the wonderful state. Have one-party rule and comrades this and comrades that, wow-wee, what a paradise, just like Cuba. Ja, just brilliant. Lemme tell you — communism makes countries into shitholes faster than anything on earth, because it is a shit idea because it is against what human nature is, and human nature never changes."

"It seems to be doing fine for most of humanity."

"It's what now?"

"Russia and the rest of the Soviet Union, plus China, I mean that alone is well north of a billion people who live in the communist system."

"Ja, and how bladdy well are *they* doing?"

"Statistics show—"

"Statistics my bladdy arse. You go and live there if you really believe it's so great. Even this Gorbachev says they have to change because it's so bad, their own leader says it. *He* knows, why don't you? You talking like a nutcase! Listen, girlie. I put my life — I fought in the war against the chazersa Nazis, you don't know what I went through and I hope you never do cos you would not sleep at night anymore. And I seen and I know that the communist lot with Stalin and all the rest, they weren't much different than Hitler's bunch. So you can take all your commies and you can chuck them on the same rubbish pile as the Nats!"

"But if you're so against the Natis—"

"Nats. *Nats!* You keep getting your basic facts wrong again, yankee doodle!"

"Nats, Mr. Helger, Nats, fine. The question is how could you be against letting people vote—"

"One's nothing to do with the other. And it's Isaac!"

"Okay, *Isaac*. How—"

"Listen," Isaac says. "The fact is they are not ready to run a first-world country, that's just the fact."

"They being . . ."

"Blacks! Who else, who else are we talking, Chinese? You cannot just turn a modern country over to them. They have to be built up first and educated proper before they ready to run it. It takes years and years to develop a first-world country, man. To have the experience and the education and the understanding. Now if the stuffing Nats had spent the last fifty years bringing the African up, developing and educating them, then maybe it would be time already and I would be agreeing with you on a vote for blacks also. But the Nats did the opposite and tried to stamp them down. When the Nats came in, in 'forty-eight, there were already some blacks on the voters roll, you know that? And coloureds also — you know what a coloured is I hope, it means mixed — those ones with some education behind them. They could have kept building that up slowly. But no! Instead they stripped them off and started with the bulldozers and the townships, they went all-out for apartheid and baaskap — being the big baas, the big boss, dominating, with the white foot always on the black neck . . . Man, they never invested in the country, they only invested in *themselves*. But you can't stamp down twenty-five million people forever. You can't!"

"I don't understand you," says Annie. "You're against the right and you're against the left, so what are you?"

"We vote PFP, dear," Arlene says.

Annie snorts, a rude sound that makes my eyebrows go up. "Progressive Party — right. They're useless."

"Who told you that?" Isaac snaps.

"I've read their platform. They wanna make a few cosmetic tweaks here and there, when it's the whole system needs to be wiped out. They're just a fig leaf."

"Beg your pardon?" says Arlene, blinking like a hundred times.

"I'm sorry," Annie says, "but maybe you feel good in the northern suburbs sending Helen Suzman or whoever to parliament there to get laughed at by all those Afrikaan men in dark suits, but . . . c'mon, it's just like a Band-Aid on a melanoma, right. All it does is make white voters feel good, it doesn't do a damn —"

"What's a Band-Aid?" asks Arlene.

"It's a plaster," I tell her. She doesn't watch as much American TV as I do. *Magnum P.I.* and *The Cosby Show* and that.

"What's a melyonia?" Isaac is asking.

"Cancer," Arlene says. "She means voting PFP is like putting a plaster on cancer."

"Aw for Chrise sake!" Isaac shouts at Annie. "You such a bladdy exaggerator!"

"Why?" says Annie. "Because I'm asking you a straight question and you don't have an answer? You can't say if you are *for* or *against*. The basic — the only — question that there *is* in this country."

"You ask me what am I?" Da says. "What am I? How about you? What about *you*?" He sticks his finger out and hammers it at her. "You're same as me, if you like it or not. You are a Jew!"

Annie opens her mouth and leans back, both of her palms going to her chest. "Um," she says. "I'm a human being?"

"Aw please!" shouts Isaac. "Do me a favour. You're Jewish. You are born one. Your name is Goldberg. You are born a Jew and you'll die a Jew. I take one look at you and I can *see* how so Jewish you are. So who you tryna kid that you not! Stop sitting there and pretending that you belong to the African people. You're not an African. You're not even a white South African. You just a Jewish girl from New York there or wherever. And you fly all the way over here to sit in my house and argue with me about African things after you have been here for about five minutes on top of it and you don't have the first clue what it is you talking about. Is that not so?"

"I —" says Annie, but that's all the space she gets. Isaac is just starting to roll.

"You should be ashamed, man! After all what the Soviets have done to our people! Look at how they suffering over there, and then you talk nice on communism? Get off it! Look at Sharansky and the refuseniks and all the rest, how they chuck Jews into labour camps in Siberia. And they don't even let them even *be* Jewish properly behind that iron window that they have there. Ja, it's true. Don't look at me like — and what about all the commie Soviet money and weapons and soldiers they are sending to all the bladdy Arab countries? Hey? Backstopping them to invade little Israel and try to wipe her out, to do another Hitler on us! And you stand there on the communist side? As a Jew? It's disgusting! Shame on you!"

Annie still seems calm, which impresses the hell out of me. "It doesn't matter," she says, "that I was born Jewish. I insist that I am firstly a fellow —"

"It matters everything! It matters everything! We are Jews here in this country and we are a tiny drop in the bucket here, and we do not belong to *that side* or to *this side*. My only responsibility is for us! For us! My family, and my people who I am born to. That's enough! That is enough of a bladdy full-time job. What do you have to go running around like a headchop chicken for? Trying to do what exactly? Save this one and that one. Run off to Africa and help the little black children there. As if the little black children are *your* children, but I got news for you — they not! They got Sotho mothers who speak Sotho and they got Zulu mothers who speak Zulu and so far as I know they don't have any mothers who speak Yiddish! If you were in trouble would those Zulus and Vendas and Tswanas come flying to America to help the Jews there? If anyone has to fight it out with chutis it is *them*" — I look at Annie to see if she understood what Isaac meant by *chutis*, our semirude word we have for Afrikaners, but the way he says it now he means the government, the Nats — "because it is *their* bladdy indaba, man!" he shouts. "That means in their language it is *their* problem, not ours. Our job as Jews is to take care of Jews! Just like every other people on this earth takes care of their own. Their own children and not someone else's, their own people and not someone else's! Listen, this here in South Africa is between the chutis and the ANC, this is not our fight. We live in the system that is here, full stop, finish and klaar. We vote PFP every election, we against the Nats, what more can you want from us? That we should all go sit in jail for the blacks? No. Let them hash it out between themselves, the terrorist communists and the bastard Nats. Zollen zey brechen zeyere kep!" This last bit was an old Yiddish saying — let em go and break their own heads — and again I wonder if Annie understood.

"Right," says Annie. "Just keeping out of it, uh? And what about your son? Isn't he in the army right now? Isn't he fighting for those Natis you say you hate so much? Isn't that the truth, Mr. Helger? *Your own son.*"

I feel myself ducking. When Arlene hisses I'm not surprised, the sound could have come from me. Arlene says to Annie, "That is enough, enough! You ganna cause a heart attack!" Isaac puts his hand on Arlene's arm and says shhh and it gets all quiet. And I swear that's more scary than anything so far. He talks softer now but very clear.

"My son Marcus is a grown man and I have no control over him. You don't have any idea how hard we tried to keep him out of that army. My whole life has been one big mission to keep my sons out that farshtunkene army. That is why I sent them to that school. That's why we had to go cap in hand to them and grovel to the Solomon board and do what we had to, for the privilege of paying them an absolute fortune, for that one reason — because *Solomon boys do not go to the army.* Oright? But you pipe down and *you* listen now. I grew up here and remember well when the Greyshirts was chucking bricks through windows of Jewish houses in Doornfontein, oright? You don't think those days could come back here? You don't think if we made enough trouble

the Nats might turn around and go for *us* next? Maybe they'll steal all
our property like Idi Amin did to the Indians up there in Uganda, and
then kick us out like dogs. Or maybe, even worse, they'll steal everything and stick us in the townships along with the coloureds and the
blacks. You don't think that could happen? You think chutis has any
kind of a *liking* for Jews? Do me a bladdy favour."

"But what about everyone else?" Annie says, her voice going up for
the first time. "What about all the ones who don't happen to be Jews?"

"That's not the point! I am born the way I am and so are you and
that's it! But I understand what I am. I *know* what we are. I understand
the position we are in! But you. You don't want to be who you are! You
don't have any clue *what* you are. That's why you fly around the world
stirring up crap for everyone else! Because if you care so much about
politics, what you should be doing is doing the right thing and going
to live in Israel, to fight and struggle for *your* people, for *your* tribe,
like everyone else does for *theirs,* if that's really what you want to do
with your life instead of settling down and having a family like any normal girl—"

"But I am normal! That's *why* I'm here."

"Like bladdy hell! You can't even make your own bed, you hypocrite! You don't think we haven't noticed! You the only one in this
household who actually *needs* a maid! And don't tell me you don't stuff
your face with meat like the rest of us, only you do it on the sly! You
bladdy hypocrite! The only reason you here is so you can feel superior
to all the rest of us when America's got plenty of racialism of its own
to deal with! Go back there and help the black Americans! Hypocrite!
It's easy for you here, if you get in trouble they'll just send you home,
but now you wanna get my other son involved? It's bad enough that the
army got Marcus now you want the bladdy security police to arrest my
Martin? He's the one who'll get stuck in a cell like a dog—not you. He's
your cannon fodder just like Marcus is President Botha's! You leave my
son alone! Hypocrite! Bladdy hypocrite!"

And that, apparently, is quite enough for Annie Goldberg. She shoves herself away from the table and walks off. Arlene goes after her. Isaac is shaking his head and muttering to his plate. Zaydi carefully eats a forkful of roasted chicken.

24

A tapping on my window and I wake up knowing it's her, I just do. Two eleven on Monday morning, almost the same time as when I saw her dancing alone that first night. Now she waves to me and I get dressed. She hasn't been back since the Friday brouhaha. Outside she tells me she came to get her stuff, can I go in the Olden Room and fetch it? I say sure. We move quietly to the garden where she'll wait for me, taking a seat on the busted old bench by the pomegranate tree that Zaydi planted years ago. Zaydi says pomegranates are moshiach fruit cos every fruit has its own little crown, and our moshiach will be king when he comes, the messiah-king, so we never eat from the tree, he wants us to wait for the Coming. Sitting next to Annie I ask where she's staying, what she plans to do. She's crashing at a friend's place in Yeoville, she'll move on to somewhere in Hillbrow, she thinks. "Things are changing there, blacks and whites mixing. The system's collapsing." I nod and she says, "Don't worry about where I'm at. I'll be moving around and you're not gonna be able to find me — yeah, well, that brings us to it."

"To what?"

"The tapes."

I look at her in the moonlight, I'd dinkum forgotten, or more like blanked it out, that I still had her four master tapes there in the Sandy Hole. "Don't worry, they're fine," I say. "I'll get them also for you with the rest of your stuff."

She says, "I'd rather you keep them here for me, for now."

I don't say anything, staring out into the garden.

"Look," she says. "I know I can trust you. And I know they're absolutely safe here. It's a lot more dangerous for me to move around with them."

"Don't you need them?"

"We're trying to figure out how we can up production to meaningful numbers. We need hundreds to start, thousands would be better. Distributing across the region is not the issue I thought it'd be. But finding a recording facility — this is tough. Can't just walk into any video place off the street. It's gonna take time to figure the right set-up. Until then I want you to keep the masters safe here for us and when the time comes — what's wrong?"

"Nothing."

"Thing is, Martin, to keep in touch we'll need to take precautions." She pulls out a little paperback. There's enough moonlight for me to read the title: *A Light for the Abyss,* by H. R. Koppel. She tells me to take a look at the first page where there's a stamp for Viljoen's Book Exchange, 125C Greenway Road.

"I know Viljoen's," I say. "I go there all the time."

"I know you do. So it won't look out of place for you to visit every Wednesday. Way it'll work for us is with a message in code that we leave inside an exchange book."

"Code?"

"You want to reach me, you put a note in a book on page one hundred, okay, and take it down to Viljoen's. There's a guy there you can trust, he's part of the Movement."

"What are you talking about? Old man Viljoen? No ways."

"Not the old guy, his son."

"Dolf."

"He's there Wednesdays. Give him the message book, and he'll give you an exchange, he'll always have one for you. You go in every week, regardless of a message or not. It's our secret post office, get it? Don't look so fucking scared."

I'm still thinking of Dolf Viljoen, a quiet young guy with glasses — him in the Movement? But he's an Afrikaner. That means he's fighting against his own. "What if Dolf isn't there that day?"

"Then just ask has he left a book for you. He will have. Make the exchange. Now — code. We're gonna use Hebrew for this, you know your aleph bet, right?" She leans over and pulls out a pencil stub and starts writing, showing me how to do a grid and convert any English word into this Hebrew code, based on the date. I can feel the brush of her hair next to me, her body heat. She tests me to make sure I have it, then tells me I need to burn every message every time, no exceptions. "It's not a real sophisticated code," she says, "but it'll work for our usage."

"Our usage," I say. She looks at me. "What's up with you?" she asks.

"I'm fine. Why?"

"You don't sound fine."

"How do I sound?"

"Like you're about to puke."

"Maybe I am." My hands are between my knees, squeezing there, I'm looking at my lap. I keep falling back in my mind to that place in Jules where everyone was shouting amandla, I keep seeing the charred bodies on the hilltop with the melted rubber and Kefiya and Ski Mask making that bomb and then there's the sick desperate feeling of being in the back of Oberholzer's Ford. It feels unreal and too real at the same time. I realise I just do not want anything to do with it. At all. I want it to disappear. I want *her* to disappear. I want to be alone in my garden forever.

I can feel her looking closely at the side of my face. "What's the problem?" she says.

"Annie, you're like a full-on ANC person, aren't you?"

"Why are you asking this now?"

I shake my head.

"Look, Martin," she says, her voice hardening. "I'm not interested in trying to convince. You're in or you are out. But if you don't want to do it, you have to let me know right now. Bring the tapes out with my stuff so I can find another safe place to stash em."

I put my forehead on my palms. "I dunno," I say. "Just hang on . . . let me think." Because, ja, I can see the bombs and the burnt people but I can also see the face of little Nosipho and I can see that can of cat food. And the whip coming down on that girl's legs. And that's all real too, that's all happening. Annie says, "Commitment is real hard, I know. But it's what grown-ups do, Martin. Make the decision and tell me now." I stay frozen and she says my name and touches my back. I feel her shifting closer on the bench, and now her soft breasts are pressing against my shoulder. "I know you're probably feeling overwhelmed, I can't blame you for that. But I also know that inside you're a good person. Do you know how I know that, Martin?" Her palm opens up like a hot flower against the back of my neck, I feel her breath on my ear. There's like hardly any space between us. "Because you told me your nightmare, and I know what it's about. What it really means. Why it keeps coming back. A message from deep inside you. It'll keep on repeating until you receive it. A dream about Nazis invading this garden right here. Attacking your house. Martin, it's so clear and obvious but you can't see it."

I swallow. "Can't I?"

"The garden is you, Martin. The garden is the centre of who you are. But the Nazis. I got news for you, Martin. The dream Nazis are you too. The dream is a warning. It's telling you the worst part of you is trying to take over everything else. You understand, Martin? The Nazis are still outside the walls, they represent all the stuff that this place South Africa wants to teach you to be, and make you into, and invade you with."

"And the Zaydi part?"

"That's easy."

"Is it?"

"He's your soul, Martin. The dream is you trying to save your soul."

Her hand rises from a pocket. A photo in the starlight, a black man behind a desk. He's smiling and has papers in one hand. "Nelson Mandela," she says. "This is him in his law office right here in sunny Joburg, before they made it illegal for an African to rent an office downtown. Keep it as a gift. Take it out and look at it when you're alone. That's not the face of an evil man, Martin. Don't believe what the Natis want you to. Don't believe your pops either. Don't let yourself get lied to."

Something is cracking inside me. The photo slips away like a petal. I can smell lemons and perfume as she drifts into me, unfolding herself, and I think again of a blossom opening up. She has so many arms all winding around me like a dozen snakes and touching hands and fingers and now the tongue which is wet and hot as blood on my neck and flicking to my lips. I lose myself and when I come back so much impossible is happening at once — she's up over me and coming down with a soft hissing sound and I feel rubbery coolness in all the heat, the flesh and skin and the weight of her so alive sinking down and down, all those arms looping me everywhere.

And I'm gone again, washed away in that tide of perfume. Somewhere in all of it her fingernails have hold of a ripe pomegranate from the tree behind and she rips out the shiny guts of it and stuffs it into my open mouth, stretching my jaw. I hear moaning and realise it's mine. The sweet pomegranate juice runs over my chin and down my throat where her long tongue is flick-flicking again, her teeth nipping. This taste of pomegranate juice. I'm never going to be able to separate it from the taste of a woman.

SCHOOL OF WALLS

25

I'm waiting at the corner of Shaka and Clovelly for Solomon school bus number eight to come and get me. The bus is a plain grey colour. It won't say Solomon Jewish Boys on it, or anything at all, and its sides are armour-plated, the windows bulletproof—obviously. Plus they change the routes all the time, so sometimes it's late. Not this morning. I hear the Leyland diesel revving and then it comes over the rise ten minutes early for the first school day of the new year, 1989. I'm the last stop before Regent Heights and even the Zulu driver sniffs at me like what is he doing having to stop *here*. The other students can see over the wall into my garden and they don't laugh or sneer or anything like they used to, but they don't have to now, they can do it all with their eyes. The thing is, this morning it doesn't bug me—not at all. For real. I know they're checking at my infamous blazer, I know what they're thinking, but for the first time in my life I do not actually give two shits. *I am no longer a virgin.* I take a seat by myself and stare out the window. The sunlight makes the blazer glitter, polyester does that. Two years ago Arlene bought it from the OK Bazaars and sewed the Solomon coat of arms onto the pocket, it's got boxy shoulders that stick out a mile. Arlene said why waste the money. She didn't understand that everyone else wears slim cotton bespoke, from Samuelson's in town. These are kids who get out of Bentleys with the driver holding the door. Who compare Swiss watches and vacations in Paris, private flights to Bophuthatswana on the weekend for gaming at Sun City or down to Plett for the beach. They come from palaces in Sandton or Houghton. Or private apartments of their own if they're not from Joburg. They carry that certain smirk that knowing you're going to inherit an actual diamond mine will give you.

I'm looking down through the glass as we swing onto Barry Hertzog Avenue. I see black people waiting in a cluster at a Putco bus stop. White municipal buses are double-deckers and mostly empty, Putcos are singles and always jam-packed. The people hold plastic bags, look tired. We pass the Solly Kramers bottle shop. R5.99 red wine special. At Bimbo's they're advertising a New Shwarma Deluxe with Chips. A newspaper board tells me, PRETORIA SPY RING BUSTED. I think about how the prefects at Solomon have their own blazers, white braids added to the purple. They choose a dozen prefects from the matric students each year. I already know I'll never be a prefect. It makes me smile to remember what I expected of Solomon before I got there, a school built last century by a goldmine tycoon who wanted an Eton for Jewish boys under the African sun. It was supposed to produce gentlemen of the highest caliber but I've never yet heard anyone use a word like *chap*. I remember my first year coming in I had this idea I'd work hard and shock everyone with my academic brilliance. They give tests for everything, that's the Solomon style, like placement tests to fit you in your class for the year — every Standard has classes ranked A to D, clever to dumb — and there are even tests *inside* each class to get your *desk*, the dumbest have to sit at the front. Basically everything at Solomon is prep for matric finals, the state exams at the end of matric, the last year. You *have* to get that university placement, otherwise it's off to the army, the government already has us all on its draft list. Plus there's that famous Solomon average that has to be kept up. When you get down to it, finals is your whole life and they let you know that at Solomon from minute one. I tried hard but I have a wandering mind. I couldn't stop myself from reading poetry and *Playing* in the garden instead of doing homework, so I barely made the C class in that first year, Standard Six, and again last year, Standard Seven. I don't expect things to be different now for Standard Eight. If I'm being completely honest I have to admit how Ari and Pats weren't too far off the mark that day at the Emmarentia Dam which I'll never forget. At least Crackcrack has pretended not to see me. My brother was never too far away, an engineering student at Wits. But by now everyone probably knows that Marcus is off in the army, and that's a different story isn't it.

Gears grate and shake me out of my memories. I should be more worried but I'm still floating and maybe this is what nonvirgins feel like all the time, floating along, not caring, maybe this is why adults don't kill themselves in greater numbers. The bus is swinging onto De Villiers Road. I catch a flash of Brandwag Park way below and I remember how Marcus and I used to walk Sandy in there when we were little, and this one time when we were caught in a storm. There's a stream down there and it flash-flooded into a raging river in front of us. Then the whole bank collapsed and this big section of tin drainage pipe was left sticking out. After a while it snapped right off. I held on to Sandy while Marcus dived in and swam after it. He got hold of it and dragged it to the side and then he used it for a slide. It was nuts — he could have been drowned so easily. But that was Marcus then, just wild, trying anything, always laughing, I'll never forget it. It's like he had his own light shining inside him all the time.

On De Villiers Road we reach the start of the school wall. It's made of these giant concrete slabs and it goes on and on like a great long cliff. On some of the slabs you can see the stamp of a Hebrew letter from when the Israeli engineers first put it in. And every thirty metres or so I see a camera in its green bulletproof box, with rings of razor wire all along between. There's only one entrance to Solomon. It's this huge gate of solid steel that could handle an atom bomb, I swear. There's an arch over the top that's the only part of the old gate left since 1982, it's black ironwork and it says WISDOM OF SOLOMON HIGH SCHOOL FOR JEWISH BOYS, with the coat of arms under and two Judean lions standing up on their back legs with our motto on scrolls, in Latin and Hebrew and English: *Justice Is Togetherness, Togetherness Strength.*

The bus stops on the driveway in front of the steel gate. We all have to get off here and go in on foot with our bags, that's security protocol, and no exceptions. I say we, but actually it's like me, and then the rest — because as we get off I'm the only one who isn't part of a group, or at least a pair. I'm alone like I've always been here. I remember in my very first week at this school, back in 'eighty-seven, I even went to Initiation. Every high school has male Initiation, where they bring in the new meat for some group suffering. Like you don't have to do it, you can duck it if you want, but I showed up on a Sunday morning cos I thought I'd get some respect at least, maybe one potential friend. I found mayhem on the rugby field. There was shaving cream, rubber whips, and cricket bats. Matric men were stalking around in Ray-Bans giving punishments to Standard Six boys. They made boys kiss heavy cinder blocks like a girlfriend and carry "her" around the field. They had to do push-ups and sit-ups while the bats were slapping their legs. They were getting their ball hairs ripped off with tape, getting walked and stomped on. I went out there and they took one look at me and someone shouted that's Helger! and that was all they had to say. *That's Helger.* The word spread like I was carrying radiation or the plague. Marcus had only just left the year before, they had come up under him. So the main man ran up with a folding chair and a nice cold can of Pine Nut. I was confused, I made a serious mistake and accepted both, sat there for a while watching all the other new boys getting the living shit knocked out of them while I sipped my nice col'drink and slowly realised this was not a trick. I left straightaway but the damage was done. From that day, I swear, I was the most hated in my Standard, upgraded from ignored. Soon I started to catch these rumours floating around myself like a bad smell. That I was a mofi, a raging homo, and I had the

AIDS. That I was not really a Helger, athletic like my brother, actually I was retarded and adopted out of pity. They said lice and that I spread it deliberately. They said not really Jewish. They said what is he doing here? And by the end of my second year I still did not have one single friend. It was not exactly the *Name* I had planned to build for myself at Solomon High.

To the left of the steel gate is this concrete pillbox thing where the uniformed guards sit with their monitors and assault rifles. There's a tall turnstile next to it with bars sticking out. You go through one at a time and it clicks off your number while a camera records your face. When it's my turn, I hold up my satchel for the guard in the little window to see. Every bag has to have a bomb tag, it's a plastic ring around the strap. This one is lavender, it came in the post in the holidays. They'll go on giving us new tags all the time, changing the colours. If anyone ever spots a bag without a tag or with the wrong-coloured one, they have to pull the alarm and cause an emergency bomb drill like the one we practice once a month. We all have to go up in *a calm and orderly fashion* to the rugby fields where our headmaster, Arnold C. Volper, will be stalking around in front with his squealy megaphone that he wears with a sling like a handbag. He's a scary man, Volper. He even has a thatch of thick yellow hair like a scarecrow made of straw. I don't believe there is a human heart inside there, honestly. He likes to read out individual test scores from the podium every week at Assembly. The eyes of the country are on us, he'll say. We must never lose our position as the brightest school in the land. We are an example. Then he'll usually give the names of the biggest dummies. You are a disgrace to us. Martin Helger. Once again. He likes to cruise around all quiet between the aisles in the school shul during prayers, looking to nab a victim by surprise. They said to us new boys when we arrived that Volper was going to get us, every single one, sooner or later. But when my turn came I could not believe it. I mean the prefect said talking in prayers, go to the office, but meantime I'm the only one who didn't have anyone to talk to even if I wanted.

They make you wait in the white passage outside the office. Talk about shitting yourself dry. My whole body was vibrating, my knees like Spanish castanets, as my breakfast kept trying to come back up, the yeasty taste of ProNutro cereal. Volper was sitting behind a polished teak desk as big as a supper table, I swear, with a huge window behind him and I remember that view of the square outside with the statue of Theodore Herzl in front of that line of pine trees, the statue being polished by three of the Zulu groundskeepers wearing their navy overalls. Volper had taken off his tweed jacket and it hung on the back of his tall leather chair. He was talking but I couldn't understand the words at first, I was too much in shock that this was happening. I remember how he removed his watch and undid the cufflinks, the slow careful way he did that. He rolled up each sleeve with exactly three turns. Like he was getting himself ready for messy work—like a butcher or a surgeon. And I remember how calm his voice was. Everything was so *civilised*. There was a nice bookshelf, there was an oil painting of a sunflower. There were silver-framed photographs of his wife and his daughters on the far side of the desk. But at the same time I knew what was coming, and it felt so impossible but *it was happening to me*. I felt oily and sick inside, I could feel the pulses in my neck pressing against my collar and tie.

Volper looked up and said, "You were whispering in prayers."

"No, sir, I was not."

"Name again?"

I told him, my voice was so soft even I could hardly hear it.

"Helger, Helger, Helger. Oh dear. This one could be that monster's little brother. From Greenside?" Volper is fat and short but he has this way of looking down on you. It's really remarkable. I mean he can do it even when he's sitting. His trick is to point his flaring nostrils. Makes em look like shotgun barrels, I swear, and he likes nothing better than to stick that shotgun right between your eyes. With all that yellow hair and that blasting nose he's a scary-looking creature all right. I told him yes sir and he sort of studied me before he went on. "Another future rugby star, doubtless." I could feel his sarcasm big time, like this wave of acid coming at me. "Your brother," he said, "used to reckon he was quite the big man when he was here, didn't he? A family like yours, it's a privilege to be here. With the right kind of people. Your parents had to make efforts to the board, I don't know what. I don't know how they managed it. You shouldn't forget that."

"Yes, sir."

"Your brother had quite the high opinion of his fine self, strutting around. But I will tell you a secret, little-brother Helger — he was not such a big man when he was alone in this office with me. *Facing the music.* All that bravado goes out of them when it comes time in here to *face the music.* When he is alone and no mates to act the big stuff in front of. No more strutting in here . . ." He kept on talking like that and suddenly I clicked that there was something *off* with this guy. How can I put it? It felt like he wasn't talking to me anymore, it was like he was talking to himself. His eyes got all heavy and half closed and his voice changed, slowing, picking up a kind of a singsong. I swear if he'd pulled out a pocket watch and told me to look at it and feel sleepy I wouldn't have been surprised. But the only thing he swung was his tall chair, he spun around and started pulling a cord and I watched the blinds go across, slowly blocking off the statue of old Theodore and the polishing Zulus. I felt jealous of them out there in the fresh air, right then I would have swapped places — or with anyone, really. Volper switched on a desk lamp. He was still talking in that weird way, about bad boys and what they are really like when they face the punishment here, not acting tough anymore, and he undid one button on his shirt and then he stuffed his tie into the gap. I remember that, the way he stuffed the tie all carefully in there, can't have it getting in the way. He took out this huge red ledger and he wrote down my punishment. I think that was about the time that I went into autopilot. Like I was nothing, a blank. It's probably how they felt when they saw the gas chambers, only times about a billion. I had to move to the corner so I moved there. I had to bend over so I bent over. I had to wait bent over, so I waited bent over. You're shaking and you're trying not to show it. Volper stood behind me for so long that I moved my feet a bit and he told me to be like a statue. Okay. Next thing I feel his hand lifting up the tail of my blazer. He did it kind of slowly and he wasn't very accurate, I mean the back of his hand, his fingers, kept brushing into me. He made a funny swallowing noise too. Next thing he was at the side by the cabinet, I saw his feet there, and the cabinet door opening. I heard wood getting knocked around, a snooker sound, and then I saw one end of the thing touching the carpet. When I saw *that,* my heart just about exploded. Volper walked around me, dragging the end of it over the carpet. It was made of yellow wood, bamboo probably, and he stopped beside me and then he let me have a good look at the whole of it, that bladdy cane. It was like as long as a fishing rod and where he held it, it was thick but it thinned down to almost a point. Next thing he was behind me again and I had to wait and wait. All I kept telling myself is that I must show nothing. *Don't let him see that he can hurt you.* That's what everyone says you have to do when you get *jacks* or *cuts* which is what everyone calls getting caned. I tried to tense even more but it was hard because the tensing made the shaking worse. I twitched big time when I heard a *woot!* But it was only his practice swing back there, that cane cutting the air like a sword as he warmed up.

When it was over, I went to the toilets and I had a look in the mirrors over my shoulder, to what had been done to me. The blood had soaked into my underpants. I had to peel them away and man that stung so much I bit my lip. Underneath, I couldn't believe what I was seeing. It looked like a tiger had raked my arse with its claws. For real, hey. No jokes. There's nothing funny about that Volper. He's pretty much a monster.

26

I come out of the turnstile and move through a zigzag of white concrete. They built it zigzag so no one can shoot through from the street
— those Israeli engineers thought of everything. After the zigzags the
school opens up in front of me, it's got one road that leads up to the
bus depot behind the swimming pool. The classroom buildings are
made of steel and glass, they're shiny and clean-looking in the sun.
To my left are what we call the Bomb Boards, basically these big cork
boards with posters. At the top of the boards it says REMEMBER MAL-
COLM STEINWAY "THE SPIRIT LIVES ON" and then the words under
are STOP! PASOP! BEWARE! STAY ALERT STAY ALIVE! and underneath
that ALWAYS REMAIN CALM. Then there're photos of different terrorist weapons we are meant to keep an eye out for, starting with round
landmines like giant tea saucers. Next are limpet mines that look to
me like car engine parts, the pale SPM and the reddish-brown mini,
both of which can be stuck by their four magnets to anything metal,
and then the safety rings and dust covers that come with them ("which
may be found discarded nearby") and the primers that look like razor
blades and come in a matchbook with Russian writing. There's detona-
tion cord and demolition charges, TNT blocks and chunks of yellow
plastic explosives that look like homemade soap. There's a Kalashnikov
and an RPG-7 with a rocket. A Tokarev pistol is held by a black man's
hand. Meantime they've finished looking under the bus with mirrors
and searching on board because the big steel gate has opened up behind me — it trundles itself across on its own track, it's that heavy. The
bus zooms through and goes up toward the depot and the gate rumbles
back across.

There's a path to the left just after the Bomb Boards and I take it.
It curves around Assembly Hall to the school shul, the Solomon Synagogue to be official about it. It's a cool building if you like science fiction,

it looks kind of like a spaceship, all white and ready to blast off. I put my satchel in the passageway like everyone else. I used to worry they would piss on my bag or put dirt and rocks inside or steal my books but all of that stopped pretty much by the end of my first year. They've gradually forgotten about me and I'm more or less just being ignored again. But this morning I'm thinking about how I was when I started here, wanting so majorly to make a name for myself that meant something. I tried but all I got was shat on. I stand there remembering, reliving what it was like that first winter when I rocked up for rugby practice.

Our coach is sportsmaster Brian Gocherovitz, who everyone calls the Gooch. The Gooch grew up as the only Jewish kid in some inbred little Free State dorp where the local Afrikaner farm boys made his life a misery by tying him to sheep and dropping him down wells and such, until he took up rugby. Eventually he played for the Blue Bulls the year they took the Currie Cup. He retired with no cartilage left in his knees and Solomon hired him to make us at least not such an embarrassment at the bottom of the league. They said he could achieve nothing for years until Marcus Helger came to Solomon. Marcus set the example, he led the best teams we've ever had. But when I trotted out onto the field on my thin pale legs for that first practice, the Gooch looked at me with much sadness. "Helger, Helger," he said. "Helger. No. Just no." He blew his whistle and everyone jogged off for laps but the Gooch held me back. I had on my brother's old-old boots that didn't fit right. The Gooch put a fatherly hand on my shoulder and walked me back to my bags. He said, "It's nice of you to put in a show, Martin, really, but you go home now, oright, my mate? And I don't ever wanna see you in a Solomon rugby jersey ever again."

"But, sir, why? I want to play."

"You know why. You not a normal boy. That name is Helger."

"But that's not my fault, sir."

"Helger. Means the level we all aim for. What I talk on before a match. Bigger than you and me, my mate. This is legacy. Must protect. No matter what." When I got moist in the eyes he patted my head.

I shake myself and go into the shul. I've given up trying. But now I start pondering how I've had a woman, a real woman, an American. I mean I had to put my hand on her mouth to stop her from waking everyone up. Nobody would believe it but I know it happened. I *am* something. More than something. If you think about it, I'm bladdy head and shoulders above. I carry heavy secrets now. I've been in a township. Man, I've come this close to actual terrorists and talked my way out of nearly getting necklaced. And all-a-sudden I'm feeling some of the old, original determination firing up in me, like one of Isaac's fixed-up Old Car engines coughing-coughing and then catching to rev hard.

Sunlight is spearing through the huge rounded windows up there inside the synagogue roof. There's a small gallery for females but it is almost completely empty, obviously, just a few lady teachers. Down below we all roll up our left sleeves and wind on the creaking leather straps of our tefillin, the three hundred boys of Solomon High. But there's only one question buzzing around and that is who will be doing hagbah, the lifting of the Torah? Whoever the matric guy is who gets to do hagbah will also be called the Strongest Lad in the School. Who's it ganna be for this new year, 1989? Obviously in his day Marcus was the hagbah guy, I mean that's a given. He was the youngest one ever, he was Strongest Lad even *before he reached matric,* a record that's never been broken. The service gets started. Prefects stand guard, Volper hunts silently. We sit and stand and praise the Almighty. Eventually the Torah gets brought out of the Holy Ark and carried to the bimah, our centre stage. Nilly Rossbaum sings this week's Torah portion as we sit and listen. When he's finished we stand up for hagbah. There's a buzz that gets so antsy Volper has to snap his lips, just once, and it goes stone quiet.

At the back of the matric block, a long, wiry guy shuffles down the pew and onto the carpet. Holy polony, it's Johnny Lohrmann — otherwise known as Crackcrack. Since that bad day at the Emmarentia Dam years ago he has filled out, his hair's gotten darker but it's the same eyes sitting deepsunk under that bony brow. As he comes along I look away, feeling those eyes slide over me. It's sort of crazy how we ignore each other, like we've both signed an invisible contract to pretend it never happened. Signed with shame. He reaches the bimah, there are seven stairs up to the gap in the low glass wall and then he crosses to the reading table where the Torah is spread open. He stands in front of it for a few seconds before he grips the wooden handles. Our school's Torah is much bigger than average, milled from heavy ironwood. At this point in the year the scroll on the left is much bigger than the right. Crack-crack shows his teeth and grunts and steps back, hiking the holy scrolls straight up in the air in one move. I have to admit it's a pretty good lift. No cheating by pressing down on the edge of the table first, just pure wrist strength. He holds it there over his head and then he spreads his arms wide to show more of the holy parchment. He makes his slow spin. You can feel the school watching carefully for any trembling. If a Torah ever fell we would all have to fast for forty days straight or be looking down the barrel of a mighty curse from above. Now everyone including me is pointing their little finger at the lifted Torah, singing the blessing. I think about how every Torah is always exactly the same as the ones that were written before, back and back for two thousand years, all those centuries of scribes like human photocopiers. The story of how God made the world and how the Jews came out of Egypt. There it is. I mean it's something. It's the reason we are here right now. The reason we *are*.

After prayers we go into Assembly Hall for our placement tests. When I get my multiple-choice paper I stare at it for a while. I know for a fact Warren Stofflemeister always gets in the A class despite being a moron deluxe, just cos his old man is on the board. My theory is they've already placed us. The tests are a sham. So I'm not going to play their game this year and don't even read the questions, circling random answers. I'm confident I'll still go to 8C — might even have earned myself a promotion. I've been lucky enough to get laid last night so why not? I wait for them to call my name but it doesn't come. Not even for 8D. Then Volper, drooling contempt, says this year in Standard Eight there is a special *overflow* class, Standard 8E. And it's right where they've stuck me. Looks like my nonvirgin cockiness just backfired big time. The school gives us a nice send-off of whoops, cackles, and whistles. Apparently our *E* stands for either Extreme Losers or Extra Dof. Waiting outside for us is our homeroom teacher — none other than the Gooch himself. They probably reckon a rugby coach is what's needed to boot some sense into a bunch of rejects like us. I look around and see guys I've mostly never seen before. It's a small group and almost every oke is a new transfer in from a different school, the reason for the overflow. Meanwhile the Gooch doesn't like the way we aren't paying him enough attention. "I swear to you all," he says, "you do not wanna start the year on the wrong footing with me. You will suffer if you do. Act like wild animals and I will gut you and eat you. I am the only tiger here. Is that clear?" We say yes sir. A boy called Stanley Lippenshmecker doesn't do it loud enough so the Gooch blows his whistle into Stanley's left ear. We march off, Stanley clutching the side of his head, and the Gooch leads us to this hill on the far side, far away from all the other classes. People call this hill the Pimple for the obvious reason it's one hell of an ugly lump of yellow rock. Our classroom is a prefab, what used to be a storage trailer, and it stinks of mould and old tennis balls and it's right at the edge of the Pimple, overlooking the rubbish dump. The Gooch threatens more bodily harm then leaves when the bell rings.

What's nice is that my new classmates don't yet know I'm the school untouchable. There's a big boy from Durban called Reginald Solovechik (Solovechik Partners, International Commodities Limited). This Reg has a head on his wide shoulders that's the size of an atlas globe, I swear. This other kid, Barry "Mouth" Horvitz (Horvitz Industrial Solutions, Pty. Ltd.), gives him his nickname in about five seconds flat. From now on Reg is Spunny — short for spanspek, a kind of sweet melon and a reference to that huge dome of his. Another new oke is Irwin Moskevitz (Moskevitz Computing: MCB on the stock exchange). This guy is paler than Casper the friendly ghost, I swear. He's got hair like that French king Louis XIV going in a split-part off his pointed head and you don't even want to know about the nose. Irwin spots a pile of dog turds and hops across and squats over it and acts like he's crapping, his thin legs shaking and his face turning red as he puts on the voice of what sounds like an old Japanese woman going hysterical. "Eeeeeh," he says. "I shitee *shitee* so good." Mouth sees this and straightaway gives him his nickname — Turdster. Others of these new okes are lighting up shmerfs around the corner. This is a class that's mostly never even heard of Marcus Helger, and suddenly I'm lank glad that I threw that test.

27

It's Wednesday arvy and I'm shaking with bad nerves. I don't want to go to the book exchange but it's time, already twenty past three. To psych myself up I think of what Annie said about me turning into a Nazi and about those people in Jules getting the police dog set on them. I remember the pomegranate tree, the promise made there in the night. Still in uniform, I unlock the gate and leave my garden behind and start walking down Shaka Road. Mulberries stain the pavement under the tree sticking over the Beechams' wall. At the Smythes's, some pink-nosed albino-looking bull terriers bang their snouts into the gate, barking hard at me. By the corner a group of maids is sitting in the shade of a municipal jacaranda tree, reminding me of Gloria — she used to strap me on her back when I was little and take me down to the shops along this route. When I was older I held her rough hand, stood there while she spoke in her language to the other maids, the giri-giri noises of Sotho, the click and pop of Xhosa. For the first time I wonder where the rest of her family was all those years when she lived in the room in the back. Some place like Jules?

I reach Greenway Road, feeling thick and clumsy with fear. Viljoen's Book Exchange is in an open mall off a parking lot, between the building society and that doggy-grooming parlour where they once burned Sandy with a hair dryer (and Marcus went back and planted the owner with one crisp left hook). As soon as I walk in, the good smell of books hits me right in the schnozz and I relax a bit. Give me books over people any bladdy day of the week. But here I'm in a bookshop looking for a person, and there he is, coming out from the back, Dolfie Viljoen. I have to cough to find my voice as I put *A Light for the Abyss* down on the counter. "I wanna swap this," I say. "Can you recommend something good?" He doesn't seem to click what this is about, maybe I should wink or something. Then he nods, says, "I think you'll like this." He goes into the back. Dolf's one of those Afrikaners who speaks like perfect English, even his accent is almost like mine. Today he's wearing a Pink Floyd T-shirt (*Dark Side of the Moon*) and his black hair is combed back, a good-looking oke with a shy way about him. He reminds me I've got a bias in how I look at chutaysim — I mean Afrikaners. They're not all huge and inbred, not all vicious and racialist. Of course Dolf's da, Oom Viljoen, he kind of *is* those things, with his blotchy face and huge white moustache — he won't serve black customers.

Dolf comes back with some science fiction book for me but also an envelope. Annie didn't say anything about envelopes. I can hardly look at him as I take both and turn around. I feel as if I should have ignored the envelope, that by taking it I've fallen into some trap. Like any second now a bunch of hard-core Special Branch dutchmen are going to be jumping on my back and dragging me away. But nothing happens except that I jog all the way home and arrive sweaty. In the garden Zaydi is clicking his false teeth and mumbling a prayer. My fingers are shaking as I open the book and riffle through all the pages but there's no note from Annie. The envelope contains a folded cheap-looking Afrikaans newspaper, an inky little tabloid called *Vryheid!*—Freedom. I can understand most of the main headline: *More* something *Truths About Our Crimes.* The story underneath says, roughly, that while our something-something units on the Border are supposed to be something heroic, the truth is that they are engaged in committing some-thingly horrendous somethings against unarmed something civilians. There are blobby black-and-white photos showing armoured trucks that are like the Casspirs in Jules. These ones are driving over the legs of men tied down. Then come more photos that are so horrible they can't be real. There's a lump of meat on a thorn tree and the caption says geskilde baba—skinned baby. Mostly the article seems to be about police units. I have to say that relieves me a lot. Marcus is not in a police unit, like the one called Koevoet—Crowbar. He's in the proper army and they don't ride around skinning babies. No ways.

I remember what it was like when he disappeared, just dropped out of varsity and enlisted without telling a soul, left behind a note and that's all. He still hasn't phoned once, or come home on leave. He sent a few letters, saying he was okay. First from Ladysmith, then Bloemfon-tein, then South West Africa. I remember how the day after he'd gone, Isaac drove his car to the Yard—a 1970 Valiant Barracuda Formula S fastback. Isaac gave him that car as a present when he got into univer-sity but we all knew it was also a bribe for not going to the army, which they'd been fighting about for a while. I remember driving in that car with Marcus and the smell of Deep Heat muscle rub and of sweat and leather from his gym bag and the big cracked boxing gloves and the bandages on the back seat. I remember one time we got tailgated by two okes in a truck and Marcus got out and this other guy got out with a wheel spanner. Marcus ducked a swing of the spanner and knocked the man down with a straight right. The other one in the truck got out and pointed a gun. Marcus just looked at him and shrugged and got back in and we drove off. That happened on Jeppe Street in the middle of town, I think it was about eight o'clock, people all around, but that's Joburg for you. The day after Marcus did his vanishing act, Isaac gave that car to Silas Mabuza who gave it to his son, Victor.

I take the tabloid to the Sandy Hole where I lift out the Quality Street tin full of secrets. First under the lid is Nelson Mandela's face, or what it used to look like. Next are the videotapes, then my notebooks full of sketches and poems. At the bottom there's a Durex effy (lubricated), a commando knife, and one of those little Barclay's plastic bank bags. In the bag is a card and a shriveled thing with a dot of gold in it. Before Annie and the bomb tapes this was my biggest secret by far. I got it one early morning when I woke from the Nightmare and heard something in the backyard. This was when Marcus was still living with us. I went out and saw him at the sink. He was washing himself like Isaac does when he gets back from the Yard. Marcus was an engineering student (we believed) but he'd also gotten himself a night job, as manager at a steakhouse in Randburg where he wore a tuxedo.

When I was sort of creeping up on him at the sink that morning, I saw the jacket and his shirt hanging from a pipe, and he was standing there barechested, scrubbing. A lump of something sticky-looking was hanging in his hair at the back. I must have got too close cos suddenly he whipped around and grabbed me by the throat and put me to the wall. After he recognised me he told me to go back to bed and not to sneak up on people. That lump had fallen and when he went back to washing, I picked it up. The bubbles in the sink were all dark from whatever he'd been cleaning off. The lump was squishy in my hand. I asked him what had happened but he ignored me. A card was sticking out of the pocket of his tuxedo jacket and as I left I took that too. I remember at the time I asked my parents what was the name of the steakhouse where Marcus is working and they didn't know. And what time do steakhouses close. I was thinking there's no need to wear a tuxedo at a steakhouse and come home at dawn. It took me a while to recognise that the gold dot was an earring, a stud, and the gooey chunk around it was a piece of an ear. I rub at it now through the plastic, it's rock hard. Soon after I got this, Marcus was gone. Secrets — where there's one there are always more, I swear. I take out the card and read over what's on it for like the millionth time. Maybe it's time I find out what it means.

28

We, the okes of 8E, get summoned on the intercom. It's still only the first month but I've been expecting this. A bunch of new boys who haven't tasted the cane yet — old Volper couldn't let *that* go on for very long. In his office he gives us a group lecture about civility and then we have to step out and come back in one by one. Waiting for your turn outside you can hear through the door every whipping cut and then the smack when it hits the trousers — sounds like a combo of Gary Player practicing his tee-offs plus the maid beating a carpet in there. But we all grin and wink at each other, pretending it's nothing, even though I know we're all just about wetting our pants. Afterwards we meet up in the downstairs bog to compare arses and thighs, to check who got the most blood drawn, the deepest wounds. We take compass needles and pick out the purple thread on the backs of our ties, making a black stripe with four fledges in it to mark the occasion — four jacks apiece received today. I already have six separate black stripes from being caned six times before, which is about par for the course for a Standard Eight. The new okes are all black-stripe virgins till today obviously, but there are a couple others in our class who aren't new. One is Boris Levin (LVK Distiller Holdings, Pty. Ltd.), who happens to take top prize for wound of the night cos the blood trickles have reached all the way to his socks and the cuts on his upper thighs look deep enough to slot a two-cent coin in. The okes are hosing themselves, having a good fat laugh at old Boris, and he looks at me and says, "At least I'm not a charity case like Helger." Everyone goes quiet and I feel shit. Not that I haven't been expecting this. Boris is a miserable douche and he's been itching to let the cat out of the bag. That he's got puffy eyes and it's clear by his already-thin hair that he's going to be very bald very early in life isn't much of a consolation at this moment. I feel my face heating up and there's a lump in my throat that won't let me talk, not that I've got anything to say. Big Spunny comes closer, his huge round head cocked to one side as he squints at me all confused. Boris takes lots of pleasure in explaining it all to him, to everyone, that I am the school poor case, that I don't belong here, that my brother was okay cos he was the greatest rugby player once upon a time, but me, I'm just a waste of space, everyone in school knows this. Spunny grins at Boris. Then he smacks the top of his head. "How's that space up *there*, hey Boris? Starting to look *unoccupied*. You bald-arse." That makes everyone kick back into major laughing mode, only it's Boris who is blushing not me. Spunny turns to me and throws me in a headlock. "Okes, Helger might be a charity case, but he's our one. Charity's a top lad." And that's when I hear a most beautiful sound, it's Mouth baptizing me right there. "Charity!" he shouts. "Charity! Cheers for Charity, okes!" I'm being spun around, I can hardly breathe, but I swear I've never felt so happy as those cheers echo on the hard white tiles.

I cruise on through the days and weeks with my new mates, a part of all the shenanigans. The starting of the fires in the rubbish dump. The baffing contest where we bend over and fart into the mike of Spazmaz Cohen's new tape recorder to make the volume meter twitch up the highest (till Katzelbaum strains too hard and kuks his pants). The punitive raids on the Standard Six lighties. The passing round of wrinkled pages from a smuggled-in-from-the-overseas *Penthouse,* porno being big-time illegal (even a nipple will bring the police). The war cries on Fridays, building school spirit.

Ugguh bugguh ugguh bugguh!
Ee uh! Uggubugguh!
Ugguh bugguh ugguh bugguh!
Ee uh! Uggubugguh!
Up with Wisdom!
Bugger the rest!

Now we get the word there's ganna be a major rawl. Big Beefus Blitzer is challenging for Strongest Lad. There's tons of betting leading up to it and when the bell goes we vikkel up to the rugby fields to secure a good position overlooking the tuck-shop square. Everything important at Solomon seems to happen around that tuck shop. In front, the square is paved with slasto and the prefects are all shoving the crowd out to make space. Here comes Lionel "Beefus" Blitzer (Blitzer Petrochemical), wheeling his short, thick arms. Beefus has the kind of wide, dark face that you can see already needs to be shaved more than once a day. And here comes Crackcrack. We the okes of 8E are standing behind the rugby fence above the square, looking down. I watch how the two of them do their warm-ups, both fighting the air and showing what they're about to do to the other. Stocky Beefus is hooking lefts and rights from way out, lanky Crackcrack keeps sucking his big lips away from his teeth which makes him look, to be honest, sort of mentally ill, as he knees the air like a hundred times and I hope old Beefus remembers to protect his goolies. Not that he seems worried. Beefus is strong as an ox, he's a definite for prop on the First Team this year. The general feeling in the crowd is Beefus all the way. The general feeling is Crackcrack deserves a fucking-up, solid. Crackcrack's got a reputation for being cruel (no surprise to me), especially among the lighties in the lowest Standards. Then the prefects are stepping back and saying go! Beefus runs across and takes a mighty swing and when he misses he's off balance and Crackcrack jumps on him. There's a wild milling of arms and legs and they go down together. Crackcrack gets ahold of Beefus's tie. I can tell he's thought this out in advance, confirmed by how he took off his own tie beforehand. He drags the knot of Beefus's tie around and starts twisting it like mad as he wraps his legs around Beefus judo-style to keep him from getting away. Choking Beefus with his own tie — I hear a buzzing in the crowd and then some okes start booing. The prefects look unsure whether to stop it or not. Others are arguing with the booers. There're ones who think this new trick is cheating and others who reckon it's pure genius. Meantime Beefus's face has puffed up all bad, his lips purple and the rest dark red. His arms go all floppy and his eyes close. Shoving matches start busting out as the chinas of Beefus try to help their man and Crackcrack's chinas are getting in their way. It takes a long while before they get Crackcrack off and they have to *peel* him, one hand at a time like he's a bladdy crab with its pincers locked into that tie.

Then his mates lift Crackcrack up, cheering. I see Sardines Polovitz there, he was at the Emmarentia Dam that day. The other one, Russ Herman, he emigrated with his family to Texas, America. They're carrying Crackcrack around on shoulders like he is getting married. Meantime old Beefus is limping away, leaning on someone. What bugs me is how people are. I mean already they are all with Crackcrack, the winner. If it had been the other way round they would have been with Beefus. People have no bladdy loyalty, they're all sheep who run after winners. It really gets to me. I'm shaking my head and I can feel my face all sour and all-a-sudden — bing! — I am looking right down into the eyes of Crackcrack himself. I know I should look away. We've got that contract of shame that goes all the way back to the Dam — *I pretend you don't exist and you pretend I don't* — but instead I make a spaz face and give it to him full stick. For a second I see the surprise hit him, the shock of it, then his eyebrows come together. He's breathing hard and he is sweating and he's just almost murdered another kid and it's probably the greatest moment of his sad life and there's me, Helger, to remind him of what happened that day at the Dam. To mock him, noch. Next thing his fist is waving at me and I hear him shouting, *screaming,* in a hoarse voice, "I'll sort you too, Helger! Your time is coming." Then they turn and carry him down the other side.

Spunny nudges me. "Looks like you made a new friend there, hey, Charity. Wow-wee. You should be a diplomat when you grow up. You got a real talent."

"What Charity's got," says Turdster, "is what we call a death wish."

"Charity, Charity," says Schnitz, shaking his narrow head. "When you ganna learn to behave yourself, hey man? When in heaven's name?" Schnitz has his cigarette style and his way of coming up sideways and talking in quick spurts. He likes to show he knows everything from the inside. He's got a wink that goes off so often it's like a medical twitch. He's the one I need to ask. I've been carrying it around for a long time, trying to find the right time, to get my nerve up. I decide, screw it, I'll do it now.

We start walking back to class. I keep rapping to Schnitz to keep him with me, dawdling a bit so we're at the back. Meantime I carefully fit it into the palm of my hand — it feels naked to have it out here in the open, away from the Sandy Hole. I take a breath and tap Schnitz to break his monologue about the various categories of vaginas and when he looks at me I turn over my hand and show him the card without letting him touch it. One of his eyebrows shoots up almost straight and starts bobbing like the hand of a keener kid with a question in class. "Not my scene," he says. "I'm a Thunderdome man."

So it's a club. I try not let any surprise show in my face. But inside I'm flashing like a pinball machine through everything I know about the clubs, everything I've ever heard. Cos Thunderdome is a club and a club is a nightclub, a kind of disco in town. The cool Solomon crowd go to clubs, they get in even if they're under eighteen. Clubs are dangerous, glamorous. I know the names and the legends but of course

I've never been. I've heard of Q's on Market Street and of Idols with its balcony on End Street. The Junction nearby and the crazy 4th World. The Doors near the Carlton Centre and Bella Napoli and the Chelsea Hotel where the frissest band in South Africa, éVoid, played some infamous concerts for their weirdly dressed-up fans called fadgets. But I've never heard of a club called Xanadu. "What's wrong with Xanadu?" I ask Schnitz. It's the one word on the card. He's trying to get hold of it but I've already pocketed it back.

Schnitz stops and sends me a lank shrewd look. "You're a Xanadu man, hey, yourself?"

"Ja, man," I say. "That spot is lank tit."

Schnitz smiles. "You scheme so, hey?" He starts talking about all the heavy jolling he has done at the clubs. The rounds of flaming sambucas. The man-crazed shiksa sluts jumping up and down under the strobe lights. The dirty action in the toilets and the *Miami Vice* suits and the time Myron Shekelovitz drove his Suzuki through the plate-glass window at the front of Jackal's. He talks about how much it costs to bribe the bouncers to let you in. "But you," he says, suddenly all sly, "you have probably got fully fake ID, am I right? Like gold-plated. A big-time clubber like you. Am I correcto, bru?"

"Hundred per cent," I say. I'm on automatic, the bullshit flowing on tap from my mouth.

Schnitz snorts. "Charity. Level with the gravel, my mate. Have you ever even been to a club? Any club. Ever in your life."

I pretend to be confused, my eyelids flapping like moth wings. "What are you asking me?"

He grins. "Charity, didn't your mommy ever teach you to tell the truth?" As he walks off what I most want to do is grab him by the shirt and shake him and say, *Take me with you next time you go!* But I'm too cool for that. My hands go in my pockets and I start whistling. Too cool for school.

29

I have my school name — Charity — but I don't have a *Name* yet, have to work for that still, find my angle. But the more time passes the more I think of the girls in Jules township, of the Struggle, and all-a-sudden I find myself swelling up with pure gratitude for the schooling that's right in front of me on a silver platter, the quality of the textbooks and the teachers, and never mind the ugly stuff. Maybe coming up on turning seventeen also has something to do with it, but for the first time in my life I start to *avail* myself of what's there, actively concentrating in classes and doing my homework first thing instead of wasting my afternoons in useless *Playing*. And every morning now I'm doing push-ups and making my bed, and at home I hang up my uniform neatly and sit down to eat a proper lunch "like a gentlyman," as Zaydi puts it. I even do shadow boxing with my shirt off in the sun, trying to remember the little bit that Marcus did teach me. Like defence first. Elbows up, fists over eyebrows. Angle off to your man. Left, right. He can't hurt you. Nelson Mandela was a boxer. He does push-ups in his cell.

This afternoon I decide to go into the Yard, I can do my homework after supper. I want to help the business, to be useful. I catch the municipal bus on Barry Hertzog Avenue and get off in Vrededorp. At the Yard, Isaac is working alone at the Old Cars just like the last time when I was here with that freak Captain Oberholzer in tow. I pass my old man his tools for a while before I notice Silas's stuff isn't there and ask about it. Isaac lifts his head with one eye shut in the sun, looking at me like he can't believe I don't know this. But no one tells me anything. He says ten days ago Silas went missing. It was a week before they found out what happened. He was driving his Peugeot 404 station wagon and he ploughed into the back of a truck on the highway off-ramp. They took him to Baragwanath Hospital in the giant township of Soweto, and there he got left on the floor, neglected in some mix-up. Eventually his family

tracked him down, and it turned out he had a broken neck and had developed bad infections on the lungs and cardiac problems. When Isaac
found out where he was, he arranged to have him transferred to a private
clinic in Illovo, their first nonwhite patient ever. "They only took him
cos I'm paying extra," Isaac says. "Plus the physician manager there is a
nephew of Errol Kramer. You know Errol." I nod. Errol's bought exhaust
systems from us for donkey's years. One time he shot three robbers dead
in his shop and was in the papers. Isaac looks sad to me and I'm not surprised, him and Silas have been glued together at the Yard since forever.

"How is he doing now?" I ask.

"You want to go see?"

So we drive to Illovo and I lose a breath when I see Marcus's car in the
parking lot. It takes a second to remember it's not his anymore, belongs
to Victor Mabuza now, Silas's son, given to him by my father after Marcus
did the unthinkable — maybe the unforgivable — and joined the army. We
go inside and Silas is lying there asleep, tubes all over the show. Isaac's already told me this is basically hospice care, Silas is no spring chicken and
we have to face it, he's not going to recover. Victor is sitting by the bed and
I can see Isaac wants to say something to him. I say I'm going to the toilet
but I listen outside at the door. I can only just hear what Isaac is saying,
his voice all squeezed. "I'm . . . very, very sorry." And Victor says, "It was
an accident." And Isaac says, "Ja, I know. But I should have looked into it
better, rightaway. He should never have lain there like a dog on the floor.
I should have looked into it when he didn't come to work. Your father . . .
I could have gotten him in here rightaway . . . Maybe it . . . I'm sorry, *I am
sorry.*" Driving home, my father's eyes are still red. "It's terrible what happens to them," he says like he's half talking to himself. "It *is* terrible. A man
should have proper doctors. Terrible. When I was a kid, I'll never forget . . ." But he doesn't go on, and I don't push it.

In the morning I realise it's Wednesday again. I'm not nervous about
that anymore, it's funny to think how I was the first time. Going down
to Viljoen's has become a routine, there's never any message from Annie

in the books. Now I think how I can go on waiting or I can make things happen myself. You can't build a Name by doing nothing. At first break I go up to the media annex where we have our Commodore 64 computers in neat rows, our library, our film hall. I've been thinking about this all night, it seemed a lot easier lying in bed — I'm shaking but I take out the steel ruler in my pocket and use the corner to unscrew the plate of an electric outlet, pulling it out and leaving it dangling, and then I go up to the top floor. Mr. Gordon is a bit of a dick and he basically lives there in the media annex, his little kingdom. I ask him about joining the video club and he looks up and talks slowly to me like I'm a moron, saying I should know it's only for matrics and only for the *very few that shall manage to qualify.* I give him a nice smile and tell him someone vandalised one of the plugs downstairs and that gets him agitated even more than I'd hoped. When he runs down to have a look, I vikkel behind his desk and through the accordion doors to the video lab. There's a video editing suite, a camera on a tripod pointed at a green screen. A steel door in the corner is slightly open. Inside is a walk-in storeroom full of supplies. There're cameras, lights, microphones — and on the far side a tall block of stacked VCRs, floor to ceiling. Hallelujah. I pump my fist. Mr. Gordon's footsteps are on the staircase so I use the outside fire escape. When I get home I hurry inside and write out the Hebrew grid Annie showed me, encoding a message: HAVE FOUND VID PRODCTN EQUIP STANDBY. It goes between page 100 and 101 of *Sense and Sensibility* which I take down straightaway to Viljoen's and do the book swap with Dolf like always. How's that for initiative, American?

30

Sunday is braai day, obviously. In the morning I go with Isaac to pick up the meat from the kosher section at the back of the Checkers on Barry Hertzog Avenue. T-bones and lamb sosaties and a jar of monkey gland sauce (Annie nearly vomited when she first heard the name, she only calmed down when I explained it's not made of monkeys, just spices and tomato and worcester sauce and such). When we get back there's a red Jaguar XJ6 parked outside. Means only one thing. Sure enough in the garden Hugo Bleznik is nicely settled in, a very large Scotch in hand and a much younger woman at his side that I've never seen before, which doesn't surprise me. Hugo with a belly like a beer barrel and about twenty-five puddly chins under his real one. He's wearing a white suit today with a carnation in his hatband. He's been Isaac's partner since the beginning but I can't think of two men more opposite. Isaac's place is the Yard — king of the rust and the wrecks — while Hugo works in nice restaurants and pretty hotels and fancy bars. He's got that warm handshake, that unbreakable ceramic smile. He knows everyone in Joburg that matters to the business and probably most of them that don't. He's never been married and he owns seven racehorses he keeps at the track out in Turffontein and a huge house in Hyde Park and another holiday house with a boat on the Vaal River. He must be getting near eighty but still has amazing energy, prefers being on the road to his office at the Yard. He not only drives all over the country, fishing for new wholesale clients and visiting dealers, he also flies to Los Angeles and Tokyo to make deals for shipments of used engines and new parts.

I help Arlene lay the table under the plum trees and after we eat and the fat black flies are parked on the gnawed bones, Hugo turns to me. Isaac has gone inside, where Arlene disappeared a while ago, to fetch another bottle. Hugo's new lady friend is in deep study of her long nails, and Zaydi's eyes are closed. Hugo says to me, "I wanna talk serious to you, boyki." His pinkie finger pointing from his glass. "You know it's ganna be you now. You the one, hey."

"How d'you mean?"

"The business. It's not ganna be your brother, it's ganna be you." I laugh. Hugo says, "Don't be modest. Shine yourself up, nobody else will. You can do it and run that business very well, one day. I got no doubt." He scrunches around in his chair to check for Isaac but the lawn is empty. "This is between you, me, and that garden wall. Your father would be miffed. He can't be whatchacallit objected about you."

"Objective?"

"There is something I want you in on it. Will be good for you."

"What is it?"

"This has to do with sorting out a problem. If you the one and not Marcus, which I believe is the case, then you need to learn how it's done. No school can teach from a book. And also being truthful to you, the way I understand this is a problem you involved us with."

"Me?"

"A problem you sort of made, Martin. As I understand to be honest."

I stare at him, waiting for a sign he's pulling my leg.

"The policeman," he says. "That you brought to the Yard." That word *policeman* like a kick in my guts.

"Don't look so pale," he says. "It'll be oright. Now I'm going back on the road next few weeks. But when I get back, next time I'm here Sunday we'll leave straight after lunch. I'll come alone. You and me. You will make up the excuse. I will wait round the corner for you."

"Come on, Hugo."

"I'm not joking here, Martin. You don't tell your father, no one."

I scratch my nose. "Go where?"

"Yes or no. But I advise yes. I think you sort of have to."

"What's this all about, Hugo?"

"I told you. That policeman of yours. Captain Oberholzer. You think on it. But when I get back, you'll be ready and you'll see. We go together and fix your problem and get it done."

Isaac is coming. Hugo touches his pinkie to his temple and winks. When he leaves, after a conference with Isaac inside, he is carrying a shoebox under his arm. It occurs to me I've watched him taking shoeboxes away with him on Sunday afternoons for all of my life, but I have no idea what's in them.

Wednesday can't come fast enough. I'm pretty sure there will be a message back from Annie but my heart still jumps in my chest when I open the book and find a little folded paper square. Her fingers left this for me. I sniff it vainly for her perfume before transferring the Hebrew letters to the decoding grid. Then letter by letter, as if in a reverse strip-tease, Annie's words gradually appear for me.

UR STAR MEET ME SAT FLEA MARKET TEAPOT STALL 11AM

A star. See what happens with a bit of trying. I know the place she means, as she knows I would, it's the market they have on the parking lot in front of the Market Theatre in Newtown. Annie. I'm going to see her, for real. I'm levitating, all my blood changed to helium. *Annie.*

But with Thursday comes news of a bombing in Fordsburg—not far from the flea market. Two dead. Blasts happen all the time, yet the place and timing of this one feels like some of kind of a message meant for me, a reminder of what's on the Fireseed tapes which chews at my mind. When it's Friday after school and I hop on the municipal bus to Vrededorp, I realise where else the bus goes. So when my stop comes I don't get off, I stay on till Fordsburg. Round here is more or less Afrikaans also, but more commercial than residential and with many Indian faces too. There're rug shops, tailors, curry restaurants. The Oriental Plaza—the Indian shopping mall—is near here. I don't know if they are allowed to live here as well cos I think it's a whites-only area but I'm not sure. I come up on a corner where cop cars are parked. Used to be a Wimpy hamburger bar here but the jolly colours are all scorched black, I see, with broken glass and melted tables in the street behind police tape. There're a few people loitering, looking. The fireblast went up to sear the brickwork of the second floor. Then my eye catches a menu blowing on the street, one of those plastic-coated ones, half burnt up and blistery but I can still read bits of it. *Cheeseburger with French Fried Chips R2.50 . . . Special Grill R3.75 . . . Shanty Salad for Slimmers . . . Hey Kids! Join the Wimpy Wiz Club . . .* "Another one," a woman near me is saying. A man's voice says, "They must really

hate cheeseburgers, hey." It's a joke about how Wimpy bars keep getting targeted. A man in front turns around and says, "You should shut
up and have some respect." The first one says, "Come make me," and
next thing the okes are swinging at each other with typical South African friendliness. The women put out their arms and shout, "Hey hey
heyyyy! Stop! Stop it!" A cop gets out of one of the parked cars and
strolls up to do just that. The sight of that uniform does something to
my stomach that it never used to. I move the opposite way. Suddenly a
hand hooks my arm. There's a square, hairy face too close to me. I can
smell sweet alcohol on the breath and the eyes are strange, not focused
on me, like he's looking at the tip of his own nose. "Stavros Christou is
my name," this guy says, all murmury. "I come from Larnaca, Cyprus,
the year 1960. For a better life, if you'll excuse me. I have a cafi on Plein
Street these thirty years. Do you know how many times I was robbed
by *them*? I say nine, you won't be surprised. But it's more, a dozen.
Have a look here . . ." He pulls down his collar. I'm moving away but he
walks with me, holding on but not hard, almost gentle. Talking to me
all softly as if we've known each other forever. "You see it? Twenty-five
stitches. Two centimetres away from the jugular, they said. I didn't even
see the screwdriver. Like always, I said to *them*, take, take everything.
I have no problem. I open the register. But *they* are against human life
in their nature. You know it was two girls it was killed with this bomb.
They put it in the rubbish bin and walked out. It was two little girls
from school here for a hamburger. Girls in school uniform just like you
are wearing. Sir, that bomb throwed them into this street here as if it
was pieces of old rubbish they was. Thirteen-year-olds. My cousin, she
does know the family of the one. Good people, sir, I can guarantee you.
The best people. The girls was in pieces. But the one was still breathing when the ambulance came. I tell you honestly, sir, this is a blessing
she died or she would have been a cabbage in a wheelchair. Did she deserve that for a hamburger? Oh what kind of place is this? Another one
person was burned on his whole entire body, lying in hospital. Now

I'm asking you a question, sir. You have an honest face. Would a genuine human being put a bomb in a hamburger place? To kill *schoolgirls*? Would a human being do such a thing? I'm asking you in all honesty, sir, because I want to know . . ."

"Let go of me," I tell him, he's breathing so close and I get the feeling he could be blind or something. He's making my skin itch. "Will you bladdy well let go of me? Will you, please?"

But he doesn't, he keeps on clinging, talking gently. "Don't you see that the government is too soft? You have a sensible face. If they are not human beings don't you agree we need to put *them* all up against a wall or it will never stop? Isn't that obvious . . ."

Some kind of a dwaal, a deep daze, hangs on to me just like that stranger, all the way to Saturday morning. I can't seem to shake it. I have to force myself out of bed. It's crazy, I know I should be excited, about to see Annie again—but I also feel all wrong in myself. I catch a different bus to the Market Theatre. This place is Liberal Central in Joburg. They have all the anti-apartheid plays like *Sarafina!* here, this is where the white Jewish kid Johnny Clegg started playing Zulu music with an ex-gardener, Sipho Mchunu, before they hit it big with their band Juluka. There's also a jazz club across from the theatre—first place I ever saw blacks and whites together in a social situation where the blacks weren't serving the drinks. I dunno, hey, the laws of apartheid they just seem to disappear around here, abracadabra. I'm under the M1 overpass and I see the tables and the people, the flea market. But inside me that Cypriot guy's voice keeps droning, and I'm seeing Kefiya and Ski Mask also, and Comrade Shaolin. In the flea market the heat sizzles on the hot asphalt around the stalls and I catch that rotteny veg whiff that I believe is zol being smoked and the more familiar pong of tobacco and the sweet whiff of beer and a dozen different songs from different speakers and the sound of a live saxophone somewhere, a guitar somewhere else, street musicians playing for coins. The crowding faces are coal-black and pig-pink and everything in between, tall, short, fat, thin, beefy. The stall I want is at the far end, towards the glass skyscrapers. But when I reach it there's no Annie so I check my watch and find I'm early. I wander up to the theatre. In the doorway there're piles of free newspapers. I recognise a stack of *Vryheid!* Next to it is one called *Liberation.* I pick it up and read about a Mass Democratic Movement rally in town. A photo shows oceans of marching people. But I can't remember seeing it on TV or in the *Star.* I turn the page and an article with the words THE JEWS mugs my eyes. THE JEWS, it says, are South African's biggest slum lords. THE JEWS are the "chief exploiters of the masses." Soweto and all the other townships, it is stated, are in fact owned by THE JEWS. Jewish banks, I read, are the reason that apartheid exists. It all went back to the Boer War and the Rothschilds and who really controlled the British Empire . . . I go sort of blank. It's like when I was a kid walking home from shul and they'd shout at us from the back of a car. Bladdy Jewsss! I put the paper down and walk away and stop and look back at the pile of them. I think of all the people who are going to pick it up and read it, repeat it, pass it on. I'm walking again but I don't remember starting out. Floating. I find myself at the stall again. Lots of teapots but still no Annie. I'm kind of relieved. Then someone taps me and says, "I think she wants you." Looking around I spy an old blue Volkswagen. Dark curly hair behind the wheel with dark sunglasses, plus a hand that keeps waving, waving.

31

She's wearing a vest so I can see her brown shoulders, and a pair of giant hoop earrings. I don't ask where she's taking me in the little Volksie and don't say anything about the quality of her driving — she jerks between lanes like she's trying to dislocate our necks and treats that brake pedal like she's allergic to it. We howl all the way down Jan Smuts Avenue and up into Saxonwold and turn onto Chester Road and come back and circle the Zoo Lake. "If you lost," I say, "just admit. I can direct you. Just tell me where we going." She smirks at me. "Oh shut the hell up, Martin." I give her an oversized shrug. "What do I know?" I say, "I only grew up here." She flaps her hand. "Everyone's a damn expert," she says. "Sit back, take your chill pill." So I keep quiet and we go around again and then she finally parks in the lot behind the lake, driving all the way to the pine shade at the far end, with no one in sight. She says, "I was making sure we're not bein' followed, you really wanna know." She clips off her seat belt and scrunches around to face me square. "Martin, Martin Helger. In the flesh. Ha!" She takes off her sunglasses and it's eyes to eyes in there and wham it hits me and I think so *this* is it. This is what all the songs and the movies are about. I'm boiling like a kettle with it.

I put my hand on her brown smooth arm and my voice comes out choked. "I missed you."

"Look at *him*," she says. "You been working out, Martin?" I think of my morning push-ups and I nod. "You got thicker around here," she says, touching my neck, my shoulder. "Looks like you've been out in the sun too, some colour. Nice. And . . . you've changed, I mean for real."

"Have I."

"You've grown. You look good."

I nod, thinking of my new friends at school. "I know, hey," I say. "Turning seventeen on Monday." March sixth it is — I haven't seen her since the pomegranate bench, two months ago.

"Really? Happy birthday."

I grin at her and next thing I've snapped off my seat belt and I'm going for it with both arms and both lips. She puts a hand on my chest to stop me. "Hoo wee," she says. "Have ta watch myself round you, don't I." I just grin like a mute idiot while she presses my hands back to my lap. She says, "So. Talk to me about how we do this. What facilities you got? When can we get the videos in there?"

It takes me a second to change gears. "Didn't you miss me too?"

She tosses her chin. "Videos, Martin," she says. "Videos."

So I tell her in detail, showing off a bit, how I got my way up into the video lab at school and what I saw there and what I think can be done with that equipment. I explain security at Solomon. The concrete walls and the armed guards, the cameras and alarms and procedures.

She nods. "Okay," she says. "So how're you gonna do this?"

I just stare. "Me?"

"What did you think? You point the way and we'll do the rest?"

I sput-sputter for a bit. "I didn't. I didn't really think about it. I'm just telling you it's there."

"Martin, listen to me. You're the only one, okay. We keep coming up against walls. We have a mission but we're bottlenecked with this copying, and falling behind. I never thought it would be this hard. You're the one who's got the master tapes. You need to get in there and make this happen like yesterday, right. You got in there already once, didn't ya?"

"That was for like a second. Mr. Gordon is always there."

"After classes?"

I'm shaking my head. "He's there till late. And there's always some after-school club up there in the media annex, it's busy till like five. Also we've got this system of in-out checking that the guards do at the gate, numbers have to match at end of day. They made it like that in case of kidnapping. So it's not like I could just hide away somewhere in the school and come out later. But even if I did, then how would I get out?"

Her big caramel eyes have squeezed down to two lines. "So what are you saying to me?"

"I'm just telling you how it is."

"You're kidding, right? You bring me all the way here for that? To tell me this is *not* possible. What's the fucking point, Martin? Jee-zus!"

I feel my back getting stiff, my face hot. "Well you the one who set this meeting."

"Because I thought you had good news and we could do this thing! That *this* was to plan it properly, in person. Duh." Her anger, her contempt — it's worse than any caning, I swear.

I fold my arms. "Well I spose you thought wrong then didn't you."

There's this silence in which her mouth hangs open. Then she says, "Don't you dare, Martin. Don't you dare attitude me, okay?"

I say, "Is that an order you giving me?"

"I'll give you some free advice, kiddo. Nobody in this world likes arrogance."

"I'm not —"

"It doesn't matter. Our emotions don't matter. We're soldiers and we are here to do a job. We need those videos copied, Martin . . . What, what is it now?"

"Nothing."

"What is it?"

"Nothing," I say. "You should go to the Wimpy in Fordsburg sometime, that's all."

"What's that supposed to mean?"

"Nothing. Order yourself a cheeseburger, well burnt."

"What?"

"Nothing. You don't even know." Then I say, "They blow up kids, Annie. Girls. For all I know that could've been from one of your Fireseed tapes."

She's quiet for a bit. Then she says, "Look, Martin. What are you tryna say, that you're going soft on me? Have you forgotten about what Jules *is* already? What this is all *about*? We're bringing down a machine here, man. This is a war. And they are the ones with the army, don't forget that."

"What do those schoolgirls have to do with any machine?"

"Civilians aren't the targets."

"Could have fooled me."

She closes her eyes, takes a big breath. Opens them and says, "Martin, if burger joints keep blowing up, people will stay home and businesses will go under. That's just a fact. Right or wrong. It spreads fear, adds pressure. Heat and tension. A revolution is like making popcorn. It has to hit a certain temperature before people start popping in masses."

"People aren't frigging popcorn, Annie!"

"It's an analogy, okay. If whites get comfortable living with apartheid why would they change it, Martin? They've had it too easy for too long. It's time they got a taste of their own damn medicine."

"Those bombs blow up blacks too," I say.

She shrugs. "The mission is to make this country ungovernable. There is no way around blood getting spilled — but that's not a choice we made. The regime did."

"I don't know," I say.

"Martin. Hey. Look at me. You remember what you agreed to with me in the garden, when I offered you a way out? I would have taken the tapes off your hands *then*, but you made a commitment to me and now it sounds to me like Martin Helger's commitments are just a buncha crap."

That stings. "I'm here aren't I."

"The world is full of fakes, Martin. Don't be a fake. Have integrity. Think of Mandela. Be an adult, be a man. Do your job. Do what you promised me, Martin. *Go and get my fucking videos copied.*"

YESOD

32

The Malcolm Steinway Memorial is in the corner of the marble lobby, it's standing panels with photos. I'm not here to look at the first part but I can't help myself. Back in 'eighty-two our buses were unarmoured and had the name of our school on them, a bad combo. In the photos from 29 September, bus number five looks like a giant can opener just went at it, backed up by about twenty hyperactive blowtorches. The driver, Ezra Thenjwayo, fifty-six, father of four, was blinded and lost his left arm. Malcolm Jerome Steinway, fourteen, reading a maths text, a boffin on his way to making prefect, was blasted into a nearby palm tree. Bystanders fainted when they saw what was left of him, dripping. A Soviet limpet mine is what did it.

Those days our school had no security guards and only a chainlink fence around it which didn't go all the way. The bomb changed everything for us, woke us up to the fact that we are a target. The board started an emergency fund and flew in a team of combat engineers from Israel to build us some top-notch security. The wall. Moving down the panels I can see the wall erecting itself in photos, the huge slabs of concrete lowered by cranes, the pickaxe teams digging, the wires and circuits and cameras and razor coils being laid down. There's a framed *Gold City Zionist* full-page feature, and some old blueprints, signed by the engineers. Some markings there have the words *original fortifications.* In the feature it mentions "uncompleted sixties-era fortifications that were never used," which the school authorities had "no intention of finishing." They wanted to make it clear that the "older security structures" were "categorically not part of the new security plan" which is described as "brand-new" and "state of the art."

Stepping back to take it all in, one fact slowly dawns — all the security is in the perimeter. All the cameras point out, not one is inside our grounds. Almost all our doors are without locks. We never see the security guards inside, only at the gate, they're not allowed in unless it's a total emergency. The builders wanted to keep the school normal except for the perimeter. They never thought of a poison bee in the hive.

I decide to walk all the way around the whole of the wall, on the inside. Maybe there's a gate or a gap or something that nobody knows about, that's not on any chart. Every break period I walk a little farther. I get up behind the rugby stands in the weeds behind the blue-gum trees. I tear my pants on thorns on the far side of the swimming pool. Always the concrete wall is at my right-hand side, rising up to block the sky. A creepy feeling the thing is watching me, looking down. Like it's a huge stone idol standing tall on the land and who do I think I am to try and challenge it. The parts of it that are more open to the school have been painted by art students over the years. One mural shows the iconic headgear of a goldmine, another a jumping springbok, another our school founder with his watch chain and mutton chops. Then there are the First rugby squads and the tennis and cricket teams in their whites, the national debating champs. Staff portraits.

Today I'm coming down the steep granite path next to the western section of the wall, passing the tennis courts, and then comes the veld — an open section of wild yellow grass. This is a part of the school that hardly anybody comes out to and I'm alone. There's a mural of my brother out here that I forgot about, a big one. But as I get closer to it I can tell there's something not right. For this portrait the art students copied a photo of Marcus from the yearbook of like 'eighty-five I think it was, showing him running with the ball under his arm and his other arm handing off a tackler. You can see the tendons in his thick neck and the ripples of muscle in his forearm. But now when I stand in front of it I see some scaly bastard has gone and spraypainted a giant yellow cock on his mouth and written HELGERS SUCK. Across his legs it says FUCK HELGERS. I stand there so long the bell rings.

In the morning after roll call I catch up to the Gooch outside our home classroom on the Pimple. As he listens to my whispered description his face gets more and more pained, the lips twisting away from the teeth. "Holy kuk stars," he says. "You not serious?"

"Fraid I am, sir."

"This is your brother, this is Marcus Helger we are talking."

"Yes, sir."

"We cannot allow this to spread. Marcus is our symbol."

"I understand, sir."

"Ganna slip you my spare office key with my left hand. I'mna tell you how to handle this personally. Be quick-quick and dead quiet. Tell no one, absolutely."

"Yes, sir."

The Gooch's office is behind the swimming pool. There are crushed cans of Lion Lager and some used pill bottles in the wire rubbish basket next to his desk. A long corridor leads back, with nails in the wall and numbered keys hanging from them. The storage room at the end is full of pool and groundskeeping stuff: ropes with floaters for the lanes in swimming galas, life jackets and polystyrene boogie boards and then lawnmowers and watering cans and fertiliser and wheelbarrows. At break I get what I need, put it in a tin bucket, and head down to the mural. The sun is stronger than yesterday, baking hot, the concrete so bright it whips at my eyes like sparks. The veld looks dusty and dry, the colour of a lion. I imagine a wounded lion waiting in there, crouched down, panting for my blood. I reach the mural and get to work. The Gooch explained that the murals have a protective varnish, so I can remove the spray paint without damaging the mural under. Still, it's tough, tricky work to scribble the red paint off with a toothbrush dipped in turps, one tiny square at a time. I'm sweating and my hand hurts and I need a drink of water. I stretch my back and look toward the school, the buildings like a mirage over the hot veld. I dry my forehead with my tie and start walking, cutting across the veld. It's rough stones underfoot, there're lizards and bits of glass, rusted cans. The land dips slightly and I'm surprised to find a wide streak of whitish sand with that swept look that dry riverbeds have. To my left it runs uphill to the high fence and tall lights of the tennis courts, to my right it goes down to what looks like a small brick oven. I lick my dry lips and head down. It's no oven, it has a grate in front. Squatting, I find chunks of old grass and dirt stuck between the bars at the bottom and shade my eyes and squint to see what's behind — the opening of a metal pipe. It slants away, off underground. My eyes are adjusting, I can see corrugations in the metal and something about this is familiar. I sit back on my heels and study the grate. It has hinges on one side and a latch on the other but there's also a little plastic box with a wire going down into the ground. In the side of the box is a keyhole and numbers stuck on by a label gun: 253.

That pipe keeps bugging me for the rest of the day, I don't know why. After school I take the municipal bus to the Yard in Vrededorp. I want to help Isaac, pass tools to him, so he won't be so alone without Silas. But when I get there Arlene says he's gone to town to see Harry Steed, his lawyer. I can have a lift back with her but she won't leave for another hour, so I wander around the warehouse upstairs while she works in her office on the ground floor. That pipe — what is it about a metal drainage pipe in the ground that makes me feel like I know it when I don't? I'm standing by the back window, thinking, when I hear the ripping snarl of an engine that can only be my brother's old car.

Down there, the Barracuda is pulling up at the back gate. Must be Victor Mabuza, maybe there's some news of Silas. I run down the back stairs and jog through the wrecks. By the time I reach the gate there's a group of maybe ten guys there around Victor, and he has a look on his face that makes me stop. They're talking loudly to him and he starts shaking his head, and then he waves with his whole arm, raising his voice. I stay back round the corner of a wrecked Isuzu bakkie and watch them, some with tools in their hands. One of the workers, Sammy Nongalo, a tall young guy, takes hold of Victor's wrist and starts tugging on it and Victor digs his heels and shakes his head. The others get louder. Victor is pulling his arm, trying to get it loose, but Sammy won't let go. The other men press in closer around them. This whole situation is giving me a bad feeling and I'd rather walk away and pretend I haven't seen anything but I remember my father apologizing to Victor at the clinic, his red eyes, so I straighten up and walk out to them.

Everyone goes quiet as I greet Victor with a smile. His eyes are flicking around and he licks his lips and I can smell his sweat and see how it's soaked right through his shirt. His chin is shaking. I look at the others but no one will look back at me. Sammy speaks in African and Victor says, "Goodbye. I must go now." He turns around and walks through the gate. I call his name but he keeps going.

I walk after him, catch him up. "Didn't you just get here?"

"I'm fine," he says. "I am fine."

"He is fine," says a voice right behind me and when I turn I'm surprised to see they are all with me, following. A guy called Phala is the one who spoke. "Everything okay," Phala says. "Okay, okay."

"Is fine," says Sammy, next to him.

"Yes, fine," says Victor. "I go now."

"He goes now," says Phala.

I want to talk to Victor alone, but the others are right there as he gets into the Barracuda. I notice now it has new hubcaps and a fat new aerial. It's a brute of a car, Marcus used to love it. Quite the score for a young black guy to have. I'm even a little jealous of him, I wonder what kind of car Isaac will give me now that I've turned seventeen and can get my learner's licence. I watch Victor reverse and drive off, the big engine gruffing like a hungry leopard. Now the others are walking back into the Yard. I catch up to Phala and Sammy and ask, "What was that all about? What were you saying to him?"

"He comes to say hello," says Sammy.

"No," says Phala. "Everything is fine."

I believe them like I believe the world is flat, but what can I do? No one's saying anything.

33

Now it's morning again on the Pimple after roll call and outside class I'm giving the Gooch an update on the mural, that I'm making progress but the work is killer. He says, "You've got to get it done pronto, Martin. Every day someone could find, and then what."

I rub my nose. "Sir, I think I know who it was who did it, hey. I'm ninety-nine per cent sure it was Lohrmann. Johnny Lohrmann. In matric."

The Gooch grimaces. He looks away from me and gives off a sigh. He's wearing his maroon shorts high on the waist. His knees are wrapped in about a thousand miles of tape each and he has at least a dozen whistles around his neck, like he's the Mr. T. of rugby. "Ach, no, man," he says. "I really didn't want to hear this kind of talk from you."

I say, "But isn't it important we find who it was, sir? To nip in bud."

"There's no nip in bud," he says. "It's exact opposite cos you put a spotlight on. People will talk and go look. If you'd leave it alone it would die off."

"But sir."

"Everybody hates a tattletale, Martin."

He's still not looking at me and we stand there in silence for a while, a blush climbing up my neck like a monkey. "Okay," I say. "Okay, sir. Forget I said it, please."

"I wish that my ears had not, Martin. But I cannot undo."

"I take it back," I say.

His whistles jingle as he shakes his head and scratches his Tom Selleck moustache. "Can't, my mate. You've put a conundrum on me." He moves off, jingling, his stocky, strapped legs bowing out like parentheses.

When I'm in his office at first break I run my eyes down the row of keys hanging on the nails and stick 253 in my pocket. In the hot veld by the desecrated mural I squat in front of the grate and hold the key to the box, my hand shaking like there's an earthquake on. Without giving myself a chance to think, I stab it in. I'm sort of praying it won't fit properly, on a level, but it slips into that keyhole like it's greased and then I wipe my sweaty hands on my shirt and stare at it some more. I'm thinking an alarm could sound, I could bring the guards here in like seconds — seriously, gunmen. It could set off a bomb drill. Parents will be called, I'll be expelled. Maybe they'll report to the police and then what. *Shut up,* I say in my breath. *Just shut up a second.* I bite into the skin of my forearm and then I turn the key. There is a hard click. There. It's done. I wait it out, sweating like a rotisserie chicken, but nothing happens. I reach up and undo the latch and pull on the grate and it creaks stiffly but swings out. I push my head inside the sloping tunnel. There's a humid musty smell of soil and rot. The corrugations on the bottom are packed with sand and stones. I roll on my back and lie there breathing in that almost familiar scent, that feeling. I reach up and touch the roof of the pipe, run my fingers over the bumps in the steel and then I rap my knuckles and — *bink* — just like that I remember it, the tin noise.

I sit up so fast I bang my head but I don't care. I'm remembering that day when Marcus and I were small and walking Sandy through Brandwag Park. And the whiteout flash of the lightning and the flash flood that filled up the creek in front of us. They always taught us to be afraid of flash floods. Kids who played in the mine dumps or the sewers got drowned like rats by them every year, they said. I'm remembering the things that flooding river carried past us so fast that day, a Pick n Pay shopping cart, a six-pack of Castle Lager, a tire, a shoe. And then the whole riverbank started caving in, it collapsed into the water and got washed away and what was left behind was a section of the pipe sticking out, as long as a car. The water kept pressing against it and when things in the current bumped into the pipe it made that tin noise — *bink!* — and then it started bending and creaking and it broke, it snapped off completely and went bobbing down, half sunk. Marcus was already hopping out of his sandals, he was woo-wooing and laughing all crazy, telling me to hold on to Sandy, pulling off his shirt. Next thing he dived in and swam after it. He caught it too, and rigged it up against the bank like a slide so he could take rides through it, yelling and howling. He was so free and loose in those days when we were little. When the storm stopped and the sun came back it felt like a new day, everything washed and dripping, and we went back to where the pipe had broken off. We could see how the rest of the pipe went back and back into the earth. There were tiny little blobs of daylight in that black hole. "Bet you a million," Marcus said, "that it's coming from all the way." And I remember now how he pointed up, up, over the tops of the trees, to the white rooftops in the distance. The Jewish school.

34

When Saturday comes, Isaac gives me a driving lesson. I wonder if I should tell him what happened with Victor coming to the Yard, but there's not that much to tell, really, and I don't want to risk upsetting him. The lesson finished, we go to visit Silas in the Illovo clinic. It's not like the last time. Silas is sort of awake, his lips moving, and Isaac grips his shoulder and puts his ear down to hear what he's whispering. Also there's a woman there I've never seen before. She says her name is Gugu, she's one of his daughters, from KwaMashu near Durban in Natal. Silas has a few wives. Gugu has a baby with her who plays on a blanket with squeaky toys. The white nurse keeps sticking her head in and looking at the kid and snapping her lips, shaking her head, and muttering *Honestly these people*. Silas falls asleep and Isaac goes off to find a doctor to talk to. I move seats to be next to Gugu. "Tell me," I say. "Has Victor been by today?"

"Yes, of course. I am staying with him. He was here when he dropped me."

I ask if everything is okay with Victor. "What do you mean okay?" she says. I tell her that he came by the Yard on Friday. She squints at me and her voice changes as she asks me what happened. I say, "What's going on, Gugu?" She looks at the door. I tell her I'm not going to say a word to my father. She grabs my arm. "You must not," she says in a hiss. I promise her I won't. She tells me I should talk to Victor.

"What's going on with him and the others?"

"I don't know," she says.

"You know," I say. "You not even asking me which others. You knew I meant at the Yard."

She gets all stiff and sits up, folding her arms. "So ask *them*. Those bustuds there."

"Why you saying they bastards, what d'they do?"

"I think you know. What did they do when Victor came to the biz-ness, heh? You said you saw."

"I'm not sure. He had to leave."

"Exactly. It's them. They are the ones." And she stares at poor Silas, all shriveled in the face lying there with the tubes. Before I can ask any-thing else Isaac's footsteps are in the corridor.

I keep my promise and go on not talking about the Victor incident with Isaac, or anyone, but in any case I have the other things on my mind and in my guts, sitting there like a lead ball. Sunday afternoon after the braai when everyone is occupied, Zaydi napping in his room, Isaac polishing the samovars with Brasso, Arlene reading one of her thick book-club romances, I take my empty school satchel to the Sandy Hole and put some things in it. There's a song by The Cure stuck in my head ("Killing an Arab"). I lower my bike with a rope over the wall cos I don't want anyone to hear the gates and then I climb down and ride into Regent Heights, crossing the RH soccer club's deserted pitch. Through a gap in the fence on the far side there's a trodden path into the wild grass. It goes downhill and comes out onto the open space of Brandwag Park. It's a nice bright day like most of ours are in Joburg and I can see all the way down the slope to where the deep-sunk stream winks in the sun. There's a group of black church people wearing blue-and-white robes, singing by the water.

I lock up the bike in the woods and walk, trying to remember, to line things up in my mind and work out where it must have been. It would be hard to believe there was ever a flooding river here but you can see the evidence of water power in how the stream trickles along the bottom of a steep donga, a trench that only years of flooding could have carved out, so deep that its walls are taller than I am. I climb down into it and walk along beside the water. Sooner or later I must come across the pipe. But it's not working out that way. I go up and down in both directions, farther out than we would have been that day, but still there's nothing. I start thinking maybe that's because it doesn't exist anymore. Maybe after it broke in the storm years ago they never repaired it, they just built a different pipe somewhere else or whatever. Up and down I march but there's no point — all I see is red dirt. Makes me feel tired and sad. I really wanted to have something for Annie.

Eventually I just give up. I'm walking back along the stream when I see something ahead — some metal sticking out, almost at the top of the trench. I've been missing it because I've been looking *down* all the time. The way I remember the pipe is that it was just above the water. But

what I forgot was that the water was *up to there that day*. Bladdy schlemiel. I start running. Here it is — a pipe of dented corrugated steel, looking thin and tinny, sticking out of the stony bank by maybe a metre. It's
angled downward and dark inside, the bottom covered in sand, exactly
what I've been looking for though smaller than I remembered, about
as round as the empty oil drums we use for rubbish at Solomon. Big
enough. Now comes the hard part. I look around to make sure I'm alone
before I get the torch out of my satchel and shine light up that black hole.
Dr. Helger the proctologist, peering into the earth's arse. Looks pretty
healthy and unobstructed to me, but I wish I had an all-body condom
cos it's definitely not clean. I take a breath and reach in all the way and
schlep myself up and in, squeezing onto my belly. It's the only way cos
there's no room to crawl with the satchel on my back. I start worming
in deeper and then I get jumped by brutal anxiety. I never knew I hated
tight spaces this much. I feel like I can't breathe, it's like being in the boot
of the Chev again. I try to keep thinking about that, about Jules. I'm
doing it for the children. Ja, right — Annie's tits have nothing to do with
it, you saint. I force myself to keep going, I'm worming my way up a hot,
filthy pipe and the corrugations start to hurt me, the bones of my arms
and my knees especially. The torch beam shows the black hole pulling
away from me like the eye of some retreating monster. What's horrible
are the cobwebs that get in my mouth, make me spit. All-a-sudden I see
something shaking like a whip on the sand in front of me. Holy God,
it's a snake. The thing is gone already but I can't go on for a long time, I
just lie there shaking, thinking what have I got myself into. In the end
I go on cos worming backwards on my belly seems much worse. There
could be things behind that I won't see till I'm on them. Things might
be *creeping up on me right now*. I start wriggling faster. It goes on and
on, I'm grinding myself bloody here. It gets steeper and more tiring. I
get so exhausted I have to rest and then I worry there's never going to be
an end. I keep on, but I'm going slower. I've been crawling by now for
what must be over fifteen minutes, I think. I'm getting a desperate, wor-

ried feeling like what if I get stuck? Or run out of air. Marcus's voice is in my head, reminding me that panic only makes things worse. But the torch beam is getting weaker or am I just imagining it? What if the batteries die? What if I hit a dead end? I can hear myself making sobbing noises, the way they echo in here. I'm soaked with sweat. I see Parktown prawns scuttling around me and making that hissing noise they do, and I also see some massive rats. But I'm too tired to freak out. I just keep slithering on. Nothing else I can do.

Eventually I make out a shifting blob of daylight ahead and sniff the coolness of fresh air. A wave of gratitude lifts in me, new energy with it. As I get closer to the light I find it slants down from above, hitting the pipe floor. This last section of the pipe rises up at a steep angle and there's a grate at the top. I've never been happier to see anything. My foot goes to the side to press off and something shifts. There's a long horizontal flap in the pipe wall down there, but I have to use my foot and all my weight to make it move just a few centimetres. I kick at it for a little bit, puzzled, and then I climb on up to the top. At the grate it's a battle to open the satchel and get the key out, dirty sweat running into my eyes. This key — 253 — is the one that I took from the Gooch's office and keep stored in the Sandy Hole. Next week I'm ganna make copies before I replace it. Right now I'm working my hand through the grate but I drop the key and almost lose it and have to get reset all over again. It takes lank tries to get it slotted into the plastic box that sits like a mezuzah on the side of the grate outside, but then it turns smoothly and it's tit-easy to open the latch. Next thing I'm crawling out into the open air under blue sky, panting like a half-drowned swimmer hitting a beach. I'm covered in filth. I stand up on shaky legs and see the veld and the tennis courts and the distant buildings and I'm completely alone. I start walking. It's like being inside a zombie movie, the end of the world. I'm the last person alive. No bells, no voices, no one at all except me and the wind. Unless old Volper is waiting with his cane in his hand, ready to rush out, lashing and screaming for me to bend over.

THE MANDELA PLOT 175

I go all the way up to the pool. In the changeroom where JT Mendelovitz likes to grab a beam naked, swing up his legs, and fart aggressively at the nearest faces, where Linky Shapiro is the undisputed towel-snap king, I use the showers, the water running black over my feet, and go out with a fresh towel around my waist. I'm starting to feel more relaxed in all this open space that belongs to no one but me. I wash my clothes and put them out to dry on the stands beside the pool, then walk down to the tuck shop. The door is unlocked so I enter and help myself to a nice selection — Aero bars and Lunch bars and Bar Ones and Chomps and Damascus nougats, a couple of cans of cream soda, a brace of Simba chips. Just like the kid in the Willy Wonka story, I swear. I go back to the pool and swim for a bit, tanning and sugar gorging till my clothes are dry. With my satchel, I head down to the media annex. At the video lab the storeroom is unlocked. There are twelve video machines but I bring out five to start, it takes me a while to work out how to connect them to the editing suite at the same time. Luckily there are tons of cables, enough to connect up every machine, but the problem is that I don't want to take too many blank tapes from the storeroom or it might get noticed. In the end I decide on only eight tapes so I only need to hook up seven machines to the suite. I get the Annie master tapes from the satchel and begin. While the forty-five minute segments are copying, I catch a nice schlof, using my Casio alarm to beep me awake whenever it's time to change a tape.

Before leaving I swipe an old tracksuit from lost-and-found and put it on over my washed clothes. After I crawl out of the filthy tunnel I ditch the messed-up tracksuit and go collect my bike. Monday I finish cleaning the mural and that afternoon I get keys copied (the Gooch's office and 253) and buy myself a miner's helmet with a light, get some overalls from the Yard, and also buy some knee and elbow pads from a BMX shop, plus a whole box of blank videotapes from the electronics shop opposite. Everything gets stored in the Sandy Hole. My alarm wakes me at two in the morning to lower my bike over the wall and ride through Greenside and up into Regent Heights. I've never ridden after dark like this. It's dead still, just the yellow streetlights and the long walls. Sometimes a television flickers like a ghost at a window or a dog howls like a wolf. There's a good chance someone is getting murdered or raped right this second. Security lights shine on razor wire. A black man lying asleep or maybe dead with his hat on his face in the weeds by a green municipal electricity substation with a sign that says DANGER! GEVAAR! INGOZI! In Brandwag Park I climb down into the trench, put on my overalls and pads, and then climb up into the pipe and switch on my miner's helmet. It would be so easy not to do this. One deep breath and then I start. This time I've kept the satchel under my belly, it makes it easier to get up a little bit higher so that I can crawl. My bones are protected by the pads and I know what to expect. The trip up takes exactly thirteen minutes. I come back out the same way before five and ride home on a bike seat wet with dew as the sky is turning light and the birds are starting to sing. I'm woken up it seems like a minute after falling asleep though the alarm says seven-thirty which is nearly two hours. On Wednesday arvy I collect a new message from Viljoen's and that night I'm back at the school. Thursday night I'm there again. And Sunday and Monday. Wednesday I pack all the tapes I've done — forty-eight of them — in a big apple box and cover the top with books and I carry it all the way down to Viljoen's where Dolf takes it off my hands. I fall into a routine after this, the days sliding by into weeks. Monday to Thursday it's early to bed, my alarm set for one. When it jabs me awake, I sneak out of the house and collect my bike and head to the Sandy Hole where I get my satchel with my pipe togs. Lower down the bike and ride to the pipe. Do it over and over. Instead of the four master tapes I use a single 180-minute copy, this lets me sleep for three hours straight. I'm out by five-thirty with twelve fresh new copies. And every Wednesday another boxful dropped at Viljoen's.

All this extracurricular action makes me cut back on visits to the Yard. Isaac doesn't say anything but I think he's hurt, sometimes he talks about visits to Silas at the clinic, wants me to come with. Silas keeps hanging on somehow. But I'm too tired to feel guilty, or to brood on what happened when Victor came to the Yard. At school I'm failing tests cos I'm not doing homework and falling asleep in class. "Charity's lost his zest," says big Spunny. "Charity needs drugs or time off." The okes are warning me that I'm *sailing for a nailing*. They say Volper has his eye on me. They also say Crackcrack Lohrmann is soeking for me big time. I do my best to avoid him by staying in the library at breaks. I need the kip anyway and there's a beanbag at the end of the mysteries stack. When the call comes over the intercom for me to go to the office I can't say I'm surprised, I only wish I had on a pair of stainless steel undies. Volper sits behind his huge desk and tells me he wants to remind me how important the Standard Eight year is, that either "the sluggards will pull up socks" and improve toward a decent matric finals or else they will "sink to the intolerable." He does not want any "rotten apples" pulling down "his" matric average. He is very proud of "his" matric average which has been maintained for decades. He points at my nose. "A horse can be brought to water but we cannot make it drink. I know you Helgers are a . . . special category, with your different circumstances. But don't let your background be a detriment, let it be a spur. If not, there is another spur that can be applied before we give up on you. Rest assured it will be. Unless we see a change in you, and soon. Are we clear, Martin Helger?" I nod, I'm starting to believe I've gotten away with just a lecture, but Volper makes me bend over and gives me two jacks, just to wake me up, he says. Looking at the blood on my arse in the downstairs bog I tell myself I've had enough of this. I'm not going to let myself be whipped anymore. But it's just talk, there's no way to stop it. Legally the police give canes that are like a thousand times more vicious than any school headmaster. If you were to threaten a headmaster that's where you'd end up. And the army is waiting. There are so many worse things than Volper all around me.

When I get back to the classroom on the Pimple there's no teacher there yet and the okes are up to their usual mayhem outside. Dice Lewinsky is at the edge of the drop, doing trash fishing, a new sport invented by Spazmaz that uses string tied to hooks made from old col'drink cans to snag items out the rubbish dump. Froggy Greenburg is causing major grief again with Baffboy by singing the milk advert to him. *Grow tall, little man.* Baffboy is short and has a complex about it. I find Schnitz and them round the corner, lighting up their shmerfs with a flick of the Bic. I tell Schnitz his lungs will turn black inside. "I wish," he says. "Like getting your black belt in karate. You got to put in like sixty a day for twenty years. Dedication." He offers me a Benson and Hedges. "Take one, Charity. Some toxin will see you right."

"Charity doesn't shmerf," says Bogroll Chernikov (C&S Minerals). "He's saving his lungs up for the right one."

"Charity's not looking so hot," says Schnitz. "What's a matter Charity?"

I tell them about the jacks I just got and that Volper is gunning for me big time. Schnitz puts his arm around my shoulders and leads me away like we're in a conspiracy. In a whisper he says, "Listen, bru, I feel bad for you. You still wanna hit the clubs hey?"

"Yes. *Yes.*"

"We going next weekend. I'm ganna stick you in the loop. You'll get a call. Don't embarrass me, hey."

"Shot, bru," I say. "I absolutely won't." And my heart jumps and there's only one word beating in my head: Xanadu.

35

Annie wants more tapes, faster. I write back, explaining I'm almost at my max capacity but if she'll come and help me we can probably work out a way to jack up production. For example, with two of us and a car we might be able to schlep in our own video machines, and then she could also take the tapes away the same night. I include details of the togs she'd need. I get a message back that they're trying to find someone. I write back and say no, it has to be her cos I don't trust anyone else. That's mostly bull — the truth is I want to see her badly. Need to.

We're in April now and the news is full of our army pulling out of South West Africa. It could mean the end of the war with the Cubans on the Border. Isaac kicks the hell out of the ottoman and shouts, "Bladdy bullshit!" He says there're too many diamonds in South West for chutis to ever give it up. Not to mention it's packed full of their fellow Afrikaners. "If South West turns into *Namibia*," he says, rolling out the African sound of it, "then believe you me it's just a matter of time before *we* turn into bladdy *Azania*. That is why I'm telling you it will never happen in a million years."

"But Da, they are saying that it *is* happening." The news even showed a UN force moving in to watch over our pullout.

"Don't be bladdy ridiculous!" Isaac says. "It's all for the cameras, Martin. Trust me, chutis has the whip hand behind the scenes. He still runs the show. Chutis will never let go." I think he's forgotten that old Botha has had a stroke and his face has turned all droopy on one side. Botha said on TV he isn't going anywhere, he's still the state president, and people believe him, I mean they don't call him Groot Krokodil — Big Crocodile — for nothing. But I'm not so sure. I heard from Stroppy Davidson at school that strokes can change a person majorly, it happened to his nice aunt who turned nasty overnight. If that's so then I think the opposite's possible too.

Next day after school I make an effort and go into the Yard. Passing Isaac tools through the hot afternoon, my eyelids start to dip and I need to stretch my legs. The sun is bright on the smashed, glittering mirrors, the twisted metal. All these broken machines are like dead bodies, with fuel pumps for hearts. Wandering through them, my head down, I almost bump right into Phala, and say sawubona — Zulu for hello but it means I see you. It's like they're not interested in what's in-side, how you are, they just want to say the fact of the moment, simple and true. I see you. Phala nods. I ask him about Victor again. He makes a show of frowning. "Victor who?"

"You know Victor," I say. "Silas's son. He was here the other day. Drives the Barracuda."

Phala shakes his head. I keep asking the question but he just shakes and shrugs, saying nothing. While I'm talking, though, I spot Winston Mathenjwa behind. He's one of the oldest guys on the staff. Winston gives me a definite look as he goes past. I leave Phala and circle through the wrecks. When I catch Winston by himself I call him softly and ask about what happened the other day at the gate. He checks around to make sure we're alone. "You mussen say for your father." I promise him I will not. Winston says, "I think Victor, he came here, he wanted to confront."

"Confront?"

"You know is good that you came out."

"Why?"

"They wanted to . . ." Winston waves his fingers across his wrinkled throat.

"What's that?"

He does it again. "They would have finish him off," he says. "Believe me." He really means what he's saying. It's hard for me to accept but he's so certain and I remember Victor's face, his shaking and sweating. How he left right away.

I ask, "But why would they?"

Winston says, "He thinks it is them who did it. He says his father would never have brakes like that. He want to see for his self, the Peu-geot wreck, maybe is here. He wanted to look."

"He thinks they did it?"

"Yuh, yuh. But you must not say your father!"

"But Winston —"

"No, this is a danger for him also. We say, even if the river looks flat it doesn't mean there is no crocodiles there. You see? These guys — the young ones here . . ." He swings his arm, taking in the Yard around us, and whistles softly over his bottom lip. "They are wanting to put this new union for us. They say is time. The olden ones like me and Silas and Oscar and those, we don't want, we are for your father, he is good, yuh. But the new ones don't respect anything. Silas he was a problem for them. Because the most follows him, even the young, and he is telling us stay away from the union, so . . ."

"So you think they messed up his brakes for him to have the accident?"

"Eeh-yuh," he says, nodding deeply "This is what is happen."

There are voices and footsteps coming closer. Winston's cheek twitches. I nod at him like thank you and he turns and heads away. All the rest of the day I keep thinking about that throat-cutting sign. I wish I didn't believe him but I do. The problem is I don't know what to do about this new info. I catch a lift home with Arlene instead of Isaac cos I'm afraid I'll say something to him, and also he might take me to visit Silas and Victor might be there — I just can't deal with this right now.

My ma looks tired behind the wheel of her Mazda. She asks me what's going on with me these days, says she's noticed a change. She calls me Toppers like she did when I was little, I can see she's in one of her dreamy moods. When we stop at a red robot she pretends to be playing the piano on the dashboard, humming away till I laugh. I think I inherited my *Playing* gene from Arlene. When she grew up in Cape Town she was going to be a great ballerina on the London stage. Her parents, the Cossingtons, had come over from England and she still always talks about going back one day. To all that style and culture that they have over there. Isaac and her met at the snake pit at Muizenberg Beach where everyone Jewish used to socialise in the December holidays. Just for fun I ask her about that now. "Wasn't Isaac a lot older than you?" I tease. She says what I know she will, what I've heard a million times before. That he looked grob, so rough and wild, he was wearing a "gruesome" peacoat. "He was like a bloomin caveman. He bopped me on the head and dragged me off by the hair up to Joburg. Ooch. *Joburg.*" And she pretends to shudder and laughs again, cos everyone knows nobody hates Johannesburg like a Cape Tonian. My grandparents from Arlene's side died before I was born. I know they were very poor, though back in England they were rich before the family went bust. They used to sell crystal to the Queen. (On the other hand, Isaac says they were kidding themselves cos there's no bigger anti-Semite than an Englishman and Ma's family were trying to be more English than the English, forgetting they were Jews till they got put in their place.) I think Arlene's parents wanted her to have a lot of class. They spent everything they could afford on her, for her lessons and dresses and that. Isaac never liked them cos they always looked down on him even though he was doing so well in business. He's still sort of bitter toward them. I think Arlene would love it if I went to live in London, and I think she wanted me and Marcus to go to Solomon so we'd have some class and be able to go back one day. All-a-sudden I want to ask her why did she marry Isaac, if he was so grob? But I don't cos I think I know the answer. She told me that once when she was little her family had to sleep in the Jewish aid shelter in Sea Point. *We always battled,* is how she puts it.

Wednesday arrives and all day at school I'm thinking about if there's a message from Annie waiting for me at Viljoen's. At second break the bell wakes me from my beanbag nap in the library. We get two bells at Solomon. First one tells you to get moving, second one comes like three minutes later. If you're not in your class or where you're supposed to be by second bell you'll get sent to Volper's office for jacks. I get off the beanbag, stretching and yawning, and head back. I'm going along the bottom corridor with my hands in my pockets when out of nowhere I'm slammed hard from the side and jammed into the brick wall on my right. Some bastard's got hold of my neck and is pinching the pressure points behind my ears like crazy, his other hand gripping the back of my arm. He starts banging my head into the wall. "Think you big stuff, hey," he says. It's Crackcrack. "Where's big brother now? You little tattletale. Run and talk shit to the Gooch on me. *This's* what you get." And he hammers me with a beaut of a dead leg. There's an art to giving dead legs and I have to admit he scores an A plus with this one — kneeing me exactly on the nerve spot on my thigh so the pain rockets up my spine as the leg goes lame. I yank my head loose and use my free hand to shove against the wall and throw my head back and manage to catch him with a little head butt as we go staggering. "You boys! You there!" Crackcrack lets me go and hoofs it out of there. There's a teacher in the corridor way down the other end. I limp-run to the stairs and keep climbing till I get away. By the end of school I can walk normally again but it still hurts like a bastard and there'll be a lekker bruise. The worry about Crackcrack stays with me — all the way until I get back from Viljoen's with a book, cos that's when I find a message. From Annie. And not just any message but one that says exactly what I've been wishing for, and then nothing else matters, nothing even comes close.

36

I'm up before the alarm, eyes open and body buzzing. I almost go around and fetch the bike before I remember and stop myself. In the Sandy Hole I collect my satchel with all my pipe togs, spending extra time checking everything. I take out the key and look at it, telling myself so long as I have control of this the school will always be mine. I shouldn't forget that. Then I climb over the garden wall. I'm expecting to have to wait but Annie's Volksie is parked there already, the engine and the lights switch on before I can turn around. "You're late," she says when I get in. I check my watch. "Four minutes?" She doesn't smile. "That's four fucking minutes too long." Her hair is tied back to show the fine bones of her face and her smooth neck, the olive skin made yellow-ish by the streetlight glow, her lips plump and shiny and her smell as it was at the pomegranate bench, lemony and musky-warm all mixed to-gether. My mouth is dry, I can't think of what to say. She pushes a tape into the stereo as she drives off. It's the old Juluka hit "Scatterlings," the Zulu voice deep and driving—*yim-boh! yim-yim-yim-boh!*—and the Jewish one going high and sweet—*oh-la-la! oh-la-la!*—singing about all of us being exiles from Mother Africa. I direct with my hand and sneak looks at her. I could bite her neck, I swear. Could scratch the clothes off her right now. I look out the window instead at the dead suburb outside, the walls.

In Regent Heights she parks at the end of the dirt parking lot above the soccer pitch and we get out and I check over what she's brought, the pads and overalls. She's forgotten goggles, I wear goggles now cos I got sick of being gunked in the eyes. I try to give her mine but she pushes them away. She's brought a duffel bag stuffed with about fifty blank vid-eotapes, four times as many as we'll be able to do. So we're schlepping a lot of unnecessary weight but I decide not to say anything, knowing how touchy she can be. We hike through eucalyptus trees and then the break in the fence and down the trodden path into Brandwag Park and I lead us straight to the pipe with no problems. Annie looks at it and doesn't say anything. A dented, thin-walled metal pipe as round as an oil barrel. Her face is grim. I don't like this tense mood, I'm going to need to find a way to relax things between us or nothing sexy's going to happen tonight. We whisper-discuss the best way to schlep the duffel bag, and in the end I decide to stick my satchel inside it also and to rope it to my waist. I adjust my goggles, switch on my helmet light and then turn back. "It's going to feel claustrophobic as hell in there, hey, your first time. Like you start thinking you are trapped. Don't let yourself. Just think of something else, pretend you're having fun. There's plenty air coming in. We'll be fine. Whatever you do, don't panic. Stay calm."

"Thanks for the advice, Dad," she says.

I blush and crawl in, feeling the rope bite into my waist as the bag slithers and drags along behind me. Then I hear her climbing in and the rope goes soft as she pushes on the bag from behind. I keep crawling and we find a rhythm between us, pull and push, with our pads scraping and knocking on the tinny steel. Getting close to the end, I twist my head to shout back and let her know, to ask how she's doing, but then my voice dies in my throat. The bag slides into me and she says, "Martin, what?"

"Quiet. *Quiet.*"

Felt something. I'm frozen, not breathing. *Felt something.* Please God let it not be. Let it not be. But it comes again and this time I shoot forward, clawing with both hands, pulling hard at the rope like some sled dog with rabies. I told her don't panic but man, I never knew what panic *is* till now. Annie starts shouting at me, what am I doing. Another faraway boom comes through the earth and into the walls of the pipe where it shivers into my hands. It can only be thunder. Big African thunder. I think I shout this aloud but it doesn't matter cos I'm already feeling wet on my fingers, seeing it ooze down out of the black ahead. Flash floods. There's a reason they call them flash — in no time the booming is coming through so fast it feels like we're being shaken by giant hands and then the wet on my hands turns into fat snakes of water, slithering cold over my arms and soaking my thighs. Branches and twigs and plastic bags and tin cans come riding down at me, and the water climbs and then living things start coming out of the dark also. A whole clump of chittery rodents all knotted together and splashing like mad and streams of shungalulus and then the huge Parktown prawns and lizards and whippy snakes go floating by and I swear I don't even glance at any of them. All I care about is go go go. The bladdy rope is cutting my waist and slowing me and I try to untie it but I can't without stopping, the knots are too tight. I'd do anything for a knife in my hand but it's in my satchel which is in the bag. I think I'm going to die I mean for real die and I'm saying Ma Ma oh mommy

Ma, I don't know why. The water now rises over my shoulders and I have to keep my chin up high to breathe. It rises some more and I pull off my hard hat to give my head some room, turning my chin to the side. The light in my hand shows the pipe slanting up ahead and I realise we've almost reached the final climb. The water smashes and tumbles here in the bend. I suck in a last big breath through my nostrils and then the cold rises up to the top and I'm under — trying to go forward but stopped in the pocket where all the weight of the water keeps churning. The bag rams into me, Annie shoving wildly from behind and there's nowhere to go. All-a-sudden I remember the part of the pipe that moves. It's on the right, at the bottom. I'm starting to really need air as I grope down there and straightaway there's a strong sucking current. My hard hat is still shining, the light strange underwater, and through my goggles I make out the flap — wide open like a mouth now, the storm water rushing through. The light is flickering out. Dropping the hard hat, I stick my foot into the opening and then the other, and sit and grab the top edge and pull and wriggle till my waist pops through. Metal scrapes my back as I drop into nothing. The rope jerks me short and I slam against a wall. But there's air here and I guzzle a breath, dangling in space. Twisting around, I plant my feet and wrench the bag through and Annie follows next and we both fall hard onto a shallow pool over a concrete floor. I slump against the wall behind us, panting. It's very dark but there's some light and I can see in front of us how the spout of water from above is hitting the shallow pool we're in. Annie is slumped back against the wall like me and I can hear even over the churning water the sobs of her breathing. It takes a while but the spout thins to a trickle down the wall while the pool drains away to show bare concrete. My eyes get more used to the dark — this is the back wall of a concrete tunnel with square sides and a high flat roof. Looking up to the flap we came through I see it's almost completely shut, there're thick springs on this side of it. In the new quiet I ask Annie if she's okay and she sort of grunts at me. I drag the wet bag across my legs and unzip it, get my satchel out and find the little torch I have in there. I don't expect it to work but it switches on first shot. I hunt out the Swiss army knife and use it to pick open the knot around my waist. The videotapes look okay, they're brand-new and all shrink-wrapped in plastic, only a few of them bashed up. I dig around till I find the stuff I packed for my night of passion with Annie. A bottle of champagne swiped from the liquor cabinet and a one-litre tetrapack of Liqui-Fruit orange. Amazing that the bottle isn't smashed. I rip open the corner of the orange juice. Annie moans when she sees it. I take a long sweet drink and pass it to her. We polish it off in two-twos and I start to feel new energy coming through but also a lot more pain as the cold numbness starts to fade. I've hurt my back and I'm scratched and bumped all over the show. Not to mention my thigh throbbing again where that arsehole Crackcrack kneed me.

I stand up and shine the torch around. There is some dim natural light seeping through from somewhere, obviously, but no visible opening except the flap above and that's fully shut now. The tunnel is wide, made of grey concrete with mould on it, with vertical beams on both sides against the walls every twenty metres or so. It stretches on straight ahead of us too far for the light to reach. Annie asks if I know where it goes. I tell her I don't even have a clue what this *is*, but thank God it's here or we'd be dead. I'm trying to remember the blueprints at the Malcolm Steinway exhibition. Annie stoops to pick up the bag. I take a handle and we carry it between us and without speaking start walking down the slightly sloped tunnel. I spot my waterlogged hard hat and fish it up and tap the headlamp but it's dodo dead. The air doesn't taste stale, fresh is getting in from somewhere as well as the dim light, but I can't feel a breeze. I know we're moving east, maybe under the Pimple, and I'm trying to picture a drain in that area on the surface but it's not something I've paid attention for. After we've been walking a while, Annie nudges me. The torch beam shows rusted ledges on the wall, two in a parallel line, the bottom one jutting out further than the top and the top one with half-moon grooves in it. Annie asks me what they are but I have no idea. We go on and then I stop and turn back. I'm remembering something, a flash from the aquarium, from inside John Vorster Square. "They're for guns," I say. "You put them like this." I show with my arm and Annie says, "Oh yeah. It's a rifle rack." She huffs through her nose, says, "You never heard of an armoury under your school?"

"Never," I say, but there was something else I'm almost remembering as we go on. We reach the end of the tunnel, a blank wall and the water here's still ankle-high, gurgling away into a large floor drain. We turn around and start splashing back the way we came. I happen to shine the light to my left and catch a thick dark line there. Closer, I find it's a narrow opening. Shining up this black slit the light shows brick walls on both sides and tons of cobwebs for like fifteen metres and then a dull green wall facing us, not brick. "Another dead end," I say.

She's shivering, hugging herself. "Hang on," I say. It's the niggling idea that I half remembered before. I shine the light back on those rusted rifle racks. "I scheme I know what this all might be. Was written on a blueprint I saw. Said, original fortifications."

"Fortifications?"

"Ja. Said they were from the sixties."

"Like before there was a school here?"

"No. Solomon goes back to the turn of the century."

She shakes her head. "Guns under a high school."

"Ja, it's a whatchamacallit — not a bunker, a bomb shelter. Didn't you in America build some nuclear bomb shelters also? In case of the Russians and that. I know that they have em in Israel. Every school has to."

"I don't know," says Annie. "This's more like a tunnel that's going somewhere than a bunker to hide out."

"That's cos I don't think they ever finished it. What I read, it said, original fortifications unfinished. Wasn't part of the new security system they put in after 'eighty-two — the wall." I shine the light down to the gurgling drain at the end. "It's got drainage, this thing. So they just joined it to the pipe for overflow, with that flap. It's a storm valve."

"And this?" She means the slit in the wall.

"Don't know. But I'd sort of like to find out." I hesitate and she tries to take the torch from me so I blow out a breath and turn sideways and squeeze into the slit and start shuffling down through the cobwebs. The rough mortaring between the bricks scrapes my front and back. I have to not think about rats at my ankles, or snakes. They could chew the hell out of me and I wouldn't be able to reach down. I get to the end, the green wall. It's metal, but thin, it pops in and out. "What's going on down there?" Annie calls. I rap on it with the torch — a hollow bang. "Martin!" she shouts. I think I know what this is. I push it hard, straightening my arm, and it rocks away and comes back. I shove it again and it falls over with a crash and dust comes boiling up. I'm glad I still have my goggles on but some grit tickles my throat even though I cover my mouth and nose, making me cough hard. Annie's still shouting what's going on as I step through.

37

The torch beam passes over boxes, plastic chairs stacked up, wooden desks likewise, racks of clothes. I've walked over a fallen filing cabinet. The beam shows other upright ones and sweeps over Hebrew on book spines and yellowed tallaysim, stacks of old papers and photos and yearbooks. The walls around all this junk are solid concrete like the ceiling. There's a light but when I find the switch on the wall and flick it nothing happens. Annie, back there in the dark, is shouting at me that I'm being an arsehole only she says it *asshole*. (Why is it everyone except Americans knows an arse is a bum while an ass is a donkey?) Anyway I'm a dick, etcetera, for leaving her back there in complete darkness. I yell at her to hang on while I look in the steel cabinets and find a box of yortzeit candles and some Lion matches. I plant lit candles around and then shine the torch down the narrow slit for Annie while she makes her way along, swearing a lot. She looks big-eyed at the candlelit jumble of *stuff*. "Creepy shit," is her verdict. Then she puts one finger under her nostrils, her eyelids fluttering. I say bless you a second before she sneezes like a cannon. "Place'll give you asthma," she says. Under a layer of dust there are framed photos, men in skinny suits and horn-rimmed glasses and women with hats and gloves. On a pile of papers, *Drum* magazine has a cover with John F. Kennedy on it. There is a radio made of bakelite, trophies for academic achievement. Some ancient curling yearbooks. I push a pile over with my foot, trying not to send up more dust. A newspaper says BARNARD HEART TRANSPLANT SUCCEEDS, 3 December 1967. I have a closer look at the Hebrew on the books, they're siddurim for prayers, mostly. I spot the word Yesod on a spine — foundation is what it means. Must be a Hebrew grammar text or else a work of Kabbalah. Dust nearly hides the first Hebrew letter of the title, almost shifting the meaning to *secret*. I look at Annie. "I think I know where we are."

"Where? Is there a way out?"

I nod, pointing up. "What dwells in heaven on high."

It's supposed to make her laugh but she gives me her bitter face. "I'm friggen tired, dude. Just speak English, okay?"

I start inspecting the ceiling more carefully. On the far side there's a metal panel with a handle. Annie helps me move a desk across. Then she climbs up first, so I hold the light, watching her twisting the handle, trying to pull. Just when I'm about to give her advice she shoves instead and it pops up. Behind is a wide rectangular chimney, with walls of wooden planks and a wooden top. It's only about four feet high. Annie asks me for a chair and I put it on the desk and she steps up. She can reach the wooden top easily now and she starts thumping on it. "Check the edges," I say. She feels all around and finds something, a catch, and works it and the top swings open and she stands up completely on the chair as moonlight rushes in with cool fresh air. "Oh my God," she says. "Would you take a look at *this*." I climb out after she does, stepping down onto the bimah, the centre stage of our school synagogue. I suspected we were under the synagogue but hadn't imagined for a second that the base of the bimah could be a hollow concrete bunker going down underground. We both stand there like we're ready to conduct a service, only the pews are empty and the windows are full of the moon and a woman would never be allowed onto the bimah — which all makes it feel even more like I'm caught in some mad dream. It gets stranger still when I look at what we've climbed out of. It's the bench — the bimah has this bench at the side against the low wall of glass, the top of it is padded leather and that's what we've opened from underneath. It's where Volper sits when he's on the bimah, where the Honoured Guest of the Week will sit on a Friday morning, waiting to address the school.

Annie is shivering, hugging herself. We're wet and filthy. I go back down and collect the bag and put out the candles and climb up again. When I climb out and shut the bench lid it locks in place. I get down on the bimah carpet and search with the light from the bottom. It takes a while but I find a knothole where you can stick your finger in and there's a tiny lever inside to open with. I pull off the sweaty goggles and we carry the bags down and cross the shul and go out through its back door. "Welcome to my school," I tell Annie, leading us to the front office in the admin block where Volper's secretary Mrs. Brune has her desk behind glass with a hole in it. Nasty Mrs. Brune who gives you that smirk when you're on your way to getting jacks and feel like you want to die. Across from Volper's office door — which I can't look at even here at night without feeling a pinch in my guts — are the staff toilets. I towel off in the gents. Annie finds a hair dryer in the ladies and we use it to dry our clothes while we stand round in towels. I get a sudden impulse to kiss her and surprise myself by going for it. What's more surprising is that she kisses back. I lose track of time and float in it and it starts to get heavy. I think it's because we both came so close to dying, it makes your body want to breed or something. But Annie stops things and we get dressed. All-a-sudden I start giggling like a madman and she says what. I shake my head, nothing. She says what, tell me. I don't want her to think I'm laughing at her or anything so I tell her the truth, that I'm laughing at myself, the great Romeo. I had this whole plan of seduction ready. As soon as the tapes were taping I was going to whip out the champagne and orange juice and mix us up some lekker mimosas which I've read are supposed to be killer aphrodisiacs. I show her the champagne and then we're both giggling so hard we can't breathe. This kind of mad laughing is also from almost dying, I reckon. Then she says, "You should have been checking the weather forecast instead" — which guillotines all humour cos she's right. I was acting like I'm the expert on the pipe but I nearly drowned us both.

I lead us up to the media annex. Annie looks inside the library. She touches the Commodore 64s in the computer room. "A little more than we have in Jules township, uh?" she says. "Just a *tad*." I show her the video lab with the storeroom and its twelve machines. I show her how they hook up to the editing suite so we can record a dozen copies at a time. With three hours of recording time I can only manage one session per night. Annie nods, asks if we can high-speed dub. I shake my head — that's not possible for video. She's looking at the editing suite, she tells me she's become convinced that the Fireseed tapes can be edited down to two hours, easy, without losing any of their effectiveness. A two-hour tape would make two tapings per session possible — doubling production. It's a good idea but while she's talking, getting excited by it, something else dawns on me and I say the f-word a few times, interrupting her. I've forgotten all about the master. That tape is deep in my satchel and it's not shrink-wrapped like all the new blanks. When I dig it out we find it's full of grit. I clean it the best I can but when we play it, Ski Mask and Kefiya are inside a bad snowstorm. So Annie adds some f-words of her own. Now there's nothing we can do tonight. We might as well leave, but I don't say that — instead I crack the bubbly. We pass it back and forth. After a while Annie gets up with the bottle and wanders back into the storeroom. There're sixteen-mil cameras and reels there also. She asks can we copy video onto film? "I don't know," I say. "I never thought about it." Annie asks me if I've ever heard of a spaza bioscope. I shrug. "A bioscope's just a movie house." She says a spaza is a little shop in someone's house in a township. In townships they have these cinemas in houses and churches. "They charge like a buck a head," she says, "and sometimes they get a few hundred folks for a screening. In the country they'll hang up a sheet off a baobab tree for a screen. Get the whole village out. If we could put our tape onto film, that would reach whatever part of the audience can't get to a VCR." I tell her I'll think about if it's doable. Meantime we've killed the bottle, standing there, and I'm feeling like maybe we could get back to the kissing. Annie seems to read my mind cos she smiles with one side of her plump mouth and walks out and wanders down into the library. I follow behind her like a needy pet. She shows me a book by someone called Larski, a famous anthropologist. Tells me he's the one who got her into politics. He "opened her eyes" to how the U.S. was responsible for South Africa because of its support for the apartheid regime going back years. She says it's her tax money, meaning she's also responsible. I ask her if he's the reason why she came here. "I have to admit that scumbag was the start of it," she says. "Even though he's just a mega-hypocrite who lives like a banker on the Upper East Side from all the royalties he makes off his writing. He's like the rest of em, he doesn't *do* a damn thing." She starts talking about how important Africa is to the U.S. That her country was built by African slaves. That all the movies and music and fashion and slang all come from black people who came from Africa. "Africa is our mother, the slave trade our umbilical cord," she says. "It really is our flesh and blood. That's why what's going on here in South Africa is so damn important to me. And should be to all Americans." She talks about Congress and votes and Reagan but I don't really follow what she's on about. I pay more attention when she switches to the South Africans "in exile" that she met overseas, blacks and whites, good friends (and I think maybe more by the way she talks about some of them) that got her caring about my country. She studied everything she could get her hands on about South Africa and she says although she's only been here months she has been heading here for years.

"Is it what you expected?"

"No," she says. "It's more. So much more."

The champagne is touching my head now and I start edging up to her so she turns around and does a flying dance step away from me. "Well," she says. "We've got plenty of time. Aren't you gonna show me the place?" So I take her on a long tour, hiking up to the pool by the bus depot, crossing the huge empty rugby fields under the wild moon. Down to my class on the Pimple, then across to Assembly Hall where we get together once a week to shout our war cries and raise our two flags and sing the two anthems while Mrs. Stanz puts long fingers to the piano, first "Hu'Tikvah" in Hebrew and then "Die Stem" in Afrikaans, first "The Hope" and then "The Voice," first the blue-and-white flag of Israel and then the four-colour of the Republic. We end up back at the front lobby and Annie wants to see the principal's office. "He's called a headmaster here," I say, and lead the way to Volper's office but when I get in front of the door I start shaking. Annie looks at me and then gives me a hug. We go in. The first thing on the right is the corner where you have to bend over. With my heart jumping in my chest I open the cupboard door. Annie says holy fuck. She's standing close behind me and can see the rack of Volper's canes all lined up like snooker cues. I tell her what it's like to be caned. She takes one out and hefts it. "Goddamn *bastards*," she says. "This is *sick*." We go over to the giant teak desk where she picks up the framed photos of the wife and daughters. She goes behind and I follow, I've never seen it from this side, the leather throne side with the big window at your back, the sun in the eyes of whoever stands on the carpet. Your victim. I try the chair out and feel all wrong, jumping up like it's dirtied me. There's a low sideboard to the right, on top is the big intercom machine with a microphone on a stand. There're rows of switches, one for each class. Volper can send his voice from here to catch hold of any boy he likes and have him brought in for some pain. Like he's a god or something. Or he can talk to the whole school. That echoing voice. Volper — just the name is enough to squeeze more sick feeling out of my guts and I want to leave. But Annie is trying the drawers, finding them locked. She picks a paper clip from a jar and straightens it. She's asking me about caning at other schools. I tell her our school is supposed to be liberal — that we have it lank easy compared to government schools. "A whole country built on whipping," she says. "Top to . . . bottom." She's working the clip wire inside a drawer lock. She's got skills I never knew about, then I remember how she opened our liquor cabinet that time. She pops open this drawer too and we find the punishment ledger. There's a fortune in pain banked up in that thing, decades of canings noted down in Volper's messy scrawl, so many it makes my head spin. Then Annie finds a ring of keys. She zooms in on one key with a funny shape, a cylinder with sides, octagonal-like. "These are for safes," she tells me. "The little kind."

"How do you know?"

"How do you think?"

"You been trained," I say.

"Help me check around," she says. We look behind paintings but find nothing until Annie rolls up the carpet and stamps on the parquet squares. There's one section where the squares are loose. She digs them up, says, "What'd I tell you?" Sure enough there's a small safe sunk into the concrete. She fits the cylinder key and unlocks it and passes me up a pile of envelopes. I empty them on the desk. Photostats of birth certificates and insurance documents. Some bright Krugerrands in plastic sleeves and a copy of Volper's employment contract with the board.

Quite a few sheets of music, handwritten, that I reckon is Volper's own composition, cos I remember he used to teach music. There's a beautiful Piaget watch. And that's about it. But when we go to return this stuff, Annie feels the bottom of the empty safe — it's a piece of carpet on wood. She lifts it and underneath there's a little wooden box carved with rhinos and mopani trees. Inside the box is a gold chain on a velvet base. I would have shut it then but Annie says wait and gives the box a shake, then she lifts the velvet base out.

Time passes in silence. I'm the one who speaks first.

"Jesus fucking Christ."

"You're taking this," she says.

"Maybe," I say.

"You can use it, man."

"Yes," I say. "But do I really want to?"

XANADU

38

There are lank ways we can catch a lift: with Mouth's cousin, with Spunny's uncle, with someone's ma. But it gets later and later and the cousin is taking the Porsche which has no room and Spunny's uncle is not in the mood and someone's ma will have a cadenza if she knows where we're going. No worries, okes, says Spunny. There's taxis, there's other okes who have their own drivers. But the drivers all have the night off and who's ganna call for the taxi and we can't get through on the phone and what do you expect it's a Saturday bladdy night. Then Mouth says that belling for a taxi is a chicken move anyway. He's had enough of all this dof backchat, he hates it when the okes can't make a simple flippen arrangement. We are worse than a pack of females. But if we are men, true men, he says, we *hitch* into town *like* men. That's the proven way to do it, and always has been. Spunny says oright. And me? Who am I to argue.

That's how come the three of us are walking at the side of Empire Road with our thumbs out and no one stopping except for black taxis which Mouth refuses to let us get into. Those combis are deathtraps, he says. And aside from the accidents didn't we know about the three teenagers who got abducted when they got into one the other day, man it was on *Police File* and all. Mouth is talking even faster than he always does, so fast I think he might actually pull a tongue muscle, telling us how the doors got locked on the teenagers who got driven to a field near some bladdy township in the East Rand where a witch doctor was waiting with strong ropes and sharp knives. The cops said they were all alive while their organs were being removed, they could tell by the way the blood sprayed, the hearts still beating. "The sangomas need the body parts fresh to make good muti," Mouth explains. "They chop your cock off and stick it in a jar to pickle. That'll give someone many wives."

"Lovely," says Spunny. "One day there's a mix-up and oke reckons it's a pickled cucumber in there. Slaps it on his hot dog by mistake."

"Bonus protein," says Mouth.

We go on ignoring the Toyota HiAces full of black people that keep slowing down for us and time passes and a white driver stops in his XR3. Ja, he'll take us into the Brow — Hillbrow, where all the action is. He's a young Afrikaner oke, tells us he's just finished his national service, two compulsory years in the army. He's playing loud Afrikaans gospel music and talking about some suicidal moments he had back there but he pulled through with a little bit of vasbyt — determination — you know? And the help of Jesus Christ his lord and saviour. Up front next to him, Mouth asks him what the army's like and he tells us how horrible it was to be a "lelike kak-smaaking troepie" — an ugly shit-tasting infantryman — who was "altyd afgekaked en opgefokked" — always getting worked and beaten. But it was praying to his lord and saviour that helped him a lot and do we pray to Jesus? So Mouth goes and tells him, no man, we are Jewish, and that makes Spunny kick the back of Mouth's seat. Meanwhile our driver's getting excited about having actual Jews in his Ford and before we can get out on Smit Street we have to accept some of his church pamphlets.

Town looks all different at night, with all the electric lights and the dark shadows. There're crowds of a kind you wouldn't see in the day, some with shiny clothes, some in rags. We walk all the way down to

Thunderdome where we are supposed to rendezvous with the rest of the okes. It's a long white building with this giant neon lightning bolt on top and spotlights swinging coloured beams at the stars. In front is a long line waiting to get in and at the front of the line by the doors are four large men that I can't stop staring at. "They wearing tuxedos," I say aloud.

"Checkit Charity," says Spunny. "The kid's in shock. Has never seen a tux in his life before."

"Those are the bouncers, Charity," Mouth says in slow-motion moron talk. "Bounce-uhs."

"Don't stare at them like that, Charity." I feel Spunny's hand on my shoulder. "First thing to learn about the clubs is the bouncers. The bouncers, they own this whole night round here. They all work together."

"Not *just* the clubs," says Mouth. "Bouncers *rule,* ay. Forget the Poras and the Lebs" — Portuguese and Lebanese gangs — "and any-one else. The bouncers are the main manne here. Forget about cops, you never smell a cop down here Saturday nights and anyway cops won't touch bouncers neither. Everyone craps bricks for bouncers." I ask them if it's only bouncers that wear tuxes and Spunny snorts and tells me, "Listen, Charity, if you see a staunch-looking oke in a tux he is not heading for the opera. Just get out of his bladdy way." They look at me like how stupid can you get — they can't read my mind and see it's filled with my brother in a tux, the jacket hanging on the pipe at dawn.

Even with all our transportation grief we've still ended up being the earliest ones here, so I say why don't we walk up to Xanadu. Spunny says only wrinkled old grots go to Xanadu, all the lekker chicks will be here. Mouth agrees. But I say I want to go check what it's like and I'm ganna head up. "You can't go on your own," says Spunny. "You a babe in woods." I say, "Watch me," and off I go. They catch up to me, calling me a schmock and retarded, saying I'm "taking lank liberties," but we all walk together up Claim Street. There are parts here that get a bit iffy and I notice Mouth and Spunny speeding up and going quiet. We pass alleyways where tons of people are sleeping on newspapers—it's true what Annie said about the races mixing in town, black people are oozing in here, apartheid breaking down like a clogged oil filter. Farther up I see a drunk man beating a woman while a drunk woman beats on him with what looks like a teakettle. There's a little mini park and people lying there and I see what looks like a grown man molesting a barefoot boy in shorts, the man cupping the crotch and the boy crying. But I keep walking as fast as the others—all those sights being flashes from a different world, the black world, and we can't involve ourselves, can't cross that line, otherwise bad things will happen. Anyway it's so much part of us to pretend that they don't exist that it's like on automatic. I wouldn't even have thought about them prolly, if not for Annie.

We pass Pretoria Street, where there are pool halls and the Hillbrow Record Centre and the Milky Lane for milkshakes. A few blocks farther up, my mates make a turn and there it is, a neon sign over a door —XANADU. Two bouncers are standing under the sign in their tuxedos. A job that makes you come home at dawn with a bloody chunk of someone's ear stuck in your hair. Meantime Spunny and Mouth are groaning and moaning cos there is also a line-up here. "Everywhere you go," says Mouth, "there's always some bladdy schvantz standing in front of you."

"Let's wait," I say.

"Ach, you mad," says Spunny. "Wait for what? By the time we get to the door it'll be time to duck back to Thunderdome." He suggests we go graze somewhere, get some chow at Fontana, maybe a roast chicken. Mouth says nawt, let's head back to Pretoria Street and jol a game of pool to kill some time. Then Mouth tunes me that anyway Xanadu is a kuk spot. You go down into a basement, it's small and dirty but it used to be this famous jazz club, there's still some photos on the walls. I can hear the thump of the dance music coming up and it sounds like house beats, the fat bass notes making me think of a giant toad burping in a cave. They start playing a dance mix of "Need You Tonight" by

INXS and suddenly I step into the road. Spunny and Mouth both shout my name, ask where I'm going. I hold up my hand, tell them I'll just be a sec, and cross to the other side and walk along to the front, passing the line-up on my right. There are women with dark purple round their eyes and glitter on their cheeks and hair all lacquered flat and spread out like mini thorn trees. There're men with brown leather jackets with the sleeves pulled up to the elbows and some with tennis headbands and everyone is white. Some of them call out things to me. "Hey, junior, over here is the line, china." "Where you scheme *you* heading, lightie?" "Check at this little wanker go." "You *go*, boy, sort them out one-time." They laugh. At the front there are some traffic cones and behind are the two men in tuxedos, one with hair cut short on the sides and left long at the back. He's the one who looks at me when I say, "I wanna ask you okes something." Now the first person in line says from behind, "Hey, what's this now, who's this little skelm scheme he is? We next man. We waiting here." The bouncer with the long hair pokes his cheek out with his tongue and says to me, "Get the fuck away."

I say, "I just wanna ask you something, man."

"He wants to ask you something," says the other one, not looking at me.

"Just, like, if you know someone," I say. "Who maybe like used to work here?"

Longhair says to the other, "Their ears never work. You notice that?"

"Never, hey," agrees the other. Longhair turns his back on me but with his face in profile, so he's keeping an eye on me but pretending not to, and when I open my mouth to speak my brother's name, Longhair steps back and hits me with his elbow, right under the sternum. He is a strong, full-grown man and he hits me full stick. It's a nasty trick of turning his back like that cos it catches me by surprise, my stomach relaxed, and all the air is smashed out of me and I fold like a mousetrap snapping shut. Drop to my knees. Can't breathe. The pain is everywhere. I hold my guts and fall over sideways on the filthy street. I can see how the streetlight has an aura around it, like an orange bubble. I move my eyes down. Mouth and Spunny are behind traffic, trying to hurry across the street as I hear a voice say, "Alley?"

"Ja, better alley him."

"Check his little mates, ay."

"I'll sort em."

A hand comes down and grabs my collar and then I'm being dragged along the pavement to the corner where the dragger goes right and takes me with into an alley smelling of rubbish. Sliding away from the street the last thing I see is the other bouncer in front of Mouth and Spunny, pointing with his whole arm. They stop, hesitating. The bouncer points again. Then I am deep into shadow. Still paralyzed. A young wildebeest getting dragged under by a big croc. There's a group of kitchen workers having a smoke break and they stop talking as I slide past, a white kid pulled by a white man — now it's me who is part of a different world to theirs, and them looking in and none of their business. My only hope is Mouth and Spunny but that other bouncer will keep them out of this alley. I try to turn myself over, get my feet under me, but can't manage it.

A young voice ahead says, "Howzit, Ray, how you?" Ray just grunts and goes on dragging. Then he says, "Head up for a minute. Ukay?" The voice says back, "Surely, man. No hassles." *I've heard that voice before.* I stare up at the stranger as he passes. Thick bushy hair, a nose like a scissors blade. He wipes it with the back of his hand, and it's that familiar gesture that makes the picture come together and all-a-sudden I see it — see *him.* Cannot believe it. I try to shout his name, but only make a gasping noise. Desperate, I wave my arms and stamp my feet and this makes him look down at me, just for a second but it's enough. He leans forward, squinting, and then his eyes go pop and he runs around and is jabbering like mad at this bouncer called Ray. Saying I know this oke and please loz it, hey, I'll make it up to you, he's a china of mine, please, hey, please, he's a lank good oke. I can't see exactly what's happening but I think he's handing Ray something. And then I hear Ray's voice. "Ja, well you tune him next time he tries causing with us he is getting planted solid. I don't give a shit whose china he is."

"Of course, of course, Ray, man. Shot, man. Thanks, hey. Thanks a million, I mean it." The hand lets go of my shirt and Ray moves off down the alley and I'm being helped up, using the brick wall too. "Come on, bru," he says. "Let's get the hell out of here before that mulet turns round and changes his mind." The back of the alley ends in a chain-link fence with a locked gate that he opens. I can more or less walk on my own by the time we reach it. There's a Vespa scooter chained to a fire escape. He turns to me. "Hop on, bru." Suddenly he grins all wide. "What are the chances, hey?" I do my best to grin back, I'm still holding my belly. He laughs and starts the engine.

39

The cold night air feels good rushing against my face and the tall, hard city is a blur that slowly gets low and green and fuzzy, turning into the suburbs of trees and hedges. I realise we are in Linksfield and soon we pull up at a high steel gate and he cuts the Vespa's engine. He punches in a security code. I help wheel the scooter to the end of the driveway and on around the side of the main house, a larney Linksfield home made of white cubes and big windows. We leave the scooter behind the servants' quarters and cross the garden. The swimming pool filter hums and the Kreepy Krauly beats underwater like a pulse, vacuuming the curved walls. In the poolhouse there's a dusty bar, a leather couch, a billiards table. When he turns on the light I see him properly for the first time. He's got some stubble on his upper lip and he looks much bonier and bigger and is about nine months overdue for a haircut but it's him all right. Patrick Cohen. The same cheeky smile I remember so well from those days playing slinkers in the foyer of the Emmarentia Synagogue with Ari Blumenthal.

"What you think of it, hey? This is all mine. I live here by myself."

"You serious?" I say. "Shweet, man!"

Pats is wearing a tie-dyed fanny pack that he takes off now and tosses on the billiard table. He unzips it and starts pulling out crumpled balls of cash. I ask whose house this is. His fingers work on the cash, straightening and making piles. "Shit, china," he says. "Can't believe you here. Old Marty Marts. You must have a horseshoe up your arse these days, know that, Mart? If I wasn't there tonight, you'd be on hospital food, know that?"

"It checked that way, hey."

"It *was* that way. Trust me, I know Ray McAlvin and he's a bladdy maniac. He was about to stomp your face in, no jokes. Hey, you still live in Greenside?"

"Of course, man."

"And that school a yours? Fancy-shmancy Solomon. How'd that work out?"

"It's oright *now*," I say. "But was helluva rough before."

"You made some chinas, hey?"

I nod. But I'm thinking, some chinas they turned out to be. Leaving me to get stomped in the alley. Pats is counting the notes. "Not a bad night so far," he says. "I'll head back in like a couple of hours when the real action starts to swing. You asked me whose place this is. S'a friend of a friend. I think it's Segal is the name, a surgeon or something. They on holidays in the overseas for like a year, not really sure. No one's ever home."

"So how've you ended up living here?" He doesn't answer, his lips moving as he counts again. I say, "What school you going to, with hair like that? Is it Milton?" Milton College is this private school in town that doesn't have uniforms and specialises in cramming for matric finals. They send dropouts there to get sorted before it's too late — a lot of times I've thought I'd end up there myself. Pats looks up and gives me this hard face, like I've said something wrong. "Stuff all that," he says. It catches me off balance, him turning so serious and I don't say anything. He asks me if I've ever smoked zol. I shake my head, starting to feel nervous. He goes into the pack, pulls out plastic bank bags full of dark green chunks and pills and also sheets of what look like stamps, and spreads them on the table. "I'm ganna have a little white pipe to mellow out my head space," he says. Then laughs at my expression. "Joking," he says. "Relax." A *white pipe* is crushed Mandrax pills smoked through a bottleneck. It turns you into an instant drooling zombie. "Mandrax is magic for my business," Pats is saying. "You know, no other country in the world uses it like we do right here in good old South Effica. We the innovators of this stuff, man. But I've also got the best zol product there is. From local growers down on the Wild Coast, the freshest Transkei heads." He gets out rolling papers and adds some green from a bank bag plus a little tobacco, then licks and rolls to complete the joint.

I think of Patrick Cohen the shul boy, the reader of strange books from his sister, the arguer of everything. I remember how he went quiet at the Emmarentia Dam that day when Sardines Polovitz headbutted him. It's all a million miles away from this zol-head in front of me and I say, "I can't believe how much you've changed."

"Once you free your mind," Pats says, "you don't go back." He lights the joint and inhales and goes over to the couch, waving me to follow. Instead I ask him how he knows Ray the bouncer and where the money comes from. He tells me it's what he does now, full-time, it's his business. He knows all the bouncers cos he supplies product to the clubs. "Product," I say. He flops on the couch, smiling at me. "Just like the song," he says. "I'm the real-life Sugar Man." Meaning the monster Rodriguez hit, the one about the drug dealer with all the magical dope to sell.

I say, "You remember that day at the Emmarentia Dam, hey Pats?"

"It was lank wrong of us," he says. There's a silence and I know what he's thinking of, remembering, but he shakes his head—he's not going there. Instead he says, "Was lank wrong for me and Ari—afterwards— to crap all over you for going to Solomon, hey. Whatever that place is, I promise you it's zilch compared to the circle of hell they call a government high school."

"Izit," I say.

"Ja, bladdy unbelievable, man. The Initiation and the jacks. Headmaster fuckface used to do his jacks *publicly*, man, during assembly. It's short back and sides all the way. March this way, run here. You fully into the sausage maker from day one. The whole bladdy system, the shitstem with a capital *S*. We had mandatory cadets. Goosestepping up and down every arvy like good little Nazis. You don't want to know what veld school was like. They sent us off in the bush with these dutchmen in charge of us that hammered the kuk out of us, brainwashing to fight the Total Onslaught and to dig out the communists vortel en tak." His voice had changed to put on a deep accent for this Afrikaans phrase, root and branch. "And when they found out me and Ari and a few other okes were a bunch of bliksem Joode" —bloody Jews—"well, china, you don't wanna know. But that was how it was in that school anyway, we had a little clique of us Jew boys and there were hard-core rawls every single day. Lebs vers Jews and Poras vers Greeks and English vers each other, this one vers that one. One time this china of mine was parked there with his back to the wall peeling and eating a naartjie all quiet, and someone rocked up and soccerkicked him full stick in the face and he half choked on that naartjie and lost his teeth, had a fractured skull. Genuine. I knew the oke, his family. Another someone had a gun in the stands for one rugby match and it went off by accident. Bang! Man, I bladdy hated it so much."

"And Ari?"

"Ari got religion hey, more and more frum. Lank of the Jewish okes get into it, hey, the religion. Me, I went shwoosh! the other way. The whole thing started to crack open for me from my sister, you remember Laurel?"

"Of course." The drama student with the crazy hair, black candles in her room and the books on UFOs and Gandhi and atheism and witchcraft.

Pats inhales and screws up his face, holding the smoke in. He waves me in with the joint. My heartbeats are heavy as I sit down beside him. He says, "See, she got arrested, hey."

"You serious?"

"Ja, man, taken in by security police, held in detention for three weeks. Twenny-two and a half days. When she came out she wasn't Laurel anymore. Never been the same. She can't even look anyone in the eyes. They did bad things to her in there, man. Just because she is against racialism, that's the only reason. And things got bad at home after that. My da moved out, he also had like a kind of nervous break-down thing, and like I don't talk to Ma anymore, cos of . . . ach, it's a whole big mess."

"So you just what? Moved out? Dropped out of school?"

"China, the day our vice-head came into our class and gave us our little army numbers for the call-up, I said fuuuuuck this. You scheme I'm ganna go into the army after what they did to Laurel? I mean I would have gone to varsity, oright, but still, just having that army draft number — no, man — no ways — ach, I don't want to talk about what happened to Laurel, but I know what they did. They put — you know those crocodile clips from a car battery? They stuck those on her — never mind, hey, no one will believe it, but I know what happened. I know what goes on. The whole shitstem is rotten, hey. We all living in one big prison and it makes us all mean. Best thing I can do is sell everyone good drugs. It's a bladdy mitzvah, man, a hell of a good deed. Get us all to mellow out and see another way. Some chemicals to try and shut the shitstem down from inside . . ." He scrunches around on the couch and gives me the joint. I lift it to my lips and inhale. Pats tells me to hold it in. The room starts to spin. Pats smokes and passes it back and I smoke some more. My scalp starts to feel crackly and a part of me is sinking down a deep well and I'm too weak to climb out and then I'm too giggly to even want to try and there's no strength in my hands like sometimes when you wake up.

But I'm still wide awake and concentrating with another part of myself, I'm asking Pats about the bouncers, how he got to know them. Pats says — his voice echoey and far away — that it all started with an oke called Declan Stone who went to his same high school. "Have you not heard of the Stone brothers?" he asks and I nod (so slowly) cos ja, I have, but not in detail. All I know is according to Schnitz there are a bunch of Stone brothers and they are like the best street fighters in Jo-burg. This is true, says Pats, and three of the oldest Stone brothers are bouncers. Liam, Stuart, and Conor. The youngest brother, Declan, he still goes to Pats's old high school. Pats says Declan used to rock up to school on a motorbike and leave his helmet and gloves on the seat and no one would ever dream of touching it. "Ever do *Great Expectations* for a setwork book in English class? You know, the Dickens? There's that bit about the lawyer, Jaggers, remember, where it says the whole of London used to shit itself for the name Jaggers. If any crook with a stolen watch was to realise it belongs to Mr. Jaggers, he would drop it like it was red-hot." Pats chuckles, his bushy head wagging. "The Stone name is like that. Legend. People know. Like one time someone shot Stuart Stone in the leg so he was on crutches for a while. So two okes decided to liberty him while he was weak. They jumped him there in Rosebank, hey. Stuart Stone *used his crutches* to put them both into in-tensive care. One of the okes was a third-dan black belt, the other one had a hammer. That is true that I know for a fact. There's a million sto-ries like that about the Stones and mostly true." It was at his government high school that Pats started to sell ready-rolled, he says, buying the zol from a friend of his sister, and that got him noticed by Declan, who didn't want anyone dealing in school. "I said no problem, I'll stop. Or if he liked, I could let him have a chunk of the profits. He liked *that*. So that's how I started into this business, how I got my in. Through Declan Stone."

I pass the smoke back and nod my crackly head. "I get it," I hear myself saying. "Cos he's a bouncer too, or his brothers are, so then the clubs . . ."

"Ja, ja, there's it." Pats leans forward. "You have to understand how it works, Marts. The clubs are the drug market. That's where all the stuff is bought and sold to all the rich boys and girls who come in from the suburbs and all over the Witwatersrand to jol in town on weekends. Now the bouncers, they control the clubs. There is no club that can run without em. If they try, that place will get burned out or smashed up. If they try bring in their own backstop, their own security, then they'll have to tangle with the Dynamite boys."

"Dynamite?"

"The bouncers. The name comes from the Dynamite Gym. That's where they all train, they all know each other, they're chinas. The Stone brothers and Jannie du Preez and Max Bronfstein and Goran Kijuc and all the rest of em. They work together but it's not like they have a boss exactly, they just operate as one unit, like. It's all about the rep. Okes have to earn that rep. They become a bouncer by planting other bouncers. Just walk up and put them away. So the ones who are in are always watching out for okes coming out of nowhere. That's why everyone is so aggro and bladdy paranoid."

"Like Mr. Longhair," I say, noticing that my middle doesn't hurt the way it did. I lift my shirt. My solar plexus has turned yellow, tomorrow it'll be a lekker purple, I reckon.

"Ja, Ray McAlvin," Pats is saying. "Perfect example. When you walked up on him he was prolly thinking you there to try your luck. That's how their minds work. He's a mean bugger that Ray." He shakes his head. "See, also, it's a lot of money and it's a lot of hectic pressure on those okes, the bouncers, to be the *hardest,* to be the *staunchest.*"

I take a deep hit of the smoke. "Ja, but tell me something. Do they all wear tuxedos?"

He nods. "It's like their uniform," he says. Then he gets up with the last bit of the joint and heads off.

I can't feel my lips as I call after him, "I was looking for Marcus. Thaz what I was doing . . . tonight . . ." I'm not sure if he heard me, my eyes closing.

When I wake up Pats is coming back from the bathroom, steadying himself on the walls. He stops and frowns. "What's that you said — you were at Xanadu to find your *brother*?"

I manage a nod, forcing myself to concentrate against the stony heaviness (so this is why they call it being stoned) and start telling him about Marcus and the tuxedo. The card and the piece of a human ear, the sink under the early morning sky. How my brother musta been working as a bouncer, maybe there at Xanadu.

"Before my time," Pats says.

"Since the army," I say, "we hear like zilch from him. He's so gone, I swear."

"Except when he comes here on leave," Pats says.

"Ach, he never gets leave."

"But I've seen him," Pats says.

I shake my weighty head. "No. No, you haven't."

"Yes I have," Pats says. "It was near the Small Street Mall there, in town, wasn't long ago."

"It wasn't Marcus. Marcus hasn't been back on leave."

"Bru," says Patrick Cohen, "I know Marcus. Don't tell me who I saw. I saw *him.*"

40

All Sunday morning I have a headache and worry that smoking drugs has destroyed major brain cells. Then I see Hugo Bleznik—he's back from his road trip, and my guts start flopping like wet sheets in a washing machine on high. At the braai under the plum trees he keeps wiggling his eyes at me and I keep pretending not to notice. The last thing I feel like doing is going with him to "fix up" that policeman problem like he told me I had to, keeping it a secret between us. Now he manages to whisper to me that he'll be waiting round the corner. I nod, but I tell myself he can wait till hell freezes.

Then after he leaves I keep thinking about how it's *my* mess—that is true. It makes my chest throb with a sick feeling of guilt. So I get changed and tell the folks I'm going to my new friend's house to swot for a physics test and I'll go wait outside for his ma to pick me up. Around the corner sure enough there's the red Jag. I get in and shut the door. Hugo asks if I've made a good excuse and I nod. He pats my leg and tells me not to worry, to "shine up" cos the problem will all soon be sorted. He reaches in the back, wheezing like an old accordion, struggling to stretch cos his belly is so damn big, I mean I'd be amazed if the seat belt fitted—not that he even tries to put it on. He brings the shoebox to his lap. "I know you've seen me collecting these from your da sometimes. You've got those noticing eyes, don't pretend you don't." I nod, not saying anything. "Your da ever tell you what's in them?" I say no. Hugo lifts the top—Adidas rugby boots, size 12. The box is stuffed with banknotes, pinkies and browns, fifty and one hundred rand notes. I couldn't guess how much total. Thousands. Hugo tells me I need to understand that a lot of business gets done with cash. "What people show in their books is one thing," he says, "but cash is the real truth. You want to get summin done in this world, stick an envelope in a man's hand. That is my first lesson to you. Exactly what we ganna do tonight."

"Where do we go?"

"To see your policeman pal. And give him this."

"What, him, himself?"

"Ja. Who else?"

"I dunno, when you said fix the problem I didn't think—"

"We're going to see Oberholzer," Hugo says. "Right now."

"Jesus, Hugo, I can't. Da'd murder me. He says I'm not even supposed to say the guy's *name*."

Hugo tells me Isaac will never know and reminds me that I'm the one who brought Oberholzer to the Yard that day. Things have happened since then that are damaging the business. "My police contacts are telling me Oberholzer is on the way up. He's pushing to get us inspected and investigated. He's got some big-shot friends and can make our life an absolute misery. Already he's had some of our staff picked up. Things keep going this way, he can end up putting us right out of business."

"No *ways*," I say, frowning with the craziness of that idea.

"Boyki, I am dead serious. You have to understand how things work in this city. Oberholzer's got contacts and he's not shy. They stick us under a microscope, you never know what'll turn up. They play dirty, these boys. Behind the scenes. Someone like Oberholzer has no bottom. Believe me."

"What do you mean, never know what'll turn up?"

"Boyki, we do what we have to, like everyone in business." He pokes the shoebox. "You need it to schmear the works so they run proper. For the insurance fellows so we get the contracts for the wrecks, for the inspectors and the licences, for the councillors so we keep our zoning. Follow me?"

I nod.

"Oberholzer's no joke. He's serious about hurting us."

"But why? I asked Da about him but he wouldn't say. I think he knows him."

Hugo takes out a hanky and mops his face, his big head shaking. "There is a whole long megillah," he says. "There was an Oberholzer that crossed ways with your father back before the war. Let me just say when your father sorts out someone they stay sorted. Let me just put it that there was bad blood with that old Oberholzer that went off all charts. That bugger was an outright Nazi and had the hell in for your old man. Now it's been passed down to this one, who happens to be — his *son*. Understand? Now he's on some kind of a revenge thing, I don't know what. I don't think a full deck of cards is being played with there, if you take my meaning. But he is a sly devil. Much worse than his father. He has brains. He's a plotter."

"What happened between his father and Da?"

"Ach, it's ancient history to anyone normal. But not to the son. What is his name again?"

"Bokkie," I say.

"Ja, that's right. Bokkie they call him. Dangerous man. A real bad bugger. It's rough luck he arrested you that day and put two and two together. You reminded him Isaac is still around and doing well. You caused him to visit the Yard and from what I hear it did not go well. So now we are on the top of the tall man's shit list and it's a big problem and it needs to be fixed. Luckily Dr. Bleznik has the cure." He picks up the shoebox and shakes it so the money rustles like an instrument. "This is why you and me are ganna go over there now and put this in the man's hands and that will be the end of it."

"Will it?"

"Boyki, I never met a man who couldn't be persuaded by a shoebox full of solid cash. Specially a chutis on a police salary."

As we drive off I ask Hugo where we're going and he tells me it's somewhere private and out of the way, Oberholzer wants to meet far from any watching eyes. We get on the highway, the N14 west, and drive for over two hours through the afternoon before we stop at a petrol station. Then we switch highways to bypass Lichtenburg. There are signs for the Botswana border. We get off and take farm roads south. There are concrete grain siloes, brown grasses, and then the land turns really dry in the orange light of the setting sun, it's full of rocks with ugly twisting little valleys and hills of gravel. Hugo tells me this area is what Afrikaners call klipveld — stone bush — and that seventy-odd years ago there'd been a huge diamond rush here. "Diamonds as big as a lion's balls were lying around everywhere for the taking. Bladdy fortunes got made. There were Yiddluch who came off the boat on the bones of their arses and ended up men of property. S'matter of fact, your father had a —" I look at him but he's stopped. Not easy for talk-machine Hugo. "A what?" I say. Hugo just shrugs and tells me to ask Da. I try for like five minutes to get him to go on but he won't budge. I say, "Has this got anything to do with that old Cadillac there in the shop?"

"Jesus!" says Hugo. "You got an eye for the raw nerve, hey, son. Listen, that Cadillac is a whole 'nother ball of wax. Like I say, you'll have to ask your da. But I wouldn't. I don't look in the rearview. Only losers in reverse do that." He asks me to get his flask from the cubbyhole. I unscrew the cap and the smell of good Scotch spills out as I hand it over. Hugo takes a large nip and offers it to me. I say no thanks. "Good man," Hugo says. "Keep a clear head on the shoulders. You here to learn."

"If we ever get there," I say, looking out the window.

"Just be patient," says Hugo, "or you end up being one."

41

Somewhere along the way Hugo uses the word *farmhouse*. This gives me a picture in my head like the Cadbury's ad (the one that goes *Come to our dairy and taste the cream* that the okes of 8E love to sing while making certain dirty gestures) showing an old stone house in a green meadow. But the real "farmhouse" turns out to be a box of concrete with a rusted metal roof standing there on the dry, flat land full of stones. There's a yellow bakkie with a rollbar parked to one side and a tin windmill is somehow turning even though I don't feel any breeze, going squeak-squeak-squeak. A man comes out and stands on the porch, his top half in shadow and his long legs wearing jeans tucked into boots. As we get closer the shadow moves up and there's his face. He says, "How goes it with you, boy?"

"Ja, good thanks, Captain," I say. "And yourself?"

"You see any uniform? Call me Bokkie out here." He goes inside and we follow and there's a sweet smell foreign to me. It takes a second for my eyes to adjust — some old furniture, a table with bottles and rags, metal pieces, a rifle. A steel thing with a knobbed handle is clamped at one end of the table. Oberholzer catches me staring. "A reloader," he says. "To make your own ammo." He smiles at Hugo. "Saves you a few shekels, hey." Hugo laughs but it doesn't sound real, more like he's pressing on that wheezy accordion I imagine living inside his chest. Oberholzer picks up the rifle, plucks a rag from the barrel and the sweet smell gets stronger. "I was jiz oiling up Claudine here. Come outside, mense" — folks — "while we still got some good light."

On the back stoep — the covered porch — all you can see ahead is open land and sky. There's a sleeping bag laid out and Oberholzer sets up the rifle there with a bipod under the barrel, lying flat on his belly in a shooting position, his eye to the scope. He hands me a pair of binoculars. Hugo rolls his eyes and taps his temple and sits down on a chair behind, mopping his face with his silk hanky, his fat knees spread and the Adidas shoebox parked awkwardly on his left thigh.

"What am I looking for?" I ask Oberholzer.

"Targets," he says. "Our little friends."

I peer through the binocs and at first it's just a moosh of colours with a spiky monster snake till I wipe the hair from the lens and fiddle with the focus ring and then a clear picture jumps at me. The hook of a thorn. Hard grains of red and yellow sand. I start tracking around and something pops up. Some furry animal, up on two hind legs like a tiny man, its smooth long neck stretched and black rings in the fur around the twitchy eyes in the neat, tiny head, claws on the ends of teeny hands. Now I know what Bokkie wants from me but I don't say anything. It doesn't help, though, cos I sense him glancing at me and he says, "Ah, you looking to the left there, hey?" Next second the rifle cracks and I see the furry little guy jump up in a twitch of blood and flop down on his back. Bokkie says, "Ja, keep looking, now is when it gets fun. His pals will come to investigate. Nou sal die poppe dans." And he chuckles. The Afrikaans saying means now the puppets are going to dance, like now there'll be hell to pay, but it has that sly double meaning cos the little creatures are just like dancing puppets as Bokkie starts to shoot. He is very quick and he never misses. We hike out there after, leaving Hugo on the porch, fanning himself with his hat. Dead meerkats are spread on the dirt in the evening light. That's what these little animals are called, Oberholzer telling me how they live underground and pop up to hunt insects while some of them stand watch, making perfect targets for his Claudine. He flicks the little bodies with the barrel. "My Claudine's a custom Anschütz," he says. "I replaced her bolt action for speed. Lightweight .22 Long ammo is all she uses. You don't need much power, you need precision. She's perfect for riot work, you can pick off a leader and not touch anyone behind. Or if you don't wanna kill, you can drill a kneecap or an elbow, drop them surgical on the spot. I got bad eyes and I wasn't born much of a blerry shot. Hard work made me one. I'm helluva good now. I was urban sharpshooter instructor on police course even. If you graft hard enough a weakness turns into your biggest strength. These meerkats let me work at range with random pop-up. Windage and bullet drop. Your stability. Your sight picture adjustment. Breathing. Not like in close like this. That's too easy-peasy for me and Claudine. Look." The rifle has a deep bend in the stock so he can use it with one hand and he points it like a long wand. A rusted can jumps off the ground maybe sixty metres away. He swings and points one-handed and makes an old paper bag flap into the wind. Then he stretches out his arm and hits whatever he names: that shiny stone, an old nail, a green chunk of bottle glass. He changes the magazine in one move and keeps going, *crack crack ping crack*. Whatever he points at gets smashed.

Hugo is on his feet when we get back to the stoep. His smile doesn't let up. "Well, Bokkie, I hope you had some very good shooting."

"With his help," Oberholzer says. "You liked that hey, didn't you, Martin?"

I just say, Ja, meneer — yes, sir — while Hugo's eyes are going like Ping-Pong balls between me and Oberholzer. Oberholzer puts his hand on my shoulder. "You remember and tell his father, Isaac, what a good learner his boy is. Tell how Captain Oberholzer is teaching him proper what to do. You make sure and tell him that."

"Um, ja," Hugo says. "Well. Actually his father. This is what I'd like to, uh, discuss."

Oberholzer reaches out with the rifle and pokes the barrel against the shoebox on the chair. "I wonder if the *discussing* has to do with zis thing over here, hey?"

"I wonder also, ha ha ha," Hugo says, wheezing that accordion. Then he frowns. "You see, Captain, I've come out here in behalf of myself and my partner Mr. Helger, whom you well know to represent the Lion Metals company. I come here on full respect, to clean up any miscomprehending that has gone between yourself and the company whichever of it may be. Captain, we want to have goodwill with any member of South African Police and —"

"And this is ganna clear things up, hey? This box here. Let me ask you something. Where is Isaac Helger right now, is he at home, enjoying his nice weekend?"

"Captain —"

"He'll retire soon, hey? And then he'll have every day off, every day will be a nice Sunday for him."

Hugo tries to laugh again, says, "Well he works hard some Sundays, so not quite."

"Does he?"

"Oh ja, he's in there at the Yard one Sunday a month, doing stock-taking himself."

"Is that a fact?" says Oberholzer.

"Yes, it is," says Hugo, "but as I was saying before, Captain. We here to bring goodwill between our firm and —"

"Shhh," says Oberholzer and he lifts up the rifle and touches the end of the barrel to Hugo's lips. Just like that. Hugo flinches back, blinking. A spear of shock goes right through my chest. Did he really just do that? "Be quiet," Oberholzer is saying. "I know why you here. I know what this is." He swings the barrel back to the shoebox and knocks it off the chair, cash sprawling out. "Let me fill you in, Mr. Goodwill who comes out here with a box of money."

"Wait a sec," says Hugo. "You invited us."

"I said quiet," says Oberholzer and pokes into the cash, stirring it, spreading it over the floor. "My father, Magnus. He died right over here, behind you, Mr. Goodwill. In this shack. Drinking himself. Full of the bitter truth of what goes on in this country. I know who killed him. I know the ones who is behind it all. Who is always behind everything. He taught me that well, and he was right. He prophesised would come the day and here we are. So I will make him proud now. Here in the flesh when you come with your pound of it, hey. Come with cash, just like he foretold me you people —"

"Ukay," Hugo says, putting his hat on. "That's enough. We hear you." He looks at me, his face red. "Boyki, let's go."

"Every scrap of your dirty paper gets off my property," Oberholzer says.

"Captain —"

"Do some real work, Mr. Goodwill. *Pick it up.*" He has swung the barrel back onto Hugo, this time against his chest. I take a step but Oberholzer looks at me and I freeze. "Cool your jets, junior," he says. "You just watch and learn." It takes a while for Hugo, groaning, to gather the money, with his bad knees and his belly. Plus it's getting dark and the notes are hard for him to see with his weak eyes. He's panting by the time he stands up with the box. "Now go," Oberholzer says, "and never come back."

"We going, believe me," says Hugo. "But I want to ask you one thing. What is it that you want with us? You said you wanted to meet. Here I am. And I brought Martin with me, just like you asked." This is news to me. What else don't I know?

"And that is what I wanted," Oberholzer is saying. "For *him*. To see *this*."

"What's he got to do with it, Captain? I mean whatever happened years ago —"

"Shut up, Jew. Go off my father's land." He turns to me. "And you go back to your daddy and send my regards. Make sure you tell him Oberholzer is the one who showed you how a man behaves — Oberholzer. You tell it to him. Tell him Oberholzer has got his eye on the Helger boys. From now on he is ganna help bring them up right."

42

In the dark in front Hugo drops the car keys. He's so anxious to get out of here he gives up the search and goes for the spare key he keeps in a little box welded under the driver's-side wheel well, but meantime I've found the dropped keys. He drives very fast — so fast we get pulled over by a traffic cop near Ventersdorp and I'm scared we'll be arrested. Just the word *Ventersdorp* is bad enough to me cos it's where the AWB, the Afrikaner Resistance Movement, is based. These guys have swastikas and brown safari suits. Their leader's called Terre'Blanche — White Earth — and he's a wannabe Adolf Hitler. They hold rallies where they shout angry speeches against the government *for being too liberal* and beat people up. But Hugo gives the cop a wad of cash from the Adidas box and the cop grins and lets us pass on. "You see," says Hugo, "that was a reasonable human being. A sane person you can do business with. This other one, Oberholzer . . ." He shudders. I'm thinking how he told me before that Oberholzer's father was a Nazi before the war and I can picture that now cos I can picture the AWB troopers, beefy bearded Afrikaans men marching with their red-and-black swastikas flying in the wind and bright as blood on their armbands, like the ones in the Nightmare. I turn to Hugo and ask him what happened there at the farmhouse. He asks me to pass him the flask and has a few long slugs from it, wiping his lips. "He was talking about his father," I say. "Who died there or something."

Hugo sighs. "Ja, Magnus was his name. I told you already."

"You said Da sorted him."

"Well he did and he didn't. Let's just say if you bite you can also get bitten back."

"I don't follow."

"It doesn't matter. What matters is what happened much later, it was in the seventies, this Magnus had quite a big mechanic shop going and your father heard about it. What he did, he decided to give Magnus some payback for all the stuff what had happened long ago, like I told you, before the war. Isaac saw it like a chance to see him right once and for all. I told him forget it but he wouldn't forget."

"What'd he do?"

"It wasn't hard. Magnus wasn't good in business. Isaac had me speak to some friends of mine who were supplying him, tell them open up the credit lines, and they piled him with goods. He couldn't say no. I mean it's not like we held a gun to his head. We just gave him plenty of rope to hang himself with. We quietly bought the property and owned his lease, we bought up his debts. He had no idea we were the ones who held all the bonds, that we owned him lock, stock, and barrel right up until your father gave the word and called them all in and put him into bankruptcy, boom. Then he had me ask all our suppliers and customers not to do business with Magnus Oberholzer again, had me spread some stories which wasn't hard because they were all true — it was just a question of letting everyone in the trade know not to do business with him or give him a job. So that buried old Magnus. I'm not surprised to hear from his son now that it broke him. But I don't shed a tear and neither should you. Like I say, the man was an absolute Nazi. They weren't called AWB back then, they were Greyshirts before the war. But there were a *lot* more of them. Storming round the streets of Joburg. They used to smash windows in Bertrams and Doornfontein. They backed Hitler to win, they had a lot of support. They bashed up Jews in the street. Those were rough days for the Jews in Joburg, lemme tell you. And this Oberholzer senior, he was a Greyshirt deluxe-deluxe. Huge bladdy ox of a man he was too. And he made your da suffer back then. So he got what he deserved in the end, for messing with Isaac Helger. Your father had the last word."

"Except that his son Bokkie is speaking up now," I say. "Isn't that so, Hugo?"

Hugo mutters something I don't catch and we drive all the way back in a strange silence. I'm supposed to be home by ten and it's late but when we get to Joburg Hugo ignores this and takes us to his house in Hyde Park, a big Tudor place with a thatched roof. The garage used to be stables. At the back is a workbench and a small fridge with enough dust a finger could sign. After Hugo parks, we sit down there and Hugo cracks open two beers from the fridge and hands me one. "This is one helluva bladdy twist," he says. "This is the twist of all twists." He looks off and shuts his eyes and rubs his face. Then he drinks some beer and says, "But lucky for us, your Uncle Hugo is a man who plans ahead for twists." I swallow some cold beer. "It's my fault," I say. "If I'd never gone to Jules with Annie . . ." I'm sort of counting on Hugo to tell me that's not true, that it would have happened anyway or something like that, but he only clinks cans and says, "Such is life, young man." Which makes me want to cry, though I don't show it, trying to smile instead. Hugo maybe sees something in my face. "Love does tricks on the mind," he tells me. "You followed that American bird. Don't blame yourself. I mean even your da—when your da was young he fell for a shiksa girl from Parktown, but she wasn't for him. Different league. Different world. You asked me about that old Cadillac he keeps around. It's because that girl's family had a Cadillac just like that and he still remembers. That's why it's there. Between you and me."

There's so much I don't know about Isaac, so much of the past that's still at play but he'll never talk about it. I sip some beer to cover my confusion. Hugo drinks too, then he puts down the can and slaps his thighs. "Right. Well. Let's lay it all out. We started today with one helluva problem on our hands. Then you and me, we went all the way and did our very best to try and fix this thing, like reasonable people. Nobody could ask for more. But it didn't work. The opposite. Now the problem is so worse it's not even funny—"

"Shouldn't we tell Da?"

"Don't be mad!"

"Why not?"

"Boyki, I don't think you understand yet. This is a police captain who is wily as they come. The only reason he had us out there was to make a point, and what is that point? That nothing can persuade this man to stop. Not money, not anything. He is ganna do his best to ruin us. But you can't tell your father. I can guarantee Isaac will go charging straight at him and it will not be pretty. For us, I mean. Oberholzer is waiting for him, he expects it. Your da could end up in prison, or worse, I swear. No, don't look at me like that. I'm a hundred per cent serious. I know what I'm talking about. A situation like this, there's only three ways. You can try to fight or you can pay the man off. We tried paying. Fighting? This bugger will win that game, big time."

"What's the third?"

Hugo takes a swig. "Lemme tell you a story," he says. "There was a doctor called Teddy Shapiro that I knew from my shul. Sweetest chap you could ever meet. Would not harm the wing on any fly by nature. He was also the biggest specialist in medicine of infecting diseases in prolly the whole world. Now this Teddy was a typical liberal-type Jew and he donated all his spare time to this free clinic he had in Soweto. He used to get tears in his eyes, I promise you, when he was talking about the blacks he was helping. It went on for years, we talking. I am saying this man was more than a mensch, he was a bladdy saint. And what did they do to him in 'seventy-six? At the clinic where Teddy Shapiro did nothing but the horrible sin of caring for them for free?" Everyone knows how bad the Soweto Riots were, in June 1976, how the police rolled in force into the townships and opened fire. Hugo says it was on the very first day of the riots that a mob ringed the little brick clinic where Dr. Teddy Shapiro was on duty. They set fire to the cars in the parking lot. Hugo explains there was a black reporter from the *Star* there, who put it all in the paper — how Dr. Shapiro recognised the faces, and knew their names and went out to speak to them, how they stripped him naked, beat him with bricks and iron bars. "Then they chucked him into the clinic and set it on fire," Hugo says. "Now think about it. That is what they did to someone who helped them. *Imagine what they'd do to anyone else.* I mean, boyki, am I a schmock? Am I a bladdy fool? No! I made up my mind then and there. I am going to leave this place. I am going to emigrate. The ship is going down. But first I had to organise things nicely . . ." Since our government makes it illegal for South Africans to move their own money overseas, Hugo says he started cutting under-the-table deals with his foreign suppliers in Japan and the States. He flew over to the U.S. and found a good lawyer, Altenberg, who has an office by Battery Park, New York City. They set up a system where the overseas suppliers would give an inflated invoice and the extra money ended up with Altenberg, who funneled it to different accounts for Hugo.

"Is it a lot?" I ask.

"Boyki, I been schlepping *hard* since 'seventy-six. What do you reckon?"

"Does my father know about it?"

"Absolutely no ways. He's not interested. He'll never leave this country. But me, I've always known these days would come. You asked what is the third option. The third option is obvious. To get the hell out. I have been on the verge of making the move for I've just told you how long. This thing now with Oberholzer, it is just the last whatchacallit that breaks the camel's leg."

"You're going to leave the country?"

Hugo stares at me. "Don't you understand? I thought you were a bright boy. This is about *you*. Martin Helger." He fishes in a jar full of bolts and brings out an Allen key. He sticks the key into a knot on the workbench and turns it and pulls a whole section of a plank right off. There's a long metal box hidden inside. "Clever, hey?" Hugo says. "Had it made special by a carpenter in Bez Valley." From the box he brings out an envelope and holds it across. I take it and I see my name typed. Inside is a letter with an imperial-looking eagle. United States Immigration and Naturalization Service. I scan the words *Re: Petition for Alien Minor* and then I see, clipped to the bottom, a card like a credit card. It has my name on it, my birth date. ALIEN REGISTRATION RECEIPT CARD, it says. I turn it over and see a photo of my younger face next to a seal and a fingerprint. The top says RESIDENT ALIEN, in blue. Hugo asks me do I remember the time, long ago, in his office at the Yard when he got me in to give a fingerprint for insurance? Well it wasn't insurance, it was for this. "I told you I've been getting ready for this day since 'seventy-six."

"What is it?"

"Important little card that, Martin. They call that a green card, don't ask me why, doesn't look bladdy green to me. Took years to get for you and for Marcus. Took bucks, plenty. It gives you the right to settle into America any time you like. You can work there, live there, for as long as you like. And it never expires. They tell me that will change, new kinds of cards coming down the pipe later this year will have expiry but yours — this one — is already permanent. Signed and sealed. Nobody can take it away."

"You're telling me you got this for *me*?"

Hugo says, "You know I've never had kids of my own to pass on to. My South African assets will go to some of the wunnerful women I have known in my lifetime which I am grateful and it's been a helluva ride, but for true blood to pass on, I've got no one. I don't know if your old man ever said, but I was raised an orphan, you know. I left that bad place when I was thirteen and never looked back. That was my only bar mitzvah. All I knew was working on the road. Sales. Being a rep. That was my life. Then I crossed paths with your father and we started in the motor game. I owe your father a lot. If I'm honest, everything. So you two — I feel you're both . . . you're like my own sons, Martin and Marcus."

This is too much, I have nothing to say, my mind spinning like a yo-yo. Hugo says come outside for some air. We follow a path into the garden and Hugo stops by a tall palm tree, half lit by the security lights. He points. "You see em?"

"See what?"

"Keep looking."

Hugo bends with difficulty and comes up with a stone. He chucks it at the palm, there's a whoosh of rushing wings, a lifting wave of those Joburg black birds with the yellow beaks. "See that. That's *us,* boy. That's like Jews. A tree is stuck here with its roots, see? Roots kill you. Roots gets you hit with stones. But the Jew birds fly. They are just fine. We know flying is survival. At least the clever ones do."

Hugo tells me his own plan is to disappear, not tell a soul, just go. That's the best way, a clean break. He says I should do the same. I have my passport, my parents got them for us that time we went to Israel to visit Auntie Rively and Uncle Yankel. I should go to New York, see Altenberg. There is a bank account waiting. "Everything is laid on for you like cake icing." It all sounds nuts to me but Hugo is serious. "Where is your adventure?" he says. "You seventeen. I was on the road for years by the time I was your age. Think about America, man! At your feet for you. You'll have your own place there, your own money. You can go to school and swot any subject you like, you can get a job, get yourself a car and drive the whole country. You know how massive America is? America is a world by itself. America — it's the opposite of Africa. You can forget about the mess we have here. America is a future. Africa is nothing but one long past that drags us down and down."

"And you? Where will you go?"

"Ach, New York is for the young. When you're an alter kukker like me you have to think of a quiet life somewhere small, with plenny of good doctors around."

I say, "You're being serious that I should just go."

"I've never been more."

"And I'm supposed to tell my parents what?"

"Are you not listening to a word? You tell them exactly nothing. The only one you tell is me, so we can both disappear at the same time, and then you get on the flight and you get off in New York and you can send them a letter. Dear Mommy and Daddy, I am *a man* and this is my life and this is what *I* have decided."

"Da will butcher you, Hugo. If he finds out about this."

"Are you ganna tell him?"

"What about Marcus?"

"When he joined the army he made his choice to stay. There's a card for him also, I was going to show it to him one day — but there's no point now."

In the end I tell Hugo I'll think about it. I won't take the envelope with me, not now. He tells me he'll keep it right there for me. "But you better hurry and make up your mind, Martin. Might be one day when the phone rings at my house and I'm not here to answer. Fershtay?"

"I understand."

"Don't put it off, Martin. I was there when your father and your late granny were battling like hell to get their relatives out of Lithuania, in 'thirty-nine. But they couldn't manage it, it was too late. And you know well what happened there. The bladdy Germans and the Lithuanians shot all the Jews like dogs and chucked them in a hole in the forest to rot. Babies and women also, the lot. I'm saying these things happen. This is the world. I'm saying when you see a stone thrower like Oberholzer taking aim, *you don't wait*. Boyki, Martin — it is time for you to leave the nest."

IF NOT NOW

43

Back at school on Monday morning, the okes are all jabbering about Saturday night at the clubs. The poonie that was pulled. The shots of flaming sambuca downed. The legend rorts — the instant-classic fights — witnessed. Schnitz is the biggest talker, according to him he was the last person to leave the Thunderdome at dawn and stepping out he saw with his own eyes a naked man standing on the roof of a moving Mercedes 500SEC, swear to God, riding it exactly like a Durban surfer on a bladdy wave. Me, I'm standing in the doorway watching this when Stan Lippenshmecker notices and looks around and everyone else turns and the class goes quiet. I walk past my usual desk, saying nothing, and take a new seat by myself in the corner. I get a book out and bury my nose in it. Gradually the jabbering starts again.

Between classes I stay in my corner desk. At first break I head for the library, but outside big-headed Spunny is waiting. He sticks his hands in his pockets and watches his shoes. "Nice to see you're oright," he says.

I say, "Where's your chicken friend Mouth? Running practice? You should go join him."

Spunny flushes. "Hey. I'm just saying I'm glad you okay."

"I'm not," I tell him. "I've been in hospital. I had emergency surgery.

My testicles are all messed up from what happened. The doctors say I'll never have kids."

"Jesus Christ!" says Spunny. Then his eyes crinkle. "Ach, you bullshitting. You fine, you never went to hospital."

"How would you know? It's not like you bothered to check up on me."

"Charity, there was stuff-all we could have done, man."

"You could have gone for help. Could've stayed and tried to find out what happened to me at least. So could the rest of the okes, having their nice fun at Thunderdome. Could have phoned my parents. Stead you pissed off and left me to get murdered in an alley."

"Hey, check — you didn't have to run over to those bouncers, china. We told you not to."

Now I feel myself flushing. "Ja, it's all my fault. I deserved."

"Be that way if you want, Martin. We were tryna be nice, inviting you with us to the clubs. Maybe the others are right about you."

As he walks away I put my fingers in my mouth and whistle hard. "Hey, big hero!" He turns and I lift my shirt, showing my stomach with its purple bruise the size of a cabbage. Then I pull a zap sign with my middle finger.

When Annie picks me up in the night I can see how nervous she is. She tells me she's checked the weather forecast like a million times and when we get to the pipe she just about vomits before she can bring herself to climb in. But the climb up goes smoothly. In the video lab we work hard together, editing down the Fireseed tape to ninety minutes, and when we're finished she hugs me, all happy. I try to kiss her neck, but she jumps up. "So great, Martin. You're all set now with this new master tape. Two tapings a night, baby!"

"Yes," I say. "We've done it."

"You can put in four sessions a week, right?"

"We can," I say. "Easily."

"*We*, sure," she says, as if I'm kidding. "Twenty-four times four, that's one hundred a week." She grins. "Boy, I'm *really* gonna miss slithering up that filthy pipe."

I'm developing a thick feeling in my throat and my smile feels stiff and stupid as my face gets hot.

"And you can work on the sixteen-mil too," she says. Then: "What's wrong?"

"Nothing," I say. "Nothing. You're not coming back."

She frowns like I've baffled her. "Martin, you can handle it all. I have full confidence."

"Thank you," I say. I turn around and walk fast all the way across the school, to the pipe where my satchel is waiting. I'm strapping the pads on when Annie catches up.

"What's your problem, exactly?" she says. "Look at me, please." When I face her she says, "This isn't date night, Martin. I've slept maybe twelve hours this whole week. I'm teaching classes and running my ass ragged all over the East Rand all the rest of the time, trying to conduct Fireseed. Meeting with the Comrades and getting your tapes out there. I've been shot at, nearly arrested, and so far I've seen two schoolkids die right in front of my eyes for this cause. So let's get real, okay?"

My voice is shaking. "You shouldn't take me so for granted you know."

"What's bugging you, Martin? You don't like the pay, uh? What do you want?"

My throat is so thick now that I can't speak at all, I just shake my head, putting my fists on my hips and rubbing my chin on my shoulder. Annie looks at me for a while and then reaches out and puts her warm hand between my legs, just like that. "This what you need? I'll give you that if it'll keep you happy." And she unzips my overalls and starts to tug on my belt, bending down. I slap her hands away. "Stop it." She looks up. "No? What, then?" She straightens up and looks me full in the eyes and then she shakes her head slowly.

My eyes are leaking. I open the grate and worm down into the pipe.

On the other side I strip off the overalls and shove them back in my satchel. I walk over to the sand wall and kick it and punch it, scraping my knuckles. After a while I hear her slithering down, breathing hard, and I quickly wipe the wet off my face and try to look bored as she climbs out and starts stripping out of her overalls. Then, instead of hiking back in the direction of the soccer club as we always do, Annie walks the other way, taking the riverbed deeper into the park. I follow behind her, puzzled. We climb out and head downhill into a clump of ash trees till I can see the low fence of green logs at the edge of the park and hear the traffic noise beyond. There's a small municipal shed in the trees. It's locked but Annie peels back the fibreglass panel just under the roof and waves me closer. On tiptoes, I can just see into the space up there. "Dolf can't handle tapes anymore, just messages. So put the tapes in a garbage bag and shove em in here instead. Someone will collect. Okay?" I nod. "Good," she says. "So we're good? We're back on track?" I nod again. "All right," says Annie. "High five."

44

Morning mist is oozing from our lawn which has little piles of sand all over it. The mole crickets are back. We deal with them by pouring detergent water. They come crawling out to lie on their backs and die, drowning in the poison bubbles. When Marcus and I were little that was our job but I remember now that Marcus wouldn't do it, he felt too sorry. This man who comes home with a chunk of human ear stuck to him, he used to be a kid who didn't even want to hurt some bugs. Now I'm the dawn returner like he was, with my own big secrets. One of the biggest is there in the Sandy Hole, just like it was there in the safe buried under Volper's carpet when Annie and I discovered it that night of the flood. I stare at it for a while. My God. I really have this. Such power. But it only adds to my sadness, makes it wider and deeper. A hopeless feeling. I put it down and put away my satchel and pipe togs and creep quietly along the giant hedge we share with the Greenbaums. There's a wall beside the back of Gloria's old room which I climb to, drop down into the backyard, and wash myself at the outdoor sink, again like my brother and my father.

Suddenly: "Shut that bladdy dog up! Shut it up!" I straighten up and run to the back fence. I know what's coming next if I don't act fast. Through the gaps in the planks I spot Mr. Stein about to start swinging a huge bladdy bell. He'll wake my folks and get me busted. I hiss like a snake. "Mr. Stein. Hey. Stop. *Stop.*" The old guy pauses and screws up his face all suspicious. "Over here, Mr. Stein, man. Here. It's me. It's Martin."

"Eh?" he says. "Who's it there? Show yourself, you swine." He's wearing a pale flying-saucer-shaped helmet, the one from the Second World War with the mouldy chinstrap, and a raggedy bathrobe tied with a piece of onion-sack string. He lifts his brass bell. "I'll brain you, you try anything." He's got eyebrows like two fat hairy caterpillars, I swear. I've never seen eyebrows that hairy. Maybe they're a symptom of insanity.

"Mr. Stein, it's me, hey. Martin. Martin Helger."

"Well you tell that bladdy dog to shut up her yapping, boy."

"We don't have a dog, Mr. Stein."

"All day the bitch yaps."

"Mr. Stein, Sandy died years ago."

"What you say?"

"Died. Sandy's dead. Long, long time."

His mad eye stares at me through the slit. I say, "Ten fingers on my Jewish Torah, Mr. Stein — she's gone. We put her in a plastic bag. Ma drove her up to Dr. Kruger. He has a cremator there."

"What happened?"

"She was just old, Dr. Kruger said."

"And you don't have a new dog?"

"Uh-uh."

"You're lying, boy. I hear her."

"No, I'm not, for real. Listen—there's no barking. Just listen." Mr. Stein turns his grizzled old head on its side. Then he drops the bell, it's heavy enough to dent the soft ground and I'm so relieved I close my eyes for a second. When I open them, he has his forearms on the fence, his head against them. He starts to sob. It frightens me cos I've never seen an old man crying before. "Mr. Stein?" I say. "You okay, Mr. Stein?" He doesn't answer and now I'm double-worried that he'll start wailing or freaking out, maybe pick up the bell again, so I climb up the fence, the same one I always never quite get to in the Nightmare with Zaydi on my back and Nazis smashing behind. I realise I haven't had the Nightmare since the night Annie told me what it means, on the pomegranate bench which itself is starting to feel like a dream, a different Annie.

From the top of the fence I can see all the way across Mr. Stein's property. His house fronts onto Clovelly Road but has no high wall unlike most on the street. Instead he's covered his lawn with fishing lines tied to tin cans. On the flat roof he keeps sandbags piled around, ready for his last stand. Looking down, I see the top of his helmet coming away from the fence. He turns and starts shuffling back to the house, leaving one slipper and the bell behind. I hesitate for a bit and then I hang by my hands and drop. Picking up the slipper and the bell, I follow after him as he zigs and zags, careful to stay in his footsteps, you never know what booby traps lie outside his safe passage. At the back door Stein shouts for Elizabeth, his maid. "Lizbeth! Lizbeth! Come make tea!" He presses his thick fingertips to the mezuzah on the doorframe, then kisses them. If Stein wasn't such a hermit he'd probably be a major shul-goer. He takes off his steel hat and sits at the kitchen table, looking at me from under his caterpillar eyebrows like he's not surprised to find me standing there in the least. After a while I put down the bell and the slipper and take a seat. Mr. Stein starts talking about Gloria. We still don't have a new maid, he says. Elizabeth told him. And our gardenboy Isaiah, he doesn't come anymore. What's going on over there? I tell him it's my da, my da's choice. After

Gloria died, Isaac just didn't want maids or gardeners anymore, doing our housework for us.

"Why not?" says Stein.

"Good question," I say. "Better ask him."

He gives me a sudden look. "Your brother? Where's he?"

"Army," I say. "All this stuff, Mr. Stein, what you're saying — it's been for years."

"I don't see him anymore either."

I nod. Stein leans forward and his voice changes, gets all low and spooky. "Your people," he says, *are not replacing anything*." It's like he's making a horrible accusation. "Things," he says, "are running down."

Elizabeth shuffles in, sniffing. She boils water and fills a teapot, adds Five Roses teabags and a huge pour of sugar. She bangs down a plate of rusks and leaves. Mr. Stein pours. "She forgot the milk, the bladdy twit," he mutters. "She's getting all ibberbottle in her old age." He doesn't get up so we sip our tea black. All-a-sudden he bangs the table. "Have you got a new dog, a puppy?"

"No."

"A new maid?"

"No."

"Gardenboy?"

"No."

"If you don't replace things when they go, that means what? Means you are disappearing. Then what are we doing here? Disappearing ourselves."

I try to smile. "Are we, hey?"

Mr. Stein doesn't get that I'm being funny. There's anger in his face, his hairy hands fly up like two jumping tarantulas, his chair scrapes. "They coming for us," he tells me. "You better get ready. I've seen it — had visions like the Nevi'im, our holy prophets, you understand? It was given to me. It could be morgen in der free, tomorrow morning, or it might be *tonight*. The electric will be gone. The radio will be out. You won't be mocking then, believe me, boy. The water cut off. We'll wake up and look out and they'll be coming down that road, right outside, a hundred thousand, a million of em. Like the waves of a dark sea. They'll be singing and doing their spears and whistling like they do. Yom Ha-Din, my boy. Day of Judgement. They'll come down turning over every car in the road and setting them on fire. They'll go into the houses, they won't leave out even one. There will be nowhere for us to run. A million of em. A million is nothing. Ten million. The justice of the Lord is sharper than any sword. They'll drag us out from wherever we're hiding. The gutters will be running red. The swimming pools will choke with bodies and the trees will snap with the weight of the hangings. They'll burn everything white from this land. There'll be nothing of us left. Like the story of Melech Shaul and the nation of Amalek. Old King Saul was supposed to wipe em off the earth. That's what the good Lord commanded him to do. But see, we are like Amalek to *them*. They will smite us and burn us. Unto the last drop of our seed. Cursed is the white man in this cursed place. Cursed is he unto the end, unto Judgement Day . . ."

Maybe I should excuse myself, but he's not going to stop and his eyes are closed now as he goes on and on, rocking on his chair, so I stand up and creep out and make my way back to the fence, feeling lucky not to get booby-trapped on the way. Madman Mr. Stein. Living alone after the wife died of cancer. Living on a pension, wearing his old tinpot helmet. Isaac always used to say he's got guns and dynamite and probably God knows what else stored away in that place. Keep away from him, Martin. One day it might all go bang.

45

Tuesday morning and the Gooch is reading roll call even though our class is so small a blind man could see who's not there. Berman, Manfred, he says. Cohen, Charles, he says. I feel something poking at my leg. Spazmaz is jabbing me with a steel ruler under the desk. I look down and see a piece of paper stuck to the end. I ignore it but he goes on poking and now I notice how all the faces nearby are watching me and they all seem to have the same compressed smile on them, like they're waiting to explode, like that piece of paper must have the greatest joke of all time written on it. I take the paper, but I've got the feeling that if it is a joke it's going to be on me. Davidson, Peter, says the Gooch.

To Johnny Lohrmann, esq. St. 10C
From Martin Helger (The Real Strongest Lad)

Dear "Crackcrack"

You are a cowardly queer. I could mess you up anyday with one hand behind my back if I wanted. But you would not have the balls to face me. In actual fact you do not have balls at all but a vagina!

I will meet you in front of the tuck shop at first break but I know you will not be there because you will chicken out, you lousy cunt.

Signed, very sincerely,
Martin Helger
The "Real" Strongest Lad

A piece of chalk cracks against the prefab wall above my desk. "Helger, Martin," says the Gooch. "Third time. Helger, Martin." I look up and the Gooch is staring at me. "Fourth time. Helger, Martin." I hear myself saying here, sir, but mostly what I hear is a tidal sound of blood washing through my ears. "It doesn't seem like it," says the Gooch. "Your carcass might be here but your brain is apparently absent as bladdy usual. Better wake up, my mate. I won't tell you again. Get your thumbnail out your arsehole or we will do it for you."

"Yes, sir."

"Kaminsky, Stephen."

The note is a photocopy. When the first bell jangles, right after the Gooch leaves, I stand up with it in my hand and my heart drumming. "Who wrote this, okes? Where's the original? Seriously."

"What's a matter, kid?" says Turdster. "You looking a bit tense, bru. You looking a little bit *concerned.*" Everyone howls — the explosion they've been holding in.

"Was it you?" I say to Schnitz. "You write this?"

"What are you talking about?" says Schnitz. "That's your note, china. Anyone can see."

"This isn't my writing, who wrote this okes? Come on. This isn't funny, hey. You okes didn't actually send this to him did you. I mean come on."

"I heard a rumour," says Baffboy Noshkin, "that note of yours, it got delivered after prayers. I heard it was pinned on Crackcrack's classroom door."

"You okes didn't," I say.

"Not us!" says Mouth. "It's *your* note, china. Don't blame others for your problems, hey. Take responsibility for your actions." And everyone booms again. The way balding Boris Levin is grinning he's like Jack Nicholson in *The Shining* when he finally gets his maniac hands wrapped around the axe in the end. "Helger, you schmock," he says. "Crackcrack already sent a message back. It's a done deal. You the only one who doesn't know what's what. The rawl is booked. First break. The whole school knows, the prefects are ready. If I was you, I'd start warming up."

"If you were him," says Stan Lippenshmecker, "you'd be changing your undies right now." He looks at me. "I feel sorry for you, Helger. Crackcrack is a total animal."

All-a-sudden my breakfast comes shooting up my throat and I have to grab my mouth as I run for the door, the okes howling and shouting after me. "Go boy!" "Get him, Helger!" "Sort him out, bru!" I make it outside in time to coch up my breakfast on the red dirt. As I wipe my mouth I hear footsteps crunching and the first-period teacher, Mrs. Snopes for maths, is there asking if I'm okay. I tell her I'm not feeling so hot and she glances at the vomit and gives me permission to go to the sickroom.

I head down the stairs off the Pimple and start to run at the bottom. I'm moving fast but thinking even faster. There is no way to avoid this — once a rawl is booked it is booked and the whole school will carry me to it if they have to. Even if I duck it now, they'll just reschedule and get me later. I'm going to have to handle this. But if I do it like I'm thinking I can, I'm going to need to get home and get the secret thing I have in the Sandy Hole because I'm going to need it afterwards. That's crucial, the afterwards. The time has come. I race to the tickey box in the corridor behind the synagogue. When I dial Arlene's office at the Yard she answers first ring. I tell her I'm in big trouble cos I left my homework at home and I need a huge favour or I might fail the whole year. Arlene's busy but after some begging she agrees to give me a lift. When she arrives at the main gate she signs for me and the camera logs my exit. At the house I run straight to the Sandy Hole and collect what I came for, placing it carefully in my blazer's inside pocket. Arlene drops me back at school with plenty of time left in the period. The classes before first break are an agony, every tick of the minute hand feels like another twist on an invisible rack. Ten minutes before the break bell, I head for the door. Adon Spitzer, our Hebrew master, shouts at me but I ignore him and start running, my satchel bouncing on my back. I force myself to slow down when I hit the stairs up to the rugby fields, I don't want to get so exhausted that I'm not thinking properly. I count the stairs to occupy my mind. Sixty-seven, sixty-eight. Even holding myself back, I'm still panting at the top. I slow even more as I walk across the wide rugby field of browned dry grass. I realise I'm still counting steps. Two hundred and eleven. Be calm and think properly. The tuck shop is a yellow-brick building with a flat roof, in front is the slasto square. But the area behind it is a patch of raggedy weeds that everyone calls the Mielies cos it looks like a patch of dry cornstalks all yellow and droopy in the sun. On the other side of it is the big athletics storeroom. When I reach its doors, I check the number on the lock, and then head up to the Gooch's office, saying a little prayer. I have my copy of his office key, but the door is unlocked and my little prayer has been answered cos I don't see anyone as I duck in and fish a key off the row in the passage behind the office.

By the time I get back to the storeroom, I'm starting to sweat and the break bell goes off. In a few minutes the whole school will be foaming up onto the rugby fields like a bubble bath overflowing. My hands are shaking so badly it takes a few tries to get the key to work. Inside, I find what I'm looking for and bring it out and lock the door. I wade into the weeds and put my satchel down and squat low and set the thing. Then I stand up, patting the bulk in my inside pocket. I take the blazer off and fold it carefully and put it down on top of the satchel. I walk out of the weeds, unbuttoning and rolling up my sleeves as I go. After a few seconds I go back in to check the thing again and then I make a mark with my heel in the ground at the edge of the weeds. Far away, across the rugby field, the first ones are starting to bubble up now, off the stairs. I step into the clear and stand there feeling my legs vibrating under me and watching the purple blazers multiply. One law of our school is that you must *always* wear your blazer outside of class. If you're busted without it on you get punished by Volper — three strokes from a cane of his choice. A lot of the blazers start pouring down toward the tuck shop, but some of them see me and stand there, staring, pointing. It takes a while for the word to spread, that Helger is over there by the Mielies. The first ones to reach me are excited, a bunch of Standard Six lighties bouncing around, some of them with cans of col'drink in their hands. "Are you seriously ganna rawl Crackcrack Lohrmann? You must be off your skull." "He's ganna stuff you up, china." "You sailing for a nailing, bru." I ignore them and they comment on that too. "He's the silent-type hero, he reckons he's Dirty Harry." "Dirty Harry was staunch, this Helger's like a twig. Bet you okes five bucks Crackcrack snaps him in half in like under ten seconds." "Nooit, hey. He won't last five . . ."

Then the prefects show up and ask me when I'm going down to the tuck, Crackcrack is there waiting. I say, "Tell him I'm waiting right here. Tell him if he doesn't come, he's chickening out."

"But rawls are always in front of the tuck, you know that."

"Tell him right here."

The prefects go and fetch the head boy, Neville Shankster. Head boy is the prefect of the prefects, Volper's favourite little prince with his steel glasses and his perfect tie knot. He tells me rawls are always in front of the tuck. "I stand here," I say. "Tell that wanker is it yes or no. I'm waiting and I don't have all stuffing day." Neville tells me I'm being a prick. "There's such a thing as respect," he says. "I can see why people want to klup you all the time." "Just run along and fetch him," I say.

I've started to walk up and down so my shaky legs don't show and my breaths are snorting in my nostrils and my insides are shaking because my heart is thumping so fast. *Be calm and think properly.* I keep looking back and making sure I can see the mark I made. Then I sort of move more into myself, looking down, forgetting about the noise and the light around me, and when I look up again there's a whole wall of blazers and faces in a big semicircle. The prefects are shoving them back. Spunny's big head is in the second row—he gives me a middle finger. Then the ranks of the blazers are splitting apart, and through them comes Crackcrack, the Strongest Lad, followed by Sardines Polovitz and some other cronies of his whose names I'm not sure of. Crackcrack stands opposite me and starts jumping up and down and wheeling his long arms and showing his teeth and biting the air. Head boy Neville moves in between us, he's saying something but I can't make sense of the words. Then he's stepping back, shouting something, and time feels sticky, like I'm trying to move as fast as I can but I'm moving through honey. Crackcrack rips his tie off and rushes at me. He's waited till the last second to pull his tie off so he wouldn't remind me to do the same, which is lank boff of him I have to admit, as I flash on what he did to Beefus. Too late now to get mine off.

"Arrrrr!" Crackcrack is screaming as he sprints in with one long arm stretched at me and the other balled up in a bony yellow fist and pulled all the way back behind him. He's already three-quarters of the way to me when I turn around and run into the weeds. This must have paused him, cos I hear him shout behind me, "Aw come *on,* you fucken puss, what's this!" Then he is crashing in after. Meantime I've bent over and I'm grabbing at the ground like mad but for like half a bad second I'm shitting myself cos I can't get my fingers around it and a kick comes smashing through the weeds, the tooled leather slices across my thigh but then my hands have it, they have it, and I'm spinning and coming up with the thing tight in my double grip and I see Crackcrack, see his face change. Then I'm lunging at him through the sticky-honey time, going all the way, as he jumps back and I'm feeling it hit and then pulling and lunging again, out of the weeds now and under the bright sun and the faces behind Crackcrack are all stretched long with shock as he trips and sits down and tries to scoot back with his arms held out. There's blood, red and red. On the dust, on the white shirt. He's screaming as he scoots back on his arse and I'm still lunging at him and everything's taking so bladdy long to happen and there is someone else who is screaming too, someone close by in the crowd, making a terrible sound, it sounds like some girl shrieking and why won't they shut her up already? But when I rub my mouth on my shoulder I feel it moving and I know who it is. It's me.

46

Nobody else makes a sound. They're all just standing there like it's assembly, a whole school paralyzed. Only Crackcrack is mewling and sobbing, he's on his side now and clawing at the ground as he drags himself, his other hand around his middle. Head boy Neville steps up slowly and steps over him and stands there in front of me with his arms out. He's the first one to speak. "Put it down, Martin. Put it down." I look down. I'm still holding the javelin in my fists. It sticks out ahead of me like a giant needle, the point of it red now. As I stare at it, some of the red drips off. I look up and see prefects on all sides, homing in on me. I make my hands open. The javelin drops. The first rugby tackle hits me from the left — it's a good one, low and hard, the Gooch would be proud. Neville jumps me from the front as I go down and they all pile on, pinning me with overkill weight. I try to tell them that I'm not struggling but they're not listening and even if they were I don't have the breath to make myself heard. They lift me up. People are shouting for the paramedic. Neville says take him to the office and they start to march me and I get walked a few feet with my hands twisted up behind my back before I dig my heels in. "Wait, okes," I say. "My blazer is there. *I need my blazer.*" I start struggling until someone says I got it and then throws it over my head. I get marched down all the way to the office like that, my notorious polyester blazer hanging over me like a hood of shame. The only one who talks is Neville. "You're going to be arrested for this," he says. "Volper will call the cops, you know. You'll go to prison. You're bladdy mad in the head."

We're in front of the office, the glass wall with the little hole in it. They unhand me and step back a little. I roll my sleeves down and put my blazer on. "You're such a fuck-up," says a prefect called, I think, Abramson. "You're such scum." He sounds sort of amazed, like he's making a discovery he still can't believe. I ignore him, straightening my blazer collars as Mrs. Brune, the wrinkled gnome, pops up behind her glass, announcing in a voice all whispery and serious, "He's ready now. He's waiting in the office." I go through the doorway to the right of the glass, into the white passage. As I pass Brune's door she clicks her tongue, a disgusted sound meant for me. The door to Volper's office is half open. I stand there for a few seconds, patting my blazer to feel the pocket even though I know it's there because I've been feeling it against my ribs. *Be calm and think properly.* This is the real part, this was always the real part of it. *You've done the other, you can do this too, Martin. Just think, thin —*

"*Get in here!*"

I step through and close the door behind me and when I turn I find Volper standing in his shirtsleeves holding a phone receiver to his chest. He waves me forward as he sits down and pivots around on his leather chair, away from me. "Yes . . . yes," he says. "Fine. Oh I will. Thank you." He swings back and hangs the phone up, tells me, "That was Mrs. Dalgleish at the sickroom. They've called an ambulance for Lohrmann." He stares at me and my eyes go sliding over the huge teak desk till they stop at the photographs with the silver frames. "That's your wife, hey," is what I hear myself hoarsely murmuring over the dumdumdum of my pulse in my ears.

"What?" says Volper. "What did you say to me?"

I move closer to the desk, like right up against it, and too softly I say, "I have. Something. For you."

He stares at me and then his eyes go slitty. "Have you been taking drugs?"

I don't answer. I lift up my right hand and put it under my blazer. Volper's eyes drop to my chest. My hand stays under the blazer.

Volper blinks fast and shoots to his feet. One shoulder starts going up and down like a sewing needle. He's frowning like I just spoke to him in Japanese or something. Slowly I pull my hand out of my blazer and when he sees what I am holding his whole face relaxes again. I look down at the yellow envelope with elastics around it. It hits me that a person could imagine it's full of money, like a bribe, and that makes me think of Hugo on the back stoep at Oberholzer's place. *Go off my land, Jew.* Volper is saying, "When I'm good and finished with you, giving you the lesson of your young life — believe me — then and only then will I be telephoning the police force. You're going home in the back of a police car today, young man. Meditate on that." I'm having trouble speaking so I just hold up the folded envelope and shake it at him and he says, "What is this nonsense?" Then he says, "You *are* on drugs, aren't you. Your parents will be — well I don't know what, actually. Helgers." He shakes his head, wincing. Then he says, "Get over to the corner. I am going to thrash some sense into your soul. And then I'm going to thrash you some more. I'm going to thrash you till my arm falls off. You could have killed that boy. You could have been facing a murder charge! You bloody imbecile!" I just keep standing there, holding the envelope out. "Helger!" he screams at me. *"Do you hear me Hel-gerrr!"*

My hand jerks, tossing the envelope. But I'm so tense the throw is pathetic, it doesn't reach him, flopping on the desk. "Take it," I hear myself rasp. Volper isn't listening, he's saying, "You get over to that corner. Right now." I clear my throat and say, "I suggest —" But it's too soft and Volper is shouting again. I clear my throat once more and when he stops I point at the envelope and speak up and say, "Suggest you look at that." I keep pointing, not moving, and Volper says, "What is this?" He leans forward and pokes at it and then he picks it up and rolls off the elastics and opens the envelope. His hand with its nicely shined nails delves inside and brings out the photocopied pages with the photos paper-clipped to them. Those photocopies were all done on the Nashua copier in the library upstairs, and the photos are colour prints of the originals that I made in the photo lab, working alone in the time after midnight when the school belongs to me, only me. Volper keeps saying *What is this nonsense* as he shuffles the pages and the photos but the way he's saying it is all weird, over and over, like he doesn't know that his mouth is in drive, and it's getting softer. All-a-sudden he drops the lot like they are burning hot. But his hands stay paralyzed, the fingers spread wide open over the pages. I say to him, "I have other copies of all of those. You know where I got them from." I look to the parquet floor in the corner, now under the rug. And Volper rotates his head like he's made of wood and looks that way too. His lips have gone white — I'm talking Lux soap white like I've never seen before on a human being. He looks down at the spilled photos and the pages and he makes this funny throttling sound and reaches for them, but then he freezes again and sort of sways there on his feet, backwards and forwards, and he says the word *no* nine or ten or twelve times, I'm not counting exactly. "Yes," I say. "I've got them. Copies. Lots. And I will send copies everywhere. I mean to everyone."

"You can't," says Volper. He sits down. Now that crazy white of the lips is starting to pop up in patches all over his face.

"I'm sorry," I say. "I just want to be left alone, you know?" I look down at the prints. From where I'm standing I can see the one of Volper with the smiling young man with the good chest muscles where the two of them are naked and hugging together, looking into the lens. The print that is half underneath this is the same young man kissing Volper's neck. Beside it is the one with the different young man, lying naked on his tummy with the shadow of the photographer next to him and the photographer — it's Volper — is in the mirror and he is naked and he's caught a major bone, his stiff thing sticking out under his fat belly, and there's a swimming pool showing through the door. It makes me remember what it was like when Annie and I first found these in the little wooden box in the safe, the incredible feeling of can this be true, can this be real? And then seeing that it was. And I even know some of the lines in those letters by heart. *I dream of you and hunger for you. I think of you every time I'm alone I want you, only you and I'm jealous of the Bitch.* That was the young man with the spiky handwriting, the other one was more flowy. That was the one who wrote, *I'm your darling I'm your whore I'm whoever you want me to be, Arn. Love and love.* I remember how Annie and I looked up their names in old year-books and worked out who they were, ex-students. One's a big-shot lawyer with his own kids now. "I'll tell you what," I say to Mr. Volper. "I'm going to go now, oright? I won't send these to anyone. Or tell any-one. And all you have to do is leave me alone. How's that?"

Volper looks up, he's still swaying. It's like he's just taken one of my brother's right hooks to the temple but somehow managed to stay on his feet. His voice is small. "How did you get these?"

"I was in here once and you left me alone. I found the safe. You had left it open. I looked inside."

He frowns. "When? No. No. How could you have?"

"I made copies and put them back."

"That's impossible."

"Well, I have them. You don't have to believe what I'm saying. Just look there in front of your eyes."

"No. Who gave these to you? Was it — one of them?"

"Nobody gave them. I got them from the safe. Nobody else knows. I'm the only one. I know about the safe, you can see that, I'm telling you it's there. Think about it."

He looks down at the photos again. His wide scarecrow head with its thick yellow thatch is nodding all trembly on his squat neck like he's suddenly got Parkinson's or something. "Oh you're a filthy individual," he says to his frozen hands. "Oh you are a maggot indeed. A filthy, dirty, disgusting individual. Oh. You filthy Helger."

"That's okay," I say. "You can call me what you like. So long as you leave me alone, I mean completely. Do not call the cops on me. And make sure I don't get charged. Talk to the parents, whoever. Just make sure. From now on I don't ever get punished for anything again. So long as you stick to that, we'll be fine. Otherwise you know what will happen, hey. I'll send copies of those to the board, to your wife. To the papers, to the cops, the government, to bladdy everyone I can." I start backing away to the door and by the time I reach it there are tears coming down Volper's white shaky face.

"Wait," he says "Wait."

"Just leave me alone," I say. "And I'll do the same. That's all."

47

Arlene is frying kingclip for supper when the phone rings and she picks it off the wall by the bread box. I'm reading *Jock of the Bushveld* for like the nineteenth time cos it makes me feel sort of cosy and I need cosy cos Jesus Christ what a bladdy day this has been. Then Arlene says it's for me and it's like a fresh kick in the guts all over again. I'm sure it's the cops with the news that Crackcrack just pegged off. *I've killed a man, Ma — just like in that song by Queen, what do you think of that, Ma?* Ja, that's right, I stuck him with a sports javelin like I was trying to make a sosatie out of the fellow. It didn't go in very deep, I pulled it short, just gave him a little prick or two in the liver (cos that's what pricks deserve ha ha) but infection got in and finished him off or I nicked an artery or — "Hellooo," Arlene is singing, "ground control to Martin, Mar-tin."

"Who is it?"

"I don't know."

"Is it someone official, like?"

She frowns at me. "No. Why're you asking that?"

"*Is it?*"

"What's the matter? It sounds like a friend of yours that's all."

I stretch the cord into the passage, covering my mouth. "Yes, who's this?"

"Martin, that you? Have you just been to the dentist or summin?" Pats. Thank God Almighty. And then I remember I gave him my phone number on Saturday night. He wants to tell me I was absolutely right, he made a mistake about seeing Marcus.

"But you were so sure," I say. "You said you would ask around. And about Dynamite Gym? Did he go there?"

There's this long silence and then he says, "Martin, does it really matter what your brother did long ago? I made a mistake, I'm telling you it wazzen him." There's a crackle and a soft whoosh — he's smoking. "Check, bru," he says. "I did swing by the Dynamite, ukay. I went there in person and those okes, they tuned me solid to loz it."

"So what if they did?"

"If *those* okes tell you let something go, you let it go."

"Fine. You know what? I'll go myself —"

"Hey hey hey. You'll do nothing. You will do absolutely zilch, man, Martin! I'm serious about that. Remember what already nearly happened to you at Xanadu."

Now I'm helping Arlene set the table, my head full of Marcus. I see him again hitting the heavy bag and behind the wheel of the Barracuda. Silent Marcus with his thick neck and his secret life. All those secrets make him heavy, like we learned in physics how a great mass pulls things towards it, that's what gravity is. Marcus has gravity. He doesn't even need to be here at home to make everything orbit him.

When Isaac gets home we can all see straightaway that he is in a dark mood. I make sure to give him an extra-large whisky as he washes without saying a word to anyone. Then it's the six o'clock news with old Michael de Morgan and the top story is about the "fruitful talks" our foreign minister, Pik Botha, says we've had with the Thatcher government. Old Pik with his trimmed moustache and his Hitler side part and his bouncy attitude. Everything is just super fine, says old Pik. He tells the camera that Commonwealth countries should watch their own backyards before criticising South Africa, like the Canadians, for instance, and how they treat their own Indians over there. The odd thing is I don't hear any stomping or shouting from Isaac. I look at him with the side of my eye and I can see Arlene is doing the same in her chair next to his. Isaac has his feet up, yes, but the legs are still. He's just sitting there staring, sunk down in his chair with his chin on his chest and his whisky glass on his belly, not moving, not saying a thing. The news stories go by — a car bomb went off outside Ellis Park rugby stadium, a black off-duty cop got buried alive by a mob in a township cemetery when he went there for the funeral of his friend and someone pointed him out as a cop — and there is not one shout of "bladdy schmocks" or "stupid ponce" or "useless bladdy twat" from Isaac, there's not even one really good, loud *bullshit!* It's so strange it makes me start to worry about him, like has he finally gone and had a cardiac or something? Arlene must be having the same type of thoughts cos right before we get up for the supper table at the end of the news, she asks him if he is all right. She has to ask him twice, like snap him out of his own little daze there. He looks around and says he dropped in at the Grand Lion Tavern on his way home. Arlene doesn't say anything but her eyebrows go up high — Isaac stopped going to taverns years ago because he was going too much. Now he says all the talk there at the Grand Lion, it really got to him. People going on about buying guns and Krugerrands and tinned food and whatnot. They're talking about emergency escape plans. They're talking visas for New Zealand, Australia — that's nothing new but now it's also Argentina, Uruguay, *anywhere else*. And he says it's all the moving vans and the FOR SALE signs he noticed on the drive back when he looked for them instead of pretending they weren't there. And the gold price dropped again and the rand did too against the dollar. We have to face it, these sanctions are really starting to bite hard. We can't go on squeezing oil out of coal forever, which is what we've been doing to keep the economy squeaking along. We can't make everything ourselves. And it's true Botha will be frekking off and in the grave any day now but this guy De Klerk who the Nats have lined up to replace him is no different, just another bald hardegat, another tough-guy Afrikaner, and it's ganna be more and more of the same. It all makes him think of Rhodesia in the last years under Ian Smith when the country tried to go it alone, but you can't go it alone, can you . . .

"This doesn't sound like you, Ize!" says Arlene. Which is so true because normally if there's any talk about emigration it comes from her, with Isaac calling her a defeatist and telling her never, *never*. But it's not only his words that don't sound like him, it's the voice too. He sounds hoarse and so tired. Arlene says, "Why did you go to the pub, Ize? Is there something wrong? Did something happen?" His eyes are red — and suddenly I realise when they were like that last, and I know what he is going to say before he opens his mouth. "Something wrong?" he says. "Ja, there is. Very wrong."

Arlene puts her hand over her mouth. I see that she's got it also, she's clicked what has happened. "Oh no," she says. "I'm so sorry."

"It's oright," says Isaac, looking away. "Oright." But it's really not.

48

I think we are the only whites here, but it doesn't feel strange because all around us are the staff. There's Winston Mathenjwa, and here's Thomas Kgase. But looking at the other faces I'm not surprised to see that Dube and Orbert and Sammy and them are not around, hardly any of those younger guys have come, even though Isaac organised taxis and closed the Yard for the morning out of respect. The women start to sing a new song, their voices are so powerful, some of them leading and the rest coming after in a harmony that goes up and up like a huge ocean wave about to crash and all the hairs prickle on the back of my neck. We're all standing on an open field of mostly dust except for the crosses and there's a priest and a deep rectangle cut into the earth under the wide-open sky, hazy blue. In the distance I can see power lines and the rooftops of Orlando East in the township of Soweto. In close is the back of a small brick building with a poking roof, the Apostles' First African

Church. The singing stops and the pastor, who has on a white robe with
a blue sash, says words in African. The mourners are wearing black, I
see Gugu in a black dress shiny in the sun and Silas Mabuza's wives —
widows — are in the row next to her, with wide black hats, and the coffin sits on the ground in front of them. I look to my left. Isaac with his
red eyes is at the end, Arlene is next to me, and Hugo is to my right.
Now the men are lifting the coffin and lowering it into the hole with
ropes. Victor is with them. The next part is like a Jewish funeral cos
the men are getting ready to take turns with a shovel to throw the sand
down onto the coffin. But Isaac takes off his jacket and hands it to Arlene and zips across and quickly grabs that shovel right out the hands
of the first guy. He starts shoveling away like a machine. When other
people tap him on the back for their turn he ignores them and keeps
going and eventually they stop trying and it's only him, working away,
the sweat coming through his shirt, breathing hard, until that hole is
filled up all the way. Arlene is crying now so I put my arm around her.
Those church women have been singing all the time and now they go
quiet and then start up with a new song that just about explodes out of
their mouths, I swear. I feel it like claws inside my chest. I close my eyes
for a few seconds and when I open them I see people turning.

There's a vehicle on the dry road, boiling up dust. Oh shit. It's a
Ford Cortina. I watch it pulling up by the church. Isaac has paid for a
little reception there and there are trestle tables put out in front by the
roasting spit, with cast-iron three-legged pots full of mielie pap. When
we all walk over we find there's a tall man by the tables and he's lifted
up the plastic cover over the meat and morogo greens, and he's shoveling food to his mouth with his bare hand. Captain Bokkie Oberholzer.
In the crisp blue uniform of the riot police with the square cap and the
yellow marks of his rank on the shoulders. The people get all hesitant,
seeing this cop, but Oberholzer comes up and shakes hands with the
pastor and then he goes over to Victor and shakes with him and then
some of the other family. He comes sauntering around and plants his

tall self in front of my father and puts out his hand. Isaac only looks at him — just like that day at the Yard. Arlene breaks the tension by reaching across and shaking the hand instead. Meantime the rest of the people have moved past to the tables and are loading their paper plates.

"Izzen this something, hey?" says Oberholzer, and he's looking at me. Arlene takes Isaac's arm and moves off with him quickly. Oberholzer turns his head to watch them go, saying, "A whole lamb on the spit killed fresh for this, I see. I don't reckon there's been such a lekker chow here in Orlando in ages. Hell, this is like better than *we* have. Your old man is really something, hey? Hey?"

"Ja, Kaptein," I say.

"Ja, *Kaptein*," he repeats, laughing at my pronunciation because I used the Afrikaans word. "So tense, hey. Such a tense young man. Hey, how you been, young Martin?" I can see Isaac behind, watching us from the table, his face getting red. Hugo starts to talk but Oberholzer holds up a hand without looking at him. To me he says, "I havun seen you in such a while. What the Americans call *a coon's age*." He chuckles. "They got some funny sayings those Americans, hey. You would be the one to know what I am talking about, hey."

I say, "Me?"

"Having yourself a juicy American girlfriend like that."

"I don't have a girlfriend."

"Oh really," Oberholzer says. "I am in mistake then." Behind him by the table I see Arlene has her hand on Isaac's arm. He twitches it off. No — he's coming back now, walking with his head down. It must show in my face cos Oberholzer looks behind. "Here comes the old man," he says. "Wants to have a lekker gesels with me, a good old chat. That is nice, I will always have plenny to talk about with Isaac Helger."

Hugo says, "Captain —"

Oberholzer swings his smile back onto Hugo and says with his voice all pleasant, "Shut your hole, fat man." Hugo doesn't say anything and Oberholzer turns to Isaac and says, "'Lo again, Mr. Helger!"

"Can you please tell me why you here?"

"Hell," says Oberholzer, "that is jus the question I have for *you*. You in my world here. Do you have permissions on you to be here in a location?"

Tiny eggs of sweat are coming through the rubbery skin of my father's face. "Look," he says. "Silas was a good, good man. We just paying respect here, that is all."

"Ja," says Oberholzer, "is very touching. But you happen to be in a war zone. You standing on a battlefield."

"Ach come off it, man," Hugo says.

Oberholzer takes off his cap and grins past them. Arlene is walking up. She looks like she really doesn't want to. She's going to try get my father away again. Oberholzer says, "'Lo there, Mrs. Helger! How are you? How is your son doing there, up on the border, keeping us all safe in our beds. It is the real grensvegters, the real fighters like Marcus Helger, that I genuine take my hat off to." And he waggles the cap in his hand.

Arlene smiles with her lips thin. "Thank you. You know his name? My son."

Oberholzer says of course. "I know *all* the Helgers." He looks at us all and it's a stiff silence, his eyes going big, like he's about to say something else but then he doesn't, he just puts his cap back on.

"Well, he's fine," Arlene says, "thank God for that. Just wish he would get more leave and come see us."

"Ja, war is blerry tough," Oberholzer says. "You know it is only out of care for your security that I come by. It might look all nice-nice with all the food and the friendly folk but you are targets out here. Funerals brings terrorists like flies to shit. They give their little speeches and then the AK machine guns come out, takka-takka. Next thing it's my arse in trouble cos a whole white family who should not be there got theyselves mowed down or even necklaced, burnt alive right here on a Wednesday morning."

"Oh, Captain," Arlene says, "but this is not a danger here, surely."

Oberholzer clicks his long fingers. "Can happen like *that,* madam. In one split of second. Belee me."

"Ukay," says Isaac. "You made your point. We only ganna stay another couple of minutes and we will be on our way."

"No," says Oberholzer, "I really think your time is up. Your scrapboy is in the ground now, so that's that." And he looks at his watch and then he sucks through his nose and spits down a coin of green snot.

Isaac looks at it and looks up and he says, "You know what, Captain? This is the funeral of Silas Mabuza, this is what this is. We don't want any trouble. All I wanna do — no, Arlene, let me, I want to say it — all I wanted to do here is to bury a man in dignity this morning. That is it."

"Ja, ja," Oberholzer says. "That is touching. I understand a hunned per cent. I tell you, I had a dog one time, fantastic dog. I remember when he died and we buried him out on the plot there, I was also very heartsore. We used to call him Kaffirtjie, you know, cos he had such black fur —"

Isaac lunges and suddenly Arlene and Hugo are between him and Oberholzer, Isaac shouting, "Keep your mouth shut! Keep your bladdy mouth off him! I don't care you got a uniform —"

Oberholzer never stops smiling, I reckon he's loving this, all calm as he says, "Listen, listen, listen. Let's not all get out of hand now. We don't need any Jewish tempers going off, ha ha. Listen. All seriousness, Mr. Isaac Helger. I also have sympathy because me too, *I don't believe it could have been a traffic accident either.*"

It goes quiet except someone gasps. Not Arlene, not Hugo — it's me. Isaac is frowning and Oberholzer shoots me a wink, so fast I wonder if it really happened. Isaac is saying, "What's that sposed to mean?"

Oberholzer pretends like he doesn't understand. "What's what mean?"

Isaac says, "What you just said, not a traffic accident."

"Da," I say, "let's just go, hey."

"It's okay, Junior," says Oberholzer. "I give a permission. You can stay for a minute more." He turns to Isaac. "Well these are just my thoughts, you know, after looking at the file."

"What file? What are you saying?"

"Da," I say, "Da, let's leave it." Cos I'm panicking now, remembering what Gugu and Winston both told me. But Isaac is sweeping his arm at me, saying shush, and he repeats his question to Oberholzer, who says, "Maybe it's not such a good idea to throw round suspicions. On those boys."

"Who's this?" says Isaac.

"You know. Sammy Nongalo. Dube Gumede. Orbert Vezi."

I look at Hugo in the silence and he has a hand over his eyes. Arlene's mouth is open. Isaac says, "How do you know those names?"

"Cos they in the file," Oberholzer says. "They are communist infiltrators. They are ANC. Labour organisers."

"Like bladdy hell they are."

"Those boys of yours know all about brake lines. And what can be done. I'm surprised you haven't heard any talk. When they want a union they stop at nothing, those kind of people. Anyway, have a nice day, hey." He touches his cap. "Enjoy the rest of the funeral."

49

Arlene insists on driving, says Isaac is too upset and had too much to drink, says they'll go straight home where Isaac can rest. Meantime Hugo steers me to the Jag. "I haven't heard from you, boyki. What's going on? When are you going to call me about your card? Have you made your plans yet?"

I get in the car in silence. Hugo wheezes his bulk behind the steering wheel and then bangs on it. "Did you see that? You see what just happened? This cop is mental! He's got a vendetta. I was looking at the way he was looking at you. Like a bladdy hyena. This is not a game, hey Martin. You coming with me to my place right now and taking that green card."

"No," I say, watching Arlene driving away with my father. "We need to go to the Yard."

"What for?"

"In case they go there instead of home."

"So what if they do?"

"Da might do something. I need to talk to him first, calm him down."

"Ja, bladdy good luck with that."

Hugo drives the long way back to Vrededorp, irritating me. It's because he wants to work on me about America, sell me on the idea I need to leave this country like now. Well, he's a salesman and that's what they do. "You need to make the leap already, man," he says. "Do it! Don't wait. This Oberholzer is one crafty, dangery son of a whore, I'm telling you."

"You've said that already, Hugo. Five times. Ten."

"Truth can never be said enough."

I'm looking out the window, at a street with low industrial units and shopfronts. Avoiding the highway, we've come into town from South Joburg. I see dirty alleys and razor wire and cracked bricks. I see peeling paint and signs with addresses. "Wait a second," I say. "This is Marshall Street?"

"Ja, that's right."

I stare at the next number. "Hey, Hugo, do us a favour?"

"Whatzit?"

"There's a place I wanna have a quick look at, along here."

"Whatzit?"

I tell him the number — not hard to remember, I looked it up in the yellow pages the day after Pats told me about it. Hugo slows down and pulls up opposite a low whitewashed building with garage doors that are rolled up. Inside I can see men moving around, wearing bright exercise clothes. I see one with a weight bar on his shoulders, going up and down. The bottom of a boxing ring is visible, the legs of fighters working in there, clashing and bouncing back. "Know something?" Hugo says. "Your daddy used to work around here when he started out, in panel-beating as apprentice."

"Ja?"

"Oh ja. Funny how things go round." He snorts. "So what, you wanna be a boxer like your brother was now? Get your brains nicely punched in."

"Hugo, have you ever heard of this place?"

"This? No, boxing's not for me, my boy. I'm one for the sport of kings. The ponies." Then he says, "Dynamite, hey." He's reading the sign. It has a logo that's bigger than the words, two sticks of dynamite inside a fist. I ask him if it rings a bell, the name. He shakes his head. "No. Why, should it?"

"I spose not," I say. "I just wanted to see it. I believe that Marcus maybe used to train here."

"I'm not sure," Hugo says, "that I like the vibes round here, boyki." He's looking into the rearview. I turn around and see a man cutting across the street. He reaches the pavement on our side and comes towards us, a big white oke with a brush cut and a thick build, wearing a tracksuit and gold chains. "He looks like he wants a word," Hugo says, his eyes on the mirror. "What is this place?"

"Maybe you should ask around, Hugo," I tell him. "I'm sure you'll have friends who have heard of it." That makes Hugo's eyebrows shoot straight up. He drops the brake and drives smoothly away. The man watches us go, his hands on his hips.

50

At the Yard, Arlene is in her car out front. Hugo drops me and leaves, he's got a meeting in Randburg. Arlene's upset, says she just dropped Isaac off. "He insisted," she says. "You know how your father is. You can't talk to the man when he gets like this. He told me to go home. Do you want a lift? I'm stopping at the Pick n Pay first." I shake my head, saying I'll come home with Isaac. "You can change at home and I'll take you to school," she says. "Still have a few hours left."

"I want to try talk to him."

I find my father sitting on the stairs at the exit doors at the back, lacing on a pair of his high boots, the steel-toed ones. On the stair next to him is a welding glove and the shaft of a pinion, a heavy chunk of greasy steel. "What you doing here?" he says. "Go home, Martin. Go to school."

"Da," I say, "you always taught me give yourself a cooling-off period. Remember that? Before you get too excited, too hitsik. You can't take things back. And you've had a few drinks."

He looks up at me. "It's fine, Martin. Go home. I'm just ganna sort this."

"How?"

"The way it's always been, when it has to be."

"Don't be silly, Da. That Oberholzer he is full of propaganda. He hates us cos of . . . what you did to his father."

Isaac's hands stop moving. "Who told you that?"

"Hugo."

"Big mouth. Big mouth, Hugo, never bladdy changes." He goes back to lacing.

"Da, can I be honest? I also heard rumours, myself, about Dube and Orbert and them."

"You heard a rumour. Why didn't you tell me? Nobody tells me a thing in my own Yard."

"*This* is exactly why, Da. Cos it's probably not true but you fly off the handle. You need to calm down, Da. Please. People didn't tell you cos they're scared you'd even close down the whole Yard. Can't you see this is what Oberholzer wants?"

"Don't talk bladdy crap. I'd never shut this place down, ever." He knots the last of it and stands up in those heavy boots. "This place is *us,* Martin. If there's a cancer, I'll cut it out. I know how to deal with it. The way we always have. Me and Silas." When he says that name his eyes get shiny. Then he bends and picks up the glove and the pinion shaft. "Da, wait," I say. "Da!" But he's already banging through the doors and all I can do is run after. I follow behind him through the wrecks and as he's marching he starts shouting for Thomas, for Winston, but they must still be at the funeral cos only old Oscar comes instead, all quiet and serious. "Yes, baas?" And Isaac tells him, "Get everyone who's here. I don't care what they doing. I want them all over there by the crusher. Right now. The lot." I have to jog every few steps to keep up with Isaac even though his legs are so short compared to mine. It's like he's walking on springs. "Da," I say, "leave it, man. If it is true what they did, then it's for the police. We can report." He snorts. "Don't make me laugh. Oberholzer *is* the cops. They even have a file, he said, you heard the man. Nothing will come of it except my boys will lose respect for me. That can't happen." He looks at me and it's almost like he's surprised I'm still there. "What you doing? Go back inside, Martin. This is not for you to see." I don't say anything, just keep on walking behind him and then he stops. "Martin. I said this is not for you."

"What *is* for me, Da?"

"What's for you is that good school I send you to. What is for you is a good education and a nice office one day. Where you can keep your soft hands clean and spend your days talking nicely. *That* is what's for you, Martin."

"Maybe this is my office, Da. If it is not ganna be Marcus."

He squints at me. "Martin, there's a rough side to how things work here. Running this place. You have to have it in you or you go under. It's not so nice, but it has to be."

"I know, Da."

"Do you?"

"Ja, I do."

"We'll see," he says, and goes on and I follow. We reach the crusher near the back wall and the sliding gate to the street, open now. Isaac stands there waiting while I keep back. After a while he sees my shadow because he waves for me to move back more which I do. The staff arrive in little groups, standing around, looking nervous. Most of the older guys are still at the funeral, so it's a young group that Isaac addresses. "Right. I want Dube and Orbert and Sammy. Come." He points, and the three step forward. "These men know exactly what they done. It was them who put Silas in the hospital. Messed up his brakes to make an accident. Why? Cos they wanna start up union shit right here in our Yard, in our *family*, don't think that I don't know all about it. Now. I always treated you all bladdy well. It was me and Silas here at this beginning. We built this place from nothing. I've always paid you better than anyone, took you on with no papers . . ." Then he switches languages, I think maybe it's Zulu but it's more probably that workplace mishmash, what they call fanagalo, and then: ". . . so Silas is gone now. Silas is dead. The funeral is over, he has passed on. These three here — quiet you! shut your mouths! — these three are the ones that done it and I been waiting to settle up. Now it's the time. Number one, you all three are finished here for good. You bladdy lucky I don't send you to police but we settle this in the family here."

"But we didn't!" says Dube suddenly. "We diden do it all. It was those other —"

"Shut up!" shouts Isaac. "You know you did! Be a man!" And then Sammy beside him speaks a few words. His voice is deep and calm and

Dube goes quiet. "You know you done it!" Isaac is shouting. The veins in his wrinkled neck are sticking out and his face looks like it's boiling over with hot blood. "We all know it. As sure as God made little green apples you bastards are the ones who cut those brakes! Now maybe you didn't mean to kill him dead — that is the only reason you ganna get off easy. But you will pay the price now. We settle like men. What you *know* you deserve." While he's speaking he is taking the heavy glove from his back pocket with one hand and the pinion shaft in the other. Then, as he gets to the end, he flips up that heavy shaft underhand. He pulls on the welding glove and grabs the pinion out the air and rushes across fast and punches that gloved fist with the steel core straight into the middle of Dube's face. There's a crunching noise and Dube's head flies back and he hits the ground stretched out, his eyes rolling back. I see teeth and pink blobs of blood on the dirt. Meantime Isaac is moving fast on his scuffling boots, kicking up red dust and going for the other two with that fisted glove cocked back behind his shoulder and his left hand reaching out. The closest man is Orbert and he sort of yelps as he tries to cover his head and turn away. Isaac grabs one of his arms and punches at him but misses cos Orbert is all hunched up and bending over. He's wailing and he goes down on one knee and Isaac swears and boots him in the side, thumping his ribs like a drum. The sleeve rips off in Isaac's hand. Orbert jumps up and runs, holding his side. All the others are behind and as Orbert runs at them, Isaac tells them, "Hold him, hold the bastard." He says it like an order, the same way he might tell them to move a front-ended Ford to the crusher. But when Orbert, making a whining sound, reaches the men, none of them do anything to stop him and he rushes through them and heads for the gate, running full stick. Isaac shouts, "What are you doing? Get the bastard! Hold the bladdy bastard! He's getting out! *Hold him!*" But the men just stand there in their Lion Metals overalls, they look at each other or at the sky or their feet. "He's getting out!" Isaac shouts. "He's a murdering bastard! Get him!" He stands there panting, glaring around all wild. Sammy Nongalo has meantime moved over to Dube lying there. Sammy kneels down and holds his head and talks to him all softly. Isaac is calling out names, pointing at different men. He seems sort of confused. Orbert's gone now, disappeared through the open gate. "What's wrong with you all?" Isaac says. "Why . . . why . . ."

Then he sees Sammy. Sammy looks up as Isaac goes at him, not running but taking deep quick steps. "You!" he says. "Wena! Umshaya wena!" Man, I'll beat you, man. "You the one, the big one behind it all." Sammy stands up straight and Isaac rushes him. Sammy sticks out his long arms and catches Isaac's shoulders and stops him. Sammy is very lean and strong. Isaac is breathing hard, the soles of the heavy boots slipping on the dust. "You can fire me," Sammy says. "I go. But no hitting." Isaac tries to headbutt him, but he's miles away. He tries with the heavy boots, going for the shins. Sammy dances smoothly and they go around. He says, "You stop it, I will leave. Stop it." Isaac, all red and shaking, says, "Bladdy murderer! You cut the brakes. You cut his brakes!" Then he fights hard again with his head down. After a while he shouts to the others, "Help me! Get him! Hold him!" And some African words. But no one moves. Isaac says, "What's the matter with you all? He's a murderer!" Then his voice breaks and he just keeps shouting, "Silas! Silas! Silas!" And every shout is like it's being ripped out of him, I swear. And I see the tears running out of his eyes over his tough old wrinkled cheeks. I start to run forward to help and Isaac sees me and shakes his head. "No! Not you, Martin. No. My boys. My boys. Help me, my boys." I stop. Sammy pushes Isaac off and steps away. Panting, Isaac sinks to one knee. Sammy looks at the men. "Silas is finish." He speaks in English, as if to make a point of using my father's language. "Is a new day now. No more baas who hits. I am going, but this place is not his. This place is yours also." On the ground, Dube is sitting up. Sammy goes over and helps him to his feet and the two of them walk through the staff who move aside for them, and then they go on out through the gate.

APOCALYPSE

51

It's like for the first time in my life I am seeing him as truly *old*. Something went out of him and now he sits crumpled in his soft chair under the full weight of his seventy years, drinking Scotch, saying nothing. The days of stamping on the ottoman are gone and never coming back, I'm sure. I mean they're talking about Botha offering *to meet with Nelson Mandela* and Isaac should be roaring at that screen, shouting it's all a bladdy con, a bunch of crap, Mandela's problee dead long ago! But he doesn't, he just sits slumped and drinking. He hasn't gone back to work since Wednesday and it's Sunday now and I missed school for the rest of last week also and Arlene says nothing about either of those things because — well, I mean we are all still in such total shock. For my dad it's a triple hit: first the death of Silas Mabuza, then what happened with his staff in the Yard (which Arlene does not know about in detail, and I don't plan to tell her), and now what has happened to all of us when the man in uniform showed up at our gate with an envelope we needed to sign for. A message from Die Suid-Afrikaanse Weermag, the South African Defence Force. Addressed to the family of the trooper with the magsnommer — the forces number — 88350343BA.

Arlene read it first, and Isaac read it over her shoulder, and then Isaac held it in one hand and held Arlene up with his other arm as she sort of fell against him in a way I'd never seen before and that's when

I ran out into the garden and started *Playing* like mad. I hadn't done any *Playing* in ages but I kept *Playing* and *Playing*, trying to block out everything and pretend I was someone else, a superhero that can fly back through time and change things, but it wasn't happening, the old *Playing* feelings wouldn't come, wouldn't sweep me away and make me feel light and happy again, just would not, and I don't think I'll ever do *Playing* again. I only felt dead and flat inside — as dead and flat as I was sure my brother Marcus now was. My father had to come out and get me and tell me, he had to physically pull my hands from my ears and say listen to me, listen to me, Martin, the message didn't say that he's killed. And I said well then what is it, then? *What the hell is it?*

That night I put it into a poem, my first poem in ages. It's a short one and I wrote it in one go, with no cross-outs.

MIA
By Martin Helger

Missing in Action
Missing in Action, man.

The best that can be said,
It's not the same as dead.

52

Getting colder. The leaves that've changed colour are falling off the trees all dry and there's frost on the ground in the mornings. Arlene kept pouring Isaac's Scotch down the sink but he just got more and put the bottles in the shed and now she's given up trying. I've never seen him drunk that it showed but he puts it away like water, and his old eyes have bloody veins in them and sometimes he doesn't shave or smells bad. He talks a lot too, going round in circles in a way he never used to, talking about how he *tried and tried with him,* my brother, to drum some sense and *make him bladdy see* what shit the army is and how *you gotta be mad in the head to join up.* But Marcus didn't believe him, *why didn't he believe me?* Or else it's how could it be that a nice Jewish boy with everything of the best that gets sent to the very best school, how could it be that he would drop out of university? For what reason, why, why? *To go and be cannon fodder for chutis? Can you explain that to me? Can anyone?* The army and war — it's the very worst thing to Isaac, it's what he always wanted most to keep us clear of and why he sent us to Solomon. Because he was in that other war, the big one, against the Nazis, and things happened to him over there that he will never ever talk about but still I've always known they're in him. I can feel it. A raw secret, like an ulcer on his soul that never heals.

Meantime Hugo has gone on the road and Arlene takes pills Dr. Slavin gave her and her face looks pale and bumpy like a mushroom. And I still haven't gone back to school. What's bizarre is how this house is full of insomniacs now. I used to be the only one, the secret tape maker — now I'm the only one who sleeps. Well, me and Zaydi. Isaac sits up with his bottle and his paper, Arlene walks around in her pyjamas like some ghost from an old English novel, her hands pinching each other, brewing up cups of tea and then leaving them around the house to get cold without drinking them. Zaydi seems the only one who hasn't changed much, maybe he prays a little more. He keeps mixing Marcus up with someone who is I think his brother from when he was a kid, in Dusat, that Jewish village that only exists in his head. I don't much listen to his stories anymore because they make me think of what Hugo told me, the bodies rotting in a pit — all those Jews murdered and other people living in their houses that they stole. But if they had left before the war they wouldn't have been killed, if they'd been able to — like I *am* able to leave if I want. And I need to talk to someone about it other than Hugo. Anyone. But I can't.

I've even missed two Wednesday visits in a row to Viljoen's, to check for Annie messages, and I do not go out at night. I just can't. Or won't. I know they're expecting bagloads of copied Fireseed tapes to be stuffed into that shed in Brandwag Park but *they* can get stuffed right now for all I care. I sleep like a log all night — I have a lot to make up for.

Now we're trying to eat supper and Arlene is picking at her food and then covering her face with her hands. Isaac gets up without a word and walks to the back door. Arlene says where are you going. In the window onto the backyard we watch him moving into the shed. He comes back with the tall wood axe. Heads straight up the passage to Marcus's old room. Arlene runs after him and I follow her, only Zaydi stays at the table with the gefilte fish. Isaac lifts the axe at the padlocked door. "I want to see it," he says. "I want to see his stuff. I want to look at my son's stuff." But Arlene grabs hold and won't let go and for a few seconds they struggle and then she swells up like I've never seen before. "Only him," she says. *"Only he will."* Isaac looks at her and then he drops the axe right there on the carpet and Arlene hugs him and I'm embarrassed to see the way they're hugging, it's too private. I return to the table, sit with Zaydi. When Arlene comes back, she tells me it's time I go back to school. Tomorrow morning. Enough is enough. I nod.

53

From the minute I get on the school bus, it's there. It's with me when I pass through security and as I walk up through the corridors and it follows me into the synagogue all the way to my pew. It's like the whole school has become this one enormous organism, a jellyfish with a million eyes all around me, watching and whispering. *See that oke? That's*

Martin Helger . . . Is that him, Martin Helger? . . . Seriously, hey, Mar-
tin Helger . . . Check, there's Martin Helger, check at him . . . doesn't look
like much but . . . I promise you, hey, he's . . . you don't ever wanna . . .
Martin Helger . . . the oke is . . . Martin Helger. Martin Helger. Martin
Helger . . . It's not about my brother anymore. It's me. I'm the kid who
put Crackcrack Lohrmann into hospital and he's still absent but I'm
back and nothing has happened to me, untouchable Martin Helger.
I can feel their rumours, their conspiracy theories. Did you hear, his
brother is missing in action. For real. I heard Marcus was a Recce, a
top commando. He got captured and is being held. On the Border. For
real . . . *There he is, hey, Martin Helger . . . Do not fuck with that oke . . .*
he doesn't look like much but he is a killer . . . he's ice cold, hey, he's in-
sane . . . nobody can touch him . . . he runs this place, hey . . . even Vol-
per is scared of the oke . . . But it's not until Nilly Rossbaum, the school
cantor, comes up to me in shul rubbing his hands all nervous and asks
me in a whisper would I like to have the honour of doing hagbah this
morning that I realise I have done it. I mean I have made myself a *Name*
like I always wanted. A thing of power like the magic words that saved
us years ago at the Emmarentia Dam. Martin Helger — the youngest
one to ever do hagbah, the new Strongest Lad.

I climb the bimah stairs (the only one there who knows what's underneath) and take hold of the carved handles of the Torah scroll on
the slanted platform, roll them apart, and pull on the long weight of
each scroll and I know I'm not going to be able to make this lift, there's
no way, the scrolls are too heavy for my thin wrists, but I don't care.
I look up at the sunlight streaming through vast windows and I hoist
the thing as hard as I can. The holy Torah raises up to about thirty degrees and then it starts to collapse. I hear the school gasping and sucking on teeth. Shouts. Nilly jumps across in front with both arms out.
He pushes up from the far side and gradually the scrolls come right.
I get it all the way over my head, balanced, and stand there grinning.

And then I start to laugh. People hiss at me, they boo, but I keep on laughing. I can see everyone down there looking to Volper, waiting for him to shut me up, they *need* him to punish me. But Volper just looks away.

When I get to class afterwards, the Gooch is waiting for me, wants a word around the side. "I am sorry to hear about Marcus," he says, "which is the only reason I don't klup your face. Don't look all smug. What's the matter with you? What do you think you are doing? This mockery in the shul. And in the first place, how d'you get into my athletics shed? You nearly killed someone with my javelin. You stole that key from my office."

"I found it open," I say. "You should tell your guys to lock up better."

The Gooch grabs my shirtfront. "Clever arse. You disgrace your name. You better wake up!"

"Let go or I report."

The Gooch goes red and trembles so much his whistles jingle. "You. You disgust me. Have you got a letter for your absence?"

"No."

"Go to Volper's office."

"Okay, sure," I say, trying to move off.

But he redoubles his grip and shakes me. "What the hell is going on with Volper and you?"

"None of your business. Sir."

"You gotten too bladdy big for your boots, Martin."

"Maybe," I say. "But I suggest you let me go. Otherwise it's you who'll get reported to Volper and not me. It'll be your job. Trust me on that." The Gooch stares and then walks off, putting his fist through the prefab wall.

In class I take my corner seat. Spunny looks away. Schnitz studies the ceiling. Turdster picks his nails. "Pack of wankers," I say. No one answers. I raise my voice. "Pack of useless wankers."

54

Now that I'm caught up on sleep and back at school, I start to think about the Fireseed tapes again. Annie needs me. Time to get back to work. I slide into the whole pipe routine as easy as kuk through a duck. Wake to my alarm after midnight. Collect my togs from the Sandy Hole and lower the bike to the street. Glide through Greenside, my Greenside, zone of the high walls, on streets dark and silent. Then the park at night and the riverbed and putting on my pads and overalls, the key to unlocking the grate tied to a string around my wrist so I won't have to go hunting for it once I'm up there. In the media annex while the video machines hum, I set up a 16-mil camera facing the TV screen and try to record directly onto film. It doesn't work at first but with some reading in the library and then some fiddling with the set-up eventually it comes right — the film speed has to be synchronised to match the flicker rate of the video image, it's not a good copy but it's usable, and there's no soundtrack to worry about. I'm shocked at how much film is needed, though, nearly four full reels. I don't think it's practical to do this on a large scale. I drop the reels off in the shed, along with the new tapes, and bike home.

Wednesday afternoon I'm heading down to Viljoen's, expecting a coded note from Annie — about the film reels but also probably a lot of cross words for me being absent. There's a yellow weaver bird building a nest in the tree next to the post office on Greenway Road. I stop for a sec to watch it work — it looks like a beaut of a nest to me, shaped like a butternut squash out of braided grass, but my opinion's not the one that counts. The female weaver bird will come and inspect, and if she doesn't like it it'll be ripped into a million little pieces and the male will have to start building all over again. A helluva life, hey. I walk on along past the doggy-grooming parlour in the open mall at the end of the parking lot and turn into Viljoen's. Straightaway I see that Dolf isn't there, it's the old man at the counter. I surprise myself by how calm I keep, I'm getting used to handling nerves, as I ask him if there's a book left for me to pick up. I start to say my name but he cuts me off. "I knows who you are, boy." He's got blotches on his cheeks and yellow hairs in his white moustache, a pouch of cherry pipe tobacco showing in his shirt pocket. "You don't come here anymore, hear me?"

"Beg a pardon?"

"You knows what I said," he says. "You want my son, go across to the Mike's Kitchen. He's there for you."

"Beg a pardon, meneer?"

"Stop pretending you can't hear. Go to Mike's Kitchen for Dolf. That's the message. And don't you come back here. Ever."

Grinning like a village idiot, shrugging as if to say *You are crazy, old man,* I turn around and exit but the calm has been squeezed out of me and my heart's tap-dancing away like whatsisname Baryshnikov and Gregory Hines in that movie *White Nights* as I stand there on the pavement. Mike's Kitchen is a chain restaurant, there's one across the road, on the upper level. I dinkum do not know what to do. Go home? Pretend like nothing's happened? What did he mean, Dolf is in there? Why would he be in there? Eventually I cross the street, telling myself I'll just peek through the window. The building has a rampway instead of stairs and at the top I find the restaurant door open. There's a booth to the right of the door and sitting there in it and looking right at me is Captain Bokkie Oberholzer. Opposite him are two other cops, bottles of Lion Lager on the table. I don't see Dolf anywhere. Oberholzer's waving me in like we're old mates and I'm expected. Well, I am, I think, going numb. The two cops, huge men both, put on their caps and haul themselves out and I sit on the warm vinyl where they'd been sweating.

"How's tricks?" Oberholzer says. "How things in the land of Helger?"

"Not so great," I say.

He's drinking Fanta, not beer. I remember him saying how his father, Magnus, died drunk in that rusty farmhouse in the klipveld, and I'll bet that's why he doesn't drink. Him and Comrade Shaolin both — they're more similar than they probably realise. He asks me how my daddy is doing. "He is fine, Captain," I say.

"Must be hard for him, after what happened to your brother now."

"You know about that?"

He smiles. "When you waltzed in here, you were looking for a different fellow, were you not?"

I'm silent.

"Lemme help your memory," Oberholzer says. "He's about this tall. Dark hair. Cocky little bastard. I know the whole family, the Viljoens from Linden, ja. Every single one of those Viljoens is henpecked by his woman. But your sad pal young Dolfie Viljoen he will never even get within a hundred kays of a woman. He's the kind of fellow whose wife will be his own right hand, you know what I mean. Collecting comics as a grown man. Terrified of the rugby field. Going into weirdo black politics with commies. Cos you know why? When you pal around with cripples you don't feel like you are limping anymore, that's why." Oberholzer leans over the table. "Black politics is for losers. I am looking at you, Martin Helger, and I am asking the question of myself, does he want to be a loser, another fokken waste of space like Dolf fokken Viljoen? Or is this one like his brother?" He lifts up a fist and shakes it. "Hard. Hard as diamond. Unbreakable. A winner."

"My brother," I hear myself say. "My brother, he's been —"

"I know what's happened to him. I am just saying a comparison." Oberholzer uses a serviette to clear his nose, wiggling it around, taking his time. "I'll tell you the difference between, let's say, a man like your brother and a dom piel" — a stupid prick — "like Dolf Viljoen. Just for hypothetics now. Now you apply some pressure to a Dolf Viljoen and he squishes on you just like the soft piece of shit he is. But your big brother, uh-uh. You cannot squeeze a war hero like that. It's another type I know well. It's like a mystery in there. You have to find the flaw. Every diamond has one. One tap — *boof* — it'll all crack right open. But you have to find it. If you try use brutal force he will not break. Put him in a machine, that machine it will break first."

"I'm not sure what you're saying, Captain."

"Kuk. You know. You been helping little Dolfie Viljoen there with the distribution of subversive literatures. Nobody in the SB even cares about a speck like Dolf Viljoen. He is a sad little legend in his own mind, that's all. But even still, I see your name on a report, I perk up, hey. I wanna know how it is you get involved. So me and crybaby we had a fatherly chat. Like I say, soft as kuk. Squish squish. He's told me everything."

Everything. *Does that mean Annie?* I say, "Honestly, I don't know anything about what you're saying, Captain. I get paperbacks from Viljoen, that's all. I'm a big reader. Oom Viljoen" — the old man — "was in there today, he told me to come over here. Said Dolf is here."

Oberholzer smiles with his lips all pressed. "Makes me very angry," he says. "Very, very angry. I thought we were friends, Martin. I even brought this for you." He reaches down and brings up a fat file with elastics around it and puts it on the table and drums his long fingers on top. "You know, I could let you take this with you. I'm sure it will be a big comfort to your family."

"Is that . . . is it my brother's?"

"So bright," he says. "I admire your brains." He swallows col'drink, his Adam's apple pumping, wipes his mouth on his sleeve, and burps. "Tell me now, when you grew up with Marcus, did the two of you share a room?"

"No."

"Where was his, next door?"

"Across the passage. My room's at the back, he had the garden one."

"The big brother. What was his room like? Describe it for me."

"I don't know. Full of boxing stuff, smelling of sweat."

"Any books?"

"He used to read comics a lot, he liked the funny ones, *Beano* and that. Then it was the boxing magazines when he went to Solomon. He changed a lot."

"Tell me, what did he care about the most? I don't mean sport, like boxing. I mean more general."

"Care about?"

"I'm talking in life in general. I mean the one thing that means — that meant — the most to him in the whole world."

"I don't know."

"Think harder, Martin. Use those brains. It's in your interest to think your hardest, believe me."

I am thinking plenty hard but not about my brother, I'm trying to guess how much Oberholzer knows about Operation Fireseed, about the hundreds of tapes, about me using the school — and Annie, of course, always back to Annie. It all depends what Dolf told him, what Dolf knows. But if they knew everything wouldn't I be in John Vorster Square right now, having that Hebrew code shoved in my face? Or else . . . I just don't know. And I can't understand why he's asking about Marcus. And why the file? I cough and say, "Well, my brother — it's hard for me to think about him now, you know, Captain. We're all in a lot of shock. My parents especially. It hurts."

"Oh, I'm sure it does," Oberholzer says. "I'm very sure of that. Especially your dad, hey." He leans forward. "He must be *really* in the hurt, hey?"

I look away, saying nothing.

"Martin, you need to talk to me. If you do, you can have this file, you can take it with you. If you don't, we'll have to have another kind of talk. And that means a trip to my office. You understand?"

I look at him again, and nod.

"I want you to do your best to explain him to me. Your brother. It's important now."

I ask as politely as I can, "And why is that, Captain?"

"You ask me why? Don't you know already, Martin? Can't you see? Because I care about you Helgers." He smiles properly now, showing all his yellow teeth. "You people, you are all such a dear project of mine."

55

Instead of going home I walk to the Emmarentia Library and find a quiet table off by myself to open up the file. From the outside it looks hell of a thick, like maybe a hundred pages. But as I turn the pages I find most of the type has been blacked out. Even holding pages to the light you can't see through these fat lines at all. Whatever there is to read is in Afrikaans, a high, technical level of the language that's hard for me to understand. So I fetch myself a dictionary and a pencil and start translating as best I can. It takes a while but slowly a picture of Marcus's military career emerges. At the beginning they sent him to 5 South African Infantry Battalion in Ladysmith, to do his basics. After that he volunteered for the paratroopers, passing the selections course and joining 1 Parachute Brigade at the Tempe base near Bloemfontein. Then came six months of paratroop training and a dozen jumps before he received his wings. After that he volunteered again, passing through another round of selections to join 44 Pathfinder Platoon, based at Murray Hill, south of Pretoria, for more specialised training. The file has a performance sheet from a commander in the Pathfinders. I read the word vertroulik — confidential — at the top, and underneath there are ten points of evaluation. Number one is verantwoordelikheid — responsibility — and two is leierskap — leadership — down to number ten, aanbeveling — recommendation — which says that the candidate should "substantiewe bevorder word" — be made substantive in his rank, which I think means he got a promotion — and begin his duties effective 01 05 1988. The evaluation remarks next to the ten points are full of words like outstanding and impeccable and first-rate. Marcus is described as highly intelligent and cool-headed, extremely disciplined and self-motivated. But at point number eight, lojaliteit — loyalty — it's noted that despite his excellence as a soldier there is *a small political question* due to certain statements about the mission of the South African Defence Force and also the candidate's Jewish background. Nonetheless he has proved himself to be thoroughly trustworthy in his actions and an exemplary leader of men. There's a note later on about a transfer to the Ondangwa base in South West Africa, but after that it's almost all black ink.

I check the time and then I start looking up all the books I can about the paratroopers and the army and that, making notes as I read. When I'm finished I consider hiding the file in the Sandy Hole with the rest of my secrets — but Marcus isn't just my brother, he's another son. When I get back home it's late and they're already at the table, worrying about me — they wouldn't have before this happened to Marcus, but everything's different now. I tell them the truth, that I was at the library, looking up military things. And then I bring out the file, telling them a military courier came and dropped it off and I signed for it. They're too excited to question my story. All Isaac says when he sees all the black ink is, "Bladdy bastids."

But at least for the first time they have some official version of his history. They knew paratrooper, they knew on the Border. They also had some idea that Marcus was in the special forces because of his two-line letters that used to come every now and then. Isaac says he thought maybe Marcus had ended up "in the Recces" because he's always been "so bladdy good at everything he does." In fact it would not surprise him one bit if it turned out he'd been captured like that famous Recce, Captain Du Toit, taken in Angola in 'eighty-five and held in solitary confinement for almost three years before his release as part of a prisoner swap deal. Du Toit had been on TV when he came out, all bony and thin-looking as he shook President Botha's hand. "Can you imagine what a hellhole that was for him," Isaac says.

"Oy Gott," Arlene says. "I don't want to think about it."

"He's not in the Recces," I say, explaining that Recces, the famous Reconnaissance Commandos, are permanent force men, in the army for life, not national servicemen doing their two years like Marcus is. "Oh thank God," says Arlene, because at least it means that he hasn't signed up to be a lifer — as if that makes any difference now.

Meanwhile Isaac is reading again. "So what's this Pathfinder?" he asks, and I explain to them what I've looked up about Pathfinders. That they're similar to Recces because they train to operate in small teams but there're only a very few Pathfinders compared to Recces, and that mostly what Recces did was hide out behind enemy lines and make observations where the Pathfinders are more trained to do raids and attacks, they get dropped in ahead of an attack to "find the path" and put down marks for the others to land on. Isaac says, "So you're telling me these guys are the first ones into the shit." And I say, "Basically, ja, I think so." And that's when Arlene starts to cry like I've never seen before and I feel terrible for bringing this stupid file home. I get the horrible idea that Oberholzer is laughing all the way back to John Vorster Square. He got me to deliver this document straight to the heart of my family, like a poison arrow.

56

Arlene has started going back to work, at least. I think it's good, more than good — I think it's what they both need, to keep themselves busy. But Isaac doesn't put on his overalls in the morning, instead he's still in bed when I leave for school. After last bell I take the bus to the Yard and sit with Arlene in her office with its big steel vault in one wall where all the cash takings are stored, while she does the books or whatever. We talk a lot. More than I think we ever have before. And we talk to each other in a way that is so grown-up it almost scares me. Especially after I confess to her what happened between Isaac and the staff, so she can understand that I think it's the main reason he can't come back to work, cos he's embarrassed to face them. Ma's worried about him and so am I and it's also a lot easier to talk about him than Marcus. She really can't even say my brother's name without crying. So I sit there with my chin on my hand as Ma's typewriter clackclacks or her pen scribbles and I listen to her hum and see the sunlight across her long neck. She stirs two lumps of sugar into her tea with milk, not the Russian way like Zaydi and Isaac who take it with lemon and seedy jam. She always wanted us to go to England where it's safe, me and Marcus. To become gentlemen. Attend Cambridge. She tells me she always wished we'd taken that *hopsy popsy* over to Britain. Arlene has her own private language like that. A hopsy popsy is a flight and the *dipsy doodles* are the restless itchy feelings she gets in her legs at night and the *wriggly boom booms* are insects that crawl and my nickname is *Toppers*. She likes to say "There's nothing like the English, Toppers," and I know she means their style, their classy way of doing things. Arlene never became the dancer on the stage she always wanted to be but now in these long talks I feel sad when she says, "I never had the West End, but I had you and Marcus," and puts her cool palm to the side of my face. "My Toppers," she says. "My Marty-Mart. I had you and you are worth more than any stage ever could be. You and your brother are more valuable than a million Londons."

We go home together and find Isaac sitting there with his bottle and his paper, in vest and underpants.

"Da, don't you think it's time to go back to work?"

"Why, are things falling apart there without me?"

"No," says Arlene. "Everything's fine. Between Hugo and Mr. Magid and myself, it's all running nicely."

"Then what am I needed for?"

It's not until the last weekend of the month that there's a change. That's when Sunday stocktaking is due. In her office Arlene tells me that she's talked it over with Isaac and it looks as if he'll come with her to do what they've always done, the two of them alone in the Yard on a Sunday morning, going in very early together, stopping for some fresh chocolate rugelach at the baker in Doornfontein, then going on to do the stocktaking carefully by hand, all the items in the warehouse totaled up by the time they're finished, and then back in time for the Sunday braai, buying the meat on the way. It's the same ritual they've had since as long as I can remember. I think it's even as old as their marriage. And because it doesn't involve the staff, it will be easy for Isaac to do, Ma says she hopes it'll break the ice and get him to start coming to work regularly the next week. So I'm not surprised when I hear their voices very early on the Sunday and then the car doors being slammed. The sky is just turning blue as I slip out and climb the dewy fig tree to look over the wall in time to see Isaac's rusted bakkie going up Clovelly Road. I see the back of Ma's head beside my father's. I wave once. Of course there's no reply. They haven't seen me.

57

A hand is pressing on my chest. I open my eyes. Zaydi is standing over me. I don't think he's ever been in my room before. It gives me a fright, this old man with his trembly mouth, his wrinkled skin so white he looks like all his blood dried up years ago. I ask him what's wrong and he says in his whispery Yiddish that there are soldiers climbing over the wall. I close my eyes cos I know I'm dreaming — a new version of the Nightmare is finally here, but my God, this one feels so *real*. I ignore Zaydi's hand prodding at me. But then I hear banging on the front door and it's loud and it doesn't stop. And I hear voices. Afrikaans, not German. They're calling for us to open up. They're saying police.

58

Maybe Annie Goldberg was all wrong about the Nightmare, maybe it wasn't all about me. The garden wasn't me and the Nazis coming in weren't me and Zaydi wasn't my soul — maybe the truth is the Nightmare was a vision, like a prophecy. Only it was slightly off, my brain confusing all the characters-to-come. These guys aren't Nazis, they're just cops in uniform, and they're not here to hurt me — at least not physically. They're here to talk softly to me, to not meet my eyes. To treat me like I've been hit with a disease so bad all a person can do is feel sorry. I get in the back of their police car and we drive to Vrede-dorp. It's Sunday, 25 June 1989. My eyes close themselves. If I were fly-ing in the air over Johannesburg I would be able to see the Ponte Tower sticking up off the ridge like a gigantic chimney made of steel and glass, and down there next to it is the ribbon of Harrow Road and under-neath the motorway there are big boulders sticking out of the ground, by the turn-off to Gordon Terrace and the way down to Bertrams. And over there is Doornfontein, Beit Street, where Isaac Helger grew up, and there next to it is the giant mushroom of Ellis Park Stadium, but me I'm flying west, to Vrededorp, and when I get over it I start falling hard. I see the big rooftop where De La Rey Street meets the 5th Street park, it's rushing up at me faster and fas —

"Martin, Martin," says the voice softly, and I open my eyes. The two cops are looking back at me from the front seat. I seem to make them frightened, it's in their faces. We're here, they say. They're asking me if I'm okay. *Okay?* I nod once and open the door and walk across the street to the green front doors of Lion Metals Pty. Ltd. It's a lovely

Sunday, the sun directly over my head. The flashing lights on the cars in the bright air look so jolly, blue and red, and the neighbourhood people crowded on the other side of the tape are looking at me with blank faces. I go around and then there's a man in front of me, wearing a suit, who says his name is Detective Sergeant van Rensburg. He's the one who is saying, "You can come through if you want, but."

"Yes," I say. "It's my right."

We start walking. I know the way past the counters, to the left, down the passage with the scratched linoleum tiles and the framed Tretchikoff print of a woman with a flower in her hair on the greasy wall. I hear myself saying, "Are you also from the Brixton Murder and Robbery Squad?"

"That's right."

At the doorway he reaches across. His breath smells of coffee. "Are you really sure?" I nod and we go in. The Austen Petersen vault door, constructed in 1928, weighing, I know, approximately five hundred kilos, is now fully open. It's quiet in this room which is my ma's office, except for the sounds of the people moving around and the shutter click from the man with the camera inside the vault. "You can see in from here, but careful and don't step in or touch," says van Rensburg. "Forensics." I go up and look into the vault from the edge. They've set lights up and everything is very clear. I am dreaming. I am dreaming. I am dreaming. I see two corpses, both are naked. The flesh looks like wax and there are these black dots everywhere which I understand is dried blood as I smell the bad butcher smell, like metal on the air. The male corpse is all twisted, it seems like it could be making a letter from an alphabet I can almost read. Hebrew. Because this is a dream and everything is a code in a dream, a symbol, that's all. The other corpse is a she. She has my mother's hair. The faces of both are like dark balloons, the eyeballs sticking out. The mouths wide open and the bellies swollen. I think: my mother, Arlene, is two fingers taller than my father, Isaac. We make jokes about this. I look at the fingers and the fingertips are black.

I don't remember backing up or turning away—how could I be in the other office now? I can hear Mr. Magid's voice from down the passage. I'm holding a can of col'drink, Fanta grape. But I don't remember anyone giving me anything. This is what happens in dreams. Right? Another detective is talking. My ma likes ginger biscuits with her tea. She gets the dipsy doodles in her legs at night. She takes milk and two sugars. I fell out of the sky and crashed through the roof. The soldiers climbed over the wall and banged on the door, they had news. This detective's voice is explaining how an anonymous call brought police, someone saying they'd seen black males fleeing the premises. Investigating officers found signs of struggle and the manager, Mr. Magid, was located to open the safe. The detective says the word *suffocation*. Someone must have made them strip and go into the vault. Probably at gunpoint. It would have happened right away when they got here, the voice says, maybe they were waiting for them, maybe they walked in on a robbery.

I hear myself say, "Suffocated. That must have taken how long?"

"That vault seals airtight, but it's big enough to last two people I'd say an hour, maybe more. But they threw in a smoker."

"A what?"

"A kind of grenade. The burning prolly et up the oxygen, on top of the smoke inhalation. We talking a couple of minutes, maximum. Like putting gas in there."

And he shows it to me, the incendiary device, sealed in a plastic evidence bag, a charred tube of steel now. This choked my parents. I'm not dreaming. I make videos that teach bombs like this. Her cool palm on the side of my face, her ginger biscuits. It's a dipsy doodle, Marty-Mart. If you scratch at steel hard enough you can grind the tips of your fingers down to blood. I'm sitting down by the window now. I don't remember moving here. I hear another detective talking to the first by the doorway, murmuring a question in Afrikaans—where is he? The other shakes his head, saying, "Daardie onnosel kameelperd. Hy't hierdie een gebring." That dumb giraffe, he brought this one. I think *this one* means me, and I start to listen hard, pretending not to. In Afrikaans they're saying:

— This is the son.

— This is the son?

— This is the son. It was him that sent the car for him. Did you show him —

— He wanted to.

— Jesus.

— Well, like he said. He has a right.

They bring in a tape recorder. I answer questions. A fat blue fly sticks on the wall. I wonder if it has been in Ma's office, in the vault. The questions keep coming, monotonous. Who had access to the building on a Sunday morning, what were my parents doing there alone. Who knew the combination of the safe, what were the names of the staff members, what were the items missing . . . At some point I'm talking about Hugo, Hugo Bleznik.

"You know where to reach him?"

I give Hugo's phone number from memory. He lives in Hyde Park, I say. But suddenly I'm not so sure that's true.

59

Some questions for the rabbi. Dear Rabbi, I know that you're supposed to sit shiva for seven days after the funeral but what if it's a double? I mean does that mean fourteen days? Because you're supposed to get all the mourning out of your system during shiva, right? Well if it's double the mourning that you have to do then shouldn't you take double the number of days? Isn't that logical, dear rabbi? With questions like that, I should be in yeshiva, right? I mean who knew I had such a talmudic mind . . . The funerals were on Thursday. Normally they would have been buried within a day or two, that's the Jewish way, but the forensic pathologist had to perform autopsies. Also, I was waiting for Auntie Rively.

Oh God. Auntie Rively.

My (late) father's older and only sister, forty years of living in Israel hasn't done much to her South African accent and she still has the same nervous giggle that I remember from when I was a kid, the same orange-yellow wig and long print dresses worn with white Dunlop tennis shoes. She came by herself, leaving Uncle Yankel and her seven sons back in Jerusalem. The first thing she did on arrival was throw a crying tantrum about the autopsies. Autopsies were a grayser aveyre, a huge big sin, and how could I, how *could I* have let it happen? How could I have stood by and let them cut up the bodies of my own parents and her own brother? Do you know how they desecrate the holy human form when they do an autopsy? What was wrong with me? And poor Zaydi *alive to have it done to his own child.* She took over all the arrangements for the funeral, for everything. I didn't care. Still don't. Someone has taken out my eyes and ears and mouth and replaced them all with big lumps of cotton wool. My arms and legs are being run via remote control. I am stuck in a huge mistake. Any second now someone's ganna rewind this video.

We had the funerals in Westpark Cemetery, near the rose gardens of Roosevelt Park at the top of the Emmarentia Dam, not far from where Gitelle Helger, my Bohbi — Zaydi's wife — is buried. Lots of people came. I had to stand there with Auntie Rively and shake the hands as the line moved up. Now we are sitting shiva — seven days total was the rabbi's answer — at my house in Greenside, which means prayers every night and people coming to say them with us. Auntie Rively's organised the catering, she hired a maid also. I hardly know anyone. Some of them are friends of Ma, some are connected to the business. But there's also a large religious bunch that Auntie Rively has brought in — and they're all strangers. They're chassidim, black-hatters, a sort we never had much to do with. I start to realise that Auntie Rively has become one of them, they have branches everywhere and she's got in touch with the Joburg lot and they've sent people. Even through the plugs of cotton wool this bugs me. I mean I don't know this strange rabbi she's brought in to run the services. Our rabbi, my parents' rabbi, is Rabbi Tershenburg from the Emmarentia Shul. He comes around but he's been pushed aside, these others have taken over, always a crowd of black hats and wigs in the lounge around the table full of smoked salmon and chopped herring and bagels and cream cheese. They want to talk to me about their rebbe and all the messianic miracles he does, want me to come and visit their synagogue or enroll in some course. I know my parents wouldn't want these strangers here. But I'm stuffed with cotton wool and Auntie Rively is running the show with her giggling and her arranging.

Now shiva is over and Auntie Rively says she's found a "properly kosher" care home for Zaydi in Glenhazel. The remote controller of my limbs sends me to bed and I lie there mostly not sleeping like I've been doing all week. This morning I find Auntie Rively showing a man around the place, he's making notes. I ask who this is and she tells me it's the estate agent. I slap barefoot into the kitchen to fetch a bowl of Strawberry Pops and milk. I notice the estate man's wearing a black hat and showing tzitzit from under his jacket—another religious one. After he leaves I lie down on the couch with a book for a while and when I hear the gates I'm up in time to see Mr. Harry Steed on the garden path, my father's lawyer, carrying two obese leather briefcases. Auntie Rively sits with him at the dining room table. When I walk over they both stop talking and my auntie asks if she can help me. Then she giggles. I shake my head and start shuffling away. But then I see my father's empty chair, the ottoman in front of it, and I can picture him clear as day chopping away with both heels and shouting *bladdy schmocks!* And it's like I can hear him saying into my ear, *Who the hell do these people think they are?* So I force myself to go back and sit down at the table. They're both quiet again, Harry looking at Auntie Rively and Auntie Rively giggling and asking me if I'm all right. I tell them I want to hear everything they're talking about. "It's just legal stuff," says Auntie Riv. "Boring for you. I'll let you know the gist."

"I want to hear."

Steed sort of rolls his eyes at her and lifts his shoulder. He's got sideburns that are like a hundred years out of fashion and full of gross grey hairs and there's some kind of skin condition on his nose. The maid brings tea and Steed unbuckles the jumbo briefcases and pulls out a load of papers. He has a low voice and he talks like a car that never gets out of first gear. It would put me to sleep, I swear, if I wasn't concentrating so hard. He reads out like a metric ton of legal words, and then I ask questions and it takes a while for me to understand what's what. How my parents' joint will leaves everything to me and Marcus — the house, their bank accounts, the business. But there's one major problem. Marcus isn't dead, he's just missing, so that means I can't get the whole lot (at least that's what I think he's saying). Then there's the other problem that at seventeen I am still technically a minor. Which brings us to other family members. Since Arlene was an only child there's no one with a claim there, but Isaac's end — well, here we have Auntie Riv. Moving onto the "corporate side," things start to get very complex very quickly. It's not just Lion Metals, there's a whole stack of holding companies, some of them bought years ago just for their accumulated losses for tax reasons, others set up by Hugo Bleznik for God knows what reason (Steed says). This brings us to the matter of the accountant, who was Hugo Bleznik's man and who has "recently schmitezed." I didn't actually know for sure that Steed was Jewish until he used that word, Yiddish slang for run away fast, disappear. Steed says he's done his best to try to "unknot all of Hugo's mess" using the books that Auntie Rively has given him.

"Wait a second," I say to her. "You mean you went to the Yard and just took them?"

"Of course," she says. "*Someone* had to lock things up and let the staff go."

"Wait a second," I say. "Wait a second."

Mr. Steed says the Yard is closed, had to be, there is no money in current accounts. "A lot has disappeared," he says. "Just like Hugo."

After Steed has gone I ignore Auntie Rively and lock myself in my room with my head going round like a carousel. This is not right, I'm being taken over — and why the hell was an estate agent here making notes? I know I've got to do something but I don't know where to start. Eventually I get dressed and head out, ignoring Auntie Rively's questions, and walk to Barry Hertzog Avenue. Since I've got like hardly any money, I take a black taxi to the shopping mall in Hyde Park and then hike the rest of the way, past the long walls and the big Rottweilers at the spiked gates, until I reach Hugo Bleznik's place. The intercom brings out a maid who remembers me and lets me in. The Tudor house is full of other maids working away as if nothing is wrong, and to them nothing is. Same for the gardeners out on the rolling lawn. One maid tells me Hugo left on Sunday, bags had been quickly packed and put into the boot of the Bentley for him.

Alone, I slip across into the garage, sliding the door shut behind me. The red Jag is parked in its usual spot and behind it at the back I put on the work lamp and dig into the jar for the Allen key. The plank slides out, but there's no tin in the hollow, and disappointment drops on me like a cold, wet sheet. But then I stick my hand inside and my heart starts thumping when I feel paper. I pull out a thick envelope. Inside are two wads of cash and some folded pages — a letter, badly typewritten.

Martl!

If you have this in hand you are well on your way as I knew it would be as you are the top 1 + never forget it. Boyki 1st how sorry I am on your loss. But how is not the time for mornning! Now is the time to act quick. Like I did the second I got the news.

Inside herew/ this is quite a few cabbage leafes for you to get by on. Also contact Webber Travel in Observatory. Maxie Webbers a good man. I have put in credit in cofidence yr 1 way ticket to New York. Your green card is here. You have yr passport. I think there is a dircet flight every day now. For now! I myself have taken another route as I will expaine below. You can leave on a weekend even Sudnay night via indirect. boyki I suggest now is the time to act do not think on the dead think on yr life there will be time later for teras which is hard now but the dead cant come back to life. Like they say in Jewish, a taytum nemt mir nit tsoorig foon besaylmem. You never bring a dead back from the "grave" Its a 1 way trip to that cemetery.What has happened has happened you need to wake up and think for yourself now.

Maybe by now you have had heard from that utter schmok Steed or other legal. They will confuse you do not be confused all is well + clear between me and you + you are protected. Your accounts are all there + kosher. You have Altenberg the lawyer in New York. I put his card. It is all there for you, boyki. The car keys to your future. All you have to do is drive.

About the other. Do not believe police, etc. What they say happened did not + if I had not LeFT in a quicky hurry probably it would be me also like that. Definitely I do not want to give that scum Captain You know who any bloody chance to get me alone in a cell and neither must you!!!

I know you understand because you are reading this which means you are alreayd thinking and moving. Good! KEEP IT UP.

Go see Webber + get out pronto. There is now nothing

for you in this broken country. Remember the birds! Make arragngements for your grandfather, bless him, you have these cabbage leafs to pay off with. From the overseas you can send more. New York will fix you up with plenty. Don't forget I been buying dollars with Rands for years whent the Rand was stronger than a dollar by a mile. Your are well taken care of but you have to go + get it!

Do not waste any time on stupid anger against me if you have it. I am looking out for you like your father wanted even if he did not understand how. You can see now today that yours truly was right + unfrtunetly yr fathe was wrong. I have seen this day coming especially since that horrible meeting with you know who + his rifle, my G-D a madman plain and simple. I have been arranging it so that what me + yr father built up has been put away in a safe places away from the bad people who run our country. Dont cry for them yr father was right they are all scum but in the meantime we have payed plenty taxes believe me but nobody should have the rigth to tell a man where he can send his own money + that is all that I did yr father would not understand but I have provisined for you.

Boyki I myself will be in Gabs, Botswasna in few hours. My plan is now drive + I will do the border run ASAP. It is getting late with me writing this + the news is terible I knoew + I you don't know how bad I feel in my heart I loved yr father + mother we were family I never had family of my own you are now my only family with Marcus gone down that bad road + that is why I am providing. From Gabs I fly to a country where I will live out my days.I leave my name behind. A good peaceful place with no more violence + mad police + all the bloody rest. REst is all I want now. I want to live out what I have left in peace. You are just starting my advice forget us all, ulter kukkers like me, forget me, you need to go <u>forward in America</u>. Maybe one day I will see you again before it is my turn to go but if not I love you, boyki.

To life! To life!!!

Hugo

PS — You must burnt all thse pages now. Trust me. Leave absolutely no trace.

PPS — I left your brother's "GREEN" card with you also. There always is hope!! You never know!!

Another page has handwritten notes — account numbers in America, a paper-clipped card for the attorney in New York City. A small envelope has the two laminated cards. Resident Aliens. One for Martin and one for Marcus. I reread everything and then I fold up the sheets and put them in my pocket, the green cards in my wallet. My vision is blurry so I wipe my eyes. I stuff the wads of cash in my pockets and then take one out again and count off some notes for my wallet and push the wad back in the pocket. I relock the plank and walk back to the house where I call all the maids and the gardeners to the kitchen. I tell them that Hugo has gone and is not coming back, that there is no one left to pay their salaries. The police will probably be coming here at some point. At the end of the month this house and the vehicles will probably be repossessed by the bank. Trucks will come and take away all the furniture and everything else of value. When I finish they are smiling at me like I'm a loony case, talking to each other in their languages. I tell them who I am and give them two hundred rand cash each — that seems to help change their minds. I tell them I am leaving now and recommend they also leave. I tell them if I were them, I would take Hugo's stuff in lieu of pay. Take the rugs, take the clocks, take any watches, jewellery, furniture, any gold fixings, whatever. "Take it now," I say, "cos if you don't other people will. Hugo's gone for real. He's not coming back." When I leave, they're arguing among themselves, waving their arms. I don't look back.

60

At home I crawl straightaway into the papyrus stand, to the Sandy Hole, to deposit my newest secrets. The photo of young Nelson Mandela stares up at me and I think of Annie and wonder if I could try to reach her somehow. I'd have to go into Jules, to the school, see if she's still teaching there — but I'm not going to do that, it exhausts me just to think about. And I have so many other problems. Inside, Auntie Rively is in a fuss, wanting to know where I've been. I don't say anything and she asks me to sit down, starts talking about Zaydi, saying things I already know. That he is happy in the old-aged home, that there is money in his own account which was managed by Isaac, his savings invested. Just when I'm starting to wonder where she's going with this, she giggles nervously and tells me the "good news" that I'm going "home" with her. To Eretz Yisroel, the Land of Israel, where all Jews belong. She's talked it over with Uncle Yankel and her sons and there's a room and a school waiting for me. We can leave as soon as she's sold off the house here, she tells me. I get up without saying a word. She follows me to the gate, talking about no more running wild, it has to stop. I need a home and a structure. HaShem has a plan for me.

This time I take the bus to town, to Harry Steed's office on Twist Street. I have to wait a long while before the secretary lets me in. Steed stays on his feet, not looking at me. I keep asking him about the house and he keeps saying I need to go talk to my auntie. "She's the one," he says. He touches my back, moving me to the door. I find myself standing outside on the street before I even know what's happened. I have the feeling he's already on the phone to Auntie Rively — Steed's not ganna be any help to me. I feel like crying, but then I think of my parents and look up and there's a post office opposite. In a phone book chained to the wall in there I turn to A for attorneys. The name Joski snags my eye for no reason other than the look of it. I dial straightaway. Back at home I fetch a wad of cash from the Sandy Hole and keep it with me in my room. Auntie Rively knocks on the door and I tell her to go away. The morning comes and I head back to town. Joski's office is nice and new-looking, full of sunlight. The secretary even uses a PC computer, you can hear the printer buzzing through the door. He's a young oke, Joski, and he laughs when I show him the cash, saying I'm not a drug dealer now am I? But he's only kidding, he takes some money and gives me an agreement to sign and says, "I'll help you. It's up to us to clean up their mess." I shake my head cos I don't understand. He says we're the younger generation, the future, it's up to us to make things right. He shows me a picture of his father who was a famous Queen's Counsel, a political guy, he says, and he also likes to take on political cases when he can as well, to do his part to "clean the mess." At home I keep to myself and by the end of the week I get a call from Joski, explaining that he received the documents he requested from Steed and has filed a motion with the court on my behalf. Another few days and a courier brings me a copy of the motion granted, with a note from Joski. Nothing can be done with the house until my eighteenth birthday. Through Joski, I am in control of the property until then, when the deed will pass into my name. If there's any trouble about this, I must call Joski at once. Best regards.

I keep this good news to myself until the day the estate agent comes back. Standing at the front door, I tell him to leave. He smiles at me and asks me where my auntie is. I take out the copy of the court document and show it to him and repeat that I want him to leave. Auntie Rively comes to the door, looks at the document, and gets all hysterical. "No, no, Martin," she says. "This is unbelievable. Where did you get this? Who gave this to you? No no no." She phones Steed and he phones back and breaks the facts of life to her. She can't sell the house — nobody can. It's my residence now. I repeat myself again to the estate man and this time he leaves, but Auntie Rively still hasn't got the picture. She starts yakking to me about Israel and studying and her husband and my cousins. How I will fit in the family and start a new life, a Jewish life, where I am meant to be. I'm her responsibility. She says this was a vow to my father, but I doubt that cos they were never that close. Then she starts almost begging me, talking about my late Bohbi and how she tried right before the war to get her sisters out of Dusat. She sounds like Hugo. "But I don't want to *try*," she says. "I want to get you *out*." She rubs her face and cries into her fingers and says, "Come on, Martin. You're all on your own. You have no family left. Come with me. What else are you going to do? *HaShem wants you to come with me.*"

She won't leave without me. She just stays and stays, forcing me to call Joski. In the end Steed has to come to escort her to the taxi with her baggage, and she's crying again, her wig sitting skew. "You're making a horrible mistake," is what she tells me as Steed shuts the taxi's door. I'm standing behind the gate. My gate. I lock it.

61

I let the maid go and I'm alone in my house for the first time. I open up the liquor cabinet and fetch out Da's Scotch, pour a glassful, and sit in his chair to watch the news. His smell oozes from the leather. My feet are on his ottoman. "Good evening," says Michael de Morgan. "Good evening," I say. The Chinese government continues to crack down following its brutal assault on the protesters in Tiananmen Square last month. The Polish workers are demonstrating. This Gorbachev with his plum-marked head is promising reforms. State President Botha has had a face-to-face meeting with Nelson Mandela, and then Mandela went back to his cell. I look at my heels on the ottoman, they haven't so much as twitched. I drink my father's whisky and fall asleep and wake up with the test pattern. I sleep a lot and when I wake I try to search in my mother and father's old cupboards. I want to sort through their things, but it's too hard, I never get anywhere. In the end the only thing I retrieve is my own passport, which was in Da's drawer along with both of theirs, from that time we all travelled together to Israel to visit Auntie Riv. I take it out to the Sandy Hole and put it in the envelope with the green cards.

Time is passing. I eat canned beans on toast. The phone is ringing —it's Detective Sergeant van Rensburg. He wants to update me on the case. I tell him to come over. He arrives with another detective and we sit in the lounge and he tells me they believe it was some of Isaac's own staff and do I have any knowledge of any of them who might have had a particular animosity towards my father? I tell them about Sammy Non-galo and the others being fired. At first I leave out the part about Isaac hitting, I don't want them to think Isaac was the kind of man who beat his staff—because he wasn't, it wasn't like that. Right? But then I tell them everything. They don't seem surprised. They say, ja, they knew about this Sammy, they are looking for him. His details are out and he'll be arrested soon, they're sure.

After they leave I lie on the couch and sleep and when I wake up I don't know what day it is. The electricity must have been out because all the digital clocks are blinking. It's dark as a bruise outside and rain is storming at the windows. I have some whisky and go back to sleep. I wake up and toast some stale bread and eat it with sardines. I have whisky. I sleep. The phone starts ringing. It's Harry Steed, he wants to tell me about what's happening with the Yard since it's almost the end of the month. I think, *Is it? How can that be?* Steed says something about the lease having some kind of clause, and there are creditors. He says the property will be taken over "unless you have some other brilliant legal tricks hiding up your sleeve." And I'm sort of surprised to realise he's still pissed off at me over Joski and the house. But then I get double-surprised as his voice changes and he says, "Martin, what are your plans? For your own self."

"It sounds like you actually care."

"Martin."

"I don't know."

"I think you must start going back to school."

I don't answer. "You can do what you like," Steed says, "but that's what I think."

I say, "The staff. What's ganna happen to them?"

"Who?"

"The guys at the Yard, the workers."

"Oh. They've found their own way by now," says Steed. "For them, for everyone, the era of Lion Metals is long over with." That pompous way he puts things, like he's giving a speech — but if he wanted to touch me I have to admit he got me there. Then I think, screw them, screw them all. The staff. *It's them who bladdy did it.* Who gassed my parents to death. And into my head flashes the waxy bodies and the black dots and the mashed fingertips. I never even want to see that fucking building again in my whole life. But something about that morning at the Yard, the vault, some little detail — it keeps scratching at me. And what was it Hugo's letter said? *Do not believe police, etc. What they say happened did not.* I should think about it more but I'm too tired. I'm lying down again. The way a car works is that the battery starts the engine and then the engine tops up the battery. But if the engine stops running the battery drains. You have to *move* in order to top up your human battery. The more you lie there, the more that's all you *can* do. While I'm lying the house starts sinking. Water pours in through the windows. Blue like the water at the aquarium in John Vorster Square. I go drifting off the couch and float down the passage. Warm as blood so you can't feel your skin. Where one things ends and another starts. A pomegranate goes floating by. It breaks open and it's full of tiny eyes, watching me. I pull out the phone cord. The gates are locked, the wall is high. I know things are rotting in the fridge but I'm not hungry. My upper lip is prickly. A moustache wants to live and I don't have the kaych to kill it. I'm shaggy, I know. During shiva they covered the mirrors. I think it's a good idea so I bring it back. Now I'm sleeping, I think, and dreaming of a clanging, a heavy bell. Some lunatic swinging a bell like Frere-oh Jacques-oh. I'm not dreaming. I go out and find it's early morning. At the back fence, the splintery planks, I say, "Take it easy, Mr. Stein."

"They coming," he says. "They coming." I put my eye to a gap showing part of his jowly chin and one eyebrow, fat and grey as an old silkworm. Suddenly that one eye flicks onto mine. "You think I'm mad. They all reckon I'm mad."

"No," I say, yawning. "I don't, really. Not anymore."

"What's going on over there? I don't see any cars coming."

"They got my parents," I say.

A long pause. "I heard," he says.

I think about this for like probably half a minute. "You couldn't bother to walk a few feet, Mr. Stein? You couldn't come to their shiva out of respect? Sis, man. Shame on you."

"Shiva," he says.

"Respect!" I'm surprised by how vicious my shout sounds, it wakes me up to how angry I must be. "You schtick drek," I call him. You piece of crap.

"I'm sorry," says Stein. "I don't go out. I got my system." I turn to leave. "Wait," he says. "No, wait, Martin. Wait here, please. I'll go and get you something. Let me fetch it for you. Please wait."

Now I'm standing in the passageway, in front of my brother's door. I remember the day Marcus first put the lock in, drilling into the doorframe. Isaac should have lost his temper but he seemed more amused, Arlene just shook her head and said I give up. The combination lock dangles like a steel scrotum. I take the box of shells out of my pocket, bright apple red with a waxy feel to them and copper bottoms. My other hand lifts up the thing that Mr. Stein gave me — it's heavy, ja, but not as heavy as I would have thought before, and then I push a shell carefully into the slot and work the pump. I click off the safety with my thumb, and aim. A voice in my head says stop, just stop. My finger starts pinching the trigger very slo —

Boof!

The explosion kicks the air and light right out of me in a storm of wood chips. My ears feel busted, ringing. I drop the long shotgun and go staggering into the bathroom. Shirt's torn. Blood, splinters. In the mirror I tell myself I'm lucky my eyes are still there. Red shoulder will bruise. I wash myself with shaky hands and go back into the passage and pick up the shotgun. There's a smell of burnt gunpowder and singed carpet. Something is smoking, I stamp it out. The door is ajar, all shredded and blown out around the smashed lock. I push it in with my foot and step inside, I can't remember the last time I was in Marcus's room. There's a wall closet on the left, a steel desk the other side. The bed with stripped mattress along the wall and the window above it. Bare floor but for the piles of boxing magazines in one corner, with cracked leather twelve-ounce gloves on top. Fight posters on the wall. Dust of years. What was the big secret? Why did he have to lock his door off? I look in the cupboard — just some neatly folded clothes. I don't know what else I expected. A diary? Like in some Victorian novel by one of the Brontë sisters, Marcus confessing his dark secrets in pretty prose. But life isn't pretty prose or even pretty and there's no confessions, no understanding, it just happens. I sit on the mattress with the shotgun across my legs. I'm thinking the police will be coming soon. Reports of a shotgun blast echoing around the neighbourhood. But people keep to themselves in Whiteland. Slowly I slide over onto my side on the cool mattress and curl up around the shotgun. When I open my eyes the moon is shining through the window. I have a look into the shotgun and there's a shell in there, it's loaded and the safety is off. Wow. I'm not thinking well. I have something else that Mr. Stein gave me along with the shotgun and the box of shells — nine cards full of pink pills. "You better take these," he said. "Amphetamine. We used to call em battle buttons in the war. Don't get caught schloffing when they come." I pop two on my palm and look at them.

Now I'm out on patrol, checking my perimeter with the loaded shotgun in my hands. I discover the mailbox is overstuffed. I empty it and start up a bonfire in the metal braaivleis. *The Greenside Shopper* is advertising a special, 99 cents on mozzarella cheese at the Spar. The United Building Society has a one-time friendly rate offer for Mr. I. Helger, Esquire. This month's *Vogue* has *Arlene Helger* typed on the label stuck to its cover. I feed these and all the rest in batches into the licking flames, like tossing chunks of meat to a demon. I watch their names turn black and blistery. I poke with a stick to get the fire's teeth into the last of it but then I see a postcard with the word *Pats* written in ink. I use the stick to flick it off but by the time I stamp the flames out it's mostly gone. I lean down and read, *All the best mate.* Above this I can just make out the last part . . . *your folks and I am very sorry and wish you long life. If I can help with anything you can bell my pager 784-112* . . . I pick up the charred scrap and wipe it off carefully on my leg and put it in my pocket. Then I dump sand on the flames and go back inside.

The problem is there's nothing in front of me but time and it just goes on and out like an infinite desert. When I get hungry I knock back a few of the pills and then the hunger goes away and the desert feeling is not so bad. I do two at a time and then three and then four. They make me feel as if someone's pushed an on-switch inside me. Alive. But they also bring a humming and an itch under my skin. I'm patrolling a lot more, I like the walking. I check on the Sandy Hole, my money, my documents. I hide the burnt scrap carefully in the pages of a notebook and leave it buried there with my other secrets. The Fireseed videotapes. Secrets have gravity, they suck in more secrets like a black hole. They accumulate. I must stay alert stay alive.

I feel hot and catch the notion of a swimming pool that won't leave my head. I can dig one out and rain will come and fill it up, like the flash floods in Brandwag Park. It makes good cool sense so I fetch a pick and a shovel from the shed and start digging into the lawn and go on until my hands bleed. I lie down awake. I'm aching, leaving sticky bloodstains on the mattress and the shotgun. I wake up low again, suffocating. I take some pills with a can of Sprite and my lungs open up again. I go out with the shovel to dig my pool but then decide to clear the garden of sightlines. I'm in the thorns, chopping and hacking. That tree has to come down. I'm chopping at the trunk with the shovel, exposing wet white wood. The tree won't fall. I get the shotgun and aim it and pull the trigger but there are no shells in the thing. I don't remember taking them out. I go inside and have some pills and load and unload and load and loadunload for so long my fingers go numb while my mind is somewhere far away. It's day, no it's dark again. I don't like the heat of the burning days. But then when it's dark the noise of the crickets in the flower beds invades my teeth. I need to bite into things, to chew. There is a six-foot Parktown prawn stalking me. I need the shotgun at all times, have to keep checking it's loaded. Got to ration my battle buttons. My jaw hurts, can't stop gnashing. On patrol again now, walking my perimeter. Belongs to me. Got my weapon. They're trying to cut the burglar bars. I can hear the wood bugs chewing in the trees. Meantime Arlene has started singing inside a little bubble deep inside my earhole. I try to clean it out with a twig but I can't reach the bubble. Arlene's voice is so high, she's doing opera. Everything I do, she starts to sing about. *He spins around but there is no giant prawn there!* It comes to me that human thoughts are nothing but a nest of little cockroaches that live at the base of the skull and the spine is a hollow tube and the cockroaches go scuttling up and down it. This is what thoughts are. *He discovers what thoughts are!* Arlene sings, wailing. If I had something sharp and antiseptic I could cut open my face and clean out the cockroaches in there, but I'm scared they'll scuttle down other holes in me and escape. I'm stuck *inside* my flesh, I'm *entombed* in it. I eat from a tub of Black Cat peanut butter. I take half a card of pills with it. Only one card left. I'm staring at the test pattern on the TV, working out that it's a giant eye, a digital watcher. Government. *He discovers the terrible truth in the test pattern!* sings Arlene inside my ear bubble. It's time to patrol. Got to. That squeaking noise in my skull is my teeth grinding.

I hear noises from the carport, gate noises. I go over the inner wall, smooth as a cat, and pad along behind the cactus bed. Someone's playing Jesus at the gate, arms out like a crucifix, shaking the bars. Then calling, "Mah-ten. Mah-ten. Are you in there?" He's a terrorist, he's got bombs at his feet. Here to lure me out. I creep up closer and put the shotgun on him from the edge of the gate where he doesn't see me. Not so clever now, are you terror boy? I start pinching the trigger. *Oh but it's wrong so wrong to shoo-oot people!,* sings Arlene. *First see what he wants! I beg and be-see-ee-ch thee!* Shut up, Ma. I'm working here. I'm surviving. But she keeps on shrilling in the bubble in my ear until I step out. He gasps and his eyes go huge in his dark face. I prod his chest through the bars with the barrel. "Don't shoot," he says. "Don't shoot me. I didn't do it, that is why I came. I didn't do it. It wasn't me. It is why I come here to tell to you. Please. Put down. Please. Mah-ten."

"Who sent you?" I ask. "Where are the rest?"

He doesn't answer, doesn't move. Ma is singing, *Maybe those aren't bombs, maybe those are shopping ba-ags.* "Just shut up, shut up a second," I'm saying aloud as I realise I've been saying other things, maybe singing also. "You," I say to the man. "You. Come closer. Who are you? *Closer* I said."

62

The house is clean and neat, the windows are open, and a clean-smelling breeze is blowing through the rooms, fluttering the lace curtains. There's a smell of Dandy floor wax and of Sunlight soap. The sun is shining but it's what we call a monkey's wedding, because it's raining from a different part of the sky at the same time. It's good to feel the soft rain, the spritzing of water on my skin, thin and cool and fresh. The sun is bright on the garden at one end and the clouds make it dark on the other. The lawn has been mowed, feels prickly on my bare feet. My digging has been filled in and neatly raked. A man comes out from behind the pomegranate tree, dragging a canvas bag. He stops to wipe his face with the back of his forearm. I know what the back of those overalls of his will say. It's Sammy Nongalo. He looks calm as he walks up. "How are you feeling?" he asks. I don't answer, I'm thinking I should have pulled the trigger. For my father. For my mother. He looks at his watch. "You have been asleep for . . . fifty hours." I just stand there. "We have some things to talk about," he says.

"I think the police are looking for you," I say.

"Yes. Is true."

We go inside. It's the first time I've ever sat at my dining room table with a black person. Gloria never sat at the table with us. She ate by herself in the kitchen or in her room. Sammy is in Zaydi's chair and I'm opposite, where Marcus used to sit. We've got mugs of tea and an open Woolworths date loaf with a serrated knife leaning on it because Sammy stocked some groceries in the kitchen. Says he took some money from a drawer in the study. "Sorry. I don't have any more of my own."

I just fold my arms.

"Are they saying to you that I did it?"

"I don't know," I say to the table. Then I say, "Yes." Then I say, "I think you did. You did do it."

"Please. Will you look me, Martin?" I look up and Sammy's face is solemn. I remember how calm he was that day at the Yard, pushing my father to the dirt.

"Why wouldn't you have?" I say. "I mean look what you did to Silas."

Sammy shifts, his chair creaking. "That was another thing," he says.

"It wasn't . . ." He lifts up his hands but lets them drop. "Okay, I will tell you what happen. The MOMSU guys—" He looks at me to see if I know that meaning and I nod, it's an acronym, the big labour union. He goes on telling me there were two men from MOMSU who came to meet with the guys at the Yard, wanting them to unionise. It wasn't just for better pay, Sammy says, they told them it was part of the freedom struggle, to liberate the economy for the people. But there was a split in the staff. "The older ones chased them out," Sammy says. "Silas was their leader. Silas very strong."

"So you decided what? Let's be straight, hey? To . . . murder—"

"No-no-no. Not me. This men, what happen . . ." And he tells me how the union guys said they would loosen a wheel and make an accident, not to kill Silas but to scare him. "We let them to the car, but they did it."

"The brakes."

"It wasn't what they said, a wheel. What they did, they put little putties on the brake lines, the safety cable, and the clutch plate. They are know how to do it but not us. These putties will go off when the car is fast, then you cannot stop with gears or handbrake. Something we couldn't do it ourselves. It was them."

I say wouldn't the police have known this, after looking at the wrecked Peugeot? Sammy shrugs. "I don't know why the police didn't look. Or ask us anything."

"Victor. When Victor came to the Yard that day, he wanted to see the wreck, to show my father, didn't he?"

He shrugs again. "I can't say."

"But you were there. You chased him out, I saw it. I was told you would have killed him. You and Phala and them."

Sammy sniffs, rubbing his nose with the flat of his hand. "Was not *me*, but the police will take me otherwise. This union guys, they told to me they have put my fingerprint there on those things and will say it was me. So I must protect myself, you see. Afterwards I am not liking this union people. I am thinking I don't know who they are, really. We don't see them again. It's maybe something else."

"What does that mean, something else?"

"I think those two was police."

"Sure," I say. "Right. Ja."

"You don't believe." Sammy leans forward, his hands going flat on the table. "Doesn't matter. I am here to say not about Silas. I am here to say for you about your parents. I did not do this. I would never do this thing. Put them like that. Your mother. No, Martin." He reaches across and picks up the serrated knife. "I am here, I am telling you I never did it. It's true maybe sometime I never liked your father. True I wanted a union. But I did not go there and kill them that morning, I wasn't there." He raises the knife to his throat. "If you want, you can even kill me, Martin. But it wasn't me." This is meant to impress, I spose. But it does the opposite. Like he's on a soap opera or something, acting.

I say, "Why should I believe you, Sammy?"

"This is why I have come here. Why should I come here? If I killed your mother and father would I do that?"

"You have nowhere else to go," I say. "They're looking for you. They'll pick you up."

"If I was a killer," he says, gesturing with the knife, "I could kill *you*, and then I could hide here."

I shake my head. "Not really. I am good cover for you."

"Do you not believe in me?"

I look away. "I don't know."

63

Sammy Nongalo moves some things from the house into Gloria's old room in the back, starts to live there like any other domestic servant of the neighbourhood. Now and then I give him some cash from the Sandy

Hole and he keeps the kitchen stocked and the place tidy. I watch TV, videos. I sleep. Read. I don't take any more of Mr. Stein's battle buttons so there are no more tiny singing voices inside my ears. Then one day I hear a woman's voice in the back, a real one. Time passes and there are other voices. I start to see faces showing up. Coming through the gate, in the backyard. A lot of them are my father's old staff, out of work. I don't tell them they have to go, I let them stay with my silence. Maybe word is getting round because more of them keep coming. I don't really mind the activity, the people-noise. I move the TV to my brother's room and keep more to myself there. Lots of time is passing, it should be scary but I don't really care. Are we in August, or is it September? I don't know. I notice the power going out, they're overloading the plugs again. I notice the toilets getting clogged. I go looking for Sammy one day and can't find him. The grass is all overgrown. There are people sleeping in every bedroom. At night I hear live music. I go out and look at the people in the lounge, dancing on the spot, sitting around, drinking, smoking, heads nodding. There's this woman from Mozambique. "Why are you doing this, letting all this people stay here?"

"Why not?"

"It will be trouble."

"Everything's coming down," I say. She comes to my bed.

I go out at dawn, to the back fence to urinate, and Mr. Stein's caterpillar eyebrow presses to the crack in the boards. "Thank you God," he says, hissing. "It is you. Hurry."

I ask him what he's talking about.

"The only reason I haven't called the cops is because those blue bulls will come charging in. They don't know how to handle hostage situations. You'll have your throat slit before they get through the gate. But for God's sake, hurry man!"

I yawn. "I'll see you later, Mr. Stein."

"Don't be a bladdy fool, Martin. Do not go back in. This is your chance. Listen to me and climb. You've got to."

"I'm not a hostage, Mr. Stein."

"They got you brainwashed," Stein says. "Stockholm syndrome."

"I'm not a hostage, I'm a host."

"You what?"

"Yes," I say. "No more movie sets. We're tearing it down." This sounds so crazy to him that even crazy Mr. Stein has nothing to say.

64

Always the whine of the brakes on the trucks and their heavy diesel panting. Always the soft rain. Always waking up in my own bed and believing it to be real. Then out of the dark the big megaphones boom and the spotlights stab like lances through the rain. The noise of jackboots hitting the wet streets as the steel-headed soldiers in their dark greatcoats come off the back of the truck and rush to our walls.

"Achtung! Achtung! Aller Juden raus! Schnell! Juden raussss!"

There is no rain when I wake up truly but the whining of brakes outside is real and so is the panting of the heavy engines. Then something starts smashing at the gate. I get the shotgun from under the bed. There's a diesel roar outside, then an almighty bang. Moving myself cautiously to the front door, I hear shouts and breaking glass from the far end by the carport. Women are screaming outside, men shouting and children crying and a dog snarling and barking. In the passage and the lounge I see people huddled low, looking frightened. Then the front door flies open and a light burns everything white and men are shouting at me to put the fokken gun down. I let it drop. Hands grab me and push me down, handcuff my wrists. They pick me up and rush me outside. I'm in my underpants and the night air chills my skin. They walk me through the carport. Two cops are holding a man down while a third keeps jumping up and down on his back, the man making an odd bleating sound. I recognise him, he is that quiet one who plays the lesiba. Up the little slope I see the front gates are busted open and a Mello Yello — a police Casspir — is stopped there. It reverses out and a police truck swings in and they start loading people up into it. They steer me a different way, to the right. There are more police cars in the street and some of my neighbours standing outside, watching and talking and nodding. It's about time, is what I'm sure they're saying. I look down to Mr. Stein's house but there aren't even lights on there. The street is gritty on my bare soles. The cops push me into the back of a parked squad car and leave me sitting by myself. Maybe an hour passes, my arms getting numb, when I see four squat, square headlights behind me. A red Jaguar XJ6 cruises slowly by. I don't need to look at the licence plate — that's Hugo's car, with a driver and passenger in-side. It parks in front of the car I'm in. The driver climbs out, so very tall it's like watching scaffolding go up. He's wearing a maroon blazer, the sleeves too short for his pole arms. Bokkie Oberholzer. I watch him move past, up toward the gate. Then I put my head back and close my eyes. Time passes. Rapping knuckles on the window wake me. Ober-holzer opens the door, he has a bundle under his arm and a ring of keys. "Out," he says. I climb out of the squad car and he motions for me to turn around. He takes off the handcuffs and pushes the bundle into my chest. It's my own clothes, wrapped around my Nike takkies. "Get dressed."

I put the clothes on and then I say, "Captain —"

"No! Can't you see, boy?" He steps back and sweeps his hands down his front, lifts one foot to show me a cowboy boot. Making sure I notice he's not in uniform. "I'm Major now," he says. "*Major* Bokkie Oberhol-zer. Special Branch!"

"Mazel tov," I say.

"Achieved my goal," says Oberholzer. "Let's go."

Since we're standing there on the pavement right outside my gar-den wall, I think he means that we are about to go back into my house. But when I take a step in the direction of the smashed gate, he snorts and leads me to Hugo's Jag. Someone's still sitting in the passenger seat. When the door opens for a second I get the sick feeling Hugo Bleznik is about to climb out but it's some young white guy. He's wearing a black T-shirt and ripped, peroxided jeans and oxblood Doc Marten boots and he's got a stud in one ear and in the streetlight as he turns I see how thick the muscles under his T-shirt are, slabs of it running into the wide neck, a weightlifter for sure. Oberholzer tells me to hop in. As I get in I catch the muscleman looking at me, lighting a cigarette. "This him?" he says to Oberholzer. His accent is English South African, northern suburbs like mine. Oberholzer nods at him. Through the glass I see the muscleman shaking his head and whistling and they both laugh. Like I'm the joke, but I don't understand the punch line. Now the muscleman is pointing to the house, talking with Oberholzer, the biceps swelling up as he lifts the cigarette and I see a tattoo there on his inner wrist — a fist holding two sticks of dynamite. I'm thinking about that, where I've seen it before, as the two of them move off.

Oberholzer comes back by himself, gets in behind the wheel. "You like my Jag, hey?"

"Not bad," I say, "for a used car."

"Ha. Good one." He starts up and drives us off. "There's investigating ongoing for your Mr. Bleznik, who run away following a double homicide involving his business partner. This vehicle was impound. When you're a Special Branch, C Section, like I am, you can have any impounded vee-hicle you want. Because people, they want to help you when you're SB. People who use to laugh behind my back, they on their knees at my shoes nowadays. No one wants to mess with a major of the Branch. I'm a powerful man now, Martin. Don't you feel good knowing I am your friend?"

I think about asking where we are going but decide not to. Oberholzer asks me how I've been keeping. I don't answer, thinking about Hugo telling me a thousand times how dangerous this man is, that he's got us in his sights. And in his letter: *Definitely I do not want to give that scum Captain you-know-who any bloody chance to get me alone in a cell and neither must you!*

"You been going through hell, I know," Oberholzer is saying. "But all that's about to end now. I'm here to help you, Martin."

"I'm sure," I say.

He says, "I understand you feel bitterness. Your parents murdered by animals. Now a bunch of vagrants move in and kuk all over your family home. You not thinking right, and you are lost. You need to understand I'm on your side, Martin. I am the one arresting these munts who took your ma and your da and stuffed them into that safe to die. What a way to go. Gas chamber is what it was. And you ganna make nice with these pieces of shit? These miserable ANC kieme." It takes me a second to remember that kieme means germs in Afrikaans and by then he's saying he's the only one on my side, catching "daardie bliksem naaiers" — those blasted fuckers — and making them pay for what they did.

We are driving east on the M2 highway. I can see the tops of the mine dumps, not so yellow at night, our sandbergs made of what we've been disemboweling from mama earth for like a hundred years, hauling out her kishkes of gold. There's some chatter from the Motorola under Oberholzer's seat. I swallow and say, "We left that guy behind, hey, Major?" He doesn't answer. I ask where we're going. "Shush now," he says.

We pass the turn-off to Jan Smuts Airport and get off the highway at the next. We find our way to a narrow road with no streetlights and fields of wild grass on either side and drive for another quarter of an hour till we come up on a perimeter of chain-link with a gate and guard. The time on the dashboard clock is five past three in the morning. I see the bright lights of the airport in the distance and hear jet engines, faintly. The guard comes to Oberholzer's window and lets us through. Ahead is a square building, a government-type block of red bricks. I haven't seen any signs. We drive around the back and park and

Oberholzer takes me to a metal door which he unlocks. There's a gross chemical smell. He flicks on fluorescent tubes overhead. The place has green tiles underfoot, bare brick walls. He's got his Motorola in his hand as he takes me left down a passage. I hear machine humming. He stops, opens a cupboard, and takes out a plastic apron and a pair of gloves, puts em on. Then I follow him through a set of swing doors into a large, cold room. There's a smell of rotting meat plus that chemical stink, both very strong. A row of air-conditioner fans is whooshing loudly from the far wall. There's a wide space down the middle and on either side against the walls there are metal scaffolds. They're full of long steel trays in rows, each as long as I am tall. On some of the trays I see long plastic bags. Full bags, full of lumpy things. Oberholzer turns and waves me closer. I'm starting to feel very bad, my skin is prickling with cold, my heart punching. For some reason I think he's about to show me Arlene and Isaac—even though I know they're buried. But I think he's dug them up, that's what he's done. *What a way to go. Gas chamber.* I step forward as he pulls a tray, sliding it partway out. The blue plastic bag has a draw cord at the top and he unties it and looks at me. "I'm sorry about this, Martin. I truly am. But it's important for you to see. She'll be going in there." He's pointing farther down. At the end of the scaffold there is a coffin made of steel sitting on a metal stretcher with wheels. "Aww," Oberholzer is saying. "Such a shame, hey. Such a waste." And I hear crinkling as I look back. One of Oberholzer's big plastic hands is gripping a handful of dark curly hair while the other one folds the plastic down over the shoulders. He sets the head back down on the tray and I am looking at Annie Goldberg. Her beautiful olive skin looks white and she's greeny blue around the lips and eyes and her eyeballs are sunk into the skull. Her mouth is open. Oberholzer is holding her head straight with his plastic fingers. I say the word *no* about twenty times and look away and when I look back I tell him that's not her, it's someone else, it's not Annie. "I'm sorry," he says, "this is the American, Martin. She's going in that coffin to be flown home tomorrow. You need to look at her. I want you to see what they done to her." He pushes the plastic down to her waist. It's like a bad model of her carved out of cold fat. Never again that shining smile, that laugh — *ha!* — with her head kicking back.

"Puncture wounds here, here, here, and here," he's saying. "See. I think they used a sharp screwdriver or an ice pick." He rolls her onto her side. "Most of them are in her back. Dozens. They just butchered away at her. She probably dropped and rolled up in a ball." I ask him who *they* are. But he doesn't hear me over the whooshing and I have to raise my voice. "Who do you think?" he says. "The same people she came here to assist. Communist blacks, terrorist blacks. She thought they were the goodies and we are the baddies like in movies where it is goodies versus baddies, but it turns out she's wrong. She learned the lesson too late. All they see is a white skin, that's it. That's how it is." He looks up. *"Exactly like they did to your parents, Martin."* I find that I'm swaying, getting black dots on my vision. One of my hands touches the scaffold, the ice-cold steel. Annie's head is turned away from me. "I am speaking the truth, Martin," says Oberholzer. "I want you to understand why I do the things I do. Why we all have to, if we are going to survive together in this place. Are you oright?"

65

That tattoo. The dynamite fist I saw drawn on the muscleman's skin — it comes back to me, pops right up to the surface like an underwater bottle as I follow Oberholzer back down the passage of green tiles. It was on the sign at the Dynamite Gym on Marshall Street. Muscleman is probably one of them. But what's a bouncer doing with Oberholzer at my house at two in the morning? The security light is shining on the red Jag and Oberholzer stands there, me next to him, as an old Valiant comes bumping down the dirt road and pulls up, three black guys inside. They get out and Oberholzer talks to them in Zulu for a while, then he turns to me and waves me closer. I shake hands. "These guys are on our side," Oberholzer is saying. "We call them Askaris, and they do a hell of a job. Nothing is more dangerous than undercover work." He speaks some more in their language and they laugh a little and go around to the boot. They open it and there's a man tied up in there with a burlap mielie sack on his head. Oberholzer gives an order and they lift him out. He starts struggling, wriggling like a fish, but his hands are tied to his feet. They slap his sack head a few times. Then they carry him over to the Jag and Oberholzer opens up the boot. "We'll take him from here," he tells me. The Askaris swing him up and dump him hard. Oberholzer pulls out a penlight and grins at me and says, "Say hello to your old pal, Martin." He plucks off the sack, shining the light into the eyes of Comrade Shaolin, who starts struggling again. There's insulation tape around his mouth. Oberholzer grabs him by the hair, the way he held Annie in there. The late Annie. "Had my eye on this bastard for a long while. Ons het hom nou." We've got him now. He puts the hood back on and slams the boot lid, says to the others, "How's about a little celebration drink, hey, fellows?" They all smile and we head in, with one of them staying behind with the cars. We climb to the second floor where there's a little cafeteria, empty. Oberholzer brings out a bottle of Klipdrift brandy and we sit at a plastic table as he pours the Klippies into three paper cups and then tops them with Coke, giving his own cup only the Coke. He lifts it and says cheers, "to a good job blerry well done." Everyone touches cups and I join in. We drink and Oberholzer says to me, with a smile, "How's business with the kill tapes, hey?" I keep my face under control, saying nothing. "That you carried for her to Dolfie Viljoen," he says. "Vidyos that shows how you build bombs from scratch. Pure evil. The kind of communist stuff when you look at it it's worse than porno."

"I have no idea about any of that," I say, my throat stiff so that my voice creaks. The other men laugh, Oberholzer only grins. "After we finish up our drinks here, you and me are going to take your pal out to a classified location in the countryside. A happy little farm we keep for people like him. There you are ganna help us get a few answers from him and then we'll show you how we dispose of our veilgoed." Trash. I take a big swallow of Klippies. He tops me up at once. "That'll be your start of your trainings," he says. "You're going to meet someone very special. Someone I know you'll be very glad to see."

I say, "Captain —"

"Major!"

"Sorry, Major."

He thumbs his chest. "Tenth floor, me. Ukay. Don't forget it. Major Oberholzer! Special Branch."

"Sorry, I understand."

"Diden I tell you that I would achieve my goal? If you focus, if you believe in yourself, you can do anything. And that's what you're going to learn with us. You want to eradicate those kieme who murdered your parents and your American girl, don't you? Hey? You're a man, aren't you? Well this is how it starts. Covert operations. We are fighting a war in the shadows here. And I want you on our side, man. The right side. We are ganna put you through your trainings at the farm, accelerated course. I've cleared it all. Then I'm ganna stick you back into that school of yours, for your first assignment."

"School?"

"Ja. That's right. Your Wisdom of Solomon."

I'm staring at him, trying to understand, and he goes into his coat and brings out a notebook and his reading glasses, licking his thumb. "Back with your little mates," he says, reading. "Solovechik and Horvitz and Moskevitz and the rest."

"Jesus. Have you been to my *school*?"

"I had a nice talk with Headmaster Volper. Following up on the murders. Turns out you haven't been there in ages. He gave me a tour. Huge! That is some place you Jewish boys have for yourselves, I have to

give it to you. Nothing but the best. Computers even, unbelievable. No
wonder you lot are so far ahead of the rest of us, hey? Anyway, it strikes
me, hell man, look around there, all these families prolly represent half
the bladdy economy of our country. We must keep a better eye on these
kids." Oberholzer leans forward. "After you have your trainings, Martin, you'll be ready to be my eyes and ears in there. Keep me posted on
all the doings of all the kids of these powerful peoples at that school of
yours, find me out their little secrets we can use. We'll work together
and make progress. You'll see. I've got new goals."

"Okay," I say. I'm thinking of Annie's skin in that cold room, her
sad, dead tits hanging sideways, and it's a terrible feeling. I want to
vomit. I take a drink to cover it.

"That Volper. He said I should come give a talk sometime. I reckon
he was trying to be clever and bluff me, make me feel small. You should
have seen his face when I said fine, ukay. He doesn't know Bokkie
Oberholzer. I look for opportunities to grow as a person. So I'm coming there. It's been booked. I am the official honoured guest and you
won't believe when for. It's coming up Friday, 29 September 1989 — the
day before your Jewish new year starts. Rosh Hashoony. Talk about
honoured guest." He lifts the bottle and pours for everyone but himself.
I give him a half-smile, like I know he's joking. "I'm serious," he says.
"I'm giving that speech." He lifts his cup. "Cheers, hey. To the Helgers!"
We all drink and he lifts again. "To memory of fathers, to strength of
sons!" We drink. He pours again. "To winning!" We drink. He turns
to me. "Listen, Martin. I want you to see the opportunity here. We are
ganna get the evil ones who did that to your parents. And we ganna
build you up as a man. You'll learn how to shoot. How to use a knife.
How to kill with your hands. You'll learn navigation and climbing and
kayaking and skydiving. They will build you from the ground up and
make you a real man. You understand the opportunity here? You'll set
some high goals. It won't be easy, it's a tough course and you are slightly

young, but I believe in you, Martin Helger. You'll report to me. You'll
be part of the action."

"Major —"

"If your brother was sitting here, don't you think he would tell you
go for it?" The brandy is in my head now. I have to concentrate to follow what he's saying, which is "Tell me what's your answer. You want
to do it? Think of your poor parents." I look at the other two and they
are grinning away at me. Maybe they're Zulu men from the hostel on
the hill in Jules, the ones we almost ran over with the BMW that time.
Maybe once upon a time they were ANC cadres themselves, before
someone like Oberholzer turned their minds inside out. Kop draai,
they call it in Afrikaans — head twisting. And now I'm the one whose
head is being twisted. Oberholzer's getting antsy-pantsy. "What's your
answer, hey?"

"I don't know."

"You know. You're coming with me."

It's my bladder that saves me, giving me the next words. "Is there a
toilet?" He snorts and points and I get up and walk to the far side of the
cafeteria. I have to go around the end of the counter and there's a tray
with knives and forks. My hand slips over the tray, snags a steak knife,
I'm expecting to hear a shout behind me but nothing comes and when
I look back the three of them are talking and laughing as I push in the
swing door and enter the toilets. I tuck the blade into my sock against
my ankle. Wait for a chance and . . . what? Try to stab him? No. I have
to get away. But there are no windows in here. And even if I could get
out, one of them is still down by the cars and there's a chain-link perimeter around this place with a guard at the gate. My bladder is throbbing,
I use the urinal. Nothing I *can* do but go along with Oberholzer to the
farm he's talking about. And then there's a part of me, a scarily strong
part, that is thinking maybe the man's got a point — maybe I should be
stepping up for my folks. I'm too soft. I did nothing to Sammy when

he might have been the one who gassed them. Maybe I'm *meant* to go with Oberholzer to this farm now and learn how to revenge. But I can't not remember his other farm where he put his rifle to Hugo's lips. And that something else that's been bothering me all along—those detectives at the Yard said that a "dumb giraffe" had sent for me the day my parents died. A giraffe—who else could that mean? And if it's him, why would he have wanted me brought to the Yard? Unless . . . but my mind is back at his farmhouse, excited now, remembering how after he made Hugo pick up the money and we were outside, Hugo dropped the car keys and couldn't find them so he gave up and went to the front left of the Jag where *he always kept a spare key.*

I'm looking up now as I back away from the urinal. The ceiling is made of those ugly white squares like Styrofoam with dimples. No time. I climb up on the sink and push, knock away some squares and stick my head into the roof. Smells of dust. I see a steel beam up in there and I reach up and grab it. I do a hard pull-up, lifting first my body and then get my legs up into the roof space. I find I can rest a lot of the weight of my legs on the panels under me, they bend down but they hold. I pull myself along, my legs sliding behind. I'm making a lot of noise but I don't care—the brandy is helping me, my fear's gone numb. When I'm sure I must have passed over the bathroom wall, I kick away the panels. It's dark in the room below, I see something bulky. No time. I let go and drop, hit something soft, sinking in. A couch. There's a window—I rush and open it. The drop is two stories. I climb out onto the windowsill and hang from it and look down and let go. My feet catch the next windowsill below and for half a second I'm scratching at the window and then I fall backwards, twisting, and land on my side on gravel hard enough to slam the air out me as grit flies into my teeth and my shoulder goes ow. The steak knife has spilled from my sock. I pick it up and run to the corner of the building where I stop and peek around. The night is dense and black beyond the dirt parking lot floodlit by security lights, the Valiant is parked next to the Jag and the Askari guy is sitting in it, smoking. In about a second I reckon they'll be in the toilets up-stairs and see where I've gone if they're not already, they'll radio down. I start moving across, bent over and as quietly as I can. If he turns his head he'll probably see me, but he's looking forward. When I get close I go to my belly and then roll onto my back and squirm my way right underneath. Without jacks, there's hardly any room to work, but my father's voice is in my memory ears, all those years passing him tools, so when I stare up into the Valiant's engine I soon spot the distributor cap with its four nubby fingers of rubber where the thick wires plug in. I move the knife up there, threading through all the engine parts, seri-ously hoping he doesn't decide to start the car cos it'll chew my arm to dog food. It's a stretch, but I get the serrated blade to where the wires are bracketed together to the body and start sawing. Just as the knife digs in a radio gives a squawk and then the man's voice sounds right over me. I bite my lip but go on sawing quietly till the knife reaches steel. This engine is a dead thing now. The guy is still talking. I manage to roll myself over, my sore shoulder seriously paining, and worm out from under the back end and then cross the gap to the Jag and around to its far side. Lights turn on in second-floor windows, my hand is feeling under the wheel well but there's nothing but grit against my fin-gers. I take a breath and make myself slow down. Maybe they searched the car and removed it. Calm down. Go slow. There. You beauty. It's a hard little box and I break a nail getting it open. The key drops into my palm. I reach up and unlock the driver's door as quietly as I can. I send my arm up and slowly push the key into the ignition. Then the steel door bangs open and one of the other Askaris comes out and shouts to the Valiant guy. Valiant guy gets out and walks toward him. I worm myself up onto the seat, staying bent over, and click the door shut and then I get one hand to the automatic shift and the other around the key. I blow out two quick breaths and turn the key and move the shifter to D and stamp the accelerator flat. The big Jag jumps like a stabbed bull. I rip the wheel around with the engine overrevving like a scream and the building flashes across the windshield with dust and gravel boiling up under the security lights. In the mirror I see one of the guys lifting his hands and then there are cracking sounds, like stones hitting the steel and the glass back there. When I realise he must be *shooting* I jerk the wheel and go off the track into the open dark of the field, the car humping up and down crazily. I hear heavy knocks from the back where Shaolin must be getting smashed around, and I smell burning. The airport lights shine beyond the chain-link fence ahead. I slow down and notice the handbrake is still on, schmock, that's what's making the burning smell, I take it off and switch on the headlights and see the ruts of a dirt road running parallel to the fence, right against it. I steer for it and turn left and start following along with the fence to my right, gunning it as fast as I can. I whip past a gate and hit the brakes. The gate is locked. I swing the Jag out and then reverse at the gate with the accelerator mashed flat. I can see the locking chain in the red of the taillights and there's a second to hope this doesn't crush Shaolin — but I don't want to risk smashing out the headlights by ramming with the front. We hit with a jingling crunch and the gates fly open. I do a three-point turn and I'm facing a dirt track into more bush, disappearing into blackness.

It's ten minutes of wobbly driving before a real road appears and then I pull over and use the boot release. It's all buckled and scraped but I can force the lid up, creaking. I still have my steak knife and lean in to cut the nylon ropes on Shaolin. I pluck the hood and help him out, he's too cramped-up to do much. I half carry him around and lay him on the back seat, telling him we've escaped and the car's stolen. He peels off the tape and asks for water and I shake my head and he asks where we are and tells me to head back to Joburg. We go on and eventually hit a sign for the highway. I take the on-ramp to the westbound lanes. Shaolin gives directions from the back. We change motorways to head south and then take an off-ramp. He tells me when to turn. Left, right, straight, and straight. I feel exhausted, adrenalin and brandy fighting it out in my system, draining me. Now we've reached a dirt road and again we go bumping through bushveld, the bright beams shining on the high yellow grass. We reach a railway bridge and park under it, killing the lights with the engine. I put my head on the steering wheel. Shaolin sits up in the back, moaning and rubbing his wrists, massaging his legs. He asks me if I was arrested and how I got away. "You lucky," he says when I tell him.

"Yes," I say. "So are you."

He says, "Any weapons?"

"What?"

"Did you get away with a gun? Is there one in the cubbyhole there?"

I lift my head and check. "No. Only got this knife."

"Help me out." I go around and open his door, and pull him out, his face all mooshed up with the pain. He's got cuts around his lips, his eyes, some lekker thick lumps and dark bruises. "Have to go that way," he says, but he doesn't move, he's leaning on the car, panting.

"Where's that?" I ask.

"This car will get you arrested. You're a fugitive now, Greenside boy."

"Yes."

"What is your plan?"

"Fly to America." And I'm surprised how simple it is now and that I couldn't see it before.

"They will stop you at Jan Smuts if you try," he says. "Oberholzer will put your name on a list."

"Can't I go to Botswana?" I say, thinking of Hugo. "Fly out from there."

Shaolin groans, his face clumping with pain again. Then: "Yes. You can walk across. Or Swaziland. Someone has to show you where. You have a passport?"

"Do you know anyone who can?"

"Give me hand here. We have to get moving."

I don't move. I'm looking at him and thinking about Annie, seeing her caramel eyes turned into those dead stones in her cold face, smelling the rot and the chemical pong. "He showed me Annie," I say. "She's dead, you know that? Stabbed all over."

He pants for a while. "Yes," he says. "I do know."

"He said it was you — your guys who did it. Is it true?"

He looks away, wipes his bleeding lips with his palm. "We need to move, Martin." He pushes off and starts to shuffle down the track. He's hurt even worse than I thought. I follow him.

"Hey," I say. "Tell me, Shaolin."

"You cannot blame the victim," he says.

"What's that supposed to mean?"

He's gasping like a fish in air, bent over like a senior citizen. He has to stop every couple of steps. "I just wanna know who did it," I say.

He pants, his hands on his knees. "Give me hand."

"I asked you a question."

"It was police who did it."

"I don't think so. You're not being straight."

"I'm not?"

"I can see you're not. What happened?"

"Will you help me?"

"What happened?"

He wipes blood off his lips again. "It was a rally. Annie was there. There were some Comrades who got carried off. Worked up. They have frustrations. It wasn't right. Someone pointed on Annie. It was not our fault. It was a breakdown in discipline. They have lost brothers and sisters. They took their rage on her, a white. Someone said spy. It was the wrong place for her to be at that time."

"You know who did it?"

He shakes his head, but I don't believe him. All-a-sudden there's a rock in my hand and I've got it cocked behind my head. I'm dizzy, brandy's still in me. Shaolin asks what I'm doing. I could do it right now, I seriously could. Nobody would know. Leave his body and drive away.

Like Oberholzer said. Get the bastards back for what they've done to you. "You're angry, Martin," he says, speaking all carefully.

"You know what was done to my parents?" It comes out like a bark from an attack dog and he goes back, lifting his hands.

"What happened?"

I step after him, telling him about the vault at the Yard, the gas on a Sunday morning. "They said it was ANCs who did it."

"Can you put that down, please. Who is saying?"

"The police."

"And you believe it?"

"Why not? They killed Annie, you just admitted."

"That was different, a rally, a situation . . . with your parents — wait. What kind of a grenade was it?"

"What?"

"You tell me they threw in a smoke grenade, to this vault. I'm asking what kind."

"I dunno. Who cares?"

"*What kind?*"

The rock is getting heavy in my lifted hand so I lower it. "The detective showed it to me," I say. "Was like this, round like a tube."

"Martin, that's a police weapon, army weapon. ANC guys don't have such smoke grenades."

"They could if they stole it."

"What is more likely, it was ANC or police guys? If that was their weapon. Think about that, Martin. But please. Now we have to move. Will you drop that thing and help me?"

I look away. "I don't buy all this crap about the grenade. It was someone who worked there. Who knew they'd be there on a Sunday morning."

"Oh you think they wouldn't know it? The police?"

"How would —" But then I stop. Cos it strikes me boom in the chest like the kick from that shotgun. That time at Oberholzer's farmhouse, he was saying something about my father having all his weekends off and Hugo mentioned no, he worked on Sundays at the end of every month, doing stocktaking. And those detectives again. The "giraffe" who sent for me. *Who wanted me to see them.*

"Please, man, Martin," Shaolin is saying. "It wasn't me who has done anything to your people or to Annie. Annie was a good comrade. I am sad for it. All of the cadres are." I drop the rock and move in on him and he makes a funny yelp, trying to get away. But when I grab his arm I only pull it over my shoulders and we start walking together down the track.

We come to a shack of corrugated iron, moths buzzing at a paraffin lamp. I'm breathing hard, wet with sweat. A tattered sign speaks very highly of Lucky Star canned pilchards. "Wait here," Shaolin says. The adrenalin's burned out of me, but it's left me with one moerse headache on the brew. Shaolin brings out a green tin of cream soda. It's warm and sweet and I kill it with four gulps. A taxi comes, Shaolin asks if I have money. I shake my head and he gives me a twenty and says, "You saved me tonight, Martin Helger." I'm thinking about what could be waiting at my house and it gives me an idea—I ask Shaolin if this little shop has any biltong, he looks at me like I'm a total oddball but he goes in and fetches a piece. The taxi takes me all the way to Greenside, DJ Cocky Two Bull Tlhotlhalemaje on the radio. I ask to get let off on Mowbray Road and then cut down to Shaka Road on foot and stop at the Greenbaums' gate, waiting for their Jack Russells to rush up and then I feed them the biltong in chunks before they can start barking. There's nothing a dog loves more on planet earth than a lekker stukkie biltong. They lick the salt and fat off my fingers and keep quiet as I climb the wall. In the fifteen-foot hedge we share with the Greenbaums there's a spot that Isaac plugged with a piece of board. I wiggle it loose and crawl through, the dogs whining and pressing their cold noses to my hands as I replace it. I'm behind Gloria's old room now, in the narrow alley where the cut grass gets dumped to compost. There's an inner wall along the backyard and I climb it and from there get onto the slanted roof of the house, lying flat on my belly on the tiles. From the apex I can check down into Clovelly Road and all along Shaka, can check meshugenah Mr. Stein's lawn, crisscrossed with the silver lines of his booby traps. There is a car parked on the street across from my smashed front gate. Could be anyone's, but people don't park outside overnight — cars get stolen or broken into. I reckon there's someone in that one, watching. I retrace my silent way to the hedge, then move along it to the corner where the papyrus grows.

Uncovering the Sandy Hole, I feel huge relief it's all there. Next, my pockets get stuffed with Hugo cash and the notebook searched for that scrap of half-burnt postcard. Then I make sure the envelope still has the American green cards and all the account info and Hugo's letter. And my passport, which is a nice extended one, good for fifteen years, the kind that Isaac paid extra to get for all of us. The pipe togs get dumped out of the satchel, replaced by the envelope and notebook, plus my commando knife. What else? The ring of keys that I copied. I hesitate about the Fireseed master tapes and the Volper pages. Then shove them in as well.

Out the same way and I vikkel all the way down to the Greenway Road shops. There's a tickey box outside George's cafi and the cafi is open already, before dawn. Stepping inside to get change, I notice three white boys at the back by the Tetris and the Space Invaders. At first it checks like they're dancing around, maybe cheering a high score or something, but then I notice the black man trying to get up off the floor. He looks drunk and the boys are probably back from some all-night jol and they keep pushing him down and kicking him. I say to George behind the high counter, "Hey, aren't you going to stop them?" And he just chuckles. I get my change and then I shout to the boys, "Better leave him go. I'm ganna call the cops on you." They all laugh at me. "Cops'll give them medals," says George.

Outside in the tickey box I dig out the half-burnt postcard and dial the number on it. The last number is burnt off, so I have to keep trying them all. I get some wrong numbers and some choice swear words before I hit the pager. It says to leave a number, so I give the tickey box's but now I have to wait here. After a while the kids come out and bang on the door, telling me they are going to smash me up. I keep the door pressed shut with my feet and repeat the word *cops* until they wander away. Then I fold my arms and wait. "Come on, come on," I keep saying. There's really no one else I can even try. Time passes and the black man staggers out of the cafi and weaves his way down the street. I slide down to sit on the dirty ground with my knees pulled up, getting cold and stiff. I drift off for a while, opening my eyes to the first sun, a nice soft pink light that mellows out my shivering as it gets stronger. A black boy with no shoes sets up shop at the intersection, selling the morning paper. Another bomb on the headline board. The streetlights switch off and time goes by and cars drive up and people unlock their shops, a few of them giving me odd looks. I'm afraid to phone again in case he is trying to get through. I haul myself up and stamp the tingling out of my feet. The phone rings. I grab it like a ratel snapping up a snake.

"It's Martin," I say.

66

I wake up in the hot, black spare room with the tinfoil stuck over the windows. When I open the door I'm stabbed in both eyes by the sun off the pool outside. Pats is cracking eggs in the little kitchen on the far side of the snooker table. He looks at me over his shoulder. I tell him shot, bru, for coming to fetch me and letting me crash here. He says no worries and asks if I want to graze. I say for sure, slipping into a wicker chair at the round kitchen table. There's a big pot of tea and I pour out a mug and tip in loads of honey. Pats brings scrambled eggs over with a bottle of All Gold tomato sauce and a plate of toast. He eats fast and I watch him tap out some white powder when he's finished. He has a tiny golden spoon on his key rings, he dips it and sniffs into alternating nostrils. He gasps, rubs his gums. "Woof," he says. "Good stuff, ay. Want a schnoff?" I shake my head. He looks at me. "I'm hell of a sorry about what happened to your parents, Marts. Hell of a sorry."

"I know, hey."

"Still can't believe it. I'm . . . also lank sorry I didn't come to the funeral. I —"

"It's oright, man," I say. "You sent that postcard, which I'm bladdy grateful for. Or I'd be in even deeper kuk now."

He shakes his head. "So crazy," he says.

"And it gets worse," I say. "Marcus."

His eyes stretch wide. "No."

"Missing in action," I say.

"Oh, *God.*"

"Ja, we got the notice at home like a few weeks ago. So he could still be alive, technically. But — let's face it, that's not bladdy likely. It was just brutal for us, my folks."

"I can imagine." He pulls on his bottom lip, avoiding my eyes.

"What's it, bru?"

"Nooit, hey," he says.

"No, what? Tune me."

"'Member I told you I thought I checked your brother, walking around in town? But then I called you later and said it was a mistake, after I went into the Dynamite Gym."

"I remember, hey. Sounded fishy though, the way you said it. Why?"

He nods. "Ja, well, I *did* see him. I'm sure of it. I spose he must have come for leave and just avoided you guys. For whatever reason." He shrugs. "Doesn't make any difference now."

"No," I say. "It doesn't. But there was a Dynamites oke there last night."

"Where?"

"My house." I tell him about the man who rocked up with Oberholzer, the tattoo on the wrist, the weightlifter look of him.

"That's Liam Stone, china," he says straightaway. "The one and only. And *with* the cops?" I nod. "That's lank weird," he says. "They come busting in your house last night and you ran away, right? Now you say this security cop Oberholzer is soeking for you, got you mixed in with all kinds of terrorists."

"That's it," I say.

"Martin, china, you sure you not just . . . like, exaggerating."

I shake my head. "Take a spin past my house and check the gate, Pats. Check the car parked outside with a cop watching."

He gnaws on his lip, sniffs more powder. "Dynamites and cops. Your brother mixed in. And he was also Dynamites, before the army."

"That's right," I say. "The tuxedo. But you know it for sure. Right?"

Pats looks at me. "He was, ja."

"Well then," I say, "that's a good place to start."

Pats snaps up straight. "What's that? What you talking about *start?*"

I don't say anything.

"You don't *start* anything," Pats tells me. "The plan is we duck you over to Gabs. Soon as we can. End of."

"It is. But first—"

"No buts, bru."

"Pats, there's some major questions that I've still got."

He is shaking his head, "What for? He's *gone*, man. What's the point? Forget all that. Now listen. I know someone who's got his own plane, flies out of Lanseria all the time. You know the little airport? It's like forty minutes from here. I'll rap with him, he's a good oke. There's no probs with security or anything there. He's taken me to Gabs lank times. I'm positive he'll take you. Oright?" I look at him and he says, *"Okay?"* I nod.

While he goes to shower and get dressed for work, I stretch out on the leather couch. He's not wrong. But leaving the country with the law looking for you is not a step you can take back. Ever. The clock on the stove says it's almost four, Pats starting his workday. He told me I should have a swim in the pool, mellow out, play some snooker, help myself to whatever I want. There's a television in the front room and some videos. If I need anything, there's a shopping mall twenty minutes' walk away. There's no one in the main house here so the place is perfect for me.

When he comes out dressed he says, "You just mellow here, bru. I'll organise you that flight, I promise."

"Right," I say. He must not like the way I say it cos he gives me a hairy-eyed skeef. "Martin," he says. "What're you plotting there, man? Tell me."

"Nothing."

"Hey. Just tell me."

"Ach," I say. "I don't want to involve you. I'll do it myself."

"Do what?"

"I don't know. Go out there. To Marshall Street, that Dyna-mite Gym."

He shakes his head like mad. "Just what I thought. Being a flippen idiot. Check here, china. That gym is bad news, oright. I nearly got my own self in heavy trouble there last time when I started asking questions about Marcus. And they *know* me there. I'm tuning you straight, Martin, whatever you do, do *not* go poking your nose into Dynamite."

"It's my brother, Pats. My parents. I wanna try. I need to understand what happened here or I'll be thinking about it the rest of my life."

"You go down there, you won't *have* a life, bru. Think about that."

All I can do is shrug and look away. Pats is fiddling with his scooter helmet now, standing by the sliding door. "Promise me, Martin," he says.

"I can't promise," I say. "I'll be leaving forever, you know. I won't be able to come back."

"Ukay, listen. I'll tell you what. I will slide by there, and I will see again if I can find out anything for you. I'll ask about this cop, Ober-holzer."

"No. I'll go."

"I know what I'm doing, Martin, you don't. *Remember Xanadu.*"

I don't say anything but being dragged down that alleyway's not something I could ever forget.

"Listen," Pats says. "I'll be in and out, too cool for school. And then you'll know. If there is anything to know."

"No."

"Don't be dof," he says. "Let me handle."

I look at him and nod, finally, and say okay.

"So I got your word, you'll park here, wait for me?"

"Yes." And then he's gone, swallowed by the afternoon sun. I realise I never even thanked him.

67

The poolhouse phone is ringing in the middle of *The Untouchables*, which I'm watching in the front room, getting depressed by this latest De Niro flick which is all about crooked cops in America. I don't want to believe it'll be the same wherever I go, want to believe what Hugo told me, that America is a clean future. America the golden. I hunt the dusty phone down behind the bar. It's past four in the morning and Pats says he's sorry if he woke me. I tell him I wasn't sleeping and he says I should be. He won't be coming home, he's too far out, he'll crash where he is. He just wanted to check in. I tell him everything's sweet and try to go back to the movie but my heart's not in it so I switch off and sit there staring at nothing for hours as the sun comes up. I make tea and listen to the morning news. There was an election last month (whites only, of course), I was so out of it then I had no idea, my house crowded with strangers. It doesn't matter, the Nats won big again. The new leader of our country is De Klerk. A new boss just like the old boss, as the song says. I get my satchel and take out the bomb tapes

and play them. Kefiya and Ski Mask remind me of Annie. I don't have
a photo of her, only memories. I feel very sad and start sobbing. Wish
I had photo albums of my folks, and of my brother, but all that's inside
my house, the one I'm never going back to. Maybe I'll be able to have
the contents sent to America once I'm there. Have Joski do it. But that's
not going to happen. Oberholzer has control of that stuff and anyway
I'd be scared to let him know where I am, they can reach overseas too
— Annie told me anti-apartheid people have been assassinated in Europe before. The spring sun rolls up, burning away the morning chill
as it always does in Joburg. I have a cold swim to shake my numb state,
and then get dressed and walk to the shopping mall. I have to remind
myself it's not like the cops will be searching for me on wanted posters,
like in a movie. Only that I'm probably on a list at the airport, at border
crossings. In the mall I buy a rucksack and fill it up with new clothes
and a vanity bag full of toiletries. When I get back I find Pats is in, eating a hot pressed sandwich from the snackwich machine. He tells me
he spoke with the oke who has the private plane. "He tuned me it's no
hassles," he says. "He can fly you out on Friday."

"This Friday?"

"No, the one after. It's the . . ." He checks the calendar on the fridge.
"The twenty-ninth. Freddy's a lank good oke, he told me once you in
Gabs he will organise you an international flight to America, no probs.
Long as you've got the dosh, hey."

"I've got it."

He grins. "Should bladdy hope so." Then he yawns and scrubs his
hair. "I'm sut," he says. "I'mna crash big time." He gives me an envelope
with numbers written on it. One is for the gate in the fence at Lanseria airport, underneath is the code for the gate and then the airplane
number, to look for on the side of the plane. Pilot's name is Fred and
he leaves at four on the dot. I nod, making myself smile to show gratitude, but I'm thinking about the Dynamite Gym — it doesn't seem like
he's made any enquiries. He reads my mind cos he tells me then that

he wasn't able to get over to the gym, but he will, and soon, I mustn't hassle, there's time.

After Pats staggers off to the bedroom, I drift back to the front room, my satchel is there with the Sandy Hole stuff. On the couch I pull out an old notebook, my eyes gliding over my poems and my sketches, scribbled little notes made years apart. What kind of a person am I? I think about Zaydi in his old-aged home, probably telling stories to no one about Dusat. Maybe I'll be like that one day, sitting there in America and muttering about Greenside, Greenside. But Jewish Dusat doesn't exist, it was wiped out by Jew haters. Like Oberholzer's father, and now his son. And they'll be in America too, don't kid yourself. And one day America could be like this place and I'll have to leave again. Or if I have a son, a daughter . . . Things don't go away, do they. Maybe Auntie Rively had a point about the Land of Israel, but there's no short-age of Jew haters there either, no shortage of war. I page through the letters from Mr. Volper's male lovers, the photographs he took with them. It makes me feel kind of sorry for him, sadistic bastard or not. I watch the tapes some more, Kefiya and Ski Mask. I cry for Annie. I doze off and when I wake up it's dark and Pats has left. There's a note on the table saying he'll be gone for a couple of days and reminding me there're frozen steaks and a braai outside. The braai's by the pool, a fancy brick one with wood and charcoal neatly stacked. I start up a fire as the last of the sun disappears. The coals glow orange and their warmth feels good. From inside I fetch the Volper letters, the photos. That sorry feeling I have for him — I dunno, I'm getting all mushy, feel like there's enough shit in the world already, maybe I don't need to add to it. So one by one I feed the pages and photos to the coals and watch them curl up and disappear. I go back in and get the Fireseed tapes. I sit there for a long time, watching the coals.

Sunday morning the ringing phone wakes me but I'm too zonked with heavy sleep and the pills to move. I remember the ringing when I wake again in the hot dark room and go out into the eye-burning sun. The pills are still spread over the top of the bar. I found them in a Jiffy bag in Pats's things, they're Mandrax — what he calls *buttons* (same as Stein called his) — the kind that gets crushed up and sprinkled to make white pipes. I've been taking them with orange juice now and then. I know I shouldn't but they've helped me to sleep and numb out the hours. At least they don't make me go on shotgun patrol and hear operas in my ears — not yet anyway. I poke the flashing answering machine. There's traffic noise, blurry voices, and then Pats's voice, all hoarse and loose and loud — he's drunk or at least a bit merry. "Bru, my china. I've been in and rapped with the boys, the you-know-whos. *Very* bladdy interesting. Woo. These okes ..." — laughing for maybe ten seconds, then snorting and coughing and some mixed-up words — ". . . ganna head back in and talk to" — some name I can't hear — "and get it sorted, aw man, lekker soos a cracker ek se" — tasty like a cracker, I say, which rhymes in Afrikaans and it's a slang joke. He's given it a heavy accent too. He's telling me, I think, that he's been hanging out with Afrikaners, people that are so stereotypically Afrikaner-like that it's too funny. But I can't be sure. I play it over a few more times. I notice I'm gnawing on my nails, my heart starting to go fast again. I decide I'll take a couple of buttons with breakfast. Okay, one, just one.

68

In my dream I say to Patrick, "Patrick, do you ever dream about the Dam? About what happened, about Crackcrack?"

"Why would you ask me that, stupid?"

"I think a wrong turn was made. We need to go back."

"You know you can't. What's lost is lost. Now let go of me. I have to go."

"But there's nowhere to cross." The lanes of traffic are full, there're highways on every side of us.

"Let go of me," says Patrick. "Your Zaydi did it, he made it through, I saw. Let go of me!" He breaks loose and runs. A red Jaguar runs him down and keeps going.

69

These last couple of days I've phoned the pager number again and again but there's never a response. I'm getting a bad feeling. Now it's Tuesday morning and I'm listening to Radio 5 — there's that ad for Jungle Oats that reminds me of Jet Jungle, the superhero radio plays I always listened to when I was little — and then the news comes on. They start talking about a murder and I feel cold hoops round my chest. I get dressed and run to the mall and buy the morning papers. I read them carefully but there's nothing about the murder. Enough to tell myself to stop panicking, but there are still no call-backs to my pages. In the arvy I head back out and buy the *National,* the evening tabloid, pro-government, big on crime. And there it is, just like I knew in my gut it'd be. Page 3, with huge headline. It's the kind of story they like, full of gore, showing the blacks as savages.

MUTI SLAYING TIED TO DRUGS
By Tina Rourke, Staff Reporter

The white teenage victim of a horrific muti-style slaying was also a suspected drug dealer, police say.

Patrick Toviah Cohen, 18, of no fixed address, identified today as the victim of yesterday's brutal attack, was a well-known drug dealer in the area, according to police sources.

"I can confirm the individual has been investigated for multiple drugs offences prior to this," said Warrant

Officer Kobus le Roux. "He had no convictions but we do believe Mr. Cohen was involved in trafficking of ecstasy, cannabis, cocaine, and other dangerous substances."

However it was unclear if the murder was related to the drug trade or not. "We have no evidence of that," said Officer le Roux. "This kind of mutilation of a body is not something common to the drug trade. It's possible he was just at the wrong place at the wrong time."

Cohen's body was discovered yesterday in the park at the corner of End Street, Hillbrow, and Beit Street, Doornfontein, not far from several well-known nightclubs. According to the coroner's initial findings, his vital organs, eyes, and genitals had been removed as well as both hands.

Police said the killing was likely the work of a group under the leadership of an experienced practitioner. They said body parts could fetch a high price on the black market. "With muti, they believe for example if you own the hand of a white man you'll never have to work for one," said Officer le Roux. "Other body parts are used to make charms what they believe can make a person immune to bullets or getting sick or arrested and that."

Investigators believe the perpetrators may have already left the Johannesburg area. "We believe they will try to go back to their homelands or possibly into Lesotho or Swaziland. We are on the alert for a party of four or five that would be possibly travelling together."

The page is all crushed up in my hand but I can't remember doing it. I flatten it out and I'm looking at Patrick's grinning face. They've got two photos, an old one, probably from his school yearbook, with a caption that says, *Bright Future in Better Days*. *Cohen was a top-marks pupil at Emmarentia High School before dropping out to pursue life in the fast lane of nightclubs and drug dealing, police say.* The other photo is a shot of a sheet with pale body parts spread out on it, most of them obscured with squares of black ink and the word CENSORED. Underneath it says, *FOUND: Cohen's sickening fate at the hands of muti killers.*

Again, I think. Again.

I'm on the ground. I can't breathe. It's got to stop.

And then I think: *Oberholzer.*

WHO BY FIRE

70

I'm big-time glad I kept my keys as I unlock the grate and crawl out, sweating in my new-bought overalls and pads, dragging a rucksack on a rope behind. I stand up on Solomon ground. I haven't been here in three months, since the end of June, when I still had parents. The tennis-court lights look like giraffe necks in the silver moonlight. I hump the rucksack through the veld to a mound of stones I remember well, and roll over a big one and dig a hole with my commando knife and put the rucksack in. I unzip it and get the smaller bag out and then head up to the Gooch's office. My torch beam roams over the storage area at the back — garden shears, rakes, mowers — and stops on the sacks of Wonderwerk fertiliser in the corner. With three of them loaded onto a wheelbarrow I head down the main road to the synagogue. Then I go back to the bus depot and fetch a big steel drum marked DIESEL and roll it down to the sacks. I return for a bus battery, a dozen cans of paint, and three bags of nails. In the science lab on the bottom corridor I dig out my sweaty notebook, read over what I've put down. These are notes I took from Ski Mask and Kefiya, stopping and rewinding again and again, before I burnt the tapes. I fetch certain compounds like magnesium from the supply room behind the blackboard. Outside the shul I empty half the diesel into a drain, then I slit open the fertiliser bags and pour them into the barrel. I use a rod to stir the mixture,

343

adding the compounds, keeping it moving like cake batter. When I'm finished, I empty the paint cans. In my bag are five hollow steel pipes wrapped with black insulation tape. Wires stick out their ends. I fill the cans with the mixture from the barrel. Then I close them and make holes in the tops and push the pipes in. I take time to clean up the work site and then carry the loaded cans into the synagogue.

Inside, the bimah is hit by white moonbeams like spotlights, holding the centre of the huge space. I climb up and find the hidden catch on the bench and lift the top and look down at the metal plate of the shut trapdoor. Onto this I pile up the loaded cans, filling the hollow bench. I pad the cans with bags of nails and set the battery next to them. Now begins the job of wiring it all together. Twist caps join the ends of exposed copper, and then I bring out the circuit board. I made this at the poolhouse, using a soldering iron, an alarm clock, and a remote-control toy car — all bought at the mall. Watching the Fireseed video, I saw how to solder the remote-control unit onto the alarm board. Now I leave the board unconnected to the cans but switch on the radio unit.

I shut the lid and head down into the pews, taking a seat in the back row of the Standard Eight block, the radio transmitter in my pocket. Amazing how small it is once you remove it from the joystick box. A little screwdriver operates it. I turn it on and listen — I can hear the faint chirping of the alarm clock inside the bench. I switch it off, move around to other seats and try it again — there're no hassles with activating the unit from anywhere inside the shul. But when I step out into the marble hallway, the signal cannot get through the teak doors. So it's as I thought, I'm going to have to be inside to do it. That's actually perfect. It means I'll get to see it with my own eyes, like I should.

Back to the bimah, to open the bench lid. Now my heart is kicking in me like a bucking zebra as I fit the positive wire from the cans to the circuit board. I take out the little screwdriver and turn the screw till it pinches the wire solidly. Then I take a deep breath and do the same to the negative. I sit there for a minute. Close my eyes and say the Shema, the first prayer you learn, the most important one. I open them and turn the radio control unit on. Nothing happens. I breathe out. Kefiya and Ski Mask knew what they were doing. I squat back on my heels and take the time to look at a fully activated bomb. This thing, just waiting for my signal to go boom. I keep looking, thinking about the amount in the cans — did I calculate it right? Did I put enough or too little or too much? I think about the blast radius and the bags of nails. The way I've worked it out the walls around the bimah of solid glass brick will confine the blast to the bimah alone. Nobody else in the school will be touched by it, not even in the very front rows. They might get some eardrum damage, but that's all, unless someone freks of a heart attack. I look at my watch. In a few hours, at about eight-thirty this morning — the twenty-ninth day of September 1989, when sundown starts the Days of Awe at Rosh Hashanah, the Jewish new year, leading up to Yom Kippur, the Day of Atonement, when HaShem Almighty judges all men and women and decrees their fate, who shall live and who shall perish, who by drowning and who by strangling, who by sword and who by fire — the only person that will be standing on this bimah will be the Honoured Guest of the Week, one Major Wilhelm "Bokkie" Oberholzer of the Special Branch of the South African Police. Giving his address to the schoolboys because Bokkie Oberholzer believes in growth as a human being, in setting goals and facing challenges.

Me too, Bokkie. Me too.

I look across to the aron kodesh, the holy ark where the Ten Commandments are etched on copper tablets. It doesn't say Thou Shalt Not Kill. It says Thou Shalt Not *Murder.* That's a legal difference that matters. Sometimes killings are allowed. Sometimes *required.* Vengeance is mine saith the Lord. Justice justice justice shalt thou pursue.

I think of hagbah, of lifting the Torah. Let them see what I have to raise up for them now. On a pillar of fire and a voice of thunder. Let them see.

71

Back outside to the rucksack. The overalls go in and a plastic bag comes out. The rucksack left well buried in the hole with rocks on top, just to make sure no one can possibly find it. To the swimming pool change-room next for a hot shower, scrubbing all the diesel dirt from my skin and hair. When I'm clean I dry myself with a stiff towel from the folded pile and get my fresh clothes from the plastic bag. One pair of black leather Bata toughies. One white dress shirt. One pair of new underwear. One pair of new grey socks. One pair of grey flannel trousers. One pur-ple polyester blazer folded flat. All this stuff bought at the mall. From the lost-and-found box by the front comes a striped tie, the owner of which was caned eleven times, according to the black stripes on the back. The sharp tip of my screwdriver cuts the school crest off a tracksuit top and some pins from my new shirt fix it to the blazer pocket. At the mirror I comb my wet hair nicely flat. All is moving smoothly. Everything is fine. Everything is . . . but now I find my hands are down even though I don't remember dropping them. My face looks too white. Then it doesn't look like my face. My watch can't be right. But the wall clock says it is. I've lost time. Be careful — maybe the Mandrax buttons are still affecting.

I pat my pockets, making sure I have the transmitter, the screw-driver, the earplugs. I stuff my used clothes in the plastic bag and then head downhill. The sky is dark blue, the colour of my Habonim uni-form from summer camp long ago. About an hour and a half and the first cars will be coming through the armoured gate. Then Oberhol-zer. Honoured Guest of the Week Oberholzer. Want to see his face when he sees me sitting there. I'll be in the pews and he'll be up on the bimah while I have my hand on the transmitter waiting for the right second. In the name of Isaac Helger and of Arlene Helger, in the name of Marcus Helger and of Annie Goldberg and of Patrick Cohen. In their names and in many others. When it goes it will be chaos. I will be as calm as a stone. Walk back to the mound and dig up the rucksack and put on the overalls and then unlock the grate and be on my way. Goodbye Solomon, goodbye forever. By five this afternoon I'll be in Botswana. After that, New York. New world, new life, new everything. Thank you, Hugo.

Black birds flap up from the dry grass of the rugby fields. I realise I've sort of gone away from myself again, I keep blanking. It's nerves and it's the Mandrax, maybe. I'll be okay. Haven't slept properly in a long while either, even with the pills. Some fuzzy shapes are crossing my eyeballs. Ignore them. I go down to the rubbish dump and toss the bag of underclothes in deep. As I step away I get hit with cramps, so bad I bend over. I start jog-walking to the shul. The cramps get worse — I'm dinkum worried I'll kuk my pants. In the marble lobby I head straight for the toilets. I sit there groaning in the stall for a long time. When the diarrhea seems to finish, finally, I go to the sink to wash my hands and I notice I'm not walking a straight line exactly. I wash up, splashing cold water on my face. Still too white — like a bladdy vampire victim. Keep calm, bru. Do what you have to. I pat myself. Transmitter, screwdriver, earplugs. There's no reason not to put the earplugs in, so I do — one less item to worry about. Must remember to take an aisle seat with the aisle to my right, so whoever is sitting next to me won't notice my right hand busy working inside the hip pocket of my blazer. When the time comes. When Oberholzer has talked for a minute, feeling safe and confident up there.

My legs are shaking. Must sit for a minute and get myself together. I should have eaten something, is there time to get something sugary from the tuck shop? No. Don't be stupid. Just wait here. At the far end there are some plastic chairs stacked up and covered with a tarp. I lift the tarp off and get a seat. When I sit down I get the icy shivers and I'm worried I'll have to run to the toilet again. I wrap myself in the tarp. My teeth are knocking. After a while the tarp warms me and I feel myself slowly unclenching.

72

I get up, it's time. I go over to the mirror. Wet my fingers and wipe my face. I'm a young man in a blazer and tie. A sharp young man looking sharp. There is nothing in this world that can stop a sharp young—

Zaydi puts his arm on my shoulders in the mirror and I scream. I start running to the teak doors. Zaydi is riding my back, trying to choke me and telling me to stop, stop. I bang through the big doors. This Zaydi is not frail, this Zaydi gives a screech and squeezes tighter. Can't breathe. My hand is working in my pocket but the bladdy transmitter won't acti-vate. I rush up onto the bimah and walk on my knees to the bench and open the catch. I lift the bench lid and there is a flash of blue sparks and wires of electricity shoot through my arms. My body jerks. I am slammed back. Flames burn the side of my face. I start clawing, screaming. Fire is eating into my jaw, the heat—

73

"Are you oright?"

"Ja, it's him, hey. It's Martin Helger!"

"What you doing here, man, Helger, are you back at school?"

"Give him space, hey okes. He doesn't look too well, hey."

The voices all muffled. I lift my head, feeling the tarp slide off my shoulders. There's a matric I recognise as Owen Roth, standing there, bending over me. Another one—Labner, Jamie Labner's his name, I think. Roth is blond, Labner's a ginger. I'm curled awkwardly on the plastic chair, my jaw hurts. I'm resting against a pipe and it's hot. I hear myself asking what the time is. My voice echoes funnily inside me. My ears are stuffed. I remember plugging them. I remember I have a watch. I look at it as I pat my pocket. Fell asleep and the earplugs kept me from getting woken. Schmock. Idiot. Owen Roth's muffled voice keeps asking me are you oright. "I thought you left school for good," Labner says. It's ten minutes to first bell. It's all right. My hand is around the transmitter. It's fine, I'm in the toilets and I'll walk out the door and across the lobby and into the shul. I'll take a seat. On the aisle. At the back. The transmitter is effective from any seat on the floor. Plenty of battery power. And a bus battery for the other. It's Friday and Oberholzer is the honoured guest speaker. Keep calm and stay prepared, just like the Bomb Board says. Stay alert stay alive. I stand up. Another matric walks in. "It is him, hey. Martin Helger. You came back to school, hey!" His face is shiny with excitement. "He is on his way, Martin!"

"Who is?" I stretch my back. Can't start cramping again. I need water. "Volper," I say. "Is that who you mean?"

"*Volper,*" the oke says, and all three start laughing. Labner says, "What were you doing in here, man, asleep?" He turns. "Okes, he was schloffing right there when we found him!"

"It's your best friend who's coming," says the other matric. "Your number-one fan, hey." More laughter.

"Jesus, is there something wrong with you, Helger, hey? No jokes, hey, you check a bit messed. What's that in your ear?"

One of the others shushes this. Tells the oke doesn't he know what happened to my parents? Meantime I'm drinking at the tap. When I go for the door, Jamie Labner makes a big show of backing away from me with his hands up. "You not chickening off?" he says. I stop, squinting — what's he mean?

Then the door bangs open and Sardines Polovitz steps in.

He takes one look at me and starts pumping up like he's about to pop with the news. He spins around and shouts, "It's him! He's here!"

I walk at him, saying, "Get out the way, Polovitz."

But Polovitz goes on shouting, his back to me, blocking the door. He's so excited his whole body's shaking like a wet dog drying itself. "He is here, okes! It's bladdy true! He's in here, s'troos God! Come quick!"

I hear running. I'm reaching to push Polovitz out the way but then he moves to the side and Johnny "Crackcrack" Lohrmann steps into the toilets. Right in my face. "Lookee, lookee here," is what he says.

74

Polovitz and other okes have their backs to the shut door to keep it from opening. They're grinning. The others are by the urinal, their faces lank serious, some with their arms folded. Crackcrack rolls his shoulders and moves in towards me and I'm stepping back. One of the okes from the side says, "He lost his parents, hey. Maybe just leave him, hey." Crackcrack stops and turns. "You think I care?" he says. "This little puss tried to kill me with a javelin! Tried to stab me dead! Maybe you forgot but I haven't!"

I say, "What do you want?" My voice croaks.

Crackcrack didn't even hear, he's busy pulling up his shirt. "Check at this!" he shouts, his voice breaking all raw and echoing round the hard room. He has a scar down his chest and onto the abdomen like a fat pink snake. Where there should've been a nipple, on the right, there's only a patch of scar tissue which he's poking at now. "You tried a kill me," he says. "You stabbed me. I lost my nipple! *I lost my nipple!*" His eyes in his skullish face are all bright and they don't look normal. And it hits me how things never go away, everything leads to something else, like a row of dominoes. Cos years ago I went down to the Emmarentia Dam with Patrick Cohen and Ari Blumenthal and I saw a Solomon rugby jersey in the willows by the mud and it was Crackcrack and Russ Herman and Sardines smoking there. They would have put us all in that filthy water but Ari spoke my brother's name and I saw the power of a *Name*. It should have ended there but it didn't. One thing nudges another thing, one domino knocks over another one and it keeps going and now it's coming up on eight in the morning the day before Rosh Hashanah in the foyer toilets of Wisdom of Solomon High School for Jewish Boys and Crackcrack is taking off his blazer and stripping away his tie. "And then I got fucking suspended!" he's shouting. "Me! Fucking Volper stuck *me* away! You — you *Helgers,* I dunno how you do it, but you fucken Helgers are controlling everything. You behind the scenes. But now you got nowhere to run — now you ganna pay, boy — big time!"

All I need is five more minutes and the bell will ring and we'll all have to go into shul. I step sideways to my left. I'm thinking hard. "Let me go or I swear —"

"Swear what?"

"I swear I'll tell all these okes what happened at the Dam. I'll tell em, Crackcrack."

Crackcrack doesn't answer but he stops and the blood leaves his face.

"I'll tell everyone here," I say. "And everyone I can. I swear I will, Crackcrack. *Everyone* will know."

There's a second or so there where I reckon maybe it's working, he's fading off, turning away. But then as he spins back, I realise all he was doing was hauling his arm back — he's zooming at me with a monster swing. I put my elbows up, fists over eyebrows like Marcus taught me so long ago, and Crackcrack's bony fist smashes down and my forearm goes numb. Don't turn away. But smashing fists keep swarming in, battering me. Some get through and my eye is thumped, my lip crushed, my ear mashed. I feel the sinks hitting me in the small of the back and I lunge forward blindly, grabbing. Our arms tangle up and we struggle together. Crackcrack is much stronger but his feet on those handmade leather soles are slipping while my cheap Bata toughies catch a better grip on the tiles. Suddenly he gets hold of my polyester lapels.

Polyester boy is what he called me at the side of the Emmarentia Dam, after he looked at the label of my dress shirt. Never knew how much a pair of words could hurt. And that water was foul and we hadn't done

a thing to them, just asked a question and by then Patrick's forehead was
all swollen and don't forget how he flattied the side of my face. Just mean.
Called Ari a shoch and painted his face black with mud. We had the
water at our backs and they would have put us in there and God knows
what all else. You have to remember all that. You have to remember he
asked for it.

Crackcrack slings me by the lapels into the ceramic sinks again and
then dives low in a tackle. I punch him in the back but it does nothing
and he is scooping my legs up, twisting, trying to put me down. I hold
on to the sinks and stay up, somehow, trying to kick him off me.

His eyes were bad. Never saw such eyes after I told him to strip. Take
it all off. He did it because he thought that'd be the end. But these things
have their own momentum. He stripped off the handmade shoes and the
Instinct pants and the Lacoste shirt and the Calvin Klein underpants. All
the armour of the brand names and he was big enough and mean enough
to beat us all up but every time he hesitated all I had to do was say Mar-
cus Helger. That's all. And then I said you made my friend go fetch his
yarmie like a dog, well now you are the dog you know that. Get down,
dog. Down and bark. And after he did and we were all laughing, Crack-
crack started to cry with a beam of sunlight on his face from a gap in the
willows. It was Ari who found the old rope, a coil of half-sunk hemp rope
curled up in the mud and reeds with the top of it dry and crackly with
dried duck shit. I lifted it with a stick with slime hanging from it and
made him tie one end around his neck like a collar.

Crackcrack drops my legs and straightens up and hammers me
with a knee in the belly. I let go of the sink that I've been clutching like
a drowning man at the edge of a swimming pool and I hit the ground
on all fours. Crackcrack drops on my back, flattening me. I feel his
hands scrabbling for something. Suddenly I realise.

I told him, Say I am a dog. Tell us what you are. He has to learn, said
Ari, but Patrick Cohen was shaking his head. I had the rope and clicked
my tongue and walked Crackcrack into the filthy water and told him

drink it. Please God stop, he said. I diden mean it. And Ari said, Ja, you did you were ganna chuck us in like rubbish and now you deserve.

I grab for my tie, snatch at the knot of it. So does Crackcrack. We both get it. Crackcrack starts to rip on it, to yank it back. I hold on with everything I have. Crackcrack gets one knee to my forearm and digs his weight down into it and my hand goes weak. Gradually the fabric is being prised out of my fingers, Crackcrack twisting up whatever comes loose. We are both breathing hard, both totally concentrated on this battle of the hands, the tie. But centimetre by centimetre it creeps away from me. Then Crackcrack yanks hard and it's gone — I snatch for it but already that knot is at the back of my neck, twisting.

One end of a log was underwater close to his head. I saw it and I looped the rope under it. I put my foot on the log and leaned back and pulled. Crackcrack thrashed around but the log was heavy and jammed and I had leverage. Ari got a stick and pushed on his head too and it went under. I held it under with the rope for a while and then I let him up just a little, to catch some air, but then I pulled again and he was gone under. I kept doing it. I don't know, it was addictive, this revenge. And his struggles got weaker.

The tie is pulled tight across my Adam's apple, so tight that no knife blade could get between it and my skin. I feel my head swelling up with blood. It makes my lips fat and I can feel the pulses ticking in them. Everything is going black at the edges. I'm aware of shouts from the side, so far away. Someone is trying to stop it but Polovitz is moving across. It's not going to stop. Crackcrack is strangling even harder.

That stick of Ari's was slick with mud and okay it was me who told Ari I don't think he's a dog, I think he's a bitch. I still had him by the rope but Ari wouldn't move. He called you a shoch, I said. He nelly drowned us. I was crazed with anger. We both looked at Patrick Cohen, but Patrick said not a word, he only fingered those lumps on his forehead and looked away. He asked for it, I said. He's the one who bladdy asked for it. And Ari's face changed but he couldn't. So I said give it here. You take this. So

Ari took the rope and held it and I took the stick. In a little while Crack-crack started to scream.

My hands give up on scratching at the tie. I can hardly feel my fingers as I start slapping and clawing all around me. All I can see now is a little smear, pumpkin-coloured, as big as a coin, and I'm feeling warm, tipping over sideways and falling, falling . . . Far away, my hand goes into the pocket of my blazer where I feel the transmitter and next to it the little screwdriver which I've forgotten all about. I reach up and feel the twisted grip at the back of my head, his hands are like a winch made of blood and bone. I bring the screwdriver up and over and stab it down and feel it go in. When it's sunk as deep as it can go I pull, gripping my own wrist, wrenching as hard as I can. The pressure disappears and the blood falls out of my head and face and I can breathe. I hear Crackcrack screaming. Just like he screamed at the Dam. I'm trying to get up. I see the white sink and the polished curve of steel pipe under. It makes a *U* shape and there's a valve on it shaped like a small star and when I reach to pull myself up, I turn back the other way and there's a blur. A dark thing. Growing wide so fast. Growing huge. As big as the world and all-a-sudd

NOTHING

GENESIS

1

In the beginning was darkness and then he created himself and he saw light and it was strange. There was light without but darkness within and he moved himself over the face of the darkness and saw nothing in it. Now he is being turned over and washed again. Powder and snap of latex. The pungent growing stench of his waste in the room. He is aware of the plastic parts that are not him because him ends where wires and tubes start. The brown hands slither over the white poles and the white poles are his parts. A sweet harsh smell, chemical — they are rubbing on the skin. Dark hands whispering with pale palms, cracked palms of calluses.

He is lying on his side. The awful ice pick of that tiny digging light, jabbing down at him, angling. He catches sight of a pink and hairy wrist under it. The controller.

It's not the first time. But he'd forgotten that.

2

Time is one solid clump that starts to break up into pieces and the pieces are all mixed up. There's the lady who puts things in his hands — a fluffy green ball, a carved wooden something from a board of black and white squares, a stick with a soft end which she dips in colours and, guiding his hand, uses to make lines on perfect whiteness. She plays music and moves his arms and legs to the rhythm. In another fragment a man buckles a helmet on his head and puts paste in a plastic semicircle that goes over his top teeth with a taste like the metal tube he places into one hand, taping the fingers around it. Then a green wide thing comes down over his mouth and nose and the man turns a tap on the tank and there's a soft hiss as the air turns cool and thin. He breathes it in and feels as if the bed is tilting. The man plugs wires into a box, twists a dial. Now there's a humming and he feels things moving inside himself, in his bones, his taped hand tingling around the tube and his muscles quivering and bunching everywhere. Another fragment: they are wheeling him upright down a wide corridor. There's a red hose coiled behind glass by the door. His rubber wheels squeak. Outside in the glaring light there is grass and there are big trees and flowers with colours that burn the air like coals. He sees people in white robes and looks down and finds he is wearing the same. And the talking man with the round face under the bald pate. Controller. He's always there in the fragments, always talking.

3

Gradually, smashed-up time starts to order itself, the fragments becoming sequential. One thing happens and then another thing comes after it, and he can look back and remember how it went together. He starts to anticipate how things are supposed to go before they happen, to feel himself living forward through minutes and hours and days. The same thing is also happening to words, they are falling into an order.

"If you understand me, blink twice. That's two blinks, like this, for *yes*. Oh gracious me. Now blink three times — three times means *no*.

Do you know what a cat is? Good. Now answer this question. Am *I* a cat, me, speaking to you? No? Good. Am I a woman? No. Good. Am I a man? Yes. Excellent. So excellent. I could cry, I really could."

In the mornings different women clean him, rub his skin. But the same one always comes to twist his limbs and he's always afraid of her because of the pain. In the afternoon it's another constant one, the one with the toys and the music. When the light is fading the man with the helmet and the gas tank arrives. In between all of them is the chunky bald controller, always talking.

"Do you recognise these? Let's take the first one. I'm going to say different names for this one. You blink and stop me if you think I've said the right name for the thing. Okay? Dee. Eff. See. Kay. Jay. Ay . . . Ay? Are you sure? Yes, you are. I can see. And you are right. *This is an* A. Wonderful. So *wonderful.*"

After the beginning most things still had no names. So they brought objects before him and pictures of objects and of living things and he was asked to pick their names. A kettle, a beach, an elephant, an egg. They brought the world before him in tiny pieces and he named the world, fragment by fragment, building it up, and forgetting and remembering and remembering again. The woman who so terribly stretches his limbs for him is Ms. Roberts. The woman with the music is Mrs. Lobenza. The one with the helmet is Mr. Rajbunsi. And the bald controller is Dr. Norman Meltzish. Call me Dr. Norm. Dr. Norm shows two hairy fists with thumbs on top, holding them vertically together in the light from the window.

"That's about what a human brain is. A little under a kilo and a half of wet matter floating in about a hundred and fifty millilitres of cerebrospinal fluid. When Leonardo da Vinci first dissected the brain in 1504 he thought the human soul was situated in the cerebral ventricles. Today we think we know better, but the truth is we're still blind — maybe that's all we'll ever be in neurology. The human brain can understand a watch or a heart because it is more complex than those simple things. We can look *down* on them and know them fully. Similarly, only something more complex than the brain can understand it. Something has to look down on *us,* to find the true seat of the soul. But that thing does not exist. We're doomed that way. We'll never grasp the human mind because we can never escape it."

It makes him so tired to hear Dr. Norm talking this way, droning, standing there by the window and looking out. And what is his own name? Who is he? He has started to make word sounds, his tongue clomping around the mouth. Moaning noises that frighten even him.

"You were a transfer from Joburg General. You were first admitted there, from Emergency, and after a lengthy stay they sent you on as a hospice case. To be brutally honest, there was no family consent to switch you off. If there had been you probably wouldn't be here. All this happened before my time. Patient Number 975-A12-89 — that's you. That's all your chart has ever told us."

His name is Patient. He is a complicated, damaged organism and his name is his essence: pure waiting.

"We have no other information about you. Whatever details Emergency might have had at the Joburg Gen has been lost in paper records that no longer exist. I'm sorry. I can tell you you were treated for significant skull fractures, including a nasty depressed bugger on the posterior right side and a *very* unfortunate basilar number. Evidently they went for a decompressive craniectomy to relieve the brain swelling. That's where they lift off a nice-size chunk of your skull like a cap and keep it on ice for a few months while you heal. They put it back. Of course."

The garden outside is terraced, falling away in levels toward the high brick wall at the base. The sun shines on red dirt and the rocks are yellow, banked at the ends of each terrace, and formed into stairs between. Down there past the flower beds and the big trees there is a sunken greenhouse that was once a tennis court and also a cactus bed in the shape of a swimming pool. Beyond the garden and the high wall is a view of the city all blotted green by the tops of the trees, a forest broken by rooftops, and stretching on toward the hazy smudge of dust on the horizon.

"The name of this city is New York, London, Amsterdam, Cairo, Tokyo, Johannesburg, Moscow. Moscow? No. That is not correct. This is not Moscow. This is Johannesburg. You've forgotten we've told you that many, many times. Johannesburg. Jo-hann-es-burg. Joburg. That is the Brixton Tower. This must be the city where you are from, Patient. Maybe you were even born here."

But there are no places in him when he tries to find them. There is only what he sees here, the institute, the grand mansion of stone with chimneypots on top and a falling garden in the front. The other patients wear whites like his and the staff are in their greens. Dr. Norm wears corduroys and no tie. He holds out a pointer and Patient opens his jaw like a rusty gate to take it in his teeth. With pain and practice he can turn it, aiming at the board full of letters. Laboriously, he communicates: WHER WE??

"You know what this place is. You've been told many times. Fight for it now, try to remember." Patient blinks twice, and waits. Dr. Norm inhales. "This is the Linhurst Institute. We are in upper Parktown, Johannesburg, South Africa. Mansion country. Up on the high ridge where the Randlords built their piles. The Linhursts are old-money Anglos. This was a family home. Donated for brain treatment research. My work here's been focused on traumatic brain injury." He smiles. "People in your line—but nowhere near."

His room is 253. This means second floor. The first thing he starts to move after his mouth and his head is the index finger of his right hand. The ability to move spreads from there, like an advancing skin rash, gradually enveloping the arm. Dr. Norm draws a diagram and tells Patient what the Glasgow coma scale is. "Your score was a three," he says.

"Pretty much the lowest you can get." By this, Patient understands that a low score is not a good thing. *Coma,* he thinks. The word feels steep in him, unassailable, like a tower of stainless steel he must try to climb. Dr. Norm is showing the bottom of a diagram he has drawn. It goes down from being dazed to being knocked down, to being confused, to being out cold. *Senseless.* "That was you," he says. "But a case like yours, Mr. Patient — there are no charts for it. It doesn't happen. You're as rare as spontaneous total remission from advanced terminal cancer."

Patient tries to concentrate, to raise the pointer again with his tingling right arm; there is a vital question that must be asked. But the question is too huge inside him, like that rearing, steely word *coma.* He sweats and trembles. The pointer falls.

4

It's only when the headache stops that he realises he has always had one, or most always, and that it's always strongest after Rajbunsi the helmet man leaves him. He communicates this to Dr. Norm and Dr. Norm says the helmet is the reason he has made his recovery. "I invented it. The Meltzish Protocols. Oxygen and mild electric current together. To stimulate neural regeneration. My thesis is that the brain is like a biological electronic device. Think of it like running a laptop on battery versus plug-in. As soon as you unplug, the screen goes dim and process speed falls off. But plug it in and it brightens up and starts zooming. This is my attempt to plug your brain in."

Labouring, trembling, moaning, drooling, Patient points at letters on the board: *LAP TO???* Dr. Norm's laugh booms and takes a while to mellow to a chuckle. "Of course, yes. I'm sorry. A laptop is a portable computer. Small enough to use on top of your lap, hence *laptop.* I'll bring one to show you." Then he leans in, narrow-eyed. "You know what computers were like, Patient. You can remember. Can you remember computers? Yes you can."

Patient blinks thrice. Dr. Norm winces. Then, ponderously, Patient raises the stick of his good arm to the letter board: *CO MU*

"Yes, coma. Comatose. That's what you have been all this time. Well. Technically a persistent vegetative state."

HOW

LONK?

Dr. Meltzish looks at him with his round bald head on one side. "You know this, Patient. I've told you. It's in you."

TEL

Dr. Meltzish shakes his head. "Not this time. You fight for it. Look for associations. Find those memories. They are in there."

TEL!!!!

"Goodnight, Patient."

Nobody understands concussion and traumatic brain injury. There is invisible trauma to the cells. Acutely, this is akin to an electric short or an emergency shut-off valve. Some view it as vascular in nature. Blood supply. There is the issue of potassium flux and calcium uptake. Dr. Norm talks of whiplash and coup and contrecoup, the way the brain slams against the sides of the cranial cavity. Shockwaves through jelly. Shearing damage of white-matter tissue. But after the swelling goes down there are often only symptoms left to deal with and no obvious visible lesions.

"My view is that there is malfunction on a microscopic level we can't pick up. Maybe one day when scans get good enough. Until then we keep working, you and I. Get our paper published. Push the frontiers of knowledge. *Onward.*"

Mrs. Lobenza takes him to the basement every day. On the mats and benches, around the weight stacks and rubber bands, he is forced to try to pull himself up, or push against her resistance as she bends him and twists him, with the musket balls of sweat popping from his trembling forehead. Afterwards he will receive a bath and a rub-down with the chemical emollients designed to combat the bedsores that still plague his flesh. He is then given breakfast. They feed him well on Dr. Norm's regimen. The brain needs fats. Eggs fried in but-ter and avocado smeared thickly on his toast. Salmon or lamb or sau-sage for supper, nuts to browse on. Sardines at lunch. After breakfast he is wheeled to the balcony on the second floor. This is his favourite time. If it's chilly the nurse will leave him with a silky Sotho blanket over the legs, but normally the sun is bright and warm. He will sit with one of the oversize-type books and try his best to learn to read again. A word at a time. A comma at a time. He can understand the individual units, but his mind keeps swiveling away from the sense held in the length of a line, a sentence. He'll put the book down and stare out above the terraced gardens of the Linhurst Institute and try not to become enraged. Rage is always there. It billows up in him like toxic smoke and there is nothing to restrain it. Just as there is nothing to hold back bouts of racking sobs and deep sorrow that come over him with no warning.

TEL HOW LONK?

"You're the impossible young man. You should be dead. We under-stand nothing of the brain. A woman in the UK was hit by a car. In a coma for eleven months. When she came out of it she spoke English with a thick Japanese accent. Never been to Japan, never knew any Jap-anese people. There is no explanation."

HW LONK?

"Try to remember, Patient."

JIS ANSER

"All right. Look at me. Watch my lips. Are you ready?"

YES!

"Six years. Nine months. Three days. The miracle kid."

5

Time passes and other limbs twitch into life, fibre by agonised fibre, just as the fibres of memory within his skull begin also to pluck and strain. Dr. Norm says memories are locked in brain cells in long chains. If one cell "comes right" it will tug its neighbours into "coming right" too. He says Patient has to listen in himself, to "pay quiet attention" for the tiny flashes of memory, those are cells "sparking up" in a dead chain. Patient is to take encouragement from this process and not lose heart. Patient wonders how memories can live inside cells which he pictures as soap bubbles filled with jelly. How can taste be written *there*? Light and noise and feeling and faces.

"We know nothing. It will happen."

His speeches by the window. His hairy fists. Patient never understands these monologues, but he appreciates them since so long as Dr. Norm is speech-making he is not testing him in some painful way and the end of another of the exhausting sessions is getting closer. He wants to please Dr. Norm with his progress, but he is always failing him, it seems. Dr. Norm and his plans for "their" paper that will stun the world. The Meltzish Protocols. Patient understands how lucky he is to be here, to have been severe enough, alone enough — and picked as the case study. He must remember to be grateful.

Months and months slip by like the brushing of the soft Sotho blanket over his shins. He is wheeled out to watch musical performances with other patients. One time he *sees* the notes, the brass sounds of a saxophone like syrup in the air. Dr. Norm says such visual-temporal hallucinations are "part of the cure." A lot of things are part of his cure. The fact that Patient still can't remember almost anything, that the flashes refuse to come together into anything coherent, is also "part of the cure," and that Patient's muscles remain stubbornly atrophied — that too is "part of the cure." Patient says — he is speaking now, slowly masticating on each syllable like a mouthful of raisins — "Why I'm. Here? How'd I get?"

"I've told you many times. All we have on your chart is Patient Number 975-A12-89. All I know is I started treating you with my protocols in 'ninety-two, never losing hope. And here we are, my friend. Making history."

"My . . . family."

"We have nothing."

They stop the last of the helmet treatments and the headaches fall off completely. Dr. Norm shows him an album cover with a picture of George Michael, a movie ad for *Top Gun* starring Tom Cruise and Kelly McGillis, a *Wielie Walie* lunchbox, a blue two-rand note with Jan van Riebeeck's face on it, a striped cricket cap from a primary school, a Super M milk carton, green for lime flavour, a Rubik's Cube. "Remember," he says. "Remember this forgotten world."

6

It's cold weather, the cold seeping through the big stone house so that people are plugging portable heaters in everywhere, when Patient first starts to walk by himself. It brings him so much pain he almost prays his motherloving legs will go back to sleep forever and ever amen. Mrs. Lobenza puts him upright between two horizontal poles and he has to work his way down, his weight shared by the arms, the hopping hands. His arms have thickened out by now, even the wrists. All those fatty meals are being turned into useful tendon and bone and muscle. The body is a most wondrous survivor. He keeps working. He begins to walk unaided. It's hot then, another season, another year, the sweat saturating his shirts. Dr. Norm has been away for a long stretch. Even before he disappeared he was there only in spurts, always seeming distracted. Now Patient can read more than a page, sometimes more than a few, and keep it all together in his head. Suddenly he remembers a dog with a name that whispers to him, just under the tongue until he dreams it and sees her: *Sandy*. Of all the family members it is the dog that comes first. He remembers riding her in diapers, with a woman's hands holding him in place, warm brown hands around his middle. These first memories change everything. He starts to see that Dr. Norm must be correct. His confidence and hope lift. His brain cells are rebuilding themselves up there above the eyes, rewiring. It's been one hell of a costly renovation job, but now some lights inside are starting to flicker back on, showing him things he has stored away in those gloomy, chaotic rooms he cannot see. Gradually he gains impressions of a childhood. The maid in the brick room in the back, she was the one who held him on Sandy, and the softness of her vast bosom. And an old man who spoke a language he couldn't understand but felt warmly toward, who sat on the sighing plastic cushion underneath the maroon branches that the sun poked through and the branches were two plum trees on the other side of the garden opposite a house. The phone in the house was green and hung on the wall in the kitchen. His room faced the garden, had a metal desk. He put a padlock on the door. He doesn't know why he would do that. His mother had her own funny vocabulary — "gribble grobbles" and the "twinkle toes" — and her dreamy ways. And he remembers the man of the house who must have been her husband, his father, that mashed mug of used-up flesh with the big lumpy ears sticking out, the steel-wool hair the colour of salted carrots. He remembers a blue hall with a high, hollow ceiling. A choir of men singing a mystery language. A feeling of awe. White robes. Letters of an alien script.

"It's a shul," Dr. Norm says. He looks at Patient. "That's a synagogue. You're Jewish. I'm not surprised."

"Why?"

He winces. "Let's just say the tribal proboscis is a gift we both share. And you're circumcised. Plus I've always had a gut feel."

"It's like I'm trying to build a bridge over a valley of mist. I can hear people on the far side, calling to me."

"Interesting," Dr. Norm says. He's back from another of his absences, but he doesn't seem all that rested. His winces a lot and his face is pale, with purple bags under the eyes. You can't call him a cheerful man anymore. He's lost some springiness, no doubt of it. He pours himself a big glass of wine — this is new — and says he is raiding bottles from the cellar. Excellent Burgundies down there. Those Linhursts had taste. "What you're describing sounds like a metaphor for the neural connections that are linking up inside your brain as we speak. But there are still dead patches of suboptimal tissue that need to be circumvented or repaired."

"Right," Patient says blankly. "But am I ganna get the rest of them back or not?"

Dr. Norm yawns and looks away. "Undoubtedly," he says. He doesn't visit in the next week.

7

Progress is no straight line. Some days he regresses, so weak he lies in bed and moves only to vomit. But other times it's the opposite, a sudden spike upward, as when he finds himself answering Dr. Norm with a feeling of fear at the speed of his own words from his own lips, like riding a precarious bike but somehow not falling, and then Dr. Norm holds up a *thing*. "Come on, think. One just like this was on your breakfast table. It's a . . ."

"A watchacallit."

"Three, two, one. You fail this round."

"No, no. Wait. I can get it. Wait!"

"Calm down."

"Wait! Fuck! What the fuck is it?"

"Sit down, chum. Don't do that. Calm down, please."

But it's too late, the tantrum is on him and he's howling and beating his hands on hard things while Dr. Norm sighs and rubs his face. This time he uses a stool on a filing cabinet with bad results. The damage surprises him, he's been so weak for so long.

"You still don't understand what you've become," Dr. Norm says. "Not truly."

"I don't?"

"Friend, you're a full-grown man now. You haven't felt what that means because your body's been so atrophied. Now you've filled out. Your nervous system is calibrating, your hormones are up to their levels. But meantime your brain still believes that you're only a teenager. Mentally you *are* still one." Patient studies his own face in the window glass. The jawline, the dark bluish stubble that would sprout into a beard if it were allowed to. His time in the sun has given him colour and the shoulders are wide.

"I think perhaps it's time we started," Dr. Norm says behind him.

"Started what?"

"Going *there*." And he points at the glass, through him, to the outside world beyond the reflection.

§

But Patient doesn't go anywhere, because Dr. Norm disappears again. This time there are no more tutors in his absence, no more nurses, just Mrs. Lobenza — and the work with her is no longer rehab but fully functional exercise. Patient can run and do push-ups, he can pull his chin over a bar. There is animal delight in the gorgeous feeling of this physical mastery, the sheer loveliness of *movement,* his body remembering what it was like to be the boxer he was, the rugby player also, and every day he feels more robust and strengthened — but then he also spends hours with his eyes closed and his fingers on his temples, rubbing, pushing, trying to force himself to remember. *Remember.*

So many months pass that he starts to think this time Dr. Norm is not coming back ever. But then he appears. And Patient can't wait to tell him he's got news. "I think I almost have my name, my family name."

Dr. Norm is unshaven. He smells bad and there are stains on his collar. He is drinking Shiraz from a coffee mug. "Almost," he says. "Almost is all you've got after all these years."

"I know. It's been a long time."

"You opened your eyes three years ago."

"My name, Dr. Norm. It's something to do with hell."

Dr. Norm sputters, burps up guttural chortling, curling forward. "Oh my. Your name is hell, hey?"

Patient's face goes stiff. "I think so, ja."

"Hell. Well, hell, man, Mr. Hell. Don't look so hurt at me."

"I don't think it's funny. I think it's the truth."

"Surely is," says Dr. Norm. "You're named after what we're all in."

"Dr. Norm," Patient says. "What's going on with you?"

He waves the mug, almost knocking the wine bottle over. "Nothing," he said. "De nada, Comrade. Session over. Session ended."

"But —"

"Get out of here, hell boy. Shut the damn door behind you."

The next time he finds that Dr. Norm has set up a television and a DVD player in the office. DVD stands for digital video disc — these have replaced videotapes. There is something important about videotapes to Patient but he has no idea what. "Pull the curtains," Dr. Norm says. They sit on the couch. There are two DVDs: one shows a documentary about the country of South Africa, the other is wedding footage, and wedding anniversary footage, and footage of children playing water sports in a place Dr. Norm says was near somewhere called the Vaal Dam. Patient doesn't have to ask him how he could be so sure, because it's obvious he was the cameraman and the children are his, the wife the same woman from his wedding, only more wrinkled and with shorter hair and wider hips. While they watch the documentary and the family footage, Dr. Norm drinks wine from the bottle and periodically breaks into paroxysms of quiet sobbing, his round shoulders shaking so violently that Patient puts his arm around them to keep him steady. Dr. Norm keeps skipping back to watch the same sections over and over.

In the first they see a flat mountain by the ocean. Cape Town. This is part of South Africa: our country. They see a convoy of vehicles, a thousand cameras, helicopters. A voice tells of Victor Verster Prison. They watch a lean old African man in a suit coming out of the prison gates, holding the hand of a woman with a thick mop of dark hair. He raises his fist. The corners of his mouth are down. His face is deeply lined. His hair is white. He looks hard, serious. Dr. Norm cries. "Nelson, Nelson," he says. The documentary tells who Nelson Mandela is. It gives Patient a strange tingling in his chest but triggers no memory flashes. The man was in prison for twenty-seven years. He had been put away because he had fought for nonwhite people to have the right to vote. But they let him out and then they had an election for all. "It was headed for total war," says Dr. Norm. "Blood in the streets. Instead we all lined up and voted together. After my wedding to Janine, and having Jamie and Simone, it was the greatest day of my life."

They watch the lines of people waiting to vote, black and white together. The tears run down Dr. Norm's face and drip on his shirt. They watch his wedding footage again, then again. It's stuffy in the room. He keeps opening wine bottles, the sweetrot smell of fermented grapes spilling on his chin. Nelson Mandela again, coming out of prison. The man had held true, he had never wavered, he had been prepared to die in there rather than give in, and he was in the right. He was let out. Justice had won. Skip back: there he was again, he raised his fist. Triumph. The first president of the New South Africa

was Nelson Mandela himself. His life story is a plot with a happy ending. "Miracles," says Dr. Norm. "Miracles and wonders." Then he says,
"Ach, screw the cynics. You have to fight them too. The so-called re-
alists." Then he says, "Just because it's like a fairy tale doesn't mean
it didn't happen. Fairy tales happened. Happy endings happen. Look
at it. Look! There it is!" They watch Nelson Mandela again. They see
South Africa win the world rugby cup and Mandela on the field with
the team. They see the first elections again. They see the prisoner become the president again. The plot is whole, the happy ending irrevo-
cable. And back to the wedding. Dr. Norm had all his hair in 1969 and
no belly — but it was him. "We believed in the same things. We were
committed to the Movement, to the struggle for a nonracial society.
We sent our kids to Swaziland for their education, we did our best to
live our principles. I was no hero but I was arrested, so was Janine. We
both did prison time. We were politicals. I can't tell you how many
times we came *this* close to leaving." He falls asleep with his chin on
his chest, snoring. Patient gets up and lowers him onto his side, then
he switches off the television and leaves the room.

9

He has his body back and so he uses its energy to rove wider in the
corridors, opening doors. He discovers old boxes full of documents in
the east wing, dust-stacked pillars without order. He excavates, reading
for days, and finds patient records, medical charts and files. He gath-
ers all the *H* documents, looking for "Hell" — from the feeling it's his
name — and after a week of looking eventually he comes across a reference to a patient Helger. M. Helger. A second document has the same
name. The patient number is 975-A12-89 — *his own.* When Dr. Norm
gets back, he tells him, "Helger — I must be M. Helger. Maybe Michael?
This *must* be me. It *is.*"

Dr. Norm sniffs, rubs his stubble. "Has the sound of it helped you to remember anything new? Any associations?"

"No."

"Where did you find these?" He nods as M. explains, and then he chuckles. "Unbelievable. They dumped the records when this place started using computers. But they were too lazy and disorganised to transfer." He looks up. "Detective Patient," he says. "I mean Detective Helger." He shakes his head. "Well, go and get ready."

"Ready?"

"Put on street clothes."

They drive down the long driveway in Dr. Norm's Mercedes and a uniformed guard opens the gate. "I didn't even know we had one," M. says. "I've never been down this far."

"Everyone has fucking guards these days," Dr. Norm says. He had never been a swearer but this too is changing. The way he spat the word makes M. glance at him. The steep road runs down alongside man-made cliffs of yellow stone until they reach the level and then drive onto the flatness of the lush treeland that is the view he's been staring down at for so long from the terraced garden. In the dappled shade under the treetops, he sees signs for ARMED RESPONSE everywhere. Certain roads are closed off, with guards waiting by gates. He notices thin wires over the walls everywhere — Dr. Norm explains they are electrified. They drive around, Dr. Norm saying he wants M. to "relax the mind" to "let the associations roll in" and "pay attention to your emotions." He says the emotions are the way that the unconscious part of the brain sends important messages to the conscious part. They are signals to take action that will result in our survival.

M. says, "What should you do if you just feel sad?"

"Suck it up," says Dr. Norm, snapping it out, bitter and quick so that M. looks at him, frowning. They are supposed to rove, to stop now and then to get out and let M. touch things, smell them. They are supposed to visit the library and look up information about the family

Helger. Instead Dr. Norm parks outside a house in Northcliff. He has a bottle between his legs and he winces and drinks from it and stares at the house. M. sees a steel gate, more electric wires. A palm tree growing over the wall and a FOR SALE sign in front. When Dr. Norm rubs the bottle against his face, all that greyblack stubble makes a scratching sound against the label. It isn't wine anymore, it's Mainstay — cane spirits. They drive to a high school and park there and Dr. Norm stares at an empty rugby field. They drive to the campus of Wits University. They visit a block of flats in Killarney. "Now what?" M. says. "What's this place?" He doesn't expect an answer, hasn't been getting any. Dr. Norm's eyes are red. "Our first," he says. He starts crying. He wipes his nose with the bottle hand and takes a long drink.

"Who's our?" M. asks.

Dr. Norm drives back to the institute in silence and drops him there.

10

He gets a stack of old newspapers from the staff and learns that Nelson Mandela is alive and well but no longer state president. He didn't run in the second multiracial election this year, 1999. The new president is Mbeki. Mandela has a new wife too, having divorced his old one, that one who met him at the prison gates, Winnie. She had been charged with child murder and convicted for kidnapping and being an accessory to an assault in a case where a fourteen-year-old township boy, suspected of being a police informant, was abducted and tortured for days at her house. Then he was dumped in the weeds nearby and murdered with garden shears. M. reads of more atrocities uncovered — hideous things done by the white government to its citizens, but also those done by the freedom fighters. Gradually, in the pages of the *Star* and the *Sowetan*, the *Citizen* and the *Mail & Guardian* and the

Sunday Times and the *Express,* he starts to discern some manner of re-flection. Like him, this whole country is trying to remember. To dig up secret buried pains and turn them over in the light. There was a kind of court where people went to confess in public, the Truth and Reconcili-ation Commission — it was the nation's Dr. Norm. But when he brings this analogy up, Dr. Norm winces. "Ach, nobody cares anymore. It's the hanky parade every afternoon. So Bishop Tutu can show off to the lib-eral wankers in London. What's the point? Either hang the apartheid bastards or not." Dr. Norm is looking like a bulldog, the weight he's put on and the pouches under his eyes. Uncut curls lean over his bald spot.

"What's going on with you, Dr. Norm?"

"Never bloody mind."

"What about me?" M. says. "When're we going to revolutionise the science of concussion?"

"If I publish what I've done they'll probably throw me back in jail. This place. These days. Close the door, please, on your way out."

"Did you find out anything about the Helgers?"

"Next time."

It's a seesaw: Dr. Norm dropping hard just as M. is picking up, fly-ing. Every morning he's been waking with a rush of new flashes. A boy's face up close with lips peeled back. A shotgun. A river in flood where a section of broken pipe bobbed along. Now he begins to have knowl-edge in whole chunks. He *is* a Helger — that's for sure. He grew up on Shaka Road, number two, in the suburb of Greenside. His father with that rough mug of a face is named Isaac. Isaac Helger. His mother is Arlene. He remembers he used to wash himself at the sink in the back-yard, the same one his father Isaac used to scrub up over, coming home in his rattletrap Datsun bakkie every evening. From a scrapyard which he owned. While he, M. Helger, he owned a tuxedo. He liked boxing, was good at it. He remembers skipping rope and hitting the heavy bag. He'd been strong and fast and vicious. He'd had a squat green car and delighted in its ugliness and power.

Then one day he says to Dr. Norm, "I've got it. My name."

"Michael? Mendel?"

"No. It's Marcus. *My name is Marcus Helger.* No middle." His hand goes to the doctor's arm. "How about you get your car keys."

11

The electric wires, the armed-response placards, the guards. The house in Northcliff no longer has a FOR SALE sign in front of it. "We lived here for nineteen beautiful years," says Dr. Norm. "Me and Janine and Jamie and Simone. A family. We met at varsity, UCT. Of all the times when we nearly left the country it was right after graduating that we came the closest. The system gave no hope, you know. But we decided we stay and fight. Joburg Jewish liberals both of us, but at varsity we turned radical. I refused to do the army. I had my degree, I would have had the rank of captain to start. They even offered me a choice of post, and reduced my national service to a year. No, I said. They stuck me in prison for three years. But I survived it. Me and Janine, we hid activists in our house. In that house, right there that you see before you. The neighbours would have had heart attacks if they knew. We were card-carrying ANC members when membership would get you twenty years hard labour. The Special Branch tapped our phones, pulled us in for questioning. We carried messages for the ANC leadership in London. We fought apartheid the best we could every single day of our lives. Took risks."

"But," Marcus says.

Dr. Norm rubs his beard. He has on yellow sunglasses. "But what?"

"I dunno. Just sounds like there is one coming."

He blows air through a sneer. "You don't know how important it is until it disappears. The Struggle *was* our life. It gave us our meaning. We were a team, it united us with our secrets, our purpose. It's like . . .

all our lives we were leaning against this wall. Then someone took that wall down and we just fell over, we were down. We couldn't get back up."

"What happened?"

"Another no-fault divorce in the New South Africa. Just sign and rinse and overs kadovers."

"I'm sorry, Dr. Norm."

"No fault. Nobody's fault. And family court judges that believe the natural order is for kids to stay with Mommy, never Daddy. That's what's happened. I'm a white male dinosaur, Marcus. Being a Jew doesn't count—the opposite actually. They just wish I'd hurry up and die off already." He starts the Mercedes and drives off. He talks about the Movement, rambling. Says where he was on that February day in 1990. February the second. The day the new president, De Klerk, stood up in parliament and changed history. "It was a dream feeling, watching those words coming out of that mouth. I know them by heart. *I wish to put it plainly that the government has taken a firm decision to release Mr. Mandela unconditionally—*"

"Wait, wait. *Stop the car.*" Marcus leans forward, pressing his wrist to the forehead. Something coming loose inside. Botha. Bald man, stroke mouth. Talking on TV. And police. A township was a place with shacks made of corrugated iron with stones on their roofs and he was there. He was running there, police after him. "I was involved too," he says. "I was in the Struggle too."

"You were just a teenager, Marcus." Dr. Norm says. "You're fantasising."

"No."

Dr. Norm shrugs and drives on, into town and then through Hillbrow. He tells Marcus to keep the window rolled up and checks the doors are locked. They drive down Claim Street and up Twist. A broken sign on a crumbling hovel says XANADU. Everything Marcus looks at is alien to him. "I don't remember," he says. "I've got nothing."

"Neither do I," Dr. Norm says. "You're not looking at the past here."

They are in the streets of an African city, the lanes jammed up with combi taxis, the pavements with crowds and people selling food and trinkets, people begging, people sleeping on the ground. Potholes full of muck. These are all black people but they don't all have the look of those he knows or can recall. He sees the long-limbed light skins from the Horn of Africa and the deep blackness and round heads of the equator and western Africa. Strange, vivid robes everywhere. The buildings have boarded windows and there are piles of trash and debris in front. Broken bricks, crumbling walls, graffiti. As he looks he finds people are staring back at him and Dr. Norm. They are the only white skins in this world. They come around to Joubert Park. There are men cutting hair with electric clippers wired to car batteries in shopping trolleys. He watches a man with no shoes scooping his hand into a rubbish bin and eating off his palm. The whole front of the park is crowded with rag people. Men leaning on the iron fences, sleeping children. "We're in danger here, you know," Dr. Norm says in a funny voice. "I know a long list of people who've been carjacked. One was shot in the head. More than a couple were raped."

"Who are all these people?"

"When apartheid fell, everyone poured in. Asylum seekers, what have you. We have a humane constitution now, better than Sweden. We also have the highest rates of HIV-AIDS in the world. We're top of the pops in assaults and robberies. Murders too. We're a democracy, ja, but we're the world's most violent one. You'd think we would have wanted to handle our own problems first before opening the borders."

They were between tall old buildings again. Marcus was looking up. "Jesus," he says.

"Ja, abandoned by the old owners. No electricity in there, no water. It's three families per unit with candles at night, crapping in buckets. Chuck the rubbish out the windows or down the stairs. I'm showing you how it is. If we came here at night, we might get shot at from up there, or a fridge dropped on our head. Here's the Carlton Centre, used to be the lap of luxury. Now barricaded, empty. What a disaster zone — *ay!*" A sweeping taxi has smashed into the back corner of the Mercedes. Dr. Norm winces and holds his expression like a paralytic. "What say we stop and talk to the gentleman, hey, swap licence and insurance info. What do you think, hey? Hey?" A forced guttural chuckle is full of sarcasm. "Okay, we've pushed our luck in here far enough." He does a U-turn and accelerates up the street. "You had enough?" he says. "I know I have. I know I didn't rot in a cell those years for *this.*"

12

He begins to remember more as they come down Joe Slovo Drive. He remembers taking other drives out this way, Sunday afternoons with his father. But it wasn't called Joe Slovo then, they used to call it Harrow Road. Slovo was from Doornfontein, Dr. Norm says. This was the Jewish ghetto once upon a time, where they all settled from Lithuania. Slovo turned into a "big macher" in the communist party, a hero of the liberation. Marcus remembers Isaac showing him a house on the corner of Buxton and Beit Streets, where Isaac grew up. Remembers his father buying him a hot beef on rye at the deli on a street behind the Alhambra Theatre. When he sees the Ponte Tower he remembers it also, only it was clean and fancy years ago, not the dirty tube with cracked windows that it is now, looming over them like a vast gun barrel. He remembers the synagogue in Doornfontein when he sees it: the Lions Shul has green scaffolding around it now, but Dr. Norm says it's still being used and nice inside. "I think my father went there," Marcus says aloud, but he's not really sure. Dr. Norm takes them past another shul, what had been one, on Wolmarans Street. The distinctive dome is still there, but it's been converted into some manner of African church. "They have a leopard skin on a throne inside where it used to be the holy ark, the original Hebrew is still there behind. Outside here, see, you can buy curry goat and get your enemy cursed."

Marcus is remembering how that shul was. The elders wore top hats and sat in the front of the bimah in a kind of wooden box, like the pilots of some strangely landlocked ship. The bimah — something there, a flicker, then it's gone. Somehow they've ended up in Killarney again, parked opposite the apartment block. Dr. Norm is crying, his face in his hands. "Janine," he says. "Oh God, Jamie! Simone!"

"Why do you keep coming back here if you want to forget?"

"Because I can't forget," he says. "That is why."

"You should try," Marcus says. "I'm a champ at it. Maybe I can help you."

"Good idea. Smash me in the head."

Wouldn't it be good if memory were like a load of sand? he thinks. Dr. Norm could unload his onto me. Win-win all round. He says, "Dr. Norm, don't forget this is the miracle country, right. You told me. The plot has a happy ending. Fairy tales come true."

Dr. Norm sniffs, puts his sunglasses back on. "You really think so?" He seems almost pathetic then, all raw. Wanting to believe it, that Janine is coming back, and the kids. Marcus could tell him it's true, make him feel better. Instead he says, "Dr. Norm, I reckon it's time for you to take me to my old house to find my people. Really. It's time."

They drive north and west toward Greenside, but Dr. Norm takes a wrong route and they have to come back down through Regent Heights first. Something fierce blooms inside Marcus's chest. Then he sees the pale concrete security wall with the perching cameras like vultures on top. "*I know this,*" he says. Dr. Norm doesn't speak but he slows and swerves onto De Villiers Road. They drive along the high wall, and then very slowly past the thick steel gate at the front with an archway above, black iron, the school crest and motto. Wisdom of Solomon High School for Jewish Boys.

Justice Is Togetherness, Togetherness Strength.

"You said your da was a scrapman and you lived in Greenside. I doubt you went here."

"I went here," Marcus says.

"Genuine?"

"Ja, this was my school."

They drive along slowly. "Just keep looking."

"It's all the same. Wall wall wall. More wall."

"Nothing but the best, hey," says Dr. Norm. "I could never have gotten in here. My old man was a dentist, Ma stayed home. The Boers never bothered us Jews, so long's we kept our heads down like good little white boys and girls. Plus they did some nice arms deals with Israel for a while. But now that we're post-racialist and Mandela's retired, you hear a lot of talk. Israel and Jews. They say the word *Zionists* but they really mean bladdy Jew. Hurts me, hey. I gave up years of my life, I mean Jews were basically the heart of the whites in the Struggle for a long time. But nowadays I got old comrades who look at me like I have to spit on Israel and denounce other Jews just to prove my loyalty to them." He shakes his head. "Maybe that's what happens to all miracles, hey, they start to rot. Like those fish that Jesus made."

He turns the Mercedes around and drives back to the gate, where he pulls up. A guard steps out with his assault rifle. "Let's hop out and make nice," says Dr. Norm. Marcus takes a breath and starts to reach for the handle. Through the iron archway he sees the top of a building, angles of stainless steel and soaring glass. He stares and then he cringes over, his arms squeezing his abdomen.

"What's the matter — what is it, Marcus? Marcus, can you hear me?"

Wheezing, he tries to explain. Something inside.

"Are you frightened?"

"I'm fucking terrified." That's what it is — he knows once he's said it: there's a terror inside the walls, a radiating Thing.

"Ahh," Dr. Norm says. "Excellent. Jackpot. Now we *definitely* go in."

"No."

"Marcus, there are big-time associations in there that you need to explore."

"No," he says. "Drive."

Dr. Norm gets out of the car. Marcus watches him talking with the guard, the guard nodding, pointing back, tucking his assault rifle on the sling with his other hand. Dr. Norm comes back and bends at the window. "I told him you were a Solomon old boy. We'll sign the register and go up to the office."

"No."

"Chin up, man. You're having stress symptoms, that's all. There's nothing wrong with you. You need to be strong and force yourself."

"I need to shit. I'm ganna vomit."

"All a good sign. The stomach is another brain."

"What?"

"Neuron-like cells in the digestive tract. Come on, out."

He opens the door and Marcus starts to scream.

13

They stop at the Greenside shops, to use the toilets, to get a coffee and something sweet. To regroup. At the table Dr. Norm starts "reframing" the event. That panic attack was not a defeat, it was a "bold first step." Dr. Norm renames it "aversion therapy" and says they would "treat it like any phobia," with "increasing exposure to the trigger site." In other words go back and try again. "Don't worry," he says. "Not your fault." When the waiter's not looking he tips a mini bottle of Johnnie Walker Red into his coffee. Marcus doesn't argue with his analysis. It wasn't just a line that it wasn't his fault, it was literal, his body had shut him down. But he had retrieved no concrete memories from what he'd seen. He shivers in the sun. Outside on the pavement he pauses to take in the sweep of the shopfronts along Greenway Road, the hookah lounge and the post office and the Woolworths in the little mall down that way, and something else, tucked in the mall, yes, a bookshop — and it was important to him, wasn't it . . . but it's gone. He gets in the car.

They drive on, Dr. Norm looping back to the main road. A reluctance there to rush on to Shaka Road, maybe fearing another episode of screaming and retching in his Mercedes. They pass a mosque complex with a huge tower and broad dome that never existed before, because looking at it Marcus remembers there had been a little park there. Dr. Norm says large mosques are popping up all over the map nowadays, most all restaurants have halal menus. Saudi money, he says. "Where slaves get lashed and women bagged. But there's no sanctions for that. Can't even say a word about it, that's just their *culture*. Everything is culture now. Used to be if you whitey you're all righty, now it's if you are browny you can never do wrongee." He mutters things Marcus can't quite hear. They keep driving, Dr. Norm sips his whisky-enhanced takeout coffee. "Ach, screw it," he says. "I just feel like it needs some truth. I'm tired of the bullshit, you know. I've stopped caring about what's correct. All we have now is right words. If you slap the correct term on the thing it'll go away. A shithole becomes developing. A murderer is a disadvantaged victim. A death cult is a culture. Man, it used to be so bladdy clear. Black and white. Evil apartheid and the good people against it. Now nobody knows which way is up and which way down. It's just a chaos of opinions. Nobody even agrees on what the enemy is. I think that's why religion is back so strong. People need their invisible god in the sky more than ever."

Marcus says, "Jews too?"

"Oh ja, more religious. The ones that haven't left. But not around here. See, what I wanted to show you . . ." They drive past some sort of office complex. "Used to have a different roof. See it? Remember?"

"No."

"That was your great Emmarentia Synagogue, Marcus."

Marcus nods, shutting his eyes. A feeling of dim coolness from an expanse of polished stone, a bottlecap sliding. Boys' voices that echo in the high dark dome. Dr. Norm makes a U-turn and takes them back. "Shuls go down, mosques go up," he mutters. He makes a right and a left onto Clovelly. Marcus is getting more flashes, they come fast. That's the library down that way, yes, and now the long straight road between the twin rows of jacaranda trees. Used to drive it sitting next to his father in the rattling bakkie and in November all the jacaranda flowers made a purple tunnel of astonishing beauty. But these jacarandas look haggard and bare. He says, "So where're the Jews now, if they're not here?"

"The Yiddluch pulled up the shtetl walls in Glenhazel there. Walking distance to the shuls, kosher restaurants for a nush. Here we are. Shaka Road." He stops the car, examines Marcus. "How you feeling this time?"

"I feel oright."

"Sure?"

"Ja."

"Let's go."

He remembers a carport. There is no carport. He remembers a lawn. There is a swimming pool and concrete paving. He remembers a garden but there is only a little of it left, enough though to make his heart jump. Not fear like at the school, but a pulse of calm joy. The walls — yes, those were them, except for the electric wires on top. An elderly woman named Mrs. Siddiqui has let them in. She is overseeing four little ones. He remembers — suddenly — a pomegranate tree, but it's gone, a jungle gym in the corner. The inside of the house is painted bright colours and the smells are of cumin and curry, the furniture low. Wait. His old room had a padlock, down at the end of the passage on the left. He hurries and finds a room with no door at all, bunk beds inside. "The girls," says the old woman, as if that's an explanation. The backyard makes his stomach tighten. There is a sink in the corner where a maid is washing clothes. *He* washed there, bending over shirtless, splashing and scrubbing. Feel of hot soapy water on the skin and the cool of the air. Night? And something else. But no. He turns away. It's this double life belonging to all things here — that which he is looking at in the sun and the other that repeats in him like a thin shadow, a familiarity that is gone when you look at it directly. Or try to. Back in the garden in front, he asks Mrs. Siddiqui when they bought the house. She starts to complain about the awful condition it was in. A disgrace. The grass this high. "We invested tousands." He asks her who she bought it from, if she'd known the Helgers. She squints at him. "Why are you asking this? We bought at auction."

"Of course," he says.

"You go now." As they are on the way out, she says, "You is Jews isn't it?"

He nods and she makes a waving gesture with both hands. "All moved out. Except the old ones. They go in Israel. They take Palestine."

Dr. Norm snorts. "I doubt that. They go to Australia."

"They have plenty money," the woman says, laughing. "They have all the money."

At the car Dr. Norm sighs. "Ja, it's everywhere. They'll teach you all about yourself. It doesn't matter what you say." He drains his coffee and shakes his head. "Just forget it. What else can you do?"

"Did you just tell me to *forget*?"

"Hardy har." He unlocks the car. "Marcus?"

Marcus is frozen, hit by a flash. "Sandy . . ."

"That was your dog, right? That came back first."

"I need to go back in there." Sandy had red fur and he rode her with his nappy on. But ants crawled on her black lips when he poked the amber eye. The old woman dressed in her shalwar kameez is standing with her arms folded now, issuing clucking noises. Dr. Norm hands some money through the gate. Marcus goes in quickly and sees at once that the papyrus patch is still there, on the far side of the pool that never was, in the corner, only looking smaller and with the fibreglass bulk of a pool filter eating into one side. "You must not be stepping on my flowers!" shouts Mrs. Siddiqui. The kids are interested in his doings. Mrs. Siddiqui calls them away as she comes up with Dr. Norm. Marcus goes around to the far side of the reeds, squats on the mud, and feels carefully. When he exposes the gap he finds it much tinier than the shadow in his mind, his shoulders scraping. He can hear the kids through the stems and Mrs. Siddiqui is shouting he must come out. Dr. Norm says here and she says, "Fifty rands. What can you buy for fifty rands these days?" The humming of the pool filter gets louder as he crawls over mud and finds an open patch and digs his bare hands in, the cold feel of the moist soil like a whisper telling him go on, go on. A wooden board against his fingertips doesn't shock him — shadow and real have merged. He hears Dr. Norm: "The old girl's getting a bit hairy out here, hey Marcus. We better make a move."

"I'll phone police!" comes the woman's shout.

"Almost," Marcus says to no one through gritting teeth, his fingers working. Almost.

14

He doesn't open the plastic bag in front of Dr. Norm, just sits with it in his lap, saying nothing, all the way back to the institute. Dr. Norm doesn't push the issue. Marcus unpacks it carefully in his room. The bag had lined the sides of the hole under the board; it contains a tin of Quality Street sweets, a set of dirty overalls, a miner's hard hat, pads for knees and elbows, goggles. The tin has only a few things at the bottom: an ancient, frayed condom, a bank bag with a hard nut of something blackened inside, an old Afrikaans tabloid newspaper called *Vryheid*, a notebook which he picks up with excitement but then finds empty — until a photograph falls out. He stares at that image for minutes at a time. Through a sleepless night he keeps getting up and switching on the light to look at the things, handle them. Dr. Norm doesn't come to the institute that day and Marcus fears he'll be absent for one of his long stretches.

When he sees Dr. Norm's Mercedes parked outside the following day, Marcus rushes up to his office. Doesn't say a word to him, just hands the photo across. Dr. Norm stares at it. "Where's this from?"

"You know where. I had it when I was a kid."

"This is unbelievable," Dr. Norm is saying, shaking his head. "I remember this picture. I had the same one, in the banned years." He's getting emotional.

Marcus says, "Dr. Norm, I'm not a virgin." Dr. Norm looks up. Marcus says, "You asked me that once, if I thought I was a virgin. If I remember any sexual experiences."

"Do you?"

He nods. "I remember a woman gave me that photo. She was older than me. Dark hair, so pretty. An American voice. I don't know how I could have known her but I did." Dr. Norm looks down again at the image, his lips twitching. Marcus says he was involved in the Movement just like you were, Dr. Norm. It was through the woman. She was the one who took him into a township, ja. And there were Molotov cocktails flying. And there was a policeman. He remembers that. A tall, thin cop . . . he remembers also there were codes written in Hebrew in a book — but Dr. Norm's left eyebrow has pronged up by now, never a good sign.

"Oright, okay," he says. "Let's slow down and be careful with this Hebrew codes business. There is fantasy and there is memory. Rule one is to be able to separate. This is one area we need strict apartheid, in your mind."

"I know, Dr. Norm. But I'm not imagining."

"You have an unusually potent imagination, we've talked about that, your fantasy playing." He puffs out air, sitting back in his long chair. "Marcus, you exhaust me, my boy."

Marcus is pacing, itchy. "I was involved, I swear. I remember fire-bombs. I remember being in jail."

Dr. Norm winces at the ceiling. Shuts his eyes. "Does not," he says, "seem plausible to me."

"I am telling you I remember."

"That a Solomon High schoolboy was involved in throwing fire-bombs at police in a township, with Hebrew code and an American woman? That you were in prison? Come on. You're probably remembering a movie, Marcus. That's why it's so vital you don't run away from the *real*."

"Run away?"

"As at that school. You can't duck these encounters, Marcus. Just the opposite. It's exactly where the growth lies."

"Okay. Tomorrow."

"Okay?"

"Yes. Let's do it."

But when tomorrow comes Dr. Norm isn't there.

15

One of the first things that Dr. Norm ever said to him was "You do un-derstand that you are a miracle. I am saying this as a complete and utter atheist. Miracle."

He is a person who went to sleep as a boy in one country and woke up as a man in another land, with a different flag, a different look, a dif-ferent everything. Dr. Norm told him once, "Your problem isn't in the brain. You can remember if you want to. But you are blocking yourself."

And he said, "That's such bull."

But maybe it isn't bull. Maybe he doesn't want to dig because dig-ging makes everything feel shaky, like attacking the foundations of who he is, what he has managed to get back so far. But on the other hand without his past he can't seem to get himself to *do* anything. Dr. Norm doesn't come back for weeks but he is not needed, for Marcus is no prisoner here. He can leave the institute, visit the school on his own. Yet in practice he is stranded in his safe and comfortable routines. Now another month passes and they are in a third. Marcus eats his fatty breakfasts and does his exercises. He naps and reads. He notices fewer patients and more staff. They seem to spend their days playing cards or listening to music on tinny radios. Matron likes to watch TV in the staff lounge. There are dirty dishes in the dining hall and giant dustballs and cat waste in the corridors. The grass is burnt dead in the sun and in the shade it grows up too high. The tomatoes rot on their vines in the greenhouse.

Now it's what? Four months since Dr. Norm last disappeared—a whole season—and a letter arrives. No return address. European stamps.

Greetings, dear Marcus,

I am hoping that if this finds you it finds you well. On the other hand, I hope it does not find you at the institute at all! I hope that you've moved on, young man. As I have told you many times, memory is overrated. You have your blocks, but maybe you don't need to crack the code. What do I know? What do any of us know? The brain is a black hole we'll never understand, and that's a fact I never hid from you, my friend. I know you've got no one now, and feel badly for it, though my leaving can't have been much of a surprise. You are a sensitive soul, young Marcus, and you could see the pain I was in and that it was no good, no good at all to try to carry on.

I realised for my own sanity I had to make a break, a sudden clean rupture before I could stop myself, in order to give my brain a chance to cleanse itself of all its many debilitating neural associations. I have to starve my memories, not be constantly reaffirming them with familiar sights and old associations, and that simply cannot be done <u>there</u>.

So I have gone and committed what a good radical, card-carrying member of the ANC should never do which is undergo the humiliation of "taking the gap." Ja, boet. I have flown the coop, done the chicken run, just like any other Whitey McFlighty out of SA. And the short and dirty answer is no, I will not be back. Not because I do not love the place with all my heart because of course I do, but because I love my sanity just a little more.

Funny. We always said we never believed in Utopia. All during the Freedom Struggle we said we are not Utopians, we merely want our country to be normal. But you know what? That was a lie. The Struggle is what made us special. We had the answer with a capital A. But now there are just a million problems and they all have a lowercase p. There is no grand drama, no great war of good versus evil. Just the chintzy schlepping of goods to market. That's what economic development means, you know. Just building more plastic water pistols or whatnot, to ship to America or China. Or filming silly movies where people pretend to kill each other.

I don't know how else to explain it but to say it bluntly, the New South Africa is a letdown. I would not have ever believed that I could write something like that with sincerity. Yet it's all just sordid now. The corruption and the greed. Good comrades in the lean years have turned into fat cats no better than any other money-grubbers with their mansions in Houghton and their Swiss bank accounts. The proportion of haves to have-nots is the same or worse, only the skin tone has altered, slightly. And the killings go on—only now it's foreign migrants who are the victims when it's not one of the 500 a week murdered for ordinary criminal reasons. To say nothing of the assaults, rapes, kidnappings. The police officer murdered every hundred hours.

So the happy ending of the Mandela story was never an ending ever after. The plot goes on. And on.

I hated what there once was, but I can see as clearly as day that I am going to hate what is coming just as much. I fought to expand the first world, not to shrink it.

My children will be what I miss most, of course, but the sad fact is that I hardly get to see them anyway. Even sadder, I believe I can best help them now by gaining a new citizenship that they may one day need to take advantage of. It's getting tough for those with pale skins to get jobs in SA and will likely only get much tougher; yet as disparity and corruption continues there's going to more populist anger directed against them. I believe it's only fair that the worm has turned, but when it comes to one's own flesh, historical justice is no consolation.

Enough of that. Let's talk about <u>you</u>, Marcus Helger. I want you to get your arse out of that institute pronto. Doctor's orders. Nobody there is going to kick you out onto the street. They are privately funded to the hilt and no one cares to rock the boat. Unless things have changed drastically, I don't believe you have to worry on that score. (I don't even think you're on the books there anyway!)

But Marcus, please don't get stuck in that honey trap. Get yourself out. Get yourself into school and get educated. Fill your blank slate with new knowledge.

Meet people. Do things. You're on your own, I know, but you're a clever fellow. Stress means growth. Pressure is what makes carbon into diamonds.

I am also on my own here in this strange country. But I too am a clever fellow. I've given up on remembering and you should too. I don't keep photographs of my past life. I shall learn a new language. Like a computer hard drive, I will "clear" my software and install a new "operating system." I want the old faces in me to hurry up and die off as quickly as possible. The old words. You've already achieved that and I suggest you go on building on that achievement, the unknowable pillar of your early life.

Certainly we can forget about publishing scientific papers together. Neuroscience will chug along fine without me! I don't want to be special anymore, I just want to be small and happy.

Marcus, I'm telling you the truth when I say I have genuine love for you. You're a good soul. Good luck and stay blessed.

Yours as ever,

Dr. Norm

P.S. Enclosed is a cash card. If you're still there, I thought you might need it. I've posted the PIN in another letter. You'll be able to draw up to R2500 a day till the account runs dry. Don't be stupid and try to use cash machines at night or in dodgy spots. Go somewhere like Sandton City, nice and safe behind electric wires.

Hugs.

When the card number arrives he hikes down to the shops on the winding Parktown roads. There's a small library there and he goes in

THE MANDELA PLOT 397

and does a search for the Helger name in old phone books, white and yellow pages, reverse street directories. This gets him the address of Lion Metals Pty. Ltd. There is a computer system called the Internet that the librarian says would help, but they don't have it at that branch. He searches periodical indexes and consults the whirring microfiche machines. This is how he finds out his parents are both dead. An index linked to an article in the *Gold City Zionist:* "Twin Murders Claim Jewish Couple." There are no back copies of the *Zionist* at that library, but he checks the *Star* around that date and finds a short paragraph on a page near the back in a column called Crime Roundup. *Isaac Helger, 70, and wife Arlene Helger née Cossington, 54, were the victims of an apparent murder-robbery. The couple had been locked in the vault of their scrapyard business in Vrededorp and died of asphyxiation, said police spokesman Lieutenant Hennie Strydom.* He stares at the words and then shuts his eyes. What had Dr. Norm written? *I want the old faces in me to hurry up and die off as quickly as possible. The old words. You've already achieved that.* Marcus makes notes, leaves the library with a roaring noise in both ears. He orders a taxi from a public phone and drives to De La Rey Street, Vrededorp. The building is no longer Lion Metals but some sort of warehouse, the front of it armoured with welded steel plates and coils of razor wire all along the second floor to stop intruders from climbing. Like a wartime fort. Graffiti everywhere. Men sleep rough in the park beside it. The sign has Chinese letters.

Marcus makes the cab drive slowly around the back. He's remembering trucks parked outside, remembering an office upstairs, his mother, Arlene. He gets out and touches the wall. It's been built up higher with new rows of grey bricks, topped with more loops of razor wire. A fat man floats into his mind. Hugo. Hugo who? Hugo Bez. Blez. He has the taxi drive him next to Westpark Cemetery. It takes a while to find a caretaker and then the graves of the Helgers. His mother and father are buried next to each other, but the grandfather, buried last, in 1990, is not next to the grandmother. Black slabs in the sunshine. Hebrew letters chiseled. They put you down in there and you never left again. When you thought about it, looked at it, it was astonishing. You had to force yourself to believe it would happen to you. He puts his pen to the notepad several times, but in the end he writes nothing except the words I AM MARCUS HELGER. When he gets into the cab he asks the driver, white guy, an Afrikaner, if he knows where Solomon High School is. The driver says, "That's the one in the news, izzen it?"

"News?"

"Where the big man's ganna visit."

"I don't know about that," Marcus says.

They arrive at the bombproof gate just as school is letting out. There's a line of waiting cars. Marcus says he wants to sit for a minute. The cabdriver says his name is Dirk, asks if he can smoke. Marcus nods and Dirk lights a Gunston and whistles softly. "Hell of a nice collection, hey?" "How's that?" "I count three Rollses and three Bentleys. Checkit that Porsche Carrera, man. I fink it's the new-new model, I mean this year." Marcus watches the kids coming out. Dirk says, "No wonder he's coming here."

"Who is?"

"Old Nelson, like I said."

Some cars in the line pull out. Marcus says, "Can you drive up closer, please?" School buses are swinging out also, without markings, each a different colour and with security grates over the windows. There had been a bomb once — he remembers that now. Someone bombed a bus. Now they are close to the driveway, the boys pouring through a turnstile in their purple blazers, their grey trousers. As in a dream, Marcus gets out of the taxi and walks up toward them, something in his abdomen clenching up like a fist. The closer he gets to the guardhouse, the stronger this bad sensation becomes. The faces are so young. Some glance at him, to most he's nothing, just an adult standing there. A guard steps out and stares through mirrored sunglasses. He tries to smile, but he is shivering. He can see through the arched iron over the gate, an apex of thrusting glass and steel beyond — the school synagogue. And suddenly memories are on him like some attacking swarm. He turns and hurries back to the cab.

He goes to a different library, to find back issues of the *Gold City Zionist*. In Observatory they have them kept in bound volumes, not microfiche, but the collection is incomplete and he can't find the issue with the article on the death of his parents. But the newest ones are stacked loose and he looks through the covers — finds a photo that stops him.

MADIBA TO SPEAK AT SOLOMON
By Candice Milner, Staff Writer

Ex-President Nelson Mandela is scheduled to address the staff and students of Wisdom of Solomon High School for Jewish Boys next month.

The address will take place in the school synagogue on a Friday morning, the way honoured guests have traditionally been received at the elite private school for close to a century.

"Madiba has consistently expressed his warm ties to the Jewish community," said school board president Samuel Leibowitz, using Mandela's clan name, a sign of affectionate respect. "It's a theme in his life going all the way back to his first legal training in a Jewish firm, and up through the Jewish comrades who shared the burden of the Struggle years with him."

Headmaster Arnold Volper said that the school has "always been a strong supporter of Mr. Mandela." He said Solomon values are the values of equal rights because "as Jews we too have suffered through the ages,

therefore it's only natural for us to feel empathy for the
plight of those in similar conditions."

The colour photo that stopped him includes Headmaster Volper.
When he sees that face he instantly remembers the cane, the whistling
cuts. Volper is even fatter and wider and his mop of yellow scarecrow
hair has turned mostly white but the chin is lifted like it used to be,
stretching a line of blubber now, to point those flared nostrils at the
camera, unsmiling. Reading over Volper's quote, Marcus snorts — he
remembers them singing anthems to the Nationalist government when
Mandela was a terrorist. Back then Volper and his lot condemned the
Jews who supported Mandela, now they praised them. Bootlickers of
the old government had new leather to shine. In the background is the
school synagogue, a long shot down through the pews toward the low-
walled platform of the bimah. He reads that Mandela will stand at the
traditional place at the rear of it. You can't tell from the photo but he
knows the waist-high wall around that bimah is made of glass bricks.
He remembers.

He returns to the institute. His parents are dead, they were murdered. The police will have a file. He will go and enquire. Tomorrow.
Maybe. He sleeps.

16

He doesn't leave the institute. He wanders around barefoot. He thinks
of a dog tied to a pole. His leash is tied to a memory, an almost-mem-
ory. It must be the knowing that his parents were murdered — but it's
not that. Without deep memories of his parents it is hard to feel real
grief. On the other hand his mind keeps flashing back to that synagogue photo, this visit of Mandela's coming up. It feels important and
dangerous but he can't say why. He dreams of fire pouring up from

holes in the ground. The woman with the dark hair is there. In an old newsmagazine he reads about how Mandela saved the country from civil war back in 1993. A white man had assassinated a popular black leader. It was right before the first election, the trigger for an all-out race war. But Mandela appeared on television and gave a speech to the nation, addressing blacks and whites, talking them back from the brink. But the question that keeps popping up unbidden in Marcus's mind is what would have happened if Mandela had not been there. What if *he'd* been killed? He puts it to Thilivhali, an older patient, a Venda from Thohoyandou. "You must not say this," Thilivhali says. "We need him. If he was taken, it would be very bad."

"Bad how?"

"She would blow up."

"Who?"

"This country."

He goes back to the items recovered from the garden. A hard hat with a torch on the front, like a mining helmet. Goggles. Why? And the pads — bizarre. Everything saturated with dirt. And he kept these in a hole in the garden, a secret place. Why? And took them out to use them. Or were they just found objects? No. He *did* use them. He feels this. He has a dream in which he floats into that synagogue photo. The pretty woman with the dark curly hair that he remembered giving him the photo — she is with him. *Her name is Annie.* Follow me, she says. She walks him around the bimah seven times. Like the walls of Jericho the glass bricks crumble. There's fire inside, she tells him.

When he wakes up he spreads the overalls on the floor and squats over them and feels them carefully. There's something hard under his fingertips that he thought was a button but there's a pocket inside. He feels carefully and brings out a key on a piece of string. You could wear this around your wrist. After a while he gets up and puts the overalls on, then he stands there, shaking.

At first light he is in a cab. As soon as he sees the school wall he asks to be dropped off. He starts walking along beside it in the dewy cool, the birdsong quiet of the new day. The key is in his hand, his heart beats hard. He can see the cameras watching down over him from the top of the wall, the razor coils. The closer he gets to the gate, the worse the sick feeling grows. He feels an irresistible tug, a compulsion. Go with it. The body knows. He veers off and starts walking across the street and then around a gated complex of townhouses and down a municipal trail, sloping towards trees below, and then on the other side of the trees the land opens up. A sign says BRANDWAG PARK. He goes on. There's something there in the fold of the land that the key in his squeezing fist is a part of. Don't think about it, just follow the impulse. When he sees the trench with the stream he makes a sound, almost like a yelp, and starts to run. There was a flood here. And a pipe broke loose and was washed down . . .

He phones the police from a tickey box. He wants to talk to the policeman in charge of Julius Caesar township. He knew the tall cop who was in charge of that place. It was where the firebombs were and Annie took him. That cop drove him home, was someone who seemed to be close to his father. So he can tell that cop about this, what he is remembering, and get some guidance. Because he has to be careful not to get himself in trouble now, if what he remembers is really true. But he also *has* to tell them. He can't just leave it. It takes a long time, being handed from voice to voice, before they let him know that the one he wants is Superintendent Lukhele. A Swazi name, yet the tall cop was white. He goes to the address after lunch, a brand-new police station, a glass cube on Peter Mokaba Crescent in the new suburb that extends Julius Caesar township. At the desk he says he has some very important information for the superintendent and gives his name, Marcus Helger, and after they send his name in he is taken at once to the office, bypassing a long line of waiting people. The sign on the door says COMMUNITY FA-CILITATOR, JULIUS CAESAR DEVELOPMENTAL REGION, SUPERINTEN-DENT JOSEPH BUZWE LUKHELE. He walks in and sees the man behind the desk looking at him and then the man's eyes expand and he jerks upright, he shoots to his feet. He's bald and quite stout, with a thick neck and a round face.

"Thank you for seeing me," Marcus says.

Lukhele just stares, his mouth open. Then he says, "They said Marcus." His voice sounds choked, hushed.

"Yes, my name is Marcus Helger."

Lukhele's face twists, his head rearing back and to the side, his eyes bulging. *"Marcus,"* he says.

"Yes. And. Well. I should probably first say before we — I mean I want to let you know that I've been a medical patient. I had a, uh, brain injury, was in a coma for . . . quite a while."

Lukhele's twisted, retracted face seems horrified, like he's staring at some monster. "I don't understand," he says.

"This is going to be hard for me to explain. But I'd really appreciate your help and if you would just hear me out, Superintendent."

"Marcus," he says again.

There is something wrong with this man, Marcus thinks. "That's correct. Like I say, Marcus Helger."

"Do you . . . ?"

"Yes?"

"Do you know me?" Lukhele says.

"Do I what?"

"Look at me," says Lukhele. "Do you know me?"

"I don't. I mean I don't think so. I —"

"You don't know me. You're not joking."

"I'm sorry?"

"You were in, what, hospital? Your brain injured, you say?"

"Ja, that's right. The Linhurst Institute. I was in a coma —"

"A coma. How long?"

"Nearly six and a half years."

"No!"

"Ja, I know it sounds . . . unbelievable, Superintendent, but that's what happened. But I'm . . . recovered — still recovering. And actually this is why I've come to see you —"

"To see me," says Lukhele. "Because . . ."

"Because they informed me you're in charge of Julius Caesar. And. Well actually, to tell the truth, I was trying to find someone else. There was a different policeman that I remember, from like years ago. I was hoping if I could talk to him. But . . ."

"Which policeman?"

"I don't remember his name, but he was in charge of Julius."

"In charge."

"Very tall, like this. A white man. Thin."

"Why is it you want to talk with this one? Marcus." When he says the word *Marcus,* the side of his mouth twitches. Then he says, "Sit down."

Marcus thanks him and takes a seat, as does Lukhele, Marcus still thinking how strange this cop is, the way he keeps staring with big eyes and his back all stiff as he sinks. Marcus says, "Sorry. Did I catch you at a bad time, Superintendent?"

"No. No, you didn't. Marcus. What is it I can do for you?"

"There's no other way for me to put this except to come out and say it. But I'll be honest. I need to trust that I'm not going to be like arrested or anything."

"Why, have you done something?"

Marcus leans forward. "I don't know if I have. See, when I came out of this coma, the brain trauma, I really couldn't remember much. Like not even my own name. It's taken a lot of work and a very long time to gain some function but I'm still not . . . a hundred per cent. With memories."

"What is it that happened to you? To put you in hospital?"

Marcus shrugs. "They think traffic accident was likely, the head trauma."

"And your people? Nobody came to find you?"

"Maybe I'm lucky. Someone could have shown up and turned the machines off."

"Come on, now."

"Really, my parents are gone. They were murdered."

"Ai. I'm sorry to hear it. What about any other family, an auntie, cousin — maybe a brother?"

Marcus shakes his head. "Not that I know of. I am still tracking down records, still trying to find those memories, if they're there."

"But you don't recall other family."

"No, I don't, as yet. I just have some vague pictures of my da and ma. That's it, really."

Lukhele sits back, his chin on his chest, one hand wrapping his fist in front of his mouth. "I think you are being honest," he says.

"Yes, I am," Marcus says. "I know it sounds crazy, but you can check with the Linhurst Institute, which is, like I said, where they've been treating me."

"Marcus, Marcus," says Lukhele.

"Yes?"

"Marcus Helger."

"Yes. What is it?"

Lukhele keeps staring.

"What?"

"Marcus Helger. You are one hundred per cent positive that is your name."

"Yes, of course."

"Because if you forgot. How could you know it?"

"There were records to help."

"I see."

"But the reason I'm here is cos I've had some memories of a, uh . . . a bomb."

"Bomb?"

"Yes. I believe. Before the accident, back in the old days, I was, I have memories of being involved in the, here, in Julius Caesar township, I was involved in the fighting. You know, the anti-apartheid stuff."

"You think so."

"Well, ja. I do. But I was also young, you see. Was also going to school. And the school I went to it's called Wisdom of Solomon High School. It's in —"

"Regent Heights. Everybody's knowing this school. Madiba is going there."

"That's right. That's sort of why I'm here, actually. Because I have these memories. I think that before, I might have been involved, before, in putting a — well, a bomb."

"You mean explosive."

"Like a homemade bomb, ja. I think it might have been me who put it in there."

"In where?"

"In the school. Well, see. In the synagogue, like really. I mean I can remember that part. I went to the school today, and I remembered there is a pipe underground that I used to crawl up to get inside the wall without anyone knowing, cos security is very full-on there, at Solomon. But I found in my old house, even, that I had stuff for going up the pipe."

"Stuff?"

"Like overalls and a mining hat and that. And a key."

"Key."

"Look, I know this sounds completely nuts —"

"Is okay. Marcus. Go on."

"The key unlocks the, uh, bars, or whatever you call them, at the top of the pipe, without setting off an alarm. And you come out inside the school. And there's no security inside. And that's what I remember. That's what I think I did. With others, maybe. We. I don't know how many. But I remember it, there was a bomb. And we stuck it. I did. Under the bimah."

"The what?"

"It's a kind of stage in a shul, a synagogue. Every shul has a bimah. And there in the school it's the place where special guests talk from. That's why I'm here, see. Why I have to be. I mean that's the main reason. What I'm scared of."

"Because?"

"Well, for him," Marcus says. And points to the wall.

Lukhele moves his eyes. The portrait hanging there is the Honourable Nelson Mandela, framed, relaxed and smiling. "I see," says Lukhele. "You are saying you think you remember putting a bomb in that place where Madiba is going to give a speech."

"Yes. Exactly. Right under where he's going to talk. I remember coming through the tunnel. I remember putting the bomb . . ."

"Can you excuse me?" Lukhele leaves Marcus in the room by himself and when he comes back he says he's checked the reports going back to the eighties, and there's never been a mention of any bomb discovered at Solomon High. He says let us assume there is a bomb there, and not something Marcus made up from brain damage. That means it's been sitting there dead for years. It's not going to suddenly decide to go off just because Mandela is standing there for half an hour on a Friday morning. The real danger is that it could go off at any time, killing schoolboys. If it exists.

"If something was to happen," Marcus says, "I would never be able to forgive myself."

"You doing the right thing, Marcus. But we have to have caution on how we proceed in terms of investigating. We don't want to spread panics to the people for no reason."

"I understand."

"So we don't talk about this outside of this room, heh?"

"Absolutely, Superintendent."

"Good. Until I have investigated."

"But Superintendent . . ."

"Yes?"

"I'm also worried that I'm going to be blamed — I mean charged, if—"

"Charged? Marcus, you think you put a bomb for the Struggle, in that school — not to kill but to go off when is empty, to disrupt the learning in the apartheid system, yes?"

"I . . . yes, I think so."

"Then you can get a medal now. Is people like *me* who are putting charges."

"Like you. I see."

"Yes. Because me, myself, I was a cadre in MK. Which that man founded." He nods to the Mandela portrait. "I also was the youth leader of the freedom fighters right here, in Julius Caesar township, in fact. You know?" He lifts his eyebrows and seems to be waiting. Marcus shakes his head. Lukhele snorts and goes on. "After liberation, MK was synthesising into our armed forces, we became the officers, ministers of defence. I was given this position. My previous leadership role was synthesised into the state command structure. One day you are on a wanted poster, the next one they put you in your own office." He shrugs, bringing his hands together. "Two opposites come like this, make something new, a new stage in history. Then it starts again."

The plot goes on, Marcus thinks, remembering Dr. Norm's letter. Even the Mandela plot. He asks, "And that tall cop that I think I remember, you know who he was? He was maybe in charge of Julius Caesar."

Lukhele smiles. "Then I can make bets he was trying to arrest me."

Marcus smiles back. "And do you know where he is now?"

Lukhele shrugs, makes a rolling motion with his hands. "Keeping afloat," he says. "Like all of us."

REVELATIONS

17

Sunday morning at first light Marcus gets picked up at the Linhurst Institute by Lukhele, driving a white BMW alone. It takes a while to find the soccer field in Regent Heights, with Marcus trying to fit the topography to what he half remembers. They park and Lukhele takes a leather tog bag from the back and then they walk through a break in the fence and on into Brandwag Park. Marcus is wearing old jeans and a T-shirt, Lukhele has on an untucked silk dress shirt unbuttoned to show gold chains, pressed khakis, snakeskin loafers, and a leather ball cap with gemstone studs. He smells richly of cologne. The land has that typical Highveld dryness, the loose yellow grass and the red sand baked hard. Marcus leads them down to the trench with the trickling stream and they climb down into it and walk along until Marcus finds the pipe. Lukhele unzips the bag, brings out new, crisply folded overalls, kneepads and torches, plastic gloves and booties and hairnets and eye protectors.

"What's all this?"

"You know what."

"Why don't we go in the front?"

"No. This is the way, to show me everything."

"You're kidding me."

"No. We must do it like this."

Marcus puts on the gear slowly, studying the filthy pipe. This is where the juice is, Dr. Norm would say. You have to. But he wouldn't be able to without Lukhele here—the official command plus his physical presence. It's easier than the front gate at least, or feels that way, so far. He climbs up into the darkness and starts worming forward, torch in hand.

He goes on through the tunnel, his shaky breaths echoing as he slithers over dirt and stones, twigs and rat shit. Eventually there is sunlight ahead and he climbs the final slant to the grate above, unlocks it with the key. He clambers out of the tunnel and turns to help hard-breathing Lukhele. They stand on Solomon ground. Suddenly memories are fighting to rise in him—but another part clamps fiercely down. Cold sweat pops out on his neck. He hides his sick feeling from Lukhele. They strip off the wet plastic and start walking. Something worse is happening inside him now, something is breaking. An overpowering sense of *wrongness* seems to shine from everything—the tall grass, the tennis courts, the distant buildings. They go down hillside stairs and cross an open stretch of grass under the sun. It's dead quiet, motionless but for black birds in the blue, wings seesawing on a breeze he cannot feel. They reach the synagogue and go down more stairs and cross the marble lobby to the teak doors.

Lukhele is ahead now and Marcus follows into the hushed cool of the sanctuary, the thick red carpets, the sunbeams through the huge windows. He feels hot, ready to faint. He climbs the seven stairs onto the bimah, through the gap in the low wall of glass bricks. The reading table is opposite. He remembers lifting the Torah there. He was Strongest Lad. A top rugby player and a boxer. *My name is Marcus Helger and my name carries fear.* Every glint of a memory comes with an intimation of panic. This breaking in him must not give way to a flood, a deep part of him holds on for its life.

Here's the little bench, just as he remembers. He kneels in front of it and tries to lift the top, but it won't move. He feels around the edges for a catch, it takes time to find, Lukhele watching him intently. When he finds the catch and slowly lifts the lid, Lukhele whistles behind him. "Yoh-yoh-yoh," Lukhele says. "Jeeee-*zus*." The stacked paint tins seem a lot smaller than the cans in his memory and they are thickly coated in white dust. Taped-up torpedo-shaped tubes stick through the tops of the cans, wires linked together with plastic caps. On the right side, resting on a car battery, is a transistor board. Bags of nails packed around. "You see?" he croaks. "It's real."

"Do not touch anything. Leave it open, like this exactly."

Outside in the bright morning Lukhele takes a Motorola unit from his bag. He holds up a palm for Marcus to stay put and walks off, talking. Marcus watches him a moment and then returns to the lobby. This wrongness, this wrongness. Everything here presses on him. Lukhele — what of him? Something . . . There's a set of boards in the corner. He goes over. Malcolm Steinway. The bus bomb — yes. He remembers this display. And over there is the door to the toilets. When he looks at it, something starts to shriek in his nerves like a metal detector. He wants to move away but he forces himself to walk toward it. He's cold sweating again. It's like it was at the front gate. He stops at the door, looks down. A puddle of blood is oozing out from under it. He takes a half step, fingernails sinking into palms. He hears something, cocks his head. Some kind of moaning. Inside. His soles are sticky on the blood. Do not open this door. He can't anyway, doesn't have the will, but then when he turns to get away dizziness wells up and he stumbles forward through the swing door.

Empty whiteness. Tiles, sinks. A urinal gutter and toilet stalls. No more blood, no ghosts. But the air feels thin and cold. He forces himself to walk to the sink. This breaking-apart feeling, this glaring of *wrongness* at him from everywhere. There is a reason that all the memories he has *are* wrong. His white face looming in the glass. Marcus Helger. I was here before. The door opens and he turns his head and a boy in uniform is walking in. A tall wiry yellow-skinned boy with eyes set deep in his skull. I know you. There are others, also in school uniforms. The wiry kid is rushing in, swinging his leg as if to goal-kick a rugby ball. But it's no ball down there. He, Marcus, is on hands and knees. The kick hammers the head into the pipe, the sharp protruding valve in the bend of it. And again, again. He watches himself lolling. "You're killing him," says someone. "You'll murder him." They pull the kicker away, eventually. But blood is oozing from the eyes and ears and lacerated scalp.

The door bangs open hard, making him jump. Lukhele. He wants to know if Marcus is all right. Marcus nods. Lukhele puts his arm around him and walks him outside into the sun. "I think I need to go home," Marcus says. Lukhele eases him down on the lawn, gives him a bottle of water, and gestures with the radio in his hand. "We'll have to stay here for now, for a while."

Marcus gulps, wipes his mouth. "Why?"

"We are going to wait here for them to arrive."

"Till who does?"

"The big guys. Must be the bomb squad, number one. And the special team. They will put the special team. You know the Leopards?"

He shakes his head. Lukhele says the Leopards are an elite national police unit, formed to fight corruption. "These guys are the best to handle this kind of business. You'll see. But we have to wait now onsite. They coming to investigate."

Marcus shades his eyes, squinting. "Do I know you?"

"What?"

"Do I know you? From before, I mean."

"Are you okay?" says Lukhele. "You look . . ."

"I don't know," Marcus says. He is fading, his eyelids closing in the heat.

"We have to wait here," Lukhele's voice is saying. "For the Leopards to come."

18

He becomes aware he is rising from a crushing blackness that is no ordinary sleep.

"Did you give him too much?" says a voice.

"It wouldn't last this long."

"How long's he been out like this?"

"All day. I'm telling you, man."

"He looks bladdy dead."

"Try wake him up."

He feels his body being prodded. He's almost there, climbing. He opens his eyes to an orange sky, it's that late in the dying day. Two men in camouflage uniforms, wearing ski masks, are beside Lukhele, leaning over Marcus as he sits up and rubs his face. He asks what the time is. Seven, says someone. His mouth is dry. Lukhele hands him a bottle of water. He swallows and then Lukhele takes it back, saying, "That's enough." Already two more men with ski masks are coming from the direction of the Pimple. They have a strange waddling walk, heavy with equipment. Dark green body armour, helmets with visors — they must be bomb-squad technicians. Lukhele is helping Marcus up and they all move together toward the synagogue. Marcus is thinking why did they come from that side? All that equipment. Didn't they drive in from the road?

In the lobby he glances at the door to the toilets, remembering what he saw. Dr. Norm once told him that the unconscious mind can dream while you are awake — it's called a vision. Now they are entering the synagogue and they all climb the bimah. Marcus watches them assembling a work light on a stand, trailing an electric cord. It's getting very dim in here as the sun sets, and they shine the burning white light on the open bench, the dusty paint cans inside, the wires and the battery. He watches them observing the old bomb for a long time, talking softly to each other and then gently touching with their gloved fingers, attaching clips and wires to meters. It goes on so long that the darkness grows solid around the light and Marcus says to Lukhele that he doesn't want to be here. It's stupid for them to be here. To stand right next to a working bomb squad. Lukhele too. "I'll stay with you," says Lukhele. "They need you. They will ask you."

"But I don't know anything." His head feels bubbly, he's drifting. He notices there are others now. More men with round black ski-mask heads standing on the bimah behind in the dark. Just standing, not moving or saying a word. Watching. Lukhele is holding his arm. The four bomb men are unrolling plastic sheets. They take out the paint cans one by one, slowly, remove some of the black stuff inside and drip some liquid from a dropper on it and watch the colour change in the white light. One of them takes the battery away. Then they replace the cans in the bench. They do other things he can't see, their backs blocking the work.

He tries to whisper to Lukhele but it comes out loud, his tongue clumsy. "Why's everyone wearing masks?"

"They fight corruptions. They keep their IDs secret, these Leopards."

When the technicians straighten up and step away, Marcus feels Lukhele tugging on his arm, pulling him forward into the light. There's a video camera in his hand. Now he's attaching a wire to Marcus's shirt collar. "Say something. I want to make a test for your voice."

"What's going on?"

"Good. That is good. We want to record on you a video statement. Go over to the bomb."

"Why?"

"Don't worry. I'll tell you what to say. Is for the record."

First he has to say that he set the camera up, the light, in order to record a statement. And provide the date. He looks down like he's told to, and in the brightness he sees small blocks of yellowish stuff that looks like putty on a plastic sheet in front of the open bench. Lukhele tells him to pick them up and he does — they're heavier than they look and there are some long silver cylinders attached to electric wires and Lukhele asks him to pick these up too. And then to take the cylinders and push them into the putty. "What is this?" he asks, trying to clear his head, to understand.

"Just do it please."

"Why do you want me to do it?"

"Is for evidence," says Lukhele's voice. All Marcus can see now is burning white light and Lukhele's voice out of the light tells him not to squint so much.

"Evidence?" Marcus says. "What do you mean evidence? Of what?"

"Your innocence. Of course. For the record. Your cooperation with us. We are the police, heh? We have to keep this on file, for the investigations. Ready now."

"I don't understand."

"Marcus, we do it all proper for legal. Don't worry about it. Just do what it is I say for you. It's fine. We are the police. But pliz control your squinting. Now, we start again . . ."

Marcus lifts the putty blocks, pushes the cylinders into them. Next he's asked to put them into the bench on top of the paint cans. He has to add a new kind of circuit board instead of the old one. They give him the camera to hold, to move around, position it as he wires in the new board for them. They explain to him how it works, the transmitter. And then they ask him to give that same explanation to the camera. It's not the bomb he made, he made a different bomb, but they want him to say that he made this bomb. He's sweating and his rubbery mind isn't working as it should. Lukhele, Lukhele. "Your name," he says to the burning light, "your name isn't that. It's something . . . I know you. I'm very thirsty . . ." He tries to walk out of the light and gets pressed back into it. The burning circle. "Please," he says. "Water."

"When you're finished your job. Do your job."

"I know you," he hears himself say. The white light is burning right into his brain, through the backs of his eyes. Having only a voice to hear has shifted things in him, a memory. It's there in him somewhere, that voice talking to him, droning, a long time ago. Saying so many things. It's coming up again — a pressing urge like the need to vomit. "I'll tell you my other name if you do your job," says Lukhele. He tells him words to say and Marcus says them, not knowing what they are, the sense of them. He points at the bomb, he explains it. How it will blow up. What it's meant to do. How he got into the school via an underground tunnel. When he's finished, he is swaying. "So thirsty," he says. But it's not the bomb he made. This is a different one. Everything wrong. "What's your name?" he shouts into the light. "I know you!"

"Is all right," says the voice, soothing. "I will tell you my name. And give you a nice cold bottle of water also. Just finish it up here now. We coming to the end. Look here and say you set this bomb in order to kill Nelson Mandela. This is the reason you have set this bomb."

He stares.

"Say it," says the voice.

"Are you mad?" he says. "Why would I set a bomb for Mandela? That's not what I *did*." But what did he do? Why did he do it? It's there, almost. They gave him something to make his head rubbery but it's lessening.

"You just say it for legal reasons," says Lukhele. "Doesn't mean anything, we do it like this, you see. What is called a legal formality for the case, okay. Is something too much to explain here but will make it easier for you, believe me. Otherwise you can be in heavy trouble with charges."

"Lukhele, Lukhele. It was something else. I know you . . . I know you . . ."

"Say, I made this bomb in order to kill Nelson Mandela. We are getting very close to the end now. Say it and you can be finish and have some water."

"No!"

"Yes, you will. Just relax and say it. Is nothing."

"No! I know you . . . I remember . . ." He turns away from the burning light and presses his eyes against his palms and crumples over and in his head the pictures start to rush and flow like sputtering water from a broken hose — fragments, flashes — Annie with her black hair in the moonlight on a bench in his garden by a pomegranate tree and that was the night she gave him the book and her full name it's . . . Annie Goldberg. God, *Annie.* American exchange scholar, teaching here. Leiterhoff School. Jules township. And down the hill was the shantytown and the cops and the firebombs that day, and that was when he met — this is him, this bald one, it's not Lukhele, it's something Chinese, it's, it's — "Shaolin!" he shouts. "Comrade Shaolin!"

A hand is grabbing the back of his neck and shaking him, pulling him upright. "Ach, enough already!" says an Afrikaans voice. "Enough!" He tries to wrench himself away from the hand. Other hands grab him. It's all collapsing in his head. And the light stand falls also and he sees men in military gear, brown camouflage uniforms, bulky vests with pouches, black masks, submachine guns. Then the light is turned again and he's held solid with an arm around his neck from behind and in front the Afrikaans voice says, "We will be here all fokken night. Put him on his arse here." They pull him down and they have his arms and there's a ski-mask face in close, the Afrikaans voice is coming from there on a waft of meaty breath, and he knows this voice also. Meantime in his head everything goes on collapsing . . . Comrade Shaolin talking in a hall where Annie brought a videotape called Fireseed. And his father in the Yard and the tall cop — the tall white cop . . . "Gee my daardie ander lig" — give me that other light — this one is saying on the bimah now, this voice that he also remembers . . . He saw himself in the toilets, on the ground and bleeding, but he was too stupid to understand he was being shown what happened to him, what put him in his coma. He was just a kid at this school. And he used to break into it every night, with Annie sometimes, using the pipe tunnel. She would fetch him in her Volkswagen or he'd pedal on his bike . . . "Hou sy bene oop" — hold his legs open — the voice is saying now . . . and then he'd make copies of the tapes. A different Ski Mask shown on them. The Fireseed tape. How to make bombs that work . . . "Now listen here to me, Mr. Martin Helger. Helger junior. You do what we tell you, oright? You hear me? You remember who I am? Of course you do. Cos I don't believe your bullshit story about bullshit amnesia for one second, mate. Not one. And you know me and you know that I do not fok around. Izzen it so?"

Martin?

Martin?

Martin.

Something cold down there. He struggles, but they're gripping him. This one in front is forcing something metal down into his pants, cool steel against his privates. "That's a halogen light, boy. It burns at thousands of degrees. You want to play games with us? I can play games all night." And there's a click and a hum and now he sees a glow shining through the fabric of his jeans and almost immediately it starts to get hot. He tries to kick, they're gripping him solid. "No!" he shouts. "Ahh! No, stop it!" . . . the sweet smell of gun oil and the dead meerkats scattered on the sand and Hugo Bleznik in his red Jag. And his name is Martin. And Hugo left him a letter. Bank accounts. The bomb wasn't to get the school. The bomb was for this one, right here, the tall man. For him. Whose name is, whose name is . . . *pain,* bright unbelievably stinging hot burning pain against the side of his penis and, worse, the soft wrinkled skin of his scrotum and the testicle nestled there, and he starts to scream and to thrash but they have him held too tight, the light is burning. "Stop it! God, please stop!" The light goes off. "We are not monkeying around here, boy," says the Afrikaans voice. "I'll burn your dick off with a smile on my face if you won't do what you are told to. Will you do what we say?" "Yes! Yes! Yes!" "I don't think you're serious enough." "No, don't. Don't do it!" But the light blinks on inside his jeans again, that sickening blue glow. "Remember this," says the voice, "while you do what you are told." It starts to burn immediately, the steel and glass is already hot. It burns so fast that a curl of smoke lifts up from the fabric and someone chuckles beside him and he starts to shriek and buck and as he screams something snaps inside his mind, he feels it cleanly break. And through the break falls an avalanche, a vast, driving avalanche while far away a tiny voice is screaming, a voice that knows, screaming over and over the same words, "You're Oberholzer! It's Oberholzer! Oberholzer! *Oberholzerrr!*"

19

Ahhh God, it stings where my cock and balls are burned, it's throbbing ten shades of red agony every second and I am stuck on a bimah surrounded by a pack of maniacs with machine guns who are trying to frame me *for blowing up Nelson Mandela,* but the truth is that on the inside right now all I'm truly feeling is relief relief relief. Swear to God. Cos I've been unclogged. The blockages in me have exploded. And what has rushed in with the flood of all my memories — at last! — is *myself.* There is no better feeling than becoming who you really are. I can see now that I have been watching myself like a stranger ever since the coma, I've been acting a part, mumbling my way through a numb life. And it was because I was too scared to face the memories that were there in me all the while. It's taken *this,* it's taken pain and near-death to force those memories up and out, to burst the blocks. And now I'm here and I am back and I am Martin Helger, I'm not Marcus my brother who dived in the river and boxed in the backyard and washed blood off his tux at dawn, and I will die here as Martin Helger, probably, and that's better than living the way I was, it seriously is. Nothing is worse than losing yourself.

I look at the camera and say my name and I say the words *Nelson Mandela has to die.* Oberholzer is directing now. He asks for another take, with more feeling. Sure. *Nelson Mandela has to die.* "That's better," he says. "Let's do another one with you explaining how you got in here, maybe we can improve on that stuff too."

"I forgot you were a video director as well," I say. "When you were king of Julius Caesar."

"Well, I was Internal Stability. Video was only a small part."

"Are you a major still?" I ask.

"They call us *police directors* nowadays in the New South Africa. To try to take away our military teeth, our rank. It should be colonel. But never mind my rank. Call me Bokkie, hey. Like old times. Let's roll."

I speak my part, gesturing to the bomb. Explaining how I entered and how I used fertiliser to augment the explosives, mixed with diesel fuel.

"Okay, we'll cut there," says Oberholzer. "You doing very well, Martin. Now when we start, you tell the camera you're a member of a Zionist commando unit."

"A what?" I say.

"Zionist. Tell the camera, South Africa must be *corrected*. Nelson Mandela refuses to do what he's told, he is taking the country down the wrong path. He gives comfort to the enemies of global Zionism and Israel and United States . . . We ganna put later a quick few shots of other masked men. Won't overdo it. Just a hint. Conspiracies need that hint." I'm really not sure what to say to this madness so I just rub my chin. Oberholzer says, "Don't have to say the word *Israel* more than once. Is better to keep it a little bit vague. Forensics on the explosion will identify the make of the detonators and that."

"Boss, I'm just ducking to the jazz" — going to the toilets — says a masked man. "Oright?"

Oberholzer shifts a bit on the far side of the light. "Ja, go. But quick now, Pienaar."

"Ja, boss."

"*Zionist power will not be broken* — try that," Oberholzer says to me. "You ready?"

"But what's it got to do with Mandela?"

"Listen, if it was a Boer, some Afrikaner like me doing it, it'd be the old story. White right-wingers. But if it is the Jews assassinating him *in one of their own temples* — ahhh now we talking, hey. Everyone fokken hates you lot. Conspiracy. Israel and Jews taking over the world. It's perfick."

I clear my throat. "I don't know."

"No? You'll see. I'm miles ahead of you, mate. Remember you made this bomb to get *me* — now look where we are." He chuckles.

I nod. "How'd the speech go, Bokkie?"

"Beg yours?"

"That speech of yours here, ten years ago." I sweep my arm like a matador.

"Excellent, thanks for asking. Headmaster Volper, he gimme a lovely introduction and I got some wunnerful applause. I spoke about goal-setting to the boys. Keeping a pure and focused mind."

"Super," I say.

"Don't get cheeky. Remember your balls. You ready to record?"

"What happens to me afterwards?"

"Now you being selfish," says Oberholzer. "Think on the good of the country. Think history. You going to be our firestarter, Martin. We need our burning Reichstag and after Zionists kill off Mandela we'll have it. You people ganna get it in the neck. But think Israel and America will stand still for that? That's how war will kick off — like it should've done in 'ninety-three." This raving gets him so excited he comes forward into the light so I can feel his spittle on my brow as I back away. I bump into waiting hands and turn to face Lukhele — no, Comrade Shaolin. He's chewing away, I can even guess what brand of chewing gum, I remember that day on the hilltop in Jules township

when he questioned me about the Annie tape and how he offered me
some Stimorol, saying he likes fresh breath, before they pulled back
the tarp on the charred bodies. The movement of history, he said then.
Thesis and synthesis and Karl Marx.

"So this is what it was all for, hey," I say to him. "Your great Struggle."

"You don't know anything," he says.

"I was there, Shaolin."

"Be quiet now."

"My people and my country is what you used to say."

He snorts. "The only country is the country of Joseph Lukhele."

"Your comrades."

"My family is my comrades."

Oberholzer comes out of the dark to lay his long hand on Lukhele's
shoulder. "You see," he says. "There it is. Even a solid old ANC man will
say it straight now. You tell it to him, Joe."

Lukhele knocks the hand off and swears at him and Oberholzer
chuckles and turns away. Lukhele glares at me. "Don't judge me, boy,"
he says. "I gave my blood for it and all what changed is the faces at
the top. The rest are down in the dirt, like always." He hits himself in
the chest hard enough to thump like a drum. "Not *me*," he says. "Not
anymore."

"But Mandela," I say. *"Nelson Mandela."*

A snarl shows teeth like jagged walls in the fierce dark circle of his
face. "How is he different? Sitting in that big luxury house in Houghton."

I blink at him, remembering. "I saved your life, Shaolin."

"You're confused," he says. "My name isn't Shaolin anymore. Your
mind does not function. You come to my office rambling how you are
your brother."

"I remember it. The red Jag."

"Let me tell you — that night I was caught it was Marcus who did it.
He was working for *him* then, he was his top man." He stabs his thumb

backwards at Oberholzer somewhere behind. "So I don't owe you Helgers. Nothing."

Oberholzer is back, drawn by the gesticulation. "Hell, those were the days," he says. "And Marcus was bladdy good. The Machine we called him. Machine Marcus. My machine."

"It was where he was taking you that night," Lukhele says, "to meet Marcus and start more trainings."

"Would have worked beautifully," Oberholzer says. "But you ran away that time, Martin. It's okay. Every negative holds a positive seed. Things happen for a reason. You've come back now with this — what a *gift*, hey."

Understanding seeps into me like a chill. I turn to Lukhele. "I went to your office and you ran straight to him. You knew I was all confused. You sold me out."

"When opportunity walks in the door," says Lukhele, "you have to think fast."

"Where's Pienaar?" Oberholzer is asking someone else.

"He's coming, boss." A masked man is pointing. I stare at him, the source of the voice, because it's another black man's accent, and I say to him, "And you also? This is *Mandela*, man."

The man's laughter is like a shout. "He'll take his offshore account over Mandela any day," says Oberholzer to me. "They all will. They're not like me — I do it on principle. The principle of payback. Eye for eye, jiz like your holy scrolls here says it. But I take good care of my men." He's walking back out of the light, to the camera. He's all legs. He's got that same rifle strapped across him, had a name for "her" back then. Picking off meerkats in the desert as the sun went down. Meantime Lukhele and another one push me back to my mark in front of the bench, in the brightness. The burn in my groin stings terribly. "Oright, chop-chop," Oberholzer is saying. "Say something like *My name is Martin Helger and I am the leader of our Zionist commando, we do this bomb to protect our world order and a free South Africa.* Try that. We'll play with it. Look straight here in the lens, man. Three two one and . . . *action.*"

There is a wet snapping noise and a man falls into the light with something spraying from his head.

20

The light swings around and in its white burning a masked man has a black submachine gun up to his cheek flickering yellow from the tip of its fat muzzle, making only a low buzzing sound and others are shouting, diving, and then the light goes out with a pop of breaking glass. Things are whirring in the air, cracking like pebbles hitting metal all around. I dive down in the blindness after the glare and someone heavy lands on top of me with the *bzzzz* noise in close and hot casings falling on my cheek. To my right one of the masked men is dropping — not flying backwards like in a movie but straight down like some string-cut puppet. Now this guy on top grabs me and starts dragging me with him across the bimah floor, saying, "With *me,* Martin. *Stay low.*" It's his voice and it paralyzes me. He curses and yanks, telling me to wake up. We slither over sprawled bodies. My hand slaps a viscous puddle of something hot with chunks in it. We reach the glass-brick wall and slide our backs along it to the stairs — a break in the wall that he starts easing around. Immediately there's a *zoop* noise and a sharp crack very close and he shouts in pain and jerks back. The moonlight is strong and my eyes are adjusting and the bimah is empty now but for the bodies of fallen men and broken glass and casings and the two of us, huddled against the wall. "Aw shit," he's saying. "Shit a fucken *brick.*" He rips off his pouched vest and his mask, starts patting at himself and pawing at the side of his head in a kind of panic. He doesn't have any hair anymore and his head is rounder, his face fatter, but it is no one else but my brother, my blood. The true Marcus Helger. I notice that the top of his ear is gone, the bleeding made oil-black by the moon. I tell him it's just the ear as he's opening a package with his teeth, a dressing he gets me to hold there while he tapes round his head to keep it in place. He's saying, "Bladdy good shot. Christ shit *fuck*."

Oberholzer's voice floats up from the pews, the open blackness on the other side of the wall — he could be anywhere out there. "Hey, hey, Martin! Is he still moving by you? He is hurt izzen he? You on your own now, Martin." I don't say anything and then Oberholzer says, "It *was* your brother, hey? The real Marcus. He's wearing Pienaar's kit. Thought he'd fox me but I'm too quick."

I can hear Marcus grinding his teeth, mumbling, "How many how many how *many*. Two, three, four. Four. Fuck shit. *Four*." I realise he's counting the number of bodies on the bimah as the echoing voice of Oberholzer floats back. "I got him," it says. "He is dead or dying there izzen he. I never miss. I put a hole in his head and I can do the same for you. You know that. So I want you to stick your hands up now, Martin. Stand up slow with your hands over your head."

I look at my hand and it's smeared with that oily black and I look at the bodies and I can smell the burnt gunpowder. It was seconds. My brother started shooting and he would have got them all but then it must have been Oberholzer who spun the blinding light onto him and jumped off. Others did too — that's why Marcus was counting. Three of them are out there including Oberholzer who was already set up and waiting for us when my brother reached the stairs. *Bladdy good shot.* I remember him firing one-handed at the farmhouse, touching a bullet to whatever he wanted. I wipe my sticky hand off on my jeans. We've lost all surprise and now we're marooned on a stage with no way off.

"Martin, come out. You know that I am a reasonable man. Let's work this through. I am a positive thinker — every adversity has an opportunity in it, you know."

Marcus twitches and his arms whip around and the submachine gun buzzes again. I look in time to see someone ducking back as bullets hit the glass-brick wall across from us, cracking hard, spraying chips. Marcus changes magazines. Oberholzer starts shouting in Afrikaans. Screaming at someone called Jannie that he needs me alive. Then Jannie shouts back, "Daar's twee van hulle!"—that it's two of us—and Oberholzer says, "Marcus! Marcus! You still there, hey? It *is* you, hey?" Marcus doesn't answer, his teeth grinding. Oberholzer calls, "Can't believe I missed. You got Jew's luck, Sergeant. Always did. You come out of nowhere, just like we trained you. You musta got Pienaar in the bog. A nice plan. Put on his kit and shoot us all in the backs. But now listen here, Marcus Helger. Hear me, you fokken traitor Jew. You failed. You didn't get us all. I am on this side and Jannie is on the other. Meantime old Joe Lukhele has gone to find the stairs up to the ladies' chairs up there. He'll be on top soon. With a lovely view down. Then the fun's ganna start."

There's a silence and then a banging, distant and steady—something heavy slamming into wood. It must be Lukhele at the locked teak doors that lead up to the women's gallery. I can picture them, they're big and solid, but if he's got a sledgehammer or something it won't take him long to bust through. Marcus grimaces and calls out, his voice hoarse, "I don't think so, Bokkie. You open fire, this thing goes boom."

"Don't con yourself," says Oberholzer's voice. "He'll pot you clean."

"I'll set it off myself. Less you back off."

"Go for it—we'll be ukay out here, we outside the blast radius. You a suicide case now, Machine? What about your little brother, you taking him with? It's over, man. Show your hands. We got you."

Now the thudding noise changes to a tearing, a splintering. There's a pause and then the thumping goes on more rapidly bangbangbang— he must be almost through—and I get a trapped and desperate feeling which is mirrored in my new-gifted memories with the time that Annie Goldberg and I were caught in a storm that filled up the pipe and nearly drowned us like a pair of unlucky kittens. All-a-sudden I've elbowed my brother and I'm savagely pantomiming but he's not getting it and I have to put my mouth right by his good ear to let him know and *then* he moves, we both slither over to the bench which is still open and we very carefully lift out the assembled bomb whole and set it down. I bend over and reach down, my hurt groin shrieking, and lift the metal trapdoor and then, staying low, I climb down into the dim space underneath. My feet find the very chair that Annie and I left there all those years ago. The banging has ceased out there, I picture Lukhele running up the curving stairway to the gallery, jumping three at a time. I step carefully off onto the desk and look up to find Marcus climbing down, lowering the trapdoor above him so that it goes black. He switches on a torch. Oberholzer is calling out again, the words muffled. I climb down off the desk. The dust and the jumbled-up stuff looks just the same, even the half-melted candles. I cross to the far side where the filing cabinet lies flat and the long slit in the brick wall behind is exposed. When I look at Marcus I can see his left leg isn't working properly by the way he hops down, stumbling, and the chair goes crashing onto the metal desk—very loud in that small space. If I can hear Oberholzer's muffled voice through the trapdoor they probably caught that. I hiss at my brother to give me the torch and he does and I head down the narrow, scratching slit as fast as I can, cobwebs brushing my face.

When I reach the main tunnel and turn around, Marcus is right there and I shine the beam up the slit. Shit—I forget to remind him to lift the filing cabinet across behind us. It's too late to go back now, I start running but then I catch myself. He has one hand on the wall to keep weight off his leg and he is hopping to keep up. "Where you hit?"

"S'fine. Go. Go." I shine the light down and see the blood on his left shin and at the calf where the bullet must have come out. I lift the beam to his chest so I can see his face. "How can you be here?" I say. "How are you even alive, man? Where the hell have you been all this time?"

"Where's this go?" he says, jerking his chin.

"Back to the pipe. Did you come in by the pipe?"

"Ja. Like them. I followed."

They all came up the pipe because their coming and going could never be recorded. My grotesque mistake was to go to Lukhele. But how could I have known what he was? What he'd become? Their plan was neat — the bomb would kill Mandela, the video would explain who and why, me and mine. The New South Africa would maybe self-destruct. Oberholzer would pay back all the hurt and rage he nursed. He'd be the winner all the way and me the supreme loser just like all those games of Slinkers back in the foyer of the Emmarentia Shul with Ari and Pats — poor Pats. Meantime I've got my head under Marcus's arm and we are hurrying down the tunnel, the torch beam stabbing around crazily. It's not too long before that yellow eye hits the blankness of a wall ahead. When I lift it up what I see is not just the spring-loaded flap that Annie and I once squeezed our ways through with a bag full of videotapes but now there is a bar of steel behind it, to keep it from swinging open too wide.

"Calm," says Marcus. "Gimme light here." He is digging into camouflage pouches on his belt. I realise he left the bulky pouched vest behind on the bimah. He comes out with three grenades, two round black globes and one long cylinder. "Phosphorus," he says of the long one. "Smoke. These two're frags." He's looking up at the steel bar. "Ja," he says. He puts down the grenades and digs out the roll of tape he used on his dressing, finds a chunk of loose concrete and wraps tape around it, and then he stretches a long piece and winds it around one of the frag grenades. Then he freezes. I've heard it too — a slow, slithering, softly crunching noise in the dark behind us. Marcus kills the light. His arm across my chest presses me to the wall beside him. It's very dark but not utterly black, some moonlight is filtering in maybe from drains and seams above. There are concrete beams that run vertically down the walls every maybe fifteen metres on both sides, and Marcus starts inching up towards the shadow of the closest one. His feet encounter something and he hands me the submachine gun which I take by the fat snout, realising it must be a built-in silencer — why these weapons buzz and don't bang. Marcus straightens up with an old half-broken plank, about as long as an arm. He takes the gun back and presses the torch into my hand and whispers close, "They won't shoot you like me. When I say, walk to them. Turn the torch on and hold up your hands but keep *it shining on them*. Got it?"

I nod. The slithering is getting closer. "This is nuts," I say, feeling numb and dreamlike around the booming of my heart.

"I need to see them," he tells me. "You go out hands up and they'll show. Keep it shining on them no matter what. Then when I shout you run all out to that side and get down. But don't stop shining. Even while you sprinting. They won't fire on you. Say it back to me." Then two things are happening almost at once. There's another slithery crunch, sounding close, and Marcus leans out and gives a burst from the submachine gun for a second and then flattens himself back against the wall. In the flare of yellow from the gun all I saw was an empty tunnel down there — they must be pressed behind the concrete beams like we are.

A shout vaults out of the dark: "Hey stupids! Come out. Where can you go?" It's Lukhele. "You stuck in here," his voice says. "Show your hands, come out."

Then comes an Afrikaans voice, it's Jannie. He says, "You left your kit and your bag behind, Marcus. We know you got stuff-all on you. Time to get real."

"Throw out the gun," Lukhele says. "Hands on your heads and come out walking backwards."

"Oright!" shouts Marcus. "Lemme just calm Martin."

"Now!" says Lukhele.

"He's scared here," says Marcus. "Tell him you won't shoot."

A pause. "Mar-ten," says Lukhele. "We not going to shoot you, okay?"

Meantime Marcus is whispering fast to me, repeating his instructions. Keep shining. Run to cover and get low. "And shout when you run."

"Shout?"

"Your bladdy head off."

"Marcus!" says Jan's voice. "We got monolenses here. We got masks. I'm rolling in a gas."

"Relax, china," Marcus calls. "Here it is." And he puts the submachine gun down flat and chips it carefully with his foot, sending it skittering out into the tunnel. "We unarmed," he calls.

"Step out! Hands on heads! Walk backwards to us!"

For a second I think Marcus is hugging me close but what he's doing is pushing some lumps of rubbery stuff into my ears and then he's turning on the torch in my hand and prodding me out into the tunnel. I step forward and lift my hands above my head, the beam slanting down as I start walking up the tunnel. They won't shoot you. Shouts come out of the blackness, telling me to turn around, turn around, but I keep walking forward slowly. Waiting for the shout from Marcus behind, waiting for them to show like he said they would, but it's just blackness and it feels like it's receding from me as I keep walking. I'm getting so far away from my brother. And then on the left a giant insect appears and I give a huff of fright and almost drop the light before I realise it's Lukhele wearing some goggling contraption over the top part of his face. A thrusting single lens — night vision. His one hand is aiming his submachine gun at my chest and his other arm is whipping down, shouting at me to drop the torch *drop it*. Jannie's voice from the other side: "I will plug him, Marcus! I will! Hear me, Marcus! Come out down there!"

I move the light a little to the right and then I see him, Jannie, he's squatting behind a beam behind the fat muzzle of his weapon. "Marcus!" he shouts. But there is no Marcus, only me, Martin, and the guns locked on me and I am surrendering truly. Marcus just wanted me to surrender, there's nothing he can do —

"Go Martin go!"

That voice hits me from behind, a voice as far-sunk as my child-hood, and I'm running with it already like I'm a sailboat punched by a sudden wind. I'm sprinting for the closest pillar on the wall and I re-member the light too late, the beam flying everywhere at the end of my winging arm, my burnt groin stabbing me. Then my shoulder slams the wall and I steady the light. I forgot to shout. Meantime at the edge of my vision, behind, something small is tumbling through the air like a hurt bird. Marcus steps out and swings the plank. The attention of the others is on me, I drew them while behind Marcus hits that thing with the plank, a full-armed swing like a cricket bat, and I hear the *clop* of the impact as Marcus ducks back behind cover. As I'm dropping low there's a hard crack on the other side, a near-instant echo, and I catch a glimpse of Lukhele's insect head snapping back and a dark piece spin-ning off and there's grit dancing on the wall in flickering yellow light — Jannie is firing, stepping out to get an angle on Marcus, and then the black tunnel turns into day.

21

My cheek is on the ground and I'm inhaling a burnt smell. Feels like the whole world just got pounded by a meteor the size of Joburg, like all the rocks of the earth are still ringing. But it's just my ears, even with the plugs, and I'm looking at the yellow eye of the torch beam on the wall, a shaking eye because the torch is still rocking on the ground. A shadow on the far side unfolds upward. It's Marcus. He picks up the torch and shines it on the submachine gun that he threw out before and he snaps up the gun and run-hops up the tunnel. I see that evil flickering in two yellow bursts. I get up and walk down, Mar-cus is limping back towards me. He pushes me to turn me back but he has the light in his hand and it flashes up the tunnel and I see what

he's come from. Superintendent Joseph Lukhele, aka Comrade Shaolin, the man with no country, is slumped oddly against the wall with
chin on chest and his head all opened so you can see inside. The other
guy, Jannie, is on the ground and looks simply butchered. Well — grenades do that. I'm helping Marcus hop towards the wall now and he
shines the beam on the other grenade, the one he wrapped with tape
to a chunk of concrete. There were two fat round grenades like that
and what he did, he batted one of them into Lukhele's face, *fired* it
across the gap with enough power and precision to nail him like a
hard punch and neutralise him for those seconds as it bounced at Jan
and blew up. That's what Marcus just did. I saw it happen. This other
stone-taped grenade he throws now, spinning up into the torch beam
and the tape wraps around the steel bar and the grenade dangles there
as we rush to cover. I press my fingertips against the earplugs. My eyes
are closed but I still catch a flash of orange through the lids, braced
better for the stomping of the earth this time.

The pipe is ripped open, moonlight pouring in like floodwater. I
help Marcus climb, boosting him up onto my shoulders. He hammers
the bent tin flat with the butt of the gun so he won't cut himself and
then clambers in and reaches down and I use his help to pull myself
up into the pipe also. We pause there, hunkered in the narrow space,
both breathing hard. Past Marcus, the pipe goes down into the earth.
All we have to do is start crawling and we'll be out in Brandwag Park
in ten minutes. Less, probably. But I look the other way. Whoever last
came through here left the grate wide open and I can see the sky and
the stars, even the tops of the wild grass. All-a-sudden I realise what's
out there — what I've forgotten and re-remembered. I start climbing
up. Marcus grabs my calf. "There's something I buried there," I tell him.
"Years ago."

"Leave it."

"Cash," I say, remembering. "My passport, a green card for America."

"Hey?" Like I've lost my mind.

"I'm serious, Marcus. A green card for you also."

"You're in shock. You're babbling. Let's go."

I kick his hand loose. "For America," I say. "Hugo arranged. Can't explain now, I've just got to fetch it."

Marcus catches me as I reach the top, flattening me to the sand just outside. "Dumb schmock," he hisses. *"Oberholzer."*

I freeze. "Where?"

"He wasn't in the tunnel. Means he stayed up. Checking for exits, to cut us off. He woulda heard the grenades. He's coming here. We go *now*."

I shake my head. I can't — I won't — forget packing that rucksack with everything I would need, in the icy calculating mood that came over me after Patrick Cohen was murdered. How I buried it under stones, along with the overalls, to make my escape to Botswana after the blast.

Marcus has fished a Motorola radio from his thigh pocket. "Pienaar's," he whispers. He presses the send button and listens and presses the button again and listens some more. But there's only static. He murmurs some Afrikaans into it. Still nothing. He pockets it and finds a stick and hangs an empty grenade pouch and then pokes it up over the top of the grass, bobbing it there like a balloon. Nothing. "He's not there," I whisper.

"He's sly," says Marcus.

"I'm going, Marcus," I say. "Take me a minute."

I start crawling but he grips me so I struggle to pull free. Finally he says, "Oright, calm. How far izit?"

"See the tennis courts, it's like halfway to them." I point. "Straight on in this direction."

"I'll take point. No talking. If I'm going off, you tap me and signal." He goes ahead without waiting for me to answer. He moves very slowly, inching along, so that it takes forever and my arms are shaking when I finally see the pyramid shape of the mound of stones. Still

there, thank God. But there's a stretch of open ground we have to cross.
Marcus keeps shaking his head but I get up in a crouch and start running and Marcus gets up too and I remember his limp so I go back and
grab him and we both reach the stones together. Marcus slumps down
with his back to them. I start turning over heavy ones, digging under.
Only dirt. I start to get scared that I'm wrong, that my mind is tricking
me again, or else someone found it over the years. But I make myself
calm down and go back to the edge and find that I've missed a big one
and when I lift it I catch a scent of wet and there're worms and mould
on the underside. Digging down, excited, I feel plastic, then a strap. I
wrench it clear — the rucksack. The fabric on the straps is rotten but
the plastic body of the thing is quite whole. I swing it around to Marcus and open it. Inside I find an envelope and in that is everything I remember: the page with the accounts, the letter from Hugo that I was
supposed to burn, the wads of cash and the passport and the American
green cards. My back is cramping and I straighten up without thinking
about it, the envelope in hand. It gives a funny shudder and there's a
soft *zoop* of something in the grass behind and Marcus is pulling me
down hard against the stones. There's a hole in the envelope now, right
under my thumb. Marcus has rolled over onto his elbows, the submachine gun aimed. The Motorola squawks in his thigh pocket. He digs
it out and we listen to soft crackling and then a voice breaks through.
That voice. "Helger boys," says Oberholzer. "What you got there, Helger boys? What's in that big letter and that bag, Martin?" Something
bad is happening to my brother. He's shut his eyes really tight and he's
shaking like we're in the Arctic Circle, I can hear his teeth chattering.
Oberholzer says, "Claudine and me could have potted you two anytime
but we let you take your little crawl. See what you up to. What did you
dig up? What's in that bag, Mighty Mart? Is it guns? More bombs? Is it
cash? What's the letter say?"

Marcus mutters something. He passes the radio to me and then he
slowly climbs up the mound of stones. "Let me educate what is what,"

Oberholzer is saying, "since we here at school. What we have is one helluva crime scene. We got five members of the Leopards murdered in cold blood plus one superintendent of the South African Police Service, who is a former ANC war hero on top of it. We got a bomb that was trying to be set to assassinate a certain ex–state president by the name of Nelson Mandela. You might have heard of him. Ja. Now with one push on my button I can have half the blerry Flying Squad down here inside five minutes flat. And you know what they ganna find? They ganna find the Helger boys was trying to put a bomb to blow Saint Mandela to a million sticky pieces. Two Jewboys on top of it. One of which used to work for the security police. Oh ja, Marcus Helger, let's not forget all the dirty stories we know you were a part of — but the Leopards, tonight we were investigating and we moved in. That is how I will explain this all. And I know the detectives who'll be investigating and they know me so who do you reckon they'll believe? I'll explain them exactly how things went bad when you opened fire on us, the two of you caught in the act. We lost our men in the line of duty, who were trying to arrest you and stop the assassination plot. Bladdy heroes the lot of them. You killed heroes, you scum. You're assassins, you're bombers. We were just doing our jobs trying to protect Nelson Mandela. You will be the ones going to prison for life."

I stare at the radio. Marcus is peering carefully around the rocks up there. "You hear me boys?" says the voice. "Better come out hands up with that bag and let's work a deal." Looking at the radio in my hand I get a sudden urge and press the transmit button and say, "We'll see who they believe when we tell the real side."

There's a pause. I hear my brother shushing me from up there, climbing carefully back down. "Hello, Martin," says Oberholzer. "I don't know what story you mean. There's only the truth. We Leopards are national heroes and your brother jiz shot four of them down in cold blood. Grenaded another one and a superintendent with him. It was you, Marcus. Marcus, hear me? Marcus Machine — you the only

murderer here tonight. You a coldblood killer, Machine. It's your nature. It's the only thing you good at. And you and me know the truth
of what you've done. Wait until everyone else finds that out too. You
might as well put your own gun in your mouth, Marcus, and pull the
trigger right now—" Marcus has reached me and grabbed the radio
back, his fingers hitting the transmit button by accident, and Oberholzer goes quiet.

Marcus says to me, "Don't talk to that devil. He's playing mind
games."

"Did you see him?"

He shakes his head. "Hate snipers. Sitting with his night eye on us."
Marcus looks at the hole in the envelope. "He meant to miss. Believe it."

The radio crackles. "Helger boys. Listen to me. I have the camera
with me. I am a master editor, you know. What I ganna do, I'm ganna
sit here and keep you detained while I make some editing on this
camera. You try to move from there, Claudine's ganna have a chat to
your backs. Meanwhile I will record over certain parts and leave the
parts in where you say Mandela must die and then tell all about the
bomb and how you put it here. Which is the truth. You put that bomb,
Martin Helger. You sneaked in the tunnel like a sewerage rat and put a
bomb because that's what your kind does. When the force shows up, I
will be the hero who saved Mandela. This vidyo is my evidence. So sit
tight while I get to work."

It goes quiet. Marcus's face is all squeezed up again and he's shaking in a scary way. "Marcus," I say. "Marcus." But he doesn't respond.
I'm seeing him clearly in the full of the moon for the first time, able to
observe his face frankly now that his eyes are closed. Truly my brother,
here and now. The freshness is all gone and life has written its lines
deep instead, replaced the soft hair with its bony cap. But he came back.

I wipe my face and look around at our reality. We're completely
pinned down here behind this hill, but I think of the security guards

at the front gate — maybe they'll investigate and save us. They're all the way over on the far side of the school and locked in their concrete pill-box, would the rumble of underground grenades have been enough? Probably not. I look at the radio resting on Marcus's chest. Is there some way to change the digital frequency and reach someone, anyone? Then it crackles. Oberholzer's tinny voice says, "Tell you what. I will give you clowns a chance, cos I am such a merciful man. Maybe what you got in that bag you dug up is worth my while. Hey? Answer please."

I look at Marcus but he's still locked up, so I carefully prise the radio from him and press transmit. "What are you saying?"

"Hello, Martin," says the voice right away. "I can let *you* go. I'll be honest, not your brother, but you. Your brother is a traitor and mur-derer. Hell, he killed six good men tonight alone. You — I say ukay. I'll take fifty per cent loss if I have to. Tell him I mean it, Machine. You know I do." Marcus seems to come back from whatever bad place he's disappeared to, reaching up and taking the radio back and shaking his head at me. Oberholzer's saying, "Just tell me what's in that bag. What's in that letter, documents?"

Marcus says, "Bag is bugging him. A loose end. Such a careful bas-tard."

The radio crisps. "Martin. Martin. Let's make a deal, hey."

I ask Marcus about using the radio to call for help and he shakes his head and says they're code-locked. Then he shinnies back up the mound. He's cupping his eyes, staring through a little gap in the stones. "Hey. Does this grass go all the way to those courts or is there a road behind?"

"There never was a road," I say. "Was grass all the way to the courts."

"Nice," he says, and slithers back down, breathing hard. He sucks his finger, holds it up.

"What is it?"

"Wind," he says, "but too soft."

"I don't get it."

He leans over and pulls out the third grenade, the long cylindrical one. "Burns at five thousand degrees. And it's a helluva dry season."

I look at the tall grass around us. "I see what you mean."

22

Marcus stays at the top position, watching. Now we are waiting for the wind to pick up — that's all there is for us. For a while the radio crackles and Oberholzer's voice drones on, but then it's just silence and I think of him observing us through a green night scope and working on his tape and sitting up there with a giggle in his heart. I look up and say, "Did you know I was in that institute all this time? You never visited."

"A vegetable, I thought. No point."

"You went missing in action."

"No."

"We got the letter."

"A trick."

"We all thought you were dead. You weren't at Ma and Da's funerals."

"I couldn't."

"What happened to you?"

"A lot," he says.

"Oberholzer called you Machine. Said you worked for security police, the SB."

Marcus says nothing. I ask how he found me here, how he managed to appear like he did. He goes on ignoring me. "Hey," I say, "you can't just — hey. You owe me something, Marcus."

Slowly he looks down.

"I want to know what happened to you."

"Not now."

"I deserve it," I say. "And now might be all there is."

He touches the dressing on the side of his head, nods slowly. He eases down quietly and then his hoarse soft voice takes me to the start in hesitant bursts. Telling me how in 1988 Oberholzer had had him flown in on special request, from Ondangwa air base where he was serving on the Border. Marcus went gladly, sick of war. In Joburg, Oberholzer offered him a role in an undercover unit — liaison man with a bouncer gang, the notorious Dynamite boys. To use them for political work, dirty ops against anti-apartheid groups. Deniable civilian muscle off the books with no official connection to the state. But he needed a liaison because they wouldn't trust cops.

"That was you?"

"Said no for a long time."

Suddenly I remember Mike's Kitchen, what Oberholzer asked me there, and I understand it better. Oberholzer had been looking for a lever, to make Marcus change his mind. "But you said yes eventually. Because."

"You know why, Martin."

"Do I?"

"You the only one who can. After Ma and Da."

The radio crackles. Oberholzer says, "You fallen asleep, Helgers? Don't sleep yet. Best is still to come, hey. I've nelly erased the bad parts. You look fantastic, Martin. Camera loves you. You a hunnerd per cent believable." He laughs.

"Utter lunatic," says Marcus, shaking his head. I want to ask what he meant about me knowing why, but he's going on already, his eyes half closed, telling me about the last apartheid years, the chaos behind the scenes after Mandela was let out but before the first elections. One world imploding, the new one uncertain. People burning documents and disappearing, others running black ops to try kill the new order before it could be born. Then the elections and disbandment. Oberholzer landing on his feet as so many apartheid enforcers did. And Marcus switching to private sector, the work the same. "You fall in a way of life. It takes you over," he says. Operating in that world, he heard my name from a contact. He followed it up and ended up tracking one of the Leopards. "It led me here."

"If you hadn't," I say. "I'd be dead now, hey."

"Might still happen, brother."

"I know it," I say.

"They'd wait till after the bomb, kill confirmed. Then bury you deep with Jeyes drain fluid poured on top. Release the video."

I nod, feeling exhausted. "Are you married, Marcus? Children?"

"I was. But hard to live with someone who screams all night. No kids." Then he says, "The problem with letting the beast out, Martin, it doesn't go back in. That's something worth knowing, brother. You have to live through a lot to learn it."

"I see," I say.

"It's not a thing you can *see* from the outside."

"Why'd you do it, Marcus?" I ask. "I mean the whole thing. The bouncing and then the army. Whyn't you just stay in varsity?"

He looks around, sniffs. "You know, it prolly started here."

"You had the *Name* here," I say. And I tell him about the time at the Emmarentia Dam, bullies running from just those two words *Marcus Helger*.

He sniffs again—a weak and cynical noise. "Ja. Well. Violence works. S'why they cane you from the start. I got here, they called me grease monkey cos of Da. Hey grease monkey. I wrapped a bike chain on my fist and gave someone twenny-two stitches. No more grease monkey. I was what, thirteen. But I found out I liked it. Gave me that taste. Started looking for it, that feeling. Rugby. Then boxing. That took me to Dynamite Gym. Then bouncing. Then the army." He stiffened. "Hear that?"

"What?"

"Wind's coming."

23

By the time Marcus has the phosphorus grenade out, there's a wide gathering hiss in the grass, the sound of our good luck. I start feeling it on the back of my neck like a cool blessing as Marcus shows all his teeth under the moon in a hard and savage grimace. "Cook his damn arse," he says. "Tries to climb that fence, my turn to pot *him*. Fuck do I hate snipers."

"We'll be gone by then anyway," I say. "Once you chuck that it'll take us like a few seconds to get back to the pipe. With this." I waggle the envelope and then tuck it under my belt under my shirt, against my belly. Quickly I paw through the rest of the bag, pulling out the knee and elbow pads and hard hat, the overalls. The squashed overalls are stiff and mouldy-looking. But the pads seem okay even after ten-odd years in the earth, so I strap them on. Marcus is silent. He has that grenade out and is rubbing it and staring at it. Black blood has dried all over the side of his face where the dressing is taped against the ear. He shuts his eyes and blows air through puckered, trembling lips. "You oright?" I ask.

"Not that much juice left in me, Martin," he says.

"You're oright."

His eyes start leaking, thin silvery streams that scare me. "I had so much of it," he says.

"There's plenty," I say. "We'll get to America, you'll see. You'll leave all this."

"Ja," he says. "But all this won't leave me."

"Marcus, there's a mural on the wall over there that's got you on it. Running with the ball. No one could stop you, man. They still can't."

He wipes his hand under his nose, says nothing, his other hand clenching the grenade.

"Marcus, chuck that thing and let's go."

"I hammered them," he says. "Made them suffer. But it doesn't help the hate. There were always more."

"Marcus, please now. Or give it to me. I'll throw."

He stares at the grenade. "Ja, like the one at the Yard, hey. You said the funerals. I saw photos of what was done to Ma and Da. I couldn't come, I was already starting undercover, hitting them back."

That gets my head tilting like a dog to a strange noise. "Hitting who?"

He frowns. "Who d'you think? *Them*. The boogs. The ANC. The PAC. The terrs. Whatever you want to call em."

"Wait," I say. "You think it was ANC guys who killed Ma and Da? Is that what you meant before, that I would understand why?"

"It wasn't just some robbery, Martin," he tells me. "Sorry if you didn't know."

"Marcus," I say. "It wasn't the union or the ANC or anyone on that side."

"What you telling me?"

"Marcus, it was Oberholzer. He did it."

There's a silence. Marcus looks at me. I say I was there, at the Yard, in the office, I *saw* them lying there. And I remember the detectives saying the "giraffe" had had me brought there and I remember that Oberholzer knew our parents would be there that Sunday and what Shaolin said on the night of the red Jag, about the kind of grenade, and what Sammy Nongalo came to the house to tell me.

The Motorola crisps and Oberholzer's voice joins us, sounding relaxed. "I've done the erasing," he says. "Nice job. Almost ready to bell the Flying Squad. Unless you want to change your mind, hey, Martin? . . . Martin?"

I'm staring at the radio, not really hearing it, my brain spinning in overdrive. "Don't you get it?" I say to Marcus. "He wanted me there. He did it because — oh Jesus." And all-a-sudden the whole thing clicks in me and I see it all. "You told me you said no to him at first, right, but then — don't you see? It was like two birds with one stone."

"Two what?" His voice has turned gruff, like he's having trouble breathing.

"Oberholzer had them killed," I say, "and then — you said you saw photos, I bet you that *he* showed you the photos, didn't he?"

He nods stiffly.

"There it is. He had Da and Ma killed like he wanted and that got you to *help* him. And me, he was planning me also. What could be a better revenge? Was *perfect* for him. You set him up with the bouncer gang and that got his promotion to Special Branch."

"You getting carried away, Martin."

"I'm not."

"You say Oberholzer's murdering people just to get someone to work for him?"

"But it's not someone. It's a *Helger*."

He shuts one eye, confused. "Hey?"

"You know how much he hates us, our family."

"What's this you saying?"

"You know that Da and Oberholzer's father were like this," and I punch my fists together. "The poison history there."

"Who told you this?"

My mouth is hanging open. I mean I cannot believe my brother's ignorance, but then I think well why *would* he know? How could he? Everything I learned I found out *after* Marcus disappeared. So I tell him — about the trip with Hugo to see Oberholzer, about how he threw us out along with Hugo's shoebox of cash. "See, Da ruined Oberholzer's old man. And so he wanted to ruin us back. It's deep with him. It's like all he cares about. And it's all my fault."

"*Your* fault."

Because I was the one who made that first contact. I got myself arrested in Jules township. I was taken to John Vorster Square where

Oberholzer realised who I was. Then we went to the Yard where Oberholzer had the run-in with Da. *But for me* none of it would ever have
happened. I was the one who put the Helger family back into Oberholzer's mind and started it going. And I'm the one who told Oberholzer about my brother being a paratrooper on the Border. "He didn't
just pull your name out of a hat, Marcus," I tell him. "He went for you
because you are a Helger. Because you are Isaac Helger's eldest son."
Just like he went for me also, tried to get me into some kind of training camp the night I ran with Hugo's red Jag, taking Comrade Shaolin along with me. "Lukhele said you would've been there at that place,
that farm, too. He probably wanted you to help train me. He would
have sprung me on you — surprise. The man is sick. That was his revenge, don't you see? To *convert* us both to his side. To *use* us. To not
only kill Da but *steal his children* and help himself doing it."

Marcus is shaking his head, saying no over and over. "Can't be. He
chose me cos I knew the Dynamite Guys . . . I'd been a bouncer . . ."

"Marcus, think about it. There're probably twenty different people
he could have used to set up with the bouncers. But it was you. He
picked you, man, had you transferred and flown out of Namibia, all
that trouble — it's because you are a Helger. The Dynamite connection
was a nice excuse and it was also a benefit to him. But then you said no.
So he was stuck. He knew he had to do something to turn you."

The radio crackles but this time Marcus twists the volume knob
and Oberholzer's monologue dies to a murmur.

"No," Marcus says. "No, this can't be right."

"Marcus, face it. Oberholzer killed our parents. It was an army grenade. He knew they would be there doing stocktaking. He did it for his
father and to screw *us* up. He made you hate. You said he showed you
photos, right? He musta talked and talked about it to you too, I bet.
Talked you right into it, didn't he? Probably said this is your chance to
get them back. The bastards who did it — am I right? But all the time it
wasn't *them*, it was *him*, Marcus. It's so obvious now. Oberholzer."

"No," Marcus says, but he isn't shaking his head anymore, and I can barely hear his whisper over the hissing of the grass but I feel the wind shifting slightly. "Throw it," I say. "Let's go." Marcus looks down at what's in his hand like he doesn't know how it got there. "You're right," he says. "What you've said."

"Let's go, Marcus."

He doesn't move, so I grab his shoulder and shake him. "He doesn't matter now," I say. "Only *this* does. And *that* does." I hit my belly and I point. The documents. The tunnel entrance. But Marcus isn't looking at me.

EXODUS

24

On the packed sidewalks between the skyscrapers he feels like a drifting cinder in a steel foundry, a feeling that never leaves him. An accent and background as a white African Jew diluted in a million foreign accents, a million other worlds and combinations of worlds. You're a nothing: this was America's prime message against which each is alone and meant to rebel.

Yet they all know Nelson Mandela. And every time he sees Mandela's face on a magazine or a screen he'll smile and think of his brother. The saviour's saviour.

He joined a college and took a diploma. Journalism. When he arrived he thought there'd be officials waiting to detain him at JFK. Thought the *New York Times* would have him on its front page with a picture of Solomon High School and the headline MANDELA BOMB PLOT FOILED, POLICE MASSACRED. But you're a nothing in America. He searched diligently for a time for any mention online and in South African newspapers, but was never able to find even a single line. No massacre, no Jewish high school, no Leopards. He checked obituaries for the name Oberholzer but it was never the right Oberholzer. And no mention of the Helger name at all. Gradually his fervor for information passed, gradually the present subsumed the past, the future rose to dominance in his psyche, his accent transformed, his old self receded. Dr. Norm would have been well pleased. So would Hugo.

His first job was digital, writing headlines for an online news aggregator. Hugo's accounts had sustained him. He has a nice apartment in Brooklyn now, an open space with a water view. This is life, it flows on like that steely river. He met Carolyn at a yoga class and by the summer they were seeing each other. At odd moments he might think of Annie. He'll try to summon the energy to investigate the location of her body, the cemetery, the family. But as always he'll put it off. He'll remember instead.

"You go," he says. "You don't wait."

"We're both going, brother."

He's wrapped his lower leg and tied it off very tightly. "Get ready," he says.

"Marcus."

He looks at me. "Swear on Ma and Da. You go and don't look back. Now."

"No," I say. "I won't do it."

"Yes, you will," he says. Then he says, "Please."

And our eyes are wet and I say what he wants me to say and he turns and throws the grenade sidearmed and it flies in a high arc over the top of the mound of stones. Out to where it lands in the hissing grasses with a soft but immutable thud.

18 June 2006. Home alone in Brooklyn he tore open a tough, strange mail package while watching a little barge towing a huge raft of garbage across his window like some machine version of an African dung beetle. In the package he found a folded newspaper article two months old and a pair of glasses with broken lenses. The frames were buckled and discoloured, as if they'd been charred in an oven. The article covered the discovery of a mass grave site, unearthed by informal residents — what used to be called squatters — in Diepsloot, an impoverished township north

of Johannesburg. A forensic team was at work identifying remains of an estimated half-a-dozen bodies. There appeared to be scraps of police uniform interred with the dead, along with traces of a corrosive agent. Attached to the bottom of the newspaper clipping was a pin with an ornament: a piece of metal painted gold. Looking closer, he saw it was a cat. Closer still were spots. A leopard. He held up the glasses and then remembered that tall, thin man putting on just such square spectacles. He'd had them on the first time he'd seen him, taking coffee with Principal Mokefi at the Leiterhoff School in Julius Caesar township, Johannesburg, South Africa. He hid the package and didn't tell Carolyn about it. Or anyone. The past is a monster you put in a closet and shut the door on and put your back to and keep pressed shut.

He was alone again when he took the package out. He poured a long drink and laid the items out. Raised his glass. He'd realised what anniversary had just passed. "L'chaim, brother," he said. "Here's to Ma, and to Da. For them."

The grenade blows up with a hollow steely bang like fireworks in a tin barrel. The flash of it hurls a ghost shadow, white as milk. There are gunshots, little cracks by comparison, that must be from Oberholzer's reacting rifle. His Claudine. I smell burning grass and something chemical. Smoke curls on the air. I have the envelope against my belly. I can hear the crackling and licking of the flames. Marcus pushes me. When I peer around the stones there is a hedge of snapping yellow taller than me, stretching out across both ways with the fireball of phosphorous smoke boiling at the centre and the grasses already beginning to roar. My brother pushes me again. Go.

I grab him. "You with," I say. But I am already resigned, it's just a gesture. He prises my hand off and checks the submachine gun. His lips are working. "He doesn't matter," I say. "We'll go to America."

Marcus shakes his head. "Ganna finish him, Martin."

"And then?"

"Go now. You already swore on Ma and Da."

I thrust my hand into the envelope and pull out his green card and push it into his pocket and tell him I will see him later. Then I run, but I stop and look back, like Lot's wife. The burning is strong in the air and it stings my eyes. He is moving up the hill close behind the moving wall of fire. Running bent over with his one stiff leg making him seem to half stumble with each step but he is moving fast. He has the submachine gun on his shoulder and he is chasing the flames and I can feel the heat even from where I am and it is bright as day on our side but with thick smoke above so that I can only just make out the tops of the tennis court fences. And smoke also rises from the ground already charred and into this my brother burrows, disappears.

An American on the outside but underneath the white skin beats the blood of an African, the heart of a Jew. He has learned only a few things. Everything you believe can be wrong. Truth is made by power. Never let the beast out. Beware of your certainties. Beware of your certainties.

He was there the night Nelson Mandela almost got assassinated. They almost made him do it. There is the history everyone thinks they know and there are the secret truths underneath it. He knows that what is black now will be white tomorrow and what white now black the next day. Annie taught him we're all living on our movie sets. Maybe it takes someone else to push us off them, to open our eyes.

In a New York rainstorm he remembers his brother when they were little and the African rain caught them as they walked their dog. Marcus was all grins, he was all laughter. He ran to the water and dived in, he could have been anything.

GLOSSARY

Afrikaners — white South Africans of mainly Dutch descent who
speak Afrikaans, a language derived from Dutch
alter kukker — old fart
amandla ngawethu — "power is ours," rallying cry of ANC supporters
Amagabane — radical youth of the black townships engaged in protests
and violence during the apartheid era, supporters of the ANC; also
called Comrades
ANC — African National Congress, a political movement that fought
apartheid as a banned organisation, eventually becoming South Africa's governing party with Nelson Mandela as state president
arvy — afternoon
aveyre — sin
AWB — Afrikaner Weerstandsbeweging, the Afrikaner Resistance
Movement, a Nazi-like political movement based on Afrikaner na-
tionalism

baas — boss, with connotations of white supremacy
backchat — truculent arguing
backstop — protector
baff, baffing — fart, farting
bakkie — pickup truck

barmy, barmies — bar mitzvah(s), the male coming-of-age in
    Judaism at age thirteen

bell, belling — phone, phoning

biltong — South African dried meat, similar to jerky

bimah — a raised platform or focal point in the sanctuary of a syna-
    gogue, on which the Torah is read

bioscope — cinema

bladdy — corruption of *bloody,* with roughly equivalent usage

blerry — Afrikaans version of *bladdy*

boet, boetie — brother, little brother; also an affectionate address be-
    tween friends

boff, boffin — clever, a clever person or someone who has mastered a
    particular subject

bohbi — grandmother

braai, braaivleis — barbecue

bru — brother

cadenza — a fit, a nervous eruption or tantrum

cafi — convenience store, corner store; corruption of *café*

Casspir — a large armoured vehicle used by South African police and
    military

cause, causing — to make trouble, to needle, to create a disturbance, to
    look for a fight

charf, charfing — to pretend, con, or flirt

chazersa — disgusting, pig-like

check — look or see

china — good friend; derives from rhyming slang, *china* being a plate
    and *plate* rhyming with *mate*

chorbs — pimples

chutis, chutaysim — disparaging South African Jewish slang term for
    Afrikaners

click — understand

coch — vomit

coloured — people of mixed black and white ancestry

combi — a minivan, often used as a taxi

Comrades — see *Amagabane*

cuts — corporal punishment, caning, strokes of the cane

dinkum — truly, genuinely

dof — stupid

donga — a dry riverbed, an eroded ravine

dorp — a small, remote village or town

dosh — money

dumela — Sotho greeting

dutchmen — disparaging South African English term for Afrikaners

dwaal — a daze or trance

effy — condom

fah fee — a form of gambling, an illegal lottery

farshtunkene — stinking

fershtay — understand

flattied or flatty — to slap hard, to strike with an open hand

flip, flippen — relatively polite curse word

freks, frekking off — dies, dying, passing away

fress — to eat hungrily, to chow down

friss — very nice, beautiful

frum — pious, adhering strictly to the Jewish religion

full stick — all-out, with maximum effort

gesels — chat, talk

graft, grafting — to work, working

grensvegter — a super-soldier, a Rambo type; literally, a border fighter

grob — rough, loud, unmannered

grot — an ugly woman

Group Areas Act — apartheid law segregating land use according to race

Habonim — Zionist youth movement

hardegat — a hardass, tough guy, rebel

headgear — tall frame that sticks up above a mine, with winch wheels on top; it powers the elevators, called skips, that are used to transport personnel and materials underground

hitsik — excitable, worked up, febrile

howzit — informal greeting

ibberbottle — senile

impimpi — a police informer

indaba — an affair or concern, also a conference

Isiqalo — the Beginning, the start of the violent uprising against apartheid in the black townships

jacks — caning, corporal punishment, strokes of the cane

Jarmans — brand of dress shoe

Jody Sheckter — South African auto racer, world drivers' champion in Formula One

jol — a party, a good time; also to party or to play

kaffir — an extremely insulting term for a black person; derived from the Muslim term for non-Muslims

kaffirtjie — diminutive of *kaffir*

kaych — energy, power

kichel — a thin, crackly cookie made of flour, eggs, and sugar, usually served with chopped herring, sometimes liver

kiddish — the Jewish blessing before a meal; alternate pronunciation of *kiddush kieme* — germs

kishkes — innards, guts

klaar — finished, done with

klup — hit or smack (both noun and verb)

koppie, koppies — small hill, hills, often rocky

kuk — shit; alternate spelling of Afrikaans word *kak*

kwela-kwela — literally, "climb up, climb up"; Zulu slang for
     police truck

lank — a lot, greatly, very much

larney — ritzy, fancy, well-off

lekker — awesome, amazing; also attractive, desirable

lesiba — a traditional African musical instrument using wind and
     strings

lighty — youngster, a junior rank; not necessarily disparaging

location — apartheid-era term for a racially segregated township

macher — a dynamic, important person

main manne — big shots, leaders, the gang in charge

Majuta — Jew, Jewish

mameloshen — Yiddish; literally, mother tongue

matla ke a rona — "victory is certain," ANC rallying cry

matric — final year of high school, Standard Ten, also refers to an indi-
     vidual in Standard Ten

mayibuye iAfrika — "bring back Africa," ANC rallying cry

Meccano — model construction toy

megillah — a long, complicated story; literally, a scroll

meshugenah in kop — mad in the head, completely crazy

mezuzah — a small object, usually a narrow tube or rectangle about
     five inches long, fixed to the doorpost of a Jewish home and con-
     taining a scroll with sacred verses

mielie — corn, often fresh corn on the cob

mielie pap — a staple dish made of cornmeal cooked to a fluffy white
   texture similar to mashed potatoes

minco — short for *minimal coordination,* as in very clumsy; a school-
   yard insult on a par with *spaz*

MK — see *Umkhonto we Sizwe*

moer — to strike hard, to beat up

moerse — enormous, mother of all

mofi — insulting term for a male homosexual

morogo — a type of wild spinach

moshiach — the messiah

muchu — insane, berserk

mulet — madman, berserker

munt — highly insulting term for a black person

muti — traditional African medicines or magical charms

Mzabalazo — the freedom struggle or uprising against apartheid

naartjie — tangerine

Nats — National Party, ruling party of apartheid South Africa

necklace, necklacing — method of killing in which the victim is
   burned to death with a tire full of gasoline around the neck; used
   in the townships during the apartheid era, often as reprisal for suspected collaboration with the government

noch — also, on top of, in addition to

nooit — no way

nush — to snack on; Lithuanian-Yiddish pronunciation of *nosh*

oke — guy

PAC — Pan Africanist Congress, militant anti-apartheid group that split
   off from the ANC

Parktown prawn — a giant brown cricket of fearsome appearance

pasop — beware, watch out, be careful

pegged off — died

plant — to beat someone up, to knock them out

ponce — slick exploiter

poonie — slang for female genitalia

pup — deflated, flaccid, flat as in flat tire; alternate spelling of Afrikaans *pap*

puss — insulting and crude slang for female genitalia; alternate spelling of Afrikaans word *poes*

ratel — honey badger

rawl — fight (both verb and noun)

robot — traffic light

rort — fight (both verb and noun)

SACP — South African Communist Party

sanctions — refers to disinvestment as well as prohibitions on trade with apartheid South Africa

sangoma — traditional healer, spiritual guide

sawubona — Zulu greeting

scaly — low-down, underhanded

schlemiel — a bungling fool

schlof — sleep, nap

schmock — an insult roughly equivalent to *twerp* or *annoying idiot;* South African pronunciation of *schmuck*

schvantz — insult meaning *penis,* equivalent to *prick*

Shabbos — the Jewish Sabbath, from Friday sundown to Saturday sundown

sharp-sharp — expression to bid hello or goodbye or to express approval, similar to *cheers*

shebeen — a tavern in a township, unlicenced during apartheid *shiksa* — a female domestic servant; also a non-Jewish female

shiva — Jewish mourning period of seven days following the death of a relative

shmerf — both a cigarette and the act of smoking

shoch, shochedika — South African Jewish slang for a black person, disparaging but not as egregious as *kaffir*

shot — thanks, nice one

shtum — keep quiet

shul — synagogue

shungalulu or shongololo — black millipede

shwank, shwanker — to show off, a show-off

siddur, siddurim — Jewish book(s) of prayer

sis — expression of disgust

sjambok — a sturdy, heavy whip resembling a tapered stick, traditionally made of rhino or hippo hide but more often of plastic or rubber

skeef, skeefing — a hostile stare, giving the evil eye

skelm — crook, thief, criminal

slasto — paving made of slate shards set in concrete

smaak — to crave, to have a taste for

soek — to start trouble, to look for a fight, to hunt someone down; from Afrikaans for *seek*

sosatie — kebab, skewer, usually with meat

spanspek — cantaloupe

Standard — school year or grade

state of emergency — the apartheid regime's suspension of ordinary legal rights, a draconian crackdown on the opposition

stoep — veranda, covered porch

stukkie — little piece; also a vulgar term for a girlfriend

sut — exhausted

swot — to study, especially for exams in school

takkies — sneakers, running shoes

tallis, tallaysim — Jewish prayer shawl(s), usually white with black
stripes

tefillin — phylacteries: a pair of black boxes, each attached to a leather
strap and containing a holy Jewish text, traditionally worn by males
at weekday prayer, one strapped on the arm, the other around the
head

tehilim — psalms

tickey box — payphone, phone booth

Tipp-Ex — correction fluid

togs — task-specific clothes, usually for sports

Tokoloshe — a hairy dwarf-like creature of African folklore, believed to
be invisible

Torah — sacred parchment scrolls containing the handwritten central text of Judaism; also refers to Jewish religious teachings more
broadly

torch — flashlight

township — racially segregated urban area reserved for nonwhites
under apartheid laws

tsotsi — gangster

tune — to tell or to say

turps — mineral spirits or mineral turpentine; also called thinners or
paint thinner

tzitzit — Jewish religious undergarment with stringy tassels at the bottom corners

UDF — United Democratic Front, a broad coalition of community
groups opposed to apartheid and sometimes described as the
ANC's aboveground wing during the 1980s, when the ANC was
banned. The UDF was itself all but banned in 1988, but this was off-
set by the creation of the Mass Democratic Movement (MDM). The
UDF dissolved soon after the ANC was legalised.

Umkhonto we Sizwe — Spear of the Nation, the underground armed wing of the African National Congress, cofounded by Nelson Mandela. It was merged with the South African military following the unbanning of the ANC in 1990.

umzi watsha — "the city is burning," opening lines of a Xhosa children's song

vasbyt — grit, stoical determination; also a term of encouragement to hang in there; from Afrikaans, literally, "bite hard"

veld — bushland, uncultivated country

vikkel — move fast, hurry; also spelled *wikkel*

voetsak — very rude way of saying *get lost* or *piss off*

wank — to masturbate; also a pathetic and pointless act

yarmie — short for *yarmulke*, the religious skullcap for Jews

Yiddluch — affectionate diminutive for *Jews*

yortzeit — anniversary of a loved one's death in Judaism, commemorated with prayer and the lighting of a candle; alternate pronunciation of *yahrzeit*

zaydi — grandfather

zol — cannabis, marijuana

ACKNOWLEDGMENTS

Grateful thanks to Lauren Wein and Pilar Garcia-Brown at Houghton Mifflin Harcourt and to Craig Pyette and Anne Collins at Knopf Canada, for all their enthusiasm, insight, and warm encouragement. Thanks to Larry Cooper and Liz Duvall for their skillful copyediting. Many thanks also to Kim Witherspoon and Maria Whelan at Inkwell Management for their expert representation.

And much love, as ever, to Nicole, Avril, and Pasey.